OTHER TITLES BY W. HOCK HOCHHEIM

Fightin' Words
Dead Right There
Don't Even Think About It!
Blood Rust: Death of the China Doll
My Gun is My Passport
Last of the Gunmen
American Medieval
The China Alamo
Be Bad Now
Impact Weapon Combatives
Knife Combatives
Training Mission Series One through Five
The Great Escapes of Pancho Villa
Face the Muzak
Takedown the Take

TABLE OF CONTENTS

Hock at an author's night, Kings School, England.

Author's Prologue

Last of the Gunslingers is third in the series of the 1890s and 1900s adventures of ex-Army, ex-Texas lawman and private investigator, gunfighter, problem-solver, Johann Gunther and his Filipino sidekick/partner Jefe Cocoy.

It was a time just after the American gunfighter, and right before the noir detective. A time when men with a certain experience were called upon to solve difficult problems, Gunther and Jefe are the owners of a special firm called Remedies Detective Agency in Fort Worth, Texas.

The series endeavors to place our hero, with his western style ethos and ethics in Texas, and in national and international problems and hotspots, all in that fascinating ever-changing, turn of the centry, era.

High adventure! Intrigue and action! Unforgettable characters.

Chapter 1: A Fresh, Clean Spot to Die

New York City, Monday, September 10, 1907...

"Don't jump!" the mother screamed.

But, the father remained on the low wall at the edge of the roof. He stood there as the wind beat and flapped his clothing and that of his son's who stood next to him.

"You let him go, Clifford Bendigo!" the mother begged.

The father held his frightened, 10-year-old son standing tight at his side. The son's face, white with shock, formed a confused grimace, his jaw dropped as if he were screaming, a soundless horror. The mother crouched with her young daughter near the center of the roof a few feet away from father and son.

"You don't understand! We are dead. We are done! Through!" the father shouted, blubbering through tears.

Earlier, the father had lured his family, dressed in finery as if going to church, first to his financial office on the fifth floor, then up to the roof of the building on this sunny afternoon with a strange offer to "show them something special" up there. But once atop the roof, the father coaxed them all to the edge, then, inexplicably, he tried to shove them all off the building! The mother and daughter, already frightened by standing so close to the edge, spun, ducked his arms and escaped. Only the son remained in his grasp.

"We have lost everything! Everything! Don't you see?" the father yelled.

"Noooo!" the mother pleaded, aghast.

"Noooo, Daddy!" the betrayed son pleaded.

"Give him to me. Let him go! And you come down from there!"

"We can't go on! We can't! We are ruined!" the father moaned.

"Please, sweet Jesus please. Let him GO!"

"We must all go. I can't leave you here. I can't be here, and you cannot make it without me. We are penniless. Completely broke! We owe hundreds and hundreds of dollars. We are homeless, Abigail. Ruined."

"Daddy!" the daughter cried.

"We have no future. No hope!"

"Your father will help us out. He has slots of money. We just need to ask him," the wife said.

"I can't ask him for help! I can't. I am a failure. A failure."

"Then I'll ask him, Clifford. He will help us, if I ask. Come down!"

The crowd of men below on the city streets yelled and moaned, but not from the drama unfolding nine floors above them. Instead, they crowded together, in front of two major banks on the same avenue, banging on the locked front doors demanding their money, demanding their investments. Their due. News of the stock market and bank crash swept through the town like a full-blown tornado destroying lives and flinging them in all directions. A lost world for those near and far.

"Give him to me!" the mother demanded, again.

"I..." filled with sobs, the father could no longer speak.

He shoved the son away from the wall toward the mother. The son fell flat on the tarred roof surface, face down, more on purpose than a trip. There he clung to the rooftop.

A gust of fall wind swept across the Hudson River and swirled over the roof blowing the bowler hat right off the father's head. With one quick swirl, it tumbled out of sight.

With a sudden, tragic face the father looked as if about to depart his cherished family for a long trip. Then, awash with a new expression of melancholy peace and an odd, quirky, quivering smile, he shook his head and back-stepped into nothingness right off the edge of the roof. He disappeared like his hat had only a second before, plummeting right over the edge, gone, forever.

Abigail, on her knees, fell too, but face down on the roof as if in a faint, only she could grasp the full impact of this retched escape. The daughter crawled over beside her mother. The three howled in horror, in almost inhuman gales of shock. Fearing to stand just yet, the trembling son crawled over to his sister and mother. There, flat on the tarred roof, the three clung together as the wind howled overhead.

The father fell into the mob of fat men standing below, all wearing three-piece suits. He burst upon the sidewalk like an oversized, sack filled with potatoes. Four of the men under him collapsed as though hit by a boulder from outer space. Those untouched leapt away from the thud, and tried to digest what had just happened to this well-dressed, mangled pile of humanity suddenly appearing before them as if by magic. Blood. Bones. Sinew. Tweed. Hair, leather. Only one groan emerged when someone poked the mass with a gold-plated, Free Masonic, walking cane.

"Another jumper!" one man declared. And the group looked up to see from whence he came, as if more might follow.

Clifford Bendigo's bowler drifted down across the street several moments later, twirling over among the angry, exiled customers. It first bounced off heads and shoulders of the money-mad citizens, then slid between stuffed overcoats to the sidewalk where shiny shoes and fine boot heels ground it into ribbons upon the sidewalk.

Clifford Bendigo, the son of one of the richest men in the world, a Texan breakfast food and train magnate, health spa master, spared his family, but still managed to kill three strangers and severely injured two more, simply by failing to choose a fresh, clean spot to die.

Chapter 2: Slipping the Veil

June 20, 1908, The Treaty West Casino and Bar, Fort Worth, Texas...

Who was this Justin Trace? Where did his endless supply of money come from? Was he a millionaire? This well dressed man, who alternately wore Parisian and New York suits, who just showed up months ago on a train from West Texas—who was he? His diamond stick pins caught the light when he walked. The spats on his shoes clicked smartly. Was he like a Carnegie? A Rockefeller? A Morgan? People wondered. Since stepping off the locomotive a year before, he had opened several classy restaurants and bars. He paid all the employees top wages, even the janitors. He'd built an orphanage. He'd started several construction companies. Rumor had it he gave money to startup business entrepreneurs, donated money to churches, even to strangers on the streets. He started a new cattlemen's association and offered startup money for new ranchers. People said he'd helped farmers buy modern equipment. How? Who the heck was he?

Some said there was bad in the mix with the good. Some of Trace's money also seemed to drift into the hands of politicians, even local law enforcement too. And some money also went to local muscle, and hired guns even, all to get the wheels and deals that Trace wanted to get done. Licenses. Permits. Approvals. Endorsements. Completions. Obstacles...they all seemed to just fade away under the powerful influence of Justin Trace.

And gamble? Lordy, Lordy, he'd gambled all over Tarrant County and lost tons of money. He didn't seem to care a twit about losing either. Not a twit.

So it wasn't too much of a surprise when Justin Trace impulsively stood up from the big nightclub poker game, right smack in the middle of a high-stakes showdown. He just stood right up and tapped an expensive top hat upon his head and grinned at the players.

"Well, sir, you leaving us?" one player asked him.

"It's a blue bonnet of an evening out there, gentlemen, and I do believe I will step outside for a breath of fresh air."

"Well, what about all this dern money here on the felt?" asked another player, hammering a fist down on the table.

"Consider it…consider it left, sir. I trust you all to share it equally. Or, winner take all. Best evening to you gentlemen. Nothing personal."

The portly Justin Trace departed the room, leaving a gallery of astonished faces behind.

He strolled through the dance hall, dining room and bar and down the long hallway of the Treaty West Casino to the entrance, opened the door and stepped outside. It was after midnight, a week night and not much ado out on the city streets around the club. Small groups of people stood about and talked. Some taxi and coach drivers waited outside for fares. He lingered there at the entrance for a second, police witnesses said later, right outside the open doors of the club and under an electric street light. He struck a match and held it to the end of a long, expensive cigar, then started to cross the street, seemingly without a care in the world.

It was a tall man, yet stout, wearing a dark suit and overcoat that rushed out from a nearby alleyway. Black hat. His hat brim pulled low over his face, he hunkered down a bit as he walked. Big collar turned up obscured his face. The man moved with an apparent mission and marched up to Justin Trace. Right up to him!

A pistol appeared! A big, black pistol, witnesses later told police. The dark man produced the handgun from inside his jacket and, with an outstretched arm and leather gloved hand, he pointed the revolver at Justin Trace's chest. Trace stopped. His eyes widened. The cigar fell from his mouth with a flutter.

"He gulped like a dying fish," a police witness said. "He dropped that cigar from his catfish lips and, before that tobacco roll could hit the ground, the man in black fired his gun into Trace's chest. I saw the explosion. The force! His shirt, all but blew up in tatters. Red tatters. I swear it was like dynamite blew out from his nipples. I think a piece of him landed on my cheek! Trace fell all the way down onto his back with a gurgle and a huff. How many times did the man shoot, you ask? Many times, that's what I saw. Yes, sir!"

Onlookers froze as they watched the tragedy unfold, and as the close explosions rattled their ears.

"Torontoola!" One man on the street cried out! "Raoul Torontoola! That's him!" He pointed his finger at the shooter.

Hat pulled low over his face, the shooter barely turned his head to look at the man who declared his name.

"He said the other night, he was gonna kill this man, and look! Looky here, he did it here in front of us! Torontoola!"

The shooter turned away like a ghost in a Shakespearean play, and made for the cobblestone alleyway he'd first emerged from.

"Sgt. Raoul Torontoola! The police sergeant! That's right! That's him! Fort Worth police! A stone cold killer!" The man continued to bellow, among the howls of the gathering crowd.

All of a sudden, this name-caller himself shut his mouth and backed away, then turned and ran off into the night too, in another direction from the shooter.

Charles Sumner, an insurance salesman placed his gloved hand on Trace's porous chest, but to no avail. He stood up and looked to the left, down the alleyway where the shooter had escaped and then turned to see where the name-calling witness had run. Then from the alleyway, he heard the sound of a small engine echoing inside the walls. Also from the right, but from a greater distance, he heard the sound of another small engine. It too buzzed off. Sounded like those new-fangled motorcycles to him?

"He's dead! A woman shrieked as she edged forward and

looked down into Justin Trace's face.

"No, he's still alive! Call the police! There's a phone in the Treaty West lobby!"

But in only seconds more Justin Trace did slip the veil.

Chapter 3: The Six Gunslingers

Afternoon, June 24, 1908. Arlington, Texas, between Dallas and Fort Worth. Just a few acres south of the Dallas, Fort Worth turnpike...

Six men.

Six horses.

Six masks.

Twenty guns in all. Twelve pistols. Six rifles. Two derringers.

The six men were all gamblers, criminals, sportsmen, drinkers and killers. Six gunmen. Six bandannas hung loose about six necks.

The horses shuffled their feet anxiously, charged with the electricity they felt flowing nervously from their riders. A sense of tense waiting filled the Tuesday early afternoon air. Anxious. Waiting to ride. Waiting to ambush. Waiting to rob. Waiting to kill.

The pickings should be so easy? The wide dirt road stretching out before them was the main thoroughfare between Dallas and Fort Worth. Nearly everyone passed down it at one time or another. The riders visually examined the profiles of traveling horses and their riders as they walked or trotted by, some going east, others going west. The occasional car rumbled by as well. And the rare truck filled with supplies – it too rattled past. The common horse and buggy or coach whirred by taking passengers about their daily business. Some folks even walked the turnpike, struggling under baskets of produce, boxes or luggage. Some people laughed and talked as they passed, or stared solemnly at the horizon, or down into the ruts of the ground, so they wouldn't stumble. Most were bound for one of the big cities at either end of the turnpike, or perhaps to the smaller towns along the highway. Restaurants and hotels lined the turnpike in those towns and some of the towns contained factories. The turnpike passed through farmland as well. In other places, like the stretch they surveyed, there was almost nothing. Nothing but flatland punctuated with a sporadic grove of trees near the occasional stream or small lake. It was in one of the occasional groves where these six gunmen waited.

"There she is," said one of the men, pointing to the west.

A black, open carriage pulled by two bay horses appeared over the shallow horizon. Two women sat in the front, both dressed in the finest fashion. It was a sleek, expensive carriage, and the horses were both admirably fine specimens. One woman spun a red parasol over her head. The other woman looked Hispanic, and she worked the reins of the two horses steering the carriage.

Hidden from view in the shallow grove of trees, six men's heads pivoted east and west almost in unison to assess how many witnesses might be close by when the actions of their guns spit bullets. Six hands fitted six masks on six faces. Six noses covered. Six hats pulled down. Twelve eyes exposed.

The carriage drew nearer. The six gunmen trotted out into view, then 12 boot heels tapped the six horses into a faster gait, then to a run. The 24 hooves clopped across the dirt and six mouths made no sound. They climbed the hilly grade to the top of the road in front of the carriage. Six revolvers were pulled from six holsters.

"Stop right there Isabella Torontoola!" one gunman declared, aiming his pistol at the woman with the parasol.

The Hispanic woman beside the lady reined in the horses, and the carriage halted. The six gunmen covered the front of the coach and spread-out in the shape of a horseshoe around it. There would be no cross-fire amongst them. People afoot on the road screamed, shouted and ran off in a pell-mell panic. Others on horses dropped off the road to get clear of the gun barrels. This commotion caused three of the gunmen to turn their attention to the witnesses, in case there was even one hero among them. One convertible automobile stopped a good distance away. Its passengers stood up to watch.

"What is it you want?" Isabella Torontoola asked.

"You know what we want, you rich bitch of a slut."

"We will vamanos, Mrs…" and the Hispanic woman attempted to ripple the reins over the rumps of their horses, for a daring charge and escape? But…

BAM. One of the six gunman shot her in the chest. It hit her with a thump and crack of bone. The two carriage horses reared from the sudden discharge, and the wagon shifted on the road. The wounded woman plummeted from her perch to the road bed, head first. Two robbers pushed their horses close to the carriage horses and grabbed the reins to stop any further attempt at escape. Some of the bystanders who remained in the immediate area shrieked and then appeared to evaporate off the road.

The lady with the red parasol made a wretched face of hate and shock. She reached into her purse. Three gunman opened fire with three handguns and seven bullets pummeled Isabella Torontoola into pieces, pinning her back into her cushioned, blue velvet seat. Her lacy white dress top filled up with red blood stains. Her parasol drifted off the coach like a hot air balloon in the wind. She sat there, clenching both of her fists in the air. Dead. Still moving, still contracting, but dead. She kicked and fell onto the seat.

"Get it!" A gunman ordered.

Three of the gunmen jumped off their horses and assaulted the coach like wild hyenas, tearing into the luggage and belongings on the open back. The other three gunmen turned their horses in slow, small circles, their handguns pointed skyward to oversee the possible witnesses.

"We'll kill any of you fools that talk!" One gunman shouted out to no one in particular.

BOOM!

A thundering blast pierced the air and the ears of all. A whistle in the wind flashed by the robbers. A piece of woodwork on the coach exploded. All six men looked east. A single, tall man standing up in the open automobile at some distance held a lever action rifle. He worked the action again. One woman and two men leapt from that topless car, no doubt expecting return fire from the highwaymen. The rifleman remained, true to his process.

Three horsemen charged the auto, yelling and cracking off wild rounds. The car's metal rippled and clanged and the windshield shattered, but the tall rifleman stood undaunted. He shot again, and this round belted into one of the three charging gunmen. The rider dropped his pistol. His arms flailed loosely at his sides, his chin pointed straight up toward the heavens. Then he tumbled off his horse. The horse wanted no more part of this mess. It never stopped and ran away at a full gallop, with such speed and determination it looked unlikely that it would stop before it reached Dallas.

Three pistol bullets hit the rifleman in the flurry, one right to his lean face. His rifle dropped onto the car's hood and he fell backward. Limp as death he fell into the back seat of the car, boots sticking up, legs up on the seat back as if on a Sunday nap.

One rider, a bulky man with a shock of visible, thick black hair on his neck, aimed his pistol at the two other men that crouched down, a distance from the car. They knew to freeze with their hands up. The other rider moved toward his wounded compadre. He leapt from his horse and grabbed the wounded man with two hands, shaking his torso. The man seemed still alive. Then he stood up with help. The rider got him atop the horse, then he crawled on himself. The rider wrapped both his arms around the wounded man then kicked the horse back toward the Torontoola carriage.

The masked man with the black hair backed his horse up several feet.

"That's a damn fool!" The man said, pointing to the old man dead in the back seat of the auto.

Then he neck-reined his horse around, and galloped back to the carriage.

The three men at the carriage held up three large, black satchels. The men slid off the wagon and ran to their mounts.

"We got it!" one cried out.

The six gunmen took off on five horses. They left the road and melted back into the grove from whence they emerged.

People on the road, prone or in the side ditches stood up and watched them go. They surveyed the carnage. A few men and women raced to the wagon to check on the two women. They ran back and forth to each woman in a frenzy. But it was too late. The ladies were dead.

Two male and the one female — travelers from the automobile — climbed back into the open car.

"Judge!" Judge Hofferman" a man pleaded.

"Rufus! Rufus!" the woman begged, her legs now astride the judge, clawing at his shirt.

But that man was dead too. He'd likely killed one of them, maybe, a moving shot, but all he got in return was his own demise. She sighed, and leaned back on the front seat, nearly atop the judge's spread legs and boots. She buried her face in her hands.

One of the companions stood in the car and with the added height could see the horsemen as they passed through the grove of trees and headed west. They all galloped at a full out pace. From a distance they looked like moving dots with legs. He turned back to his dead friend and placed a fast hand on his forehead, almost knocking his Stetson off. Tears fell.

"My God," he fretted, "when will all this meanness end?"

Chapter 4: The Bloody Fandango on Lake Tahoe

Night of June 27, 1908, Lake Tahoe...

"Are you Johann Gunther?" the woman asked, "Can you help me? There are two men here tonight who want to kidnap me, or kill each other trying."

Johann had been staring out over Lake Tahoe and its surrounding mountain ranges from the broad balcony of the ballroom off the corner of a millionaire friend's house. The evening party and guests, numbering at least 50, were all inside and chattering just behind him. It felt just a bit chilly out there, as did so many of the evenings. With a glass of sherry in his hand, he took his gaze off the shimmering lights from the Nevada side of the lake and turned to the woman beside him.

She looked exquisite. Tall, with thick, lush black hair. Beautiful eyes and red, full lips. Her body poured into a silvery gown of red sparkles that almost matched the very sparkles on the lake. Gunther had to blink twice to adjust his eyes to the nearest flashes. Like her accent, she looked oriental.

"I am afraid I have not had the pleasure of your acquaintance," Gunther said, ignoring his, this, standard opening remark.

"Michelle Smith."

She looked at Gunther's long blond hair brushed back over his ears, as if to confirm he was indeed the tall blond man she needed to find for help before extending her hand.

He took her red-gloved hand and kissed the velvet top of her fingers.

"I gather, given your ethnicity, your name is an adopted one?"

"Yes."

"And you are from the Celestial Empire?"

"Yes…China," she said impatiently. "People here tonight. They tell me you are a problem-solver, Mr. Gunther, that you have helped Mr. Pendergast in the past..."

"That is why I am a guest tonight, yes. A return of many favors."

"I need a favor. I am…I am in a terrible situation. I am from Los Angeles. There are people there who want me back in Los Angeles."

"People. Bad people?"

"Very bad. They have paid men to come catch me like an animal and take me back there. I see two of them here tonight."

"And where are these two…"

"Johann!"A voice boomed from Gunther's left. "I see you have met my son's fiancée, Michelle!"

Willard Pendergast, owner of this palatial mansion on the shore of Lake Tahoe and purveyor of this 25-year business, anniversary party walked toward Gunther.

Gunther had saved Willard a lot of money years before with a theft investigation, and they had remained friends ever since. It was more than fitting that both Gunther and Jefe were invited to the occasion this evening.

"Keith's fiancée?" Gunther said wryly. "I am indeed disappointed with this news." He really was, but he said it with such a smile and light-hearted charm, the compliment hung feather light in the air without causing offense.

"Let me borrow Michelle and introduce her to some friends." He took the lady's arm and guided her back into the ballroom, where they faded off into the group. She glanced back at Gunther, over her bare shoulder, a desperate curve to her lips.

Gunther sipped his sherry, and watched.

Jefe, his best friend since the Philippine War where the Filipino served with Gunther, and now his partner in Remedies Detective Agency, walked up to him. He noted Gunther's transfixed stare and his own gaze followed the direction Gunther's held.

"You see that woman with Pendergast?" Gunther said. "The oriental one?"

"Oh no, not another lady for you to get fish bowl eyes over? Someone you have sex with maybe four or five times, don't have kids with, don't get married to, and you leave like the alley cat that you are."

"Five times? Oh, oh she's at least a 15-er."

Jefe shook his head in disgust.

"She said she's in trouble. She said there are two men here tonight that want to kidnap her and cart her back to some bad men in Los Angeles."

"Oh?"

"Where is Maria?" Gunther asked about Jefe's wife.

"She is eating in the dining room. I was coming to get you to eat. Your favorite. Barbecue. Very good."

"Might tell her to stay there for a bit. You have a gun?"

"No. No, I do not have my gun. I have my knife. You have your Luger?"

Gunther tapped his armpit under his tux, "But, I'd like to get out of this without shooting people. Shooting up this place."

"Poor Mr. Pendergast," Jefe lamented. "A Texas shoot-em up at his big Nevada party. Very civilized people…and then they invite you, the cave man that plays with fire."

"They invited you too."

"They need me to watch you."

"She's engaged to Pendergast's son, and she's in trouble in L.A. Who do you think doesn't fit?" Gunther asked. "Who looks…LA?"

Michelle continued to look back at him with compelling glances from time to time as Pendergrast moved her around to introduce her to various guests, never quite releasing her arm.

"That kano under the chandelier. The third chandelier

from the bar. Wrong clothes. Slight stubble," Jefe noted.

They looked over at this kano, or "white boy" in Filipino Tagolog, taking in his appearance from top to bottom. He wore a decent enough jacket and pants, but his hair was pressed in at the top of his head. The man spent too much time in a hat to match the well coifed hairdos of the rest of the group. Also, a little too much sun. Some questionable boots?

"I'll tell Maria to stay in the dining room," Jefe said.

"There are some hiking and walking sticks by the front door," Gunther suggested.

Jefe nodded. As a Filipino martial artist, he loved sticks.

Michelle now stood in a group, a strained smile on her face. She looked again at Gunther. Gunther touched his nose with a finger then quickly pointed at the miss-dressed suspect. She nodded it was him.

Gunther walked across the ballroom to the kano.

"Well, good evening!" he said.

"Good evening," the man answered, preoccupied.

"My name is Johann. Family friend. How is it that you know the Pendergasts? Do business with them?"

When the man glanced at Michelle, Gunther scanned his torso. Definitely had a gun on the right hip, under a jacket.

"Ahh, yeah. Yes. Business."

"Ahhh business…"

Gunther spied Jefe sorting through some 30 or so hiking and walking sticks propped in a decorated oversized barrel in the front foyer. Like a kid in a candy store, the Filipino finally selected one.

"…what business is that?" Gunther finished.

Jefe approached the man from the rear.

"What business is it of yours?" the man said, with an impatient sneer.

"Ha! Oh. Well. You know…that…is the wrong answer."

Jefe dropped down to all fours behind the man, and Gunther shoved the man hard on the chest with both his hands. The man fell over the top of Jefe and sprawled out onto the floor.

"Gun, right hip," Gunther whispered.

Jefe, deft as a cat, slipped to his side, and he and Gunther each grabbed an arm and stood the man up as they walked toward the foyer. Whoever saw this, let loose with a few gasps, but most people missed the whole trick. It looked like they were helping a man who had suddenly fallen.

"Ha! Too much brandy!" Gunther said to a few with a big smile as they went by. Mr. Pendergast spun to see the minor commotion, but seeing Gunther in charge, confidently returned to his conversation.

Out of view, they shoved the kano again, this time up against the foyer wall. Jefe took the revolver from the holster, tucking it into his own belt line under his tuxedo, and then brandished the walking stick with two hands before the man.

"My business is finding out what your business is. Mr. Pendergast is my business. Now what do you want here?" Gunther asked. Smiles all gone.

"That woman."

"What woman?"

"That Chinese whore of a woman in there. She was the head of a prostitution ring. A hooker herself years ago. She is..was…Rooney Mick's girlfriend. You know who Rooney is?"

"No."

"You should! You better! He runs a lot of things in L.A., you see. And he wants her back. And she ran off with a stack of his money too."

"I see. And Mick promised to pay you to bring her back?"

"Like a bounty. Look, if you help me, I could see if I could get you some money too. Both of you."

"Share and share alike," Gunther repeated. "Hmmm. You got a partner in there too. More to share with?" Gunther asked.

"Nope. I don't. But there is an L.A. police captain in there. He's a Mormon, son of a bitch originally from Utah. Name's Astler. Corrupt. Lap dog for Rooney."

"You're not working together?"

"Shit, no, I just said. We are not. No partner of mine. He wants all the money. And he won't share any of his money with you, but I will. I don't know how he found out Ling was here tonight."

"So, Ling's her name. Ok, which one is he?" Jefe asked.

"He's big. He's got black, curly hair, Fat face. Black suit. He's got a black, walking cane. Just for show. He don't need it. He was my biggest problem tonight until you two goons showed up."

Jefe stepped back so he could see into the ballroom. He scanned the crowd. He spotted the man with a cane and black curly hair. He nodded to Gunther.

"Goodnight, mister…what was your name?" Gunther asked.

"Louis."

"Goodnight, Mr. Louis."

"Huh?"

And Jefe clubbed him in the head with his stick. Louis slid down the wall.

"Jesus, did you kill him?" Gunther complained.

"No! No, just love tap," Jefe smiled.

"Looked like a kill tap to me," Gunther said, as they hauled Louis down a hallway off the foyer.

"He will just dream of the Los Angeles beaches and beautiful women of his homeland for awhile."

"More like nightmares."

They dumped him on a rug in a dark room behind some plants.

Back in the ballroom, a piano player started some low-key, Claude Debussy arrangement. Gunther and Jefe split up and maneuvered around the room in opposite directions until they flanked Captain Astler. Astler appeared a complete charmer. Drink in one hand, fancy cane in the other, talking with several couples, all of them smiling.

"Captain Astler!" Gunther said with a big smile. "Is that you?"

Astler turned his head to better study Gunther, looking a bit confused.

"Astler? Los Angeles Police Department?"

"We've met?" Astler asked.

Gunther shook his hand and stepped closer, "no, but

Rooney Mick and I have. Might we have a word?"

"Yes," Astler said with a big, forced grin. "Please excuse me folks," he told the couples.

The two walked across the room and out onto the balcony. Jefe hovered nearby, just in range to cover any action. Just behind Astler.

With his back to the party, Astler's face turned downright menacing.

"She's mine. I know Mickey's hired a bunch of scum bags like you to find Ling, but I found her, see! She's mine. I have a badge and a gun, and I swear I'll walk her out of here like she's been arrested. Mine! See!"

Gunther just stared at him, blank-faced.

"Well, you gonna play?" he said. "What's your play, scallywag? Or stand clear of me."

Silence.

"Well, I'm taking her out of here, and I swear to Christ I'll shoot anyone who tries to stop me."

"How much is this Mickey paying?" Gunther finally spoke up.

"You know how much!"

"No I don't. How much is he paying for Ling?"

"One hundred dollars."

"What if I could hand you 150 dollars here, tonight, to leave her alone, what would you do? Would you take it and leave?"

Astler shuffled his feet, and his gaze wandered.

"Would you take it and walk away?"

"I don't know."

"No one would know anything about this and you would have 150 dollars."

"Well, I have a…a relationship with Mickey, and I…"

"No one will know unless you tell him."

"Yeah. I guess."

"Wait here," Gunther said.

Gunther walked back into the ballroom and up to Pendergast.

"Mr. Pendergast, may I have a word with you for a moment."

"Well, yes," Pendergast said, a bit surprised.

"Michelle. Keith. Will you join us?"

Michelle didn't look like she wanted to. Son Keith agreed to go.

"Let's all go into my study," Pendergast said.

They stepped into a the nearby room, indeed, a well furnished study.

"What is it, Johann?" Pendergast asked.

"Sir, you have an unconscious thug from Los Angles laying on the floor of one of the adjacent rooms temporarily stashed behind some plants."

"I…do?"

"Yup. Jefe rendered him so. We stuffed him in there for safe keeping. And on your balcony right now stands a Los Angeles police captain, armed with a cane and pistol and a big badge, who will not leave unless he can take Michelle…that is…Miss Ling here, back to L.A. with him."

"What?" Keith said. He turned to her, "are you wanted by the law?"

"No," she said, "I…"

"I believe," Gunther interrupted, "that Michelle has some very serious explaining to do, to the both of you. She is not wanted by the law. She is wanted instead by a notorious gangster named Rooney Mick. The bounty is 100 dollars. To sweeten his fast exit, I offered him $150."

Gunther turned to Pendergrast, "I believe if we pay him 150 dollars here, right now, he will leave tonight, and your party will not turn into a bloody fandango."

"I …we shouldn't pay anything! Maybe we should shoot him!" Keith said.

"We? You mean, maybe *I* should shoot him, Keith? The man is a police captain."

"He's right, Keith," Pendergrast said.

"Keith, I understand you are confused, but the best outcome now is to give me 150 dollars. I will pass this to the captain and get him out of here for tonight."

"What will stop him from getting her tomorrow? Or the next day?" Keith asked.

"Nothing. He may still try." Gunther turned from the son

to the father. "Is it worth a hundred to save your anniversary party? How much have you paid for the drapes here? The catering tonight? Is it worth a hundred to save the night?"

"You're right, Johann. Save the night. Tomorrow is another day." He walked over to his desk and sat, pulled out some drawers and opened several small metal boxes.

"Ling," Gunther said, "you've been discovered here. Your past has caught up to you. It's a race you cannot win. You need to fully explain yourself to these men. What happens next…happens."

She grimaced. Keith grimaced. He glared at her profile.

Mr. Pendergast approached Gunther. He handed him a thick wad of money. Gunther nodded and left the room, and left the father, son and whore to fend for themselves in their own little personal tragedy the best they could.

Outside in the ballroom, the piano played on. Captain Astler was still standing alone on the balcony. He looked curiously at Gunther. Gunther scratched his forehead with his fingers holding the wad of money. Astler nodded. Gunther walked to the foyer. Astler did too. Jefe flanked him along the way.

The three men met in the hall and filed outside the mansion through its giant, double doors. The darkness of the courtyard enveloped them, broken up only by the faint porch lights. The night air felt chilly with a touch of mountain humidity. Three valets and handlers dressed in smart, gray uniforms caroused near some cars, horses and carriages nearby.

"One hundred dollars," Gunther said. He handed Astler the money.

Astler smiled, but with a curious eye. He rested his cane against his leg as he thumbed the cash for a quick count, then he looked Gunther in the eyes.

"What's your name?" he asked.

"Gunther."

"Where you from?"

"Fort Worth, Texas."

"What do you do down there?"

"Jefe and I own a company called Remedies. We solve problems."

Astler looked for Jefe, but the Filipino was off again busy talking with the handlers. Two of them ran into the house.

"Problems. Like a detective solves problems? You solved a big problem here tonight, cowboy."

"Temporarily."

"Fort Worth, huh? You ever wear a badge?"

"In Paris, Texas for a few years."

"A cowboy shamus," he shoved the money into his pocket and smiled again.

"This ain't temporary, Gunther. I ain't coming back for the woman," Astler said matter-of-factly. "You might think little of me, think I am a paid-off, crooked cop. A racketeer. Or, some kind of scum or something. But you have no idea where I work, see, and what I have to put up with all around me."

"I can imagine."

"Los Angeles is as wild as any Wild West town you know of east of here. Maybe even wilder. But I am a man of some honor. Through a series of misfortunes I just ended up owing the wrong people. Some honor. Some money. As much honor…as I can have and stay alive." He shook his head.

"You saved me a lot of work and a lot of worry here tonight. You saved a lot of work and worry for Pendergast, too. I don't wanna mess up this place. Shoot up this place. Haul a scratching, biting woman up the side of this mountain, and then all the way back to Burbank. And you got me a lot of money, see.

I came here because I needed money. Badly. A mess I got into back in L.A. A bad mess. A gangster mess. Now…" he fanned the money. "Now, I got some money that will pay my way out of it. I appreciate it. And that means my wife and kids appreciate it, too."

He turned to the remaining handler in the yard, "hey, boy!" The handler ran for a small carriage.

"I am impressed with your problem-solving skills. You did a real nice job here."

He stuck out his hand, and Gunther shook it. "My name is Barry Astler. They call me 'Barry the Cane' in L.A." He lifted the cane up till the round, silver, ornate handle was chin-high, then he flicked it an inch forward.

"If you every need any help in Los Angeles, you just let me know."

The handler brought up a single-horse carriage from nearby. Astler climbed in.

"Hey!" Jefe called out from the front stairs.

They turned to him to see two of the valets, each with a shoulder under the babbling and stunned Louis. He obviously did not know who or where he was yet.

"Can you maybe drop off your fellow Californian somewhere, anywhere away from here would be fine?" Jefe asked.

"So, is he about dead?" Astler asked.

Gunther shook his head, no.

"Throw him in the back," Astler said with resignation. They watched the two haul the man up and drop him into the small luggage area behind the front seat. Astler studied his face "I don't know this mug. Never seen him around."

"Louis something, or something Louis," Jefe said.

"They know she's here," Astler warned them. "And others will follow. That's what Mick wants. Mickey usually…"

"…gets what he wants," Gunther finished for him.

"Yeah," and with that, Los Angeles Police Department Captain "Barry the Cane" Astler reined his horse to the left and drove off.

They watched him driving away for a moment.

"One would think," Gunther said, "that as a city evolved into the size of Los Angeles, it would grow into a cleaner, safer place. Not a wilder place. I guess crime just evolves right along with it."

"What next?" Jefe asked. "Do you think Pendergast will ask us to stay?"

"Can't stay forever. This Ling girl is going to have to take care of this mess somehow."

"Maybe they will hire us to solve her problems?" Jefe said. "Maybe deliver some money to Mickey."

"Maybe. I don't know. I think they might be through with the girl though after tonight. But then, you know true love."

"I know true love," Jefe said. "You don't know true love."

They started back inside when Jefe stopped and tapped his belt line.

"Allah be praised, I still have dey Louis pistol!"

"Maybe that is a good thing for awhile."

They walked back inside where it all remained a big ballroom party, minus a dad and a son, and a mysterious lady from the Celestial Empire, now conspicuously absent.

A waiter's gaze scoured the party, searching for faces. He spotted Gunther and jogged over to him.

"Mr. Gunther! Mr. Gunther. You have an important phone call."

"I do?"

"Yes, sir. It is from the governor of Texas. Can you follow me?"

The men walked into a side room. Gunther picked up the earpiece of the phone that was hanging at the end of the cord. He spoke into the mouthpiece on the wall.

"Governor? Hello? Governor?"

"Yes. Johann?"

"Yes, sir, this is he."

"Johann, we have a problem down here, but I hate to bother you while you are at the Pendergast party."

"What is it, sir?"

"Johann, there has been a murder. Well, three murders, on the highway between Fort Worth and Dallas. A robbery and murders. Two women were shot, and a man on the road with his family tried to intervene, and he was shot and killed too. That man was a former judge and a former Louisiana congressman named Rufus Hofferman."

"Yes?"

"The congressman was a good friend of the Louisiana governor. As am I! Of course, I have been speaking with the governor and I have promised him a full investigation. And I swore the murderers would be caught and strung up. I told him about you, and how you saved the lieutenant governor's life at the Fort Worth opera house a few years back. I told him of my faith in you, and I promised him I would also engage you in the investigation, to…help the local authorities in all the ways that the local authorities need help."

"I understand, sir."

"How soon can you be back, Johann?"

"Three, four days by train, sir."

"I will have an updated report at your office in three days."

"Yes, sir. I will tell you now I will need substantial reward money to pass around for information. The police will not have this kind of money," Gunther said.

"You have it. Johann, this is a messy affair. It is not just a simple highwaymen hijack. One of the murdered women is the wife of a very controversial Fort Worth police detective sergeant named Torontoola. This detective is a powerful...and corrupt...figure in the area. His hands are muddy. I am told he is currently incarcerated in the Tarrant County Jail, held without bond, accused of the murder of a local businessman."

"Raoul Torontoola. Yes. I read about him in the newspaper. Accused of shooting a rich gambler on the street in cold blood last week."

"How can this be a coincidence? This highway robbery goes off like an anarchist's bomb in about six different ways, Johann. And I need an ear and an inside hand outside of the police department there. Even outside the Texas Ranger's office. I will tell them you are helping and to consider you part of the team. When you dig in a shovel load into this one, you'll see why I need an outsider. I will hear from you soon?"

"Yes, sir. Goodbye, sir."

He hung up. Jefe stood near him.

"Troubles in Austin?" Jefe asked.

"Troubles in the home town, Cow Town. Stretches to Austin too. Tell Maria to pack. I think I'll have barbecue first. Then I'll pack."

Chapter 5: The Whispering Wind

Remedies Investigations Office, Fort Worth, Texas...

The meeting was at the behest of governor. A meet and greet and also to get Gunther up to speed on the investigation. No problem for Tarrant County Sheriff's Office Investigator William Wiley Lewis, known by all as just "Wiley."

He walked in and sat in the chair in front of his friend Gunther's ornate office desk. The Texas Ranger however with him, a grimacing Chester Winch, was a stranger to Gunther until they were introduced, after which he stood a distance off from the desk, obviously annoyed at having to be there. The thin, boney Ranger wore a red bandana around his neck, a leather vest, and an ornate, two-gun, sienna brown gun belt, and looked everywhere in the room but into Gunther's eyes.The office was full of military regalia and items from his world travels in Cuba, India, Afghanistan, China and South Africa. Winch looked it all over and snorted.

Jefe entered the room and dropped into a big leather chair to the side of the desk hanging a leg over the arm, under the watchful glare of Winch.

"Have a seat Ranger," Gunther offered.

The grimace deepened. The message was clear, but he did finally sit and crossed one lean ankle over the other long legged knee. A fancy, expensive spur attached to a fancy boot wagged in the air. Gunther heard them when he came in, but now he heard the spur spin slightly on the lifted boot. Winch ran his tongue all over his teeth like a caveman toothbrush, and absently spun the spur on that high boot with a long boney finger.

Mesha, the Hindu maid that Gunther had rescued from flaming death in India a few years earlier, and who then later rescued Gunther from certain death in an Afghanistan fort, entered the room and poured four glasses of sun tea from a glass pitcher then distributed the glasses. Hand cracked ice swirled and tinkled in the glasses.

"You want the Fort Worth Star Telegram newspaper version of this mess?" Wiley asked.

"I want the *Whispering Wind* version," Gunther said, referring to the local tattler, sensationalistic gossip rag.
Wiley pulled a bound, log book from a leather satchel beside his chair and opened it. He read the contents on the Torontoola case. It seemed no coincidence that Torontoola was arrested in a murder, then his wife was murdered a few days later. After hearing the report Gunther knew little more than what the governor first told him on the telephone days before while he was still in Tahoe.

"Six gunman. Three citizens dead. One robber shot. Dead? We don't know if'n he's dead," Wiley Lewis summarized, then he slapped the book closed.

"Presumed dead," Gunther added. "Anybody missing around here? Any talk about this at all?" Gunther asked.

"Nobody seems to be missing yet, that we know of. At least here-abouts."

"What about that horse?"

"The horse?" Wiley asked.

"The robber's horse? The one that just...ran off."

"Well, I don't know anything about that horse. That horse just run plum off. Could be anywhere, from here to Dallas. It's a horse. A horse in horse country."

"Or not. The horse had a saddle on it. Somebody had to see or find a riderless horse with a saddle on it."

"How in Hades are we going to find one horse in Fort Worth, Arlington or Dallas, Texas?"

“The Whispering Wind,” Gunther said with his eyebrows up. “The horse may have a brand. A personalized saddle. Saddlebags with identification in them. Who knows what all?”

“What about the dropped pistol?” Jefe asked.

Ranger Winch sneered at him.

“The dead cowboy’s pistol? We got that. Can’t trace it, no how,” Wiley said.

Jefe reached for a pad and a pencil on the desk. He started writing. Out in the long foyer, Mesha’s small pet monkey scampered about, chattering. The monkey stopped at the office doorway and looked in. It looked longingly at Gunther. Gunther waved a high hand at it, made a “sho” sound for it to go away. It did.

“Then there’s Raoul Torontoola,” Wily said.

“Yeah, he must have something to do with this. Tell me about that murder.”

“Not a good case of murder on him. Weak. Lame,” Wiley said. “He was born in Mexico. Forty-three years old. Been on the city police force for 14 years. We all know Torontoola is as dirty as get out. Protection racket for many of the gambling houses and saloons at Hell’s Half Acre and parts outside of it.”

Hell’s Half Acre was known publically as “a rough and rowdy district filled with saloons, dance halls, gambling parlors, and bordellos.” A section of downtown no bigger than half an acre actually, the Fort Worth Democrat described the customers as “...lewd women of all ages 16 to 40... the most respectable of citizens, the experienced thief... the ordinary murderer, the average cowboy and the ordinary young man of the town.” Add to that list, judges, lawyers, politicians and corrupt police detectives like Sgt. Raoul Torontoola.

“Torontoola’s got em a day job at the city police department,” Wiley continued, “detective bureau, but he gets all fancied up just about every night in a black, three-piece suit and works the Acre’s streets like the devil himself. In and out of the bars. Over-seeing. Watching. Glad-handing. During which times, he gets all kinds of cross-ways with a gambler and enterp…ontrip…entis…”

“Entrepreneur?” Gunther offered.

"…from Lubbock with this Justin Trace feller. Trace moved here trying to set up a little honey pot of his own in our city like he'd done so well with in Lubbock. We think anyway. Running games in some smaller clubs and bars. He started businesses for people. But his aims were not small time here. No. Pissed a lot of locals off. There he was, running a gambling house and forgiving some of the gambling debts! I'm just saying, who in hell runs a money house like that? People left the other gambling joints and went over to his two places.

The local bosses told Torontoola to, you know, get rid of him. Run him out of town. Vamoose. They have had a few confrontations, a bad one in public too. Trace would not leave. Killing words crossed betwixt them, and in front of various witnesses. It started to look like Torontoola was going to have to kill him to get shed of him. That, mi amigo, is the *Whispering Wind*, gossip version."

"You'd think Torontoola, a city policeman, would be smarter than to just walk up like that, in front of witnesses, and shoot the man."

Wiley took a sip of his ice tea. Ranger Winch stared at his kneecap, his boot and spur shaking the spur impatiently. He reached down and spun the star on his spur again.

"You say the murder case is lame?" Jefe asked.

"Yup. One night two weeks back, Trace stood up from a roulette table at the Treaty West Casino…"

"Been there," Gunther added.

"…and muttered something about needing some fresh air. He put on his top hat. Stepped outside. Lit a cigar and was shot dead. A man had jumped out from an alley, strutted up to him, pulled a big-assed revolver and shot him down graveyard dead, and then fled."

"Was it Torontoola?" Gunther asked.

"Nobody knows! Nobody knows for got damn sure. There were some witnesses standing around, and they described a man looking like him. Tall as him. And dressing like Torontoola usually dresses. One man there? One man shouted Torontoola's name to high heaven. Made sure everyone heard it. Then he disappeared too. "

"He did? That ain't much a nothing," Gunther said.

"I know. I know, but Lord knows I have seen men hung for less over the years."

"Not in Fort Worth," Gunther said.

"No, not in Fort Worth, not lately anyway. Not for many a year. But somebody heard somebody say something that the District Attorney has a surprise witness that will lynch Torontoola."

"Think he did it?" Gunther asked.

"Hell if I know. He can get real testy. Maybe he flipped his cork all night and drunk - shot the man? He ain't talking to nobody. They've got him in a special cell on the top floor of the Tarrant County Jail. No bail. Being a police detective, the judge entertained the notion that his life would be in danger if incarcerated in the regular jail amongst the regulars. His eats are brought-in, and he's still dressing like a show horse. Stirs around in fancy silk pajamas. They say he's got a rope strung across the cell with all his suits hanging on it. A big mirror. Smoking pre-mo cigars from foreign countries."

Jefe leaned forward. "We need at very least the color of dis missing horse." He looked at the pad in his hands and read aloud,

"Wanted. A horse involved in a murder and robbery at..." we'll need the location, and we'll need the date and time. "This horse lost its criminal rider and ran off. There is a....."

"One hundred dollar," Gunther said.

"One hundred dollar reward for information that leads to the recovery and the location of the horse and, or its tack."

"One hundred dollars!" Wiley said, then whistled, "that is a lot of money."

"It'll raise eyebrows. That's the point. We'll print posters. We'll buy ads in all the newspapers. Small town and big. Dallas, Arlington, Fort Worth."

"And included, 'a reward for any information leading to the arrest and conviction of the six robbers.'"

"How much," Jefe asked Gunther, jotting down his own notes.

"Six men. Five hundred dollars."

"Damn, that's a lot of money," Wiley said.

"What I want to know," Ranger Winch finally spoke up, "is why the governor asked you and your little Mex here in on this investigation. At all?"

Gunther stared at him. Deadpan. This lasted until Wiley shifted in his crunchy, leather seat. Jefe ignored the "Mex" remark and wrote on his pad.

"And you giving away taxpayer money to people on an opium, pipe dream of finding a lost, damn horse," the Ranger said. "Rewards. You, in control of it all. I mean what are you anyway? Who? A…a…fancy pants? You ain't a gunfighter. You ain't a lawman. And what is this place here? Remedies. Shit. Are you some kind of pharmacist without any drugs? Remedies!"

Gunther still looked deadpan.

"I want that reward money now." He pounded a finger on the desk. "I will take control of it, as an official Texas Ranger representative of this state. I should be in control of it and I alone will apportion it out accordingly as I see fit. Officially."

In a very low voice, extra calm, Gunther said,

"Ranger…I don't have the money."

"Don't have it? Well, where is the money?"

"In the governor's back pocket. If you want that money, you can ride to Austin and ask him directly for it."

"Sheeet!" Winch said and stood up, leaned forward and rested his two fists on Gunther's desk. "I might just do that," he said while rolling his head around over his shoulders.

They stared at each other, then Winch reached for his first sip of ice tea. The sip turned into a long gulp.

"Thanks for the tea," he said when he finished the glass. He did not slam the glass down. Instead, he set it ever-so-gently on the desk. Then he pivoted on his boot heel and walked out of the room. Gunther watched him cross the hall. The monkey was chasing a ball up and down the hall there with Jefe's kids. Gunther saw him pass.

Gunther watched the monkey with no small degree of concern, he said, "If he hurts that monkey, Texas Ranger or not, I will kick his ass into next week."

The Ranger did not bother with the monkey. He detoured around it instead and went out the front door. No slam.

"Is that your pet monkey?" Wiley asked.

"No. He just lives here." Gunther sat down. "Mesha's monkey from India."

"He just likes to play games with you."

"He's a monkey! Monkey-en around. Smart little bastard too. He thinks I'm a big monkey. But, I'm just a monkey's new uncle according to Darwin."

"Dar-who-won-what-now?" Wiley said.

Gunther laughed.

"As any monkey can see," Wiley said." Governor also assigned the local Ranger Captain and company to help us," Wiley explained. "Winch is that help. *Sorry-ass,* help, too. Worthless. Winch worked as an inspector for the Tarrant County Sheep and Goat Association. And he was a sorry, lazy coot at that, too. Rangers needed a brace of men years ago for a border problem. They hired him in a batch, awhile back for that mess."

"And let me guess. Down and back from the south. Border wars. Mexican killer," Gunther growled, still watching the front door. It opened again, but it was just the mailman.

"That's about right. Winch won't be much help. In fact he'll probably be a hindrance. Sad to say Gunth, he just… wants…the money," Wiley said, "he figured you'd chicken up a money box or something. Then he'd have it. And he would…"

"…keep it. Somehow. With a made-up story," Gunther growled. Then asked, "But you are in charge of the investigation?"

"Well, I am in charge of the highway robbery investigation. Officially. Not the city case. That's city police business. A detective named Reno Burton has that murder case."

"Big Ears Burton?"

"That's him."

Gunther sipped his tea. "He's a good man."

"He is a good man. I am the big chief in charge of the highwaymen robbery, but I got nobody, no money to run to all these newspapers to place ads you are talking about,"

Wiley said waving a finger at Jefe's pad. "Nobody to hang posters all over Dallas and Tarrant counties. I am working three other robberies and a murder just outside of Weatherford right now. Plus all this shit here now."

"We'll take care of the ads and the posters. We'll hire people to do it if we need to," Jefe said.

Mesha brought the mail in and laid a few envelopes on the desk.

"Thank you," Gunther said fingered though them casually, then settled in seriously on one. He pulled a knife from the top drawer and sliced it open.

"What?" Jefe asked.

"Well, shit fire and save matches. It's a letter from Sgt. Torontoola, at the jail." Gunther scanned the lines. "He wants…he wants to meet me at the jail. To talk. He wants to…" he looked up at Jefe and then to Wiley. "He wants to hire us to solve the murder of his wife."

Chapter 6: The Wailing Man

Deputy Hanniken and Gunther climbed a stairwell of the Tarrant County Jail to the fifth floor "perch" as they called it, that housed Fort Worth Police Detective Sgt. Raoul Torontoola.

"Whew," whispered the overweight Hanniken, "they are building an elevator shaft on the other side of the jail."

"They are?"

"They are, but…I don't know. I don't know. You ever been on an elevator?"

"Yes, I have," Gunther said.

"I don't know. I don't know iffin I'll ride it once't it's finished. Is it…is it kinda like flying or somethin?"

"No. Not really. It's like a small room. You might feel the movement in your legs a bit."

"So, it's not like taking off in a circus balloon?"

"I have also been in a balloon…"

"You have?"

"Yeah, and it's different than an elevator. Elevators run straight up and down. A balloon…bounces around a bit. Sort of drifts."

"Oh, shitfire!" He shook his head. "Gunther? What kind of name is that, sir?"

"It's German. I was born in Germany."

"I'm from Finland. Well, I myself was born south of here in Mansfield, but my parents are from Finland."

"We left Germany when I was very young."

"Lots of Germans in Texas."

"Yup."

"Have you ever been on a, on a esca…escaliner?"

"Escalator?"

"Yeah!"

"No, I haven't."

"Reckon someday they'll replace every flight of stairs with an escalator in the USA?"

"Maybe, huh?"

"Some fire out there, huh?" Hanniken said. "Look out here."

They stopped at a window on the wall of the stairs and both of them looked out. A slow burning fire had engulfed part of Hells Acre working its way through a serious number of structures despite efforts over almost two days running to contain it. They could see the flames topping the heights of the nearby buildings.

"Yes. They are bringing fireman in from Dallas to help."

"It's a lulu!" They continued up the stairs. "It is a shame about Sgt. Torontoola," Hanniken said. "Seems like just the other day he was bringing in prisoners to the jail. Booking them in. Now he is one his own self. Every night you know. He just cries. Cries and cries. Moans. He cries out loud. So loud that folks say they hear him from down on the street. He wails and cries. Kinda creepy. Kinda like a fairytale. Like a wounded man in a tower or something out of a Grimmer Fairytale."

Gunther nodded when Hanniken looked over at him. They reached a short hall at the top of the stairs. They were both a bit out of breath. There was a chair and some newspapers by the door.

"I'll sit right there while yer here. Don't be a rushing. " Hanniken pulled a key from a chain attached to his belt and unlocked a big iron door. The key opened it silently with little to no effort.

"I greased this…Monday," Hanniken said with a smile. Gunther entered the large fifth floor of steel and bricks. There was a room outside of a very large jail cell, and a hallway ran beside the cell.

"Good morning, Sergeant!" Hanniken shouted in.

"Good morning deputy!" A cheery, deep voice with a Hispanic accent answered from within the cell.

Hanniken shut the big quiet door behind Gunther.

Gunther walked down the hall. The cell inside was indeed giant, like a residence. There were maroon velvet chairs and a sofa inside. A dining table. Lamps. Books and newspapers scattered about. A long, decorative cord stretched across the cell and dozens of outfits, shirts and pants hung on hangers from the rope. A fat, yellow cat appeared from behind the furniture and walked across the cell toward the sofa. It ignored Gunther.

"Hello, Señor Gunther!" A tall dark man, about 45 years old, emerged from behind the clothesline. He wore lightweight wool dress pants and a white, well-tailored shirt. He had waxed back, thick, black hair and a black moustache also waxed to fine points at the end. He appeared stout and just a bit majestic.

"Have a seat. Have a seat."

Gunther sat at a wooden oak table in an oak, leather-back chair in the hallway near the cell door. One side of the table pressed up flush against the bars. There was an ashtray full of ashes on the table, and a coffee mug. An ornate, wooden, cigar box sat in the middle of the table. A dirty shot glass contained wooden matches. A deck of cards lay alongside the shot glass. The incarcerated man sat on the other side of the bars in his own chair. He crossed one of his legs over the other revealing a red velvet slipper dangling on one foot.

"We have never met, but I have seen you around town. The opera? Some events here and there," Torontoola said.

"Probably so. No, we have never met. But I recall seeing you, too. And I've heard quite a bit about you."

"Oh my."

"Especially, lately."

"Oh my, then I would guess it has not been good talk. But I have heard about you and that messy shooting at the opera house years ago. You saved the lieutenant governor's life. And you also have been in some wars, have you not?"

"Yes, some."

"A war hero?"

"No. No a war survivor. Sometimes, just barely."

"Hmmm. I wonder…I wonder why a man such as yourself is not down south fighting in the Banana Wars or the Mexican Revolution. It is never over. I understand there is good money in the soldier of fortune business, especially if you know how to operate these new machine guns. And you graduated from West Point!"

"Yes. Well, I shoulda been killed in Cuba. Shoulda been killed in the Philippines and certainly China. Didn't do much in South Africa. Was damn near killed in Afghanistan. So, I've had my fill of foreign wars on foreign soils."

Torontoola nodded. "But you still stay…'active.' You are still a professional for hire. Sometimes, you know, we grow strong on the battlefield, but we slowly disintegrate in peace. So you stay…active?"

Gunther let that remark lay. And he was not going to ask him if he had been in any wars as he knew it was sometimes uncomfortable for men who were not. But Torontoola spoke up on the subject.

"I have fought in the Revolution in the '90s. It was a crazy time. My unit changed sides several times. Bribes or promises. It all became very confusing, this revolution. Everyone changing sides like the wind. So, tell me, Mr. Gunther. Do you gamble?" He flicked a finger at the deck of cards on the table.

"No, gambling is a total waste of time for me."

"Good! Good, because if you gambled, and if you gambled here in Fort Worth, I do not think I could trust you."

"I hear that Hells Acre is on fire. The sirens and bells! When the wind changes, I can see the smoke go by my window. What have we lost so far?"

"The Shamrock Saloon is gone. All three stories."

"Madre de Mia!"

"Dew Drop Inn. Bunch of smaller places. Homes, too." Torontoola nodded.

"I am sorry to hear about your wife."

"Yes. Thank you. I guess you have heard that I…cry out every night. Deputy Hanniken loves to tell every visitor that I cry. But I must confess that I do. I have lost my beautiful wife. She was the garden of my life. And of course, too, the horror of losing our simple housekeeper—it breaks my heart. She was so innocent. It is our…my fault. She was a mother and a wife herself. Very loyal to us. But, I cry too because, I had a very, very good life.

Such freedom. At night, I put on these very fine clothes behind me and went about the city. The night clubs. Restaurants. Everywhere. Ahhh…working, as I am sure you have heard about me. So, when the night falls here to me in this caged cell, you know, it creeps in the windows like the absence of air. Like death. Another death. I just can't seem to stand it anymore. Being in here like this. I am filled with such…anguish. And pain. I feel the loss of my wife the most at that time. And, yes, I cry. I do cry out."

The cat leapt up on the prisoner's lap and froze like a still life. Gunther lifted his left booted foot up and placed it on a nearby, empty chair to relax.

"Mr. Gunther, I want to hire you to investigate the murder of my wife."

"Well Raoul, I am already working on that."

"No, not for me you are not. You are working for the governor on that. You will only report to the governor. You will not tell me what you know, what you discover. And, of course, I will not tell you what I know. Unless of course, you are working for me. Then I must tell you." He smiled. "And there is little question you need to know what I know."

Gunther smiled. "Well, I guess it doesn't matter if I have two clients on the same investigation."

"It is a smart decision to decipher, sir. You will be paid twice. And, of course it does not matter that you have two clients. How much will you charge me for this work?"

"Two hundred dollars. And any extra expenses."

"Two hundred dollars! That is a lot of money. And you will see it through to the end?"

"To the bitterist of ends. And I hope some of the expenses will be for five bullets."

"I hope not. I am not a regulator, nor am I an assassin."

"I am joking."

But, Gunther could tell if he was or if he wasn't.

Torontoola shoved his hand through the bars and Gunther sat up, leaned forward and shook it. And a deadly deal was sealed on the fifth floor of the county jail that day.

The cat jumped to the floor, let out a howl and slipped through the bars to the sunshine beaming outside.

"Look at her go! I wish I could do that. All day and all night she torments me with the ease by which she escapes my cage. In and out. Out and in. My sister brought her up here to keep me company. There is no one left at my house to feed her, until my father-in-law comes in from Monterrey."

"Did you kill that gambler?"

Torontoola sighed. "I have killed men. Yes. But I did not kill that gambler," he said solemnly. "I have killed some, yes, but I have never walked up to someone like that and just shot him. Not even in the Revolution have I done this. Have you ever done such a thing?"

Gunther remained quiet.

"And who does this? And who kills? Rides up and just kills two women. Rob them! Ok? Rob them, but kill them? You know, sweet Jesus, rob them and not shoot them! Why shoot them? Like such wild, animal outlaws. It is 1908! These men are the last of some gunmen who would do such a thing, I think."

"Who killed the gambler?" Gunther asked.

"I do not know. Let me inform you that this gambler, this Justin Trace is a very suspicious man. He came here from Amarillo with a lot of money. A lot. He opened some small gambling operations in some bars and clubs off of downtown. He paid some oil roughnecks who are out of work or who have been fired, to protect the games and the businesses. But it is the damdest thing. You see, he overpays them all." Now Torontoola leaned forward. "And, he spent even more money. He gives money away to the business owners for improvements. Buys equipment. I mean to say, a lot of money. No strings attached to this money. He is like a bank that no one ever pays back. Like a bank gone mad. A rich man gone mad."

"Is the gambling business that good for him?"

"No! No it is not. I saw that it was not. Others too. It

would seem this man has unlimited money. I have heard that when some of the gamblers lost a lot of money at his game tables, he gave it back to them! This is most unusual practice of a gambling house. He seemed to be a charity not a business man. He has donated money to foster homes. Orphanages. Churches. Hospitals. I tell you he is a mystery man."

A tea kettle whistled, and Raoul jumped up.

"Tea, Mr. Gunther?"

"Don't mind if I do. Plain."

"Of course, this news of generous and forgiving gambling houses caught fire in my end of the city," Torontoola said from where he stood making tea at the portable stove on the far wall. "My friends have lost business to these new places. My friends wanted me to do something about this man."

He approached the bars with a large cup.

"This gonna fit?" Gunther asked, eyeing up the approach.

"Yes, yes, I do this all the time. Here, here…" and he barely squeezed the cup through the bars. Gunther grabbed the handle. They both sat down, their cups in hand. "I wanted to deeply investigate Justin Trace. I could find no source for his endless money. I threatened him a time or two. Yes, yes. One night at the Black Cat Club, he even pulled a revolver on me. I stared him down. I told him if he did that again I would kill him. There were witnesses to this. These, these careless words, are the cause of all my trouble now."

"And the night of his murder? Where were you?"

"Elsewhere. I was elsewhere in our fair city. I cannot say exactly where I was at the exact time. I was visiting many places."

"Alone?"

"Alone. Si."

"We are going to have to collect the names of the places you visited that night. You need to make a list."

"If they will just let me testify before the grand jury…"

"You need more than that," Gunther said. "More than words."

"I tell you that my wife would be alive today if I were not locked up in this place the day when she was robbed and shot. There is no way this would have happened if I were free. Mr. Gunther, every Tuesday morning my beautiful wife and I take a wagon ride to a bank in Dallas."

"Dallas?"

"We have an account in a bank in Dallas. It is far enough from Fort Worth that few people can track or find my money easily. We deposit my money into this bank from my work week. My weekend work is very good."

"How much a week?"

"About a hundred a week."

"A hundred dollars? A week?"

"Yes! Yes, sometimes much more! Are you now ever so sorry that you only asked for only two hundred? That particular Tuesday morning there was some 13 hundred in the chest - these thugs stole."

"Who knew you did this? Who knew she made this weekly run?"

"No one I could tell you for sure. The list of suspects grows the longer I sit here and think about it. Maybe the housekeeper told someone who told someone else? Maybe my wife was followed?"

"Do you have enemies at the district attorney's office?"

"Ha! I have enemies everywhere in this county. There are people in the DA's office that do not like me or my lifestyle. Yes."

"I have heard that there is a surprise witness against you."

"I do not want you to involve yourself with my problems. I want you to find the killers of my wife."

Gunther leaned forward and asked, "what do you know about Texas Ranger Chester Winch?"

"Ohhh, Chester Winch," he said slowly with disgust.

"He is a corrupt buffoon. Why?"

"The governor wanted a Ranger on this case. The local Ranger Captain has assigned him to follow this case."

"Oh no, oh you try to keep him in the dark. Keep him on the outside. He hates all Mexicans. He hates me because I am Mexican. He will hate you if you try to help me. He is corrupt and a con man. If he has a winning card to play, you can bet he will gamble with it. He will use it to make money any way he can. If he gets in the middle of what you are doing it will only spell trouble. Caramba, this news of Chester Winch troubles me." He stared at the floor.

"Give me the name of your best informant. Someone who will know the whispers of the city. Someone well-connected."

"Best? I cannot call anyone the best. But, there is Beau Kershaw. He plays the blues and jazz piano in a quartet many nights a week in Bociferous on Holly Avenue near the baseball stadium. He will go out drinking and smoking the Mexican marijuana at the after-hour parties and gambling houses. He can walk amongst all of them, and does.

He is well-liked, but it is also because he is a pimp. He runs two girls, sometimes as many as three girls. He finds country girls and befriends them. He keeps them out at his rooming house and gets them hooked on laudanum. Then he works them into the trade. Right now, I think he has three girls. Cousins from Midlothian. I only know one. A girl named Betha."

"What rooming house?"

"You know the Abby Holland House? On Jacksboro?"

"Yeah. Big place. All the rooms are on the first floor. Restaurant in the center. Been there."

"Each girl has a room. Kershaw has a room. But the girls, and they are young girls, will trade anywhere he sends them."

"Didn't know that about Abby."

"Abby is in on the trade. If there is sex in her place, she gets a cut. But few know this."

"Damn straight? Such good fried chicken too."

"Oh, yes! And the pies!"

"I can't imagine that the murder of Justin Trace, setting you up is not a clever plot. It has to be connected to the robbery and murder of your wife," Gunther said. "So, I will be troubling with your troubles. I have a partner, a Filipino named Jefe."

"El Capitan! That is his first name?"

"Yes. He is also a war vet. He will come up here and ask you some more questions soon. Tell him anything. You can trust him with your life. I have many times."

Torontoola grunted and nodded. "Does he play cards?"

"Yes, he does. But he won't gamble with you. He is a devout Muslim."

"Then I will talk to him, and we will play cards, with matchsticks maybe."

"If you need anything? Get word to me," Gunther said and pushed the old and new cups across the table close to the bars. Torontoola's finger sipped out from the bars like a fast worm and caught the handle of each cup, slipping them back inside his cage.

Gunther stood and walked to the door. The cat, who had reentered the cell through the bars some time earlier, charged the door in hopes of escape by that route.

"Take care not to release my cat, please!" Torontoola shouted. "He must share with me, and share my pain."

Gunther knocked on the iron door for the deputy. He moved a booted foot near the cat and threatened him in a whispery voice, "go on, go on, now. Geet!"

The door opened and Deputy Hanniken, aware of the cat's past escape attempts, put his foot at the low end of the opening too, kicking it a few inches. Gunther exited, as Hanniken pushed the door back into the frame, Gunther heard Torontoola say aloud to himself, "Dear mother of God."

Hanniken must have heard it, too. "I sure hope he doesn't commence to crying," the deputy said as they descended the stairs. "It's only early afternoon, and it just breaks my heart to hear him fuss so."

Chapter 7: Circulation

Spanky Runyan made a clean power swing with the bat. The wood hit the sweet spot and the ball took off for the bleachers like a shooting star. He knew its destination the minute it came into contact with the bat. It was an amazing hit, especially for practice, and the hulk of a man with thick, wavy, black hair, placed the end of his bat on the ground and rested on it like a cane just watching the ball soar, enjoying the simplistic beauty of the thing. Home run!

"Ha, haa!" he chuckled. His head bobbed up and down.

He stepped back into the batter's box, and the practice catcher dropped down behind him for the next pitch.

Ranger Chester Winch appeared from the Bobcat's dugout and walked onto the field. He nodded to a few of the players and walked about halfway to home plate. He caught Spanky's eye. But The Spank looked back on the ball right away and ripped another one into the bleachers; and another cracking sound of ball on sweet wood echoed across the field.

Then Spanky left the box, signaled the awaiting hitter he was up and approached the Ranger. Once beside him, they did not look at each other, just stared out over the field and the empty seats of the stadium.

"Chester."

"Spank."

"Whatcha find out?" the ballplayer said.

"I found out that this Gunther says he does not have in his possession, the governor's money. It's in Austin, he says."

"You believe 'em?"

"I don't. He is a slick German, prick. All prissy up there in his fancy-ass, office. Got some Mexican looking side-kick, assistant who acts like a genius. He's got a gotdamn monkey in his office. Can you believe it?"

"A monkey?"

"A gotdamn monkey running around."

"He's some kind of a war hero, ain't he?"

"Shit. They say." He curled his lip in disgust.

Spanky laughed at Chester's answer. "They say…" he repeated and shook his head. "Well, what's he say then?"

"He says he's gonna hunt down that horse that ran off."

"Hunt the...hunt the horse down? How's he gonna do that? It's 30 miles of almost nothing out there. How's he gonna find one horse?"

"Proclaims he is gonna advertise for it."

"Advertise?"

"Advertise."

"Advertise how? Like in a newspaper?"

"Yup."

They stood quiet, watching the hitter knock balls to the fielders.

"Whatcha think?" Spanky asked.

"I think he'll never find one horse between Fort Worth and Dallas, that's what I think."

"Lotta horses between Dallas and Fort Worth alright, I think too," Spanky said, almost in a boyish giggle.

"Says he will offer up 100 dollars for information on the horse and 500 dollars for information on the robbers."

"Five hundred dollars. Five hundred. That's a lot of head-turning, money," Spanky said, suddenly more concerned.

"If I could get ahold of that money? I could shrink the reward. I could control the tips that come in too. See that the good ones die a quick death. Also see who the spies are and pay them a visit."

"If you could. Can you?"

"I have to go over the head of my captain. Go to Austin. Speak with the governor. That's a tricky step."

"Hmmm.

The batboy, a lad about 12 years old wearing a smaller version of the Bobcat uniform, with a ball cap too big, wandered around nearby.

"Hey runt!" Spanky shouted to him. "Runt!"

The boy reluctantly looked up at him, but he wouldn't hold any eye contact.

"Come here to me!" Spanky demanded.

The boy came nearer.

Spanky flipped the bat in his right hand and held the heavy end, offering the handle to the batboy.

"Here, do yer job," Spanky said with a sneer.

The boy lifted his hand for the bat and Spanky quickly hit the kid on the side of the head with the handle. Not a knockout shot, but not a light tap either.

"Haaa, what's a matter, little runt? Ain't cha fast enough to do yer job?"

The boy looked down at the grass.

Spanky hit the brim of the boy's ball cap with the handle. The hat popped off the boy's head.

"Do yer job!" he growled.

Spanky more or less hit the boy's open hand with the bat handle. The boy took the handle. The boy picked up his hat and ran off to the dugout.

Spanky and Chester looked at each other, grinned and chuckled.

"They got anything else?" Spanky asked.

"They got nothing else."

"So that County Detective Wiley. He sound like he got anything?"

"He's got nothing. Nothing but a big casebook of unsolved crimes. This is just one headache."

"Well, ok. You coming around the house tonight?"

"I think I will stop in for a whiskey. Is that little ol' gal gonna be there?"

"Betha?"

"Betha."

"Oh I guess so. It's Thursday. I think so."

"I think I'll stop by later tonight."

"Got anything else on the fishing hook?" Spanky asked.

"I got a preacher on the hook. Monsignor Hoolahan at the Catholic Church. He be lovin him some pussy and whiskey."

"We gonna rob a church?"

"Who's got more money than God?"

"Ha!"

"I think I might introduce Betha to the Monsignor."

"Ok. See ya later Chester."

Chester walked off leaving the way he came, through the dugout. The bat boy tried not to look at him either.

"BOO! Ya-ha!" Chester yelled as he got close to the boy, and the lad shrank away, fearing more abuse. Half the players in the dugout laughed. The other half didn't laugh at all. And that interaction quickly told the tale to anyone who cared enough to look who was with whom on the team.

The Whispering Wind...

The Whispering Wind newspaper office was a new, red, brick building on the northeast side of Fort Worth. Jefe's imported Filipino cousin Louis from Manila, now the official Remedy's carriage driver, bearing the nickname "Quick-some' yanked the reins back on Darlene, the company's carriage horse, and pulled the wagon to a halt out front of the paper. Gunther jumped out.

"Ten minutes," he told Quick-some.

"Lickity-split," the Filipino said. It was a new English term he picked up somewhere, and he liked the sound of it. No one was quite sure he knew what it really meant, but he used it in place of all sorts of answers.

Outside, leaning up against the wall, were about 15 bicycles. The front door burst open and just as many young men charged out with pads of paper in their hands. They dashed to the bikes, jumped on them, and in a scattered, tangled mess, eventually managed to take off heading down the road.

Gunther watched them with curiosity, then entered the building and stood before a long wooden counter in the lobby. Behind it, numerous men and women scurried about; and the strong smell of ink and cleaning solvent lingered throughout the office, stirred in waves by the ceiling fans.

"Can we help you, sir?" a redheaded, teenage boy ran up

and asked.

"What was all that?" Gunther asked, pointing his thumb toward at the door.

"The news crew, sir," the teen clerk said. "The Hendersons called the police and reported that their son was kidnapped. They're off to cover the story. Can I help you?"

"Oh. Ah, yes, you can. I need to put this ad in your paper." Gunther laid a sheet of paper on the counter.

"Yes, we can do this." The teen took the sheet and ran off toward an office in a row of offices to the left. A man dressed like a banker, came out of the office with him in only a few moments and walked to the counter.

"Let's see," the man said reading the words on the sheet. "Hmmm. Hmmmm. One moment."

Then he left the sheet on the counter and made for another office doorway down another row. The teen remained, smiling broadly at Gunther. Gunther smiled back.

A tall woman with long, black hair and thin, black-rimmed glasses emerged from that office door, wearing a starched white blouse and brown pants - not a common sight. On her feet she wore ornate cowgirl boots. When her eyes met Gunther's, she smiled big and bravely at him, and Gunther found it a beautiful smile. He returned it instinctively with just such an honest one of his own. She was — in a word — beautiful.

"Johann Gunther!" she said, stretching out her hand in greeting. Her silver, Indian bracelets slid up her forearm as she reached out.

"That's me."

"I am Carmella Davis. I am very pleased to meet you. I am a feature reporter here at The Wind."

"Well, as lovely as it is to make your acquaintance Carmella, I think I need to see that feller over there in advertising. Not a feature reporter like you say you are?" Gunther leaned on the counter for a better look. She was about 30 years old. No wedding ring. Her thick hair framed her face and bloomed about her shoulders as though she'd just walked away from posing for a hardware store calendar painting.

"We'll be glad to handle that for you, sir," and she motioned for the ad man to return to the front desk. He did. He picked up the sheet on the counter and walked off with it.

She remained.

"You are quite the famous gentleman. We haven't met yet because you seem to stay gone a lot."

"Yes."

"And now, here you are right in my office! We've heard that you are working for not one, but two state governors to find a gang of robbers and killers."

Blue eyes. Black hair. Blue eyes and black hair! Did Gunther say that twice in his mind?

"Ahhh…yeah."

"That is one heckuva feature story, Johann. May I just cut to the chase and call you Johann?"

"Sure. Cut away."

"That'll be one heckuva story, if you can catch them, that is. And I see by your ad you are trying to hunt down the horse of the injured criminal. Good idea."

"Got a picture?" the ad man asked as he returned.

"Picture of what?"

"A horse? A saddle? Anything?"

"No. we're looking for them. To get a picture. We don't have a picture."

"What Chuck is saying," Carmella interrupted, "is that we here at the Wind like to attach some artwork or a photo to every story or ad we can. It's newspaper policy. People like to see something, arty. We always try to catch their eye, if possible." She took off her glasses and rested the tip of one temple on her full lower lip.

"Ok, well, can you add something to catch eyes?" Gunther said.

"We can, sir," the ad man said.

"The horse was brown."

"We have an adequate drawing of a running horse. Black and white drawing."

"Riderless? With a saddle?"

"Yes, sir. Can do."

"Can you run that for two weeks? Half page."

"Yes sir. That will be 18 cents a day."

“That’ll be fine.” Gunther put the dollars and some change on the counter along with his Remedies business card. Can you mail us a receipt to this address?”

“Surely,” the ad man said.

“Do you have good circulation…in Arlington?” Gunther asked Carmella.

“I try to keep the circulation moving everywhere.” She arched her left eyebrow.

“I’ll bet you do. I will certainly leave here with the good feeling that my circulation is moving.” He couldn’t help saying it and couldn’t help but chuckle a bit.

“Good stuff means good circulation,” she said. “Like you. Like you and this story. I would like to check in on you and ask you some questions about your progress. Does that sound like a plan? A…date?”

“Uh, yeah sure, when the time is right. Timing is everything.”

They looked at each other for a few seconds and Gunther rapped his knuckles on the counter twice as if to break a spell, and nodded as if to say to goodbye. She remained in place, her hands now on the counter, arms straight, hip cocked out to the right.

His look at her lingered a bit longer than necessary as he turned to go. He couldn’t help himself, and he also wanted her to see him do it. She did, while watching him closely. He walked out the door back onto the street. The teenage clerk stood outside on the wooden sidewalk, smoking a cigarette with one hand and holding a bottle of Dr Pepper in the other.

“She’s a real doll, ain’t she? Huh?” The kid said aloud with wide-eyes and a wide grin, smoke floating out of his nose and mouth.

Gunther stopped and looked at the kid, shook his head then made for his carriage.

“She…ain’t…married!” the clerk said in a sing-song voice. “Near as I can tell she ain’t in l-o-v-e either,” he said.

“Today’s gossip from the Whispering Wind,” Gunther added.

“That’s what we do best here.”

Gunther climbed into the carriage, recovered his Stetson

from the seat and put it on.

"Let's get back to the office," he told Quick-some.

"Lickity-split!" Quick-some said.

He glanced at the building's front windows as they pulled away from the curb. He saw Carmella watching him leave. Even through the bright reflections on the glass, she was a sensual vision, more beautiful than any sculpture or mannequin in any window he'd ever seen. He knew he'd buy anything she was selling.

Chapter 8: A Man Named Clemency

Ten days later, Arlington, Texas...

Gunther, Jefe and County Detective Wiley Lewis stopped their horses on the Arlington country Farm-to-Market Road 28, right beside the metal and wood gate to a farm. Beyond the wide gate was a long, straight road bordered by mature oak trees on both sides. Within sight of the road sat a residence and off back, some barns. A wind kicked up the thinner branches on the trees. Black and white spotted goats and longhorned cattle wandered in separate pastures on each side of the road.

"This is the place," Jefe said.

"Clemency Rag," Wiley said. "Farmer. Church deacon. Arlington police said he shot a feller in 1902 at a political rally. Wounded him. No charges filed though. Nothing much else on record for him."

Gunther reined his horse around to get a better view of the house. He stood in the saddle stirrups. Gunther's city clothes, were replaced by Western garb, and he looked more like someone just in from the Pecos, complete with his semi-auto Luger pistol in a visible gun belt. The men each sat astride an Arlington police horse, borrowed by arrangement through Wiley. Policing arrangements had been made so the horses were waiting for them when they stepped off the train earlier at the Arlington station.

Jefe had been in the area all day the day before working

the letters and phone call tips from the missing horse newspaper advertisements. The best sounding tip said their missing horse was at the Rag Farm.

"Well, let's see if a man named Clemency is actually interested in some clemency," Gunther said.

Jefe slipped off his horse and opened the gate. The other two rode their mounts through, and Jefe led his horse through the gate after them. He shut it quickly, wary of the 20 or so goats nearby inside the pasture. Gunther and Wiley slowly rode down the road. Jefe did not remount his horse and instead made the walk. As was his way since Cebu and Manila, Jefe spread out from Gunther when the going got a little hot. The army called it "covering."

All three ate up the scenery with keen gazes looking for trouble. At the road's end, it all opened to a large front yard before what appeared to be a rather old, ramshackle, main house.

"WHO in hell are you?" a growling voice sounded from behind them.

They turned to see a man with a rifle, crouched by some stacked hay bales they'd passed. The gun was pointed right at them.

"He ain't alone!" another man warned them. Also armed with a rifle, he stepped out on the front porch.

"Now who in hell are ya?"

"Here I'm the law and, if things don't go well, I may be the last law you see before you see hell," Wiley said. He slowly opened his jacket to display a police badge pinned on his vest.

"That badge don't make me no never mind, as to the fact that you are on my private property," the man standing by the bales answered. "What do you want?"

"To talk to a Clemency," Gunther said. He stepped down from his mount and walked toward the man.

"Oh yeah, you take another step. Yeah."

Gunther ignored the threat. He kept walking.

"Clemency we are looking for a brown horse. We heard it was here."

"A brown horse. What? Are you calling me some kind of a

horse thief?"

"No. Not a horse thief at all. A horse finder."

Silence followed this statement. Gunther stopped walking. He knew that by now, with the distraction of his approach, Jefe was well behind his horse, off to his left with his gun out and at the ready.

"A horse finder?" the man repeated with a slight air of confusion.

"Yeah. A horse lost its rider and ran away from a robbery, murder scene up on the Dallas, Fort Worth turnpike about three, four weeks ago," Wiley said, his hands resting on his saddle horn. "It belonged to one of the robbers. That robber is likely dead. Shot right off of it. That robber and his accomplices shot a Louisiana judge and killed two unarmed women in the coldest of blood."

"Heard of it."

"Good. Well, that horse and all tack attached to it at the time it ran way is important to the investigation," Wiley said.

"Clem!" the man on the porch called out. "That Chinese-Mexican has a gun out."

Gunther smiled because he knew that would irritate Jefe. He shook his head.

"What's so funny to you, creeper?" The man on the porch asked.

Gunther, still smiling shook his head. "Long story."

"Well, what's so damn funny about two guns a pointed at yer head?"

Gunther could tell his calm and easy smile had unsettled the two men.

"There a reward?" the man by the bales asked.

"Yes, there's a reward," Wiley said with a sigh. "Don't nobody do nothing anymore without cashing in on it?"

The man stepped away from the bales and lowered his lever-action rifle to hip height.

"If such a horse and such tack existed, how much would it be worth?"

"One hundred dollars," Gunther said.

His barrel dropped. "Yeah, we got that horse, yeah. Come on here. I didn't steal it! My daughter found the horse in our north pasture. Over there." He gestured. "He was hungry and lost."

Wiley stayed aboard his horse. Jefe and Gunther followed the farmer afoot, when he walked past them to the trail beside the house. The other man jumped off the porch, lowered his rifle and followed all of them.

"I am from the Philippines. Not China. Not Mexico," Jefe told him.

The man just looked at Jefe, as though he were from Mars.

The five walked around the house down a path to a fairly solid looking, gray weathered barn. Clemency opened the door and motioned toward a stall, and there stood their horse happily munching hay.

"He's a good horse. My daughter has adopted him. She's grown real fond of it."

Wiley and Jefe combed over the horse looking for markings.

"What about the saddle, bridle, blanket—anything the horse came in with?" Gunther asked.

"Yonder." Clemency pulled up at a sliding door and inside a side tack room atop a tree stump sat the saddle with a bridle and blanket thrown over it.

A tomboy-looking teenage girl appeared in the barn door.

"Daddy?" her voice sounded breathless and a bit shaky from a run.

The man looked at her.

"Daddy, are…are they here for Charlie?"

Gunther looked the girl over and then circled the saddle. He flipped it over onto the ground.

"Whatcha got here?" Wiley walked up and asked.

"Got a saddle maker," Gunther said, after kneeling and examining the saddle. "Lawrence Sureline Saddles. And a number. Number 727." He looked at the blanket and bridle but found no markings that would identify their makers. Both could be bought at any local feed store, so he set them aside.

"Were there any saddle bags?" he asked, standing and placing the saddle back on the stump.

"Nope, that's all there twas," Clemency replied.

"No brand on the horse? Either?"

Gunther walked back over, opened the stall door and examined the horse closely but could not find a brand.

"Guess this will have to do," he said.

"I know that outfit. They're in Fort Worth alright," Wiley said.

"Are you taking the horse, mister?" the girl asked him, solemnly, lips pursed, with a quiver.

Gunther watched that lip quiver for a moment. "Detective Wiley? If we were to take this horse, how would we get it back to Fort Worth?"

Wiley noticed the quiver too. He looked out the door away from Gunther as if seriously considering the situation. "Be a lot of trouble. Have to lead it all the way. You know how cantankerous horses can be on a lead. Don't always get on with the lead horse. Kicking and fighting and such. Even if we got it back to the police stables in Arlington, somebody would have to feed it. Ride it. And every day, too. Shovel up its excrement. Considerable trouble."

"Considerable. What if we left it in the custody of these folks. This girl's custody, for instance?"

"I am thinking that would save my police force and the Arlington police force a lot of horsing around, frankly."

"Young lady?" Gunther said. "Reckon you have a saddle?"

"Yeah."

"Because, we will need to take this saddle with us."

Gunther pulled out his wallet. "By the power invested in me by the governor of Texas..."

Her eyebrows rose.

"I am giving you this 10 dollar bill. So, you can take proper care of this horse. Until such time as we might need it. If we ever do need it."

"Can I buy this horse?"

"Maybe. What is your name, little lady?"

"Clementine."

"Sir," the dad reminded.

"Clementine, *sir.*"

"We'll see what we can do, but you know, there might be another girl in Fort Worth. One about your age, maybe. The daughter of the man that fell from this horse, and she may love this horse, too and…may want him, too, because it was her daddy's horse. She may love it too and has loved it for a longer time than you have. I don't know yet. Do you understand what I mean?"

"Yeah. Yes, sir."

Gunther nodded. "I am inclined right now to see that you get to keep this horse. But I don't think either of us want to break another little girl's heart, you know? Especially if she's younger than you and all. And she really misses her dad."

"Uh-huh."

Gunther handed the 10 dollar bill to Clementine. He took four 20s and a 10 out of his engraved wallet and handed it to the father. The man's jaw dropped an inch.

"That is a beautiful wallet," Clementine said.

"Yes. It was made for me in India. I was in hospital there for too long a time. A dog. A very, very big, ugly dog attacked me," Gunther said. "Have you ever read The Hound of the Baskervilles? A story about Sherlock Holmes?"

"No, sir."

"Well I wish you would. It's a little scary, but it's quite a popular book. To me that dog that got me was as big and scary as the Baskerville hound," Gunther said as he lifted the saddle and tossed it over his shoulder.

He left the barn first. It was now obvious to the two farmers that these men were far from simple intruders and were nothing to worry about. The rest of them followed him out of the barn, except the girl who remained talking cheerfully to her new charge. The three returned to their horses waiting for them out front. Gunther tossed the saddle over the back of his horse and used some leather straps to connect it to the main saddle. He climbed aboard.

"I might apologize for the rough treatment at first," Clemency said.

"Mister Clemency, I've been shot at, shot and hit and almost eaten alive...by that dog I told you about! So, a few rough words don't bother me much at all."

"Sorry I called you something you ain't," the second man said to Jefe, as the Filipino leapt smoothly onto his horse.

Gunther tipped his hat, and the three men turned their horses toward the road.

"You all have been a big help. Thank you," Wiley said over his shoulder.

"Thank you for this reward!" Clemency said and then quick stepped up to Gunther, "And thank you for, you know, ...for…the...horse."

"Thank you for making my day on two counts. The saddle and getting to make a little girl happy. I'll do what I can to see she keeps that horse, and if not? I'll buy her a new one."

The three didn't speak until they reached the gate. This time Jefe leaned over and opened the latch.

"I guess we'll have to brief the Ranger that we've got our hands on the saddle," Wiley said.

"Eventually. Eventually. Let's save him some work and check it all out first, so we won't be wasting his precious time."

Wiley nodded.

"No sense wearing down those spurs, and wrinkling all that starch," Gunther said. "Wiley, let me ask you something; where are the bullets they removed from Torontoola's wife? And did they remove the bullets from the maid's body as well?"

"Nope. In 'em."

"In 'em? So they were buried with all bullets still in them?"

"Yup. The witnesses all said the gunmen used revolvers. So we know they were pistol bullets."

"How about Justin Trace?"

"Bullets? Witnesses say the shooter used a revolver on him too."

"The bullet is still in Trace's body, as well? In the grave?"

"How about Judge Hofferman?"

"Buried. In the grave. Why?"

"Well, they are learning some amazing things from bullets taken out of bodies nowadays."

"Who's they?"

"Scientists in Boston. New York. In Europe."

"And what is so amazing?" Wiley asked as the trio turned

onto the county road.

"They can, with the use of a microscope and some tests, match some bullets up directly to the pistols and rifles that fired them. To the barrels. Firing pins, too. And even match bullets up with other bullets sometimes."

"Huh?"

"I'm going to call on our attorney, Norman Spinks. Get something going on this."

"Going on what?"

"We need to dig up those bodies and retrieve those bullets."

"You'll need an order from a district judge to exhume bodies," Wiley said. "We do it once in a while. Not often. But it can be done."

"We'll have to dig up the three bodies and pull the bullets out. Then we'll get all of Torontoola's guns we can find."

"You don't think Torontoola shot his own wife and maid...?"

"Oh no. He was in jail right?"

"Yup, he was in jail when his wife was shot."

"It would help build a defense. Do you ever just pull the bullets out of bodies and keep them?" Gunther asked.

"What fer? If'n we don't know about the murder weapon? Yes. We take a look to see if it's a rifle bullet or a pistol bullet. If the bullet's been pulled out for a look-see, then we stick it in the evidence room. Can't stick it back in the body. Kinda silly. And can't throw it away. Until later maybe. We lock them up for awhile."

"How many bullets like that do you think you all have locked up from all shootings?"

"Oh, maybe 20 over the last three or so years."

"Who does the cemetery digging?" Jefe asked.

"The judge orders the cemetery workers to do the digging. The County Doc looks over the body."

Gunther nodded.

"That's some nasty work right there," Wiley said.

"Yes, it is. Did I tell you when I was working as a deputy in Paris, Texas years ago we had a big case on a mad doctor selling body parts to hospitals and labs?" Gunther asked.

"No!"

"Yeah! Got to the point this doctor was killing people on special order for medical school bodies and body parts. Money was that good. The bodies and parts were shipped coast to coast to medical colleges and labs. I think some even went to Europe. This doctor hired the local Klu Klux Klan up there to do the killing. Helleva deal. Anyhow, I caught them all. A real mess. In fact, if the family of those KKK guys ever find me? They might still try to kill me. The governor of Oklahoma – we solved some murders up there too – got me out of there and away from the Klan. He got me appointed to West Point and that is how I went to West Point."

"I did not know that," Wiley said. "I thought all this time you were just a rich kid."

"He was not rich until he met me," Jefe said.

They rode on quietly for a piece.

"Jefe?" Gunther asked,

"Yes?"

"Remind me to send that girl the book, "The Hounds of the Baskervilles."

"Sounds like something your old friend Stinky Moses has done," Jefe said.

"That's right. Stinky sent many books to kids in Paris, Texas."

"Sinky...Moses?" Wiley said.

"Yup, " Gunther said, "best deputy I ever worked with. Stinky was not a nickname."

Chapter 9: The Hot Pepper Sureline

"Who owned Saddle number 727," Gunther told Lawrence Sureline, after some opening, how-do-you-do, owner-customer conversation.

That was not a question Mr. Sureline anticipated. He seemed too old to make saddles anymore, but by the looks of things, business continued to boom. Looking past him Gunther could see he had several men in the open back shop toiling away, and he counted at least a dozen saddles in various stages of construction.

As Gunther watched a middle-aged man wearing a leather smock threw down his tools and strutted from the back to the front of the leatherworks building coming up to where Gunther stood, with Lawrence Sureline.

"My son, Abbott Sureline," the elder Sureline made the introductions of the angry worker. "He pretty much runs this place now."

"What makes you think you can walk into our shop and demand information about our customers?" the man asked. His jaw jutted out at an angry angle. He put his hands on his aproned hips and flexed his big chest.

Gunther nodded and said, "Ok." He looked at Abbott, and said calmly, "I am not demanding anything."

"Well, demand or not, what makes you think you can just two-step on in here and collect confidential information about our customers?"

"This is part of a murder investigation and we…"

"I don't give a Christmas fuck what it's about!" His chest got a few inches closer to Gunther's chest. "Are you the sheriff? The police?"

"Abbott, if you get any closer, you'll be behind me," Gunther said, letting the clock tick a bit on that remark. Each second made Abbott seem a little more foolish.

"No. I work for the police. But, I'll just come back with the police and with a search warrant."

"A what?"

"A search warrant."

"A search what? A piece of paper? You're gonna come back here with a piece of paper, and you think that will make *me* release information about my customers?"

"A search warrant and the county detectives will collect the information on EVERY son of bitch that's walked through your front door for the last ten years and bought a peppermint from that jar, least of all saddles. Other than that, you should feel lucky that I can go and will get a search warrant," Gunther said, turning away to leave.

"Lucky? I should feel lucky?" Abbott asked.

"Yeah. Lucky." Gunther stopped and turned back at him. "Lucky. Lucky we live in this civilized city. Lucky because if we were just about 20 miles west of here? Out in the country? I'd kick your ass all up and down this fucking shop, and while you laid out on the floor gasping for breath like a fish out of water and looking up your teeth, I'd break open your file cabinet over there, make a pot of coffee and read every fucking invoice on every fucking customer you've ever had, while I rested my boot on your head. So yeah! I would say that you're real fucking lucky you live in this city."

Abbott's face turned red. His fingers flexed in and out of fists.

"Yeah," Gunther growled, "yeah, you take that swing, shop boy."

The shop went dead quiet, everyone had stopped working, maybe even stopped breathing as they turned to watch. Gunther pivoted and headed for the front door.

The senior Mr. Sureline followed him out of the show-room.

Shaking his head, he said, "hold on now, hold on there, Gunther. Come here. Come back here." Sureline waved his hand toward a wooden cabinet behind a counter. "Number 727, you said?"

Gunther turned and followed Mr. Sureline back into the show room and over to a cabinet behind the counter. He looked over Lawrence's shoulder as he unlocked the cabinet and searched through the receipts. Abbott shook his head and ambled back to his work table, picked up a cloth and started to buff the leather on one of the saddles with a bit more intensity than seemed necessary, all the while he kept his gaze fixed on Gunther.

"I, for one, do know what a search warrant is, and I don't want a bunch a got-damn badges swarming all over my place. They might stumble upon all the Spanish gold bullion I have buried under the back steps." He smiled.

Gunther smiled and nodded back.

"Anyway, this is about a murder, and I have always helped the police. And here it is. Ahhh. Owww. Say there. It's Billy Joe Farks." He handed Gunther the receipt. Gunther took out a piece of paper and a pencil from his jacket and wrote down the name and address.

"Remember anything about him?" Gunther asked.

"Remember him? Shit. He's one of my son's best friends."

They stared at each other, and then Gunther glanced back into the shop. Abbott was polishing away, his face a bright red, clearly the man was flustered.

"That explains all the puffed up, bravado. But you say, he is?" Gunther said, folding the paper back into his breast pocket. "He…is, or he…was? Is Farks still alive?"

"Alive! Is? Was? I haven't seen him around in a few weeks. I don't know. I think I would have heard if he died. But we made him that saddle two years ago. He's in my son's motorcycle club. Made him a seat for his motorcycle too and saddlebags for that contraption."

"Ok."

"I'm glad nothing happened back there. Abbott is a red,

hot-pepper-head. My grandson, his boy, works back there too. He'd a seen a helleva mess if there'd been a fight. My son's a pretty tough tamale. You'd a had a scrap on your hands. Fighting him wouldn't a been easy."

"I'll bet. Ohh, hell, I was just bluffing, ya know?"

"The hell you say. I've seen angry fellas, but yer a cool and angry fella. I caught me a scent of piss and vinegar, not bullshit."

Well then I am lucky for your help, sir." Gunther patted his jacket pocket with the handwritten note. "You do nice work here. Someday, I will have you make me a saddle."

"Anytime. I'll have someone other than my son make it for ya though. He's liable to stuff some firecrackers in the cantle."

Gunther chuckled at that and walked outside to the busy side street. He looked up and down the sidewalk. On the side of the saddle shop sat an Indian motorcycle with what looked to be a custom-made, leather seat. He walked over for a closer inspection. On the back hung leather saddlebags. On the bags read "The Home Run Kings," and under that a drawing of crossed baseball bats. A baseball under the bats had a flaming trail. To the side was a laughing human skull. A symbol. A brand. The skull was laughing just a bit too hard for Gunther's taste. he'd seen a lot of skulls and didn't take the use lightly.

Dusk...

Abbott Sureline rode up to the two-story wooden house on Reckon Road on his 1907 Indian motorcycle. The double front doors stood open. Some men and women sat on the front porch drinking. Someone more or less successfully picked out a tune on a piano inside.

Abbott parked near the other motor cycles, peeled his goggles and gloves off, rested the bike on the kickstand and walked up the old, busted steps. He spoke to the folks on the porch then entered the big front room. Men and women filled the room, some standing around, others playing pool, all of them drinking and talking. Four men played cards in the corner at an enormous table.

"Spanky around?" he asked.

"In the kitchen," one said.

Abbott walked into the kitchen. Spanky Runyan sat kicked back in a wooden chair, drinking booze straight from the bottle. Ranger Chester Winch sat at the kitchen table too, surrounded by empty beer bottles. A girl Abbott knew as Betha, a local prostitute, cooked meat on a gas stove near a big pot of beans steaming on a back burner.

The lean, lanky Johnny Cleveland, the star Bobcats pitcher, leaned against a nearby kitchen wall. Newspapers lay spread out all over the table. Abbott sat down at the table. Sitting at the big table was none other than Texas Ranger Chester Winch, smoking a cigar, holding a glass of whiskey on his thigh.

"Man came into the shop today. Named Gunther. Said he worked for the police."

This caught every man's full attention. They looked at Winch.

"He's working fer the Governor. He is. So's the county too," Winch said.

"He had a number. A saddle number from a saddle we made. It's Billy's saddle."

"He found that fucking horse," Spanky muttered, shaking his big head.

"You tell him who it belonged to?" Johnny Cleveland asked.

"No, I tried to run em off, but he wouldn't scare. he sadi he would return with a passel of police and papers to look up our ass. My father told him. My father showed him the paperwork."

"What's on the paperwork?" Winch asked.

"Well, his name. His job at the meat factory. This address. His home address. After he left, my daddy came to me and asked if Billy was alright. Said Gunther asked him if Billy was dead?"

"What he say?"

"He said he didn't know. Said if Billy was dead, he'd probably know about it."

"And this address is listed on the paperwork?" Cleveland asked.

"Standard. It's…it's standard. Home address. We collect everyone's home address."

"Shit," Cleveland said.

Betha came by and picked up the empty beer bottles. Winch grabbed the left cheek of her ass and she swatted him away. Not smiling.

"Betha," Spanky said, "why don't you skedaddle for a bit?"

"What about these steaks?"

"I got em," Johnny Cleveland said as he stepped over to the stove and picked up the meat fork. He took up her position over the steaks.

Betha left and Spanky leaned on the table.

"You know about this saddle shit?" Spanky asked.

"Nope. They's hiding stuff from me," Winch said.

"We're gonna have to kill this Gunther," Spanky said.

"Yeah," Winch said, "I'd like to skin that college boy."

"Hey now, I've been to college," Spanky said.

"Johnny's been to college too."

"Y'all ain't like him," Winch flashed back.

"We are going to have to figure out a way to set this Gunther up and kill him. Maybe this Wiley feller, too."

"And their mud friend, that little smart-ass Mex," Winch said. "Leave that to me. But Wiley? Wiley is just gonna work his pile of cases. He'll forget about this one like he forgets about all the other cases. He gets new ones and starts off on them, then the newer ones make the older ones peter away. He's busier than a one-legged man in an ass-kicking contest. I know him, and I like him right where he is. I can count on him and his kind."

"Inept in place," Spanky said.

"Yeah. That."

"They are liable to walk right up to this front door! Tonight or tomorrow," Cleveland said stirring the onions around the meat, "asking questions."

"That's why we have to be sly about this! We will set him up," Spanky said. He leaned back in his rickety chair, "like we've done before. Okay. Settled. Now Ranger, anything new with the preacher you got on the hook?"

Winch grinned and started in on the next caper, "Monsignor Hoolahan has collected a few girlfriends from the rounds he makes, checking on the poor. He meets needy women and then he talks them up, and sneaks them back to the rectory at night and needles them up, but good. He gives them money fer it. I know a girl that can get Betha into the rectory."

"And this will eventually…?" Spanky asked.

"Church has all kinds of money," Winch interrupted. "I get him in a corner and put the bear trap on him."

"How much?" Cleveland asked above the sizzling meats.

"Reckon I'll find out when the trap closes."

BAM! Gunfire sounded in the front room!

Spanky pulled a small revolver from his pocket, stood and bolted for the room. Chester followed into a round of male and female laughter that immediately followed the shot. Chiseler Kovaks, the Bobcats' star shortstop, sat holding a derringer in his hand, pointed at the floor. He looked drunk. Then he laughed. Then he saw Spanky.

Spanky fired off another round narrowly missing Spanky's foot.

"You think that's funny!"

"Damn! It's new! Sorry Spanky! Ha! I didn't know about the…I didn't know about the safety. It was an accident!"

Spanky looked at holes in the floor.

"It's your foot, but it's like you almost blew a hole in *my* foot," Spanky complained. "You almost blew a whole season for me, for us, you stupid fuck."

"Awww, maybe he shot a rat under the house!" a woman declared. More chuckles.

Spanky shook his head and returned to the kitchen.
Betha walked out on the porch and announced to the people sitting there, "It's alright. Chiseler shot a hole in the floor by accident. Everyone's ok."

"Haaa," the drunks outside laughed.

But it wasn't alright for the two prone men in the empty lot across the street from the house. They were about to cross the street and crawl under that very house to spy on the inhabitants just as soon as complete darkness fell. They exchanged glances after overhearing Bertha's explanation. They easily could have been the rats under the house.

Chapter 10: Jazz is Always New

The Bociferous Jazz Saloon had a frontage of brass and dark wood, set on the street corner, and cut in to the city block like a piece of pie. Two torches on brass poles, fed by streams of gas, lit the cement sidewalk outside and warmed the night air. A man in a three-piece suit, western hat and boots stood outside the double doors, his thumb hooked in the fob pocket of his vest. His sole purpose was to stand guard and ensure no riff-raff, bums or homeless people wandered into the establishment. And, there were plenty of them about on the downtown streets. No doubt a revolver rested under his jacket, Gunther thought as he climbed the one steep sidewalk step and approached the doors, feeling the rays of heat from a torch warm his face.

The doorman eyed him from boot to brim, and sprang to attention, yanked on the brass handles of the heavy doors and opened them for Gunther.

"Good evening to you, sir," he said.

"Thank you," Gunther replied. He stepped inside and slipped off his Stetson.

Ten p.m. The jazz bar and hall were full of men and women, talking, smoking, drinking, standing and sitting. Dancing. Dancing in a strange, drunken way. Gunther felt he'd stepped into New Orleans, and he'd never even been there! But, this was how someone would imagine the southern city at night. Seven musicians played this disorganized-sounding thing called jazz on a stage.

An ornate cloakroom counter stood off to the right, and Gunther walked over and laid his hat on the counter. A teenage girl, her face caked deep in powder, snatched up his hat and handed him a small piece of paper with a number.

"Fifty-three," she declared.

"Fifty-three. Say, which one of those gentlemen on the stage is Beau Kershaw?"

"Huh? Oh. That man playing the piano."

Gunther nodded, and moved toward the bar, eyeing the piano man. Middle-height, middle-aged. Black curly hair. Beard. Moustache. Smiling in ecstasy with every piano note. Big mouth. Big teeth. Small nose.

Gunther got a Mexican beer, lit a Cuban cigar and took it all in.

"So, this is jazz," he mumbled. It was different. Rambling. Loose. Connected, but not. And some people near the stage were somehow dancing to this? Shifting. Like they were lost in a dream. Like he'd seen some Oklahoma Indians do in ceremonies.

The set ended. The crowd applauded and whooped. The musicians bowed. They meandered off the stage. Exit stage right, with Kershaw giving the last wave and one more giant smile.

Gunther left his beer on the bar and made for the stage right exit. He walked down the hall, peeking into half-open doors until he found Kershaw reclining on a couch, holding a drink in his hand.

"Beau Kershaw?" Gunther asked.

"Tis. That's moi, colonel."

Gunther walked in, and shut the door behind him.

"My name is Johann Gunther."

"Hmmm..."

"And a friend of yours told me to come see you. Raoul Torontoola."

"The sergeant! Yes. What about?"

Gunther looked around for a chair and found one. A tall, thick one with a big winged back, and he hauled it, with some effort, over near the couch.

"You know the sergeant's in jail."

"Yes, I do, colonel."

"Do you know anything about that?"

Kershaw stared at Gunther, probably sizing him up.

"Do you know he was set up?" Gunther continued.

"Why you askin?"

"He asked me to ask."

"He payin you to ask?"

"He's paid me to ask."

"I sees." Kershaw smiled. His teeth didn't look so good up close.

"There's some talk about town, about dat. Nobody thinks the sergeant did it."

"And his wife…?"

"Terrible story. Terrible news. Shot down on the road like dat. Like a mangy dog." He took a drink from his cup, and Gunther could see a tea bag string hanging over the edge.

"You think they are connected?"

"Hmmm, well, you know. Yes. Yes I do," Kershaw said.

"Do you know Abbott Sureline? Billy Joe Farks?"

"Hmmmmmm. I've met them. Dey come here sometimes. Dey frequent where I frequent after hours. Sometimes. Sometimes I sees them here and there about town."

"You know anything about them."

"You mean colonel, are dey outlaws and the like?"

"I mean just that."

"They are members…well…part of a group of men, that can get in and out of trouble from time to time."

"Robbery trouble?"

"Can't say."

"Murder trouble?"

"Can't say, either. Don't know."

"Have you seen Farks around lately?"

"Not in a dog's age."

"Where do they frequent?"

"Frequent? Frequent. Well colonel, if you'll stick around? After my last set? I'll take you to some places, some clubs or two. They are there a lot. Carousing. Frequenting. You have transportation?"

"No, I am afoot tonight."

"It's a bit far to walk. For me away. I am in no kinda condition." He grinned. "If you'll be so kind as to get us a coach?"

"I will do that."

"and…and the drinks are on you!"

"The drinks are on moi," Gunther said.

A very large woman stuck her head in the door and said, "five minutes, Mudcat."

Kershaw swung his legs off the couch and the soles of his shiny shoes hit the floor.

"My ladies call me 'Mudcat.' You enjoying the show, colonel?"

"Interesting. Interesting. I am new to jazz."

"Ha-haaa! You know what, colonel? Jazz is always new."

Midnight. The doorman arranged for a coach, and when the night was over at the Bociferous, other clubs were just beginning their nights, presumably the ones that Sureline and the dead or half-dead Farks caroused in.

Gunther wanted to find Farks alive and well. He got his hat from the over-caked girl and stood by the doorway. Kershaw appeared from the back hall, and made his way to the front, shaking a few hands and accepting compliments in passing from the crowd. He nodded at Gunther and the two forsook the club in favor of the night air.

"Over there, sirs." The doorman pointed to a black coach across the street.

The two crossed the paved street and climbed into the open buggy.

"Sir Lancelot's Pub, mon amie."

"Señor," the driver said, rippling a rein lightly over the horse's rump.

"I like to cool down there after work with a spray of gin. And I sometimes see these gentlemen thereabouts."

Gunther nodded. He sure hoped this would not be a long night. His Tex-Mex-French was very limited.

Sir Lancelot's was not that far, but still on the outskirts of downtown. Cars were parked along the streets and horses stood tied at the curbs. There was even a horse tied off to the back of a car. The men-about-town dismounted from their cab. Gunther paid the driver. The area was more open and the buildings single-storied. Gunther could see the city's baseball stadium across an empty cornfield.

Out front, across from the bar stood a British knight's suit of armor near the door, and an English flag was mounted to a metal sign over it.

"The owner's from London," Kershaw said. "Nice chap."

As they got close, Gunther spotted some bullet holes in the armor. He imagined how they got there and chuckled. The architectural and interior layout and decoration did their best to replicate a British pub. Gunther had been inside several real pubs. The place was half full and about a third as noisy as the jazz joint. A woman wearing a Victorian dress in royal blue with thick auburn hair piled high on her head played the piano. Classical music, but something off the norm, Gunther did not recognize the melody.

Kershaw and Gunther walked toward the bar. Once there they ordered drinks. Kershaw smiled at Gunther, winked, then strutted across the room and sat down on a high stool next to the piano. He rested an elbow on the top.
Then he tipped his hat back and smiled at the woman playing. She nodded and smiled back. They talked. She changed her tune to some Southern style music as soon as they spoke. Suddenly while playing with one hand, she grabbed a beer glass and took a long swig, set the mug down, and the beer hand flawlessly melted back into keyboard work. Gunther smiled at that skill too.

Kershaw and the woman looked about the bar, and each nodded at someone a time or two. Then Kershaw left the piano and strolled to the far wall where some men stood drinking and talking. He struck up a conversation with a tall, lanky man. Gunther watched as the two spoke and both cut their eyes back at him at different times. The man looked and listened as Kershaw spoke. Then Kershaw left him and made for the bar once more. The tall man headed out the front door.

"That gentleman knows a man, who knows about the two

men you asked me about."

"He does?"

"Yes. Do you have some money?"

"He wants money?"

"Probably not a lot. You have two dollars?"

"I do."

"That will do. Well, two for my friend and two for the man we are going to meet. Four dollars."

"When and where are we meeting him?"

"In one hour." Kershaw sipped his beer. "At the ballpark across the street. There is no one there at this hour. Tis a safe place to meet."

"Fast work, Kershaw."

"Twas a fast riff. It twas, it twas."

One hour later, Kershaw and Gunther left the pub and walked north to the large sports arena. The field itself stood fenced in. There were open bleachers down the sides of the ball field diamond and one large covered building containing more bleachers in the outfield. Painted in giant letters on the outside of one side wall they could read – McIntrye Windmills, with an enormous windmill on a sunny dairy farm drawn alongside it.

"Whew, well…" Kershaw gasped. This was a man not accustomed much to walking. "There is no gate here. Just an opening that runs under the bleachers in the main stadium building. They like the children to come anytime and play baseball on the field. It helps promote the sport."

"Good idea."

The stadium was indeed wide open, and they walked up to one of the main, wide concrete entrances under the bleachers leading into the ball field, a shadowy tunnel through the covered bleachers. Gunther could see the ballfield spreading out before them in the moonlight. He could smell the grass from inside the tunnel.

"Hello?" someone called inside the tunnel.

Just before the entrance to the open arena itself a man stepped out of the shadows of the tunnel and into Gunther's view. It was the same tall man Gunther had seen at the bar.

Gunther turned to Kershaw, expecting to see him beside him, but Kershaw wasn't anywhere nearby. He was a good 20 feet or more behind Gunther. Out of breath? Why so far back? He turned back to the tall man.

"Couldn't find your friend….?" Gunther started to ask.

Wham! Gunther was hit across his right arm by what felt like a 2 x 4. The ambush knocked him clear across the large, open hallway-like tunnel. He crashed into the far wall. He looked back. It wasn't a 2 x 4. It was a baseball bat and in the hands a big stocky man with a wild shock of black hair, a flat face and big, yellow, toothy grin.

"Lookin' for someone, Pally?" the big man said with a Yankee accent.

This man was not alone. Three others stepped out of the nooks and crannies of the dark hallway.

Gunther reached for his shoulder holster, his right arm to his left armpit. His arm hurt, but he made the draw. His German Luger came out at about waist high. It held the four men at bay. Kershaw still remained 20 feet or so back.

"Lookin for trouble, pally?" the batman said again, staring at the pistol.

Gunther stumbled back toward the wall and inched toward the entrance.

"This your idea, Kershaw?" Gunther growled, glancing at him.

Kershaw grinned and shrugged his shoulders.

Then from nowhere, almost as if by magic, Gunther felt a blast in the left shoulder and neck from something. Like he was shot. The shock caused him to discharge the Luger into the cement floor. And then something smashed his head. Like a bullet to his head. No one was even near him! What? He fell to his knees and dropped the pistol in this blank, painful moment.

On his knees, in a stunned, numb, lost world, his jaw dropped, he saw a baseball slowly rolling in front of him.

"Steee-rike!" the batsman yelled, then laughed.

Gunther looked to his left and saw the tall man, now pushing away from his perch against the wall. The man shook his arm as if to loosen it up. He was…the pitcher. He held another baseball.

Gunther looked up. His bullet hadn't hit any of the men. He saw his pistol just two feet in front of him laying on the cement. Right there! His Luger! He reached for it as fast as he could. That was when the next bat swing descended, smack on the top of his right forearm. He pulled his arm back in agony.

Another raucous laugh. Then a round of cheers roared from the others. Even in his dull, stupor, Gunther knew he was done for. Done! He couldn't think straight, he just knew he'd had it.

Another fast ball hit his left torso.

"Steee-rike!" the big man yelled out.

There were other blows. Other hits. His arms stopped working. Legs stopped working. He was bashed around like a rag doll. Up. Down. Over. He threw up his guts. Flattened. All the while he saw Kershaw standing there smirking at the entrance. Then for a few flashing seconds, he thought he actually saw Texas Ranger Chester Winch there too. Standing in the background up against the far wall. Just out of the dark. Standing there, smiling. Just smiling at him as he was beaten to death.

"They are killing me," Gunther thought.

Then he passed out.

Chapter 11: Beat Me Out to the Ball Game

"Oh my God! Gunther! Gunther! Are you alive? Are you alive?" It was a female voice, yelling at him, inches from his numb face.

Gunther heard the questions, but it seemed like they came from within a deep tunnel. He imagined the hallway in the stadium. Was he still there? Or, it all sounded like his head was wrapped in a thick, wet towel.

"Johann. Johann!"

He felt some impacts across his face. Were they slaps? What? Were they still beating him?

"Ahhh…"

"Thank God!" she gasped.

He felt his back curiously arched. His stomach was his highest point. He was almost upside down? He choked. Then he gagged on lumps in his throat. Bloody lumps of spit ups.

Carmella Davis came into his view, like the focus of a telescope. Her long dark hair framing her pretty face over his. He smiled. It hurt. Then he saw stars - the stars of the night sky above.

"Now you are smiling?" she asked aghast.

"Where am…where…"

"You are on the pitcher's mound at the ball park."

"The…"

"The mound. The pitcher's mound. Where the pitcher stands. They left you here for dead."

"Dead. Like a graveyard mound…like a what? The pitcher's mound?"

She grabbed the lapels of his jacket and hauled his upper body up to a sitting position. He gasped out in pain and spit up more blood.

He looked around. He was on the baseball diamond of the ballpark. He was sitting on the pitcher's mound. His mouth hurt. His head hurt. His chest hurt. Arms hurt. Who knew about his legs? They were too far away right now to even consider. If he even had any legs anymore? Feet?

This was not right! Not right at all. He knew there was some trouble, but what? He reached for the Luger in his shoulder holster. It was gone.

"What…?"

"They beat you up, Johann."

"Who…now…who beat me up?"

"About half the ball team."

"The…ball team?"

"Some of them had bats."

"Was I at…a baseball…game, or something? What…what happened?"

"No, no. You were at a bar. Two bars. I followed you there. You and a piano player…"

"Kershaw!"

"…walked over to the stadium. You tried to talk to some men. Some were ballplayers drinking at the last bar."

"Yeah, yeah. Ballplayers. The ballplayers?"

"You know…Spanky Runyan? He beat you the most."

"Spanky. With the bat? The black hair? Yeah. Yeah. What, what, how did you…?"

"I followed you tonight Johann. I am sorry. I knew you'd be working on the murder cases, and I followed you from your office. It was the only way I could get any new leads on the Torontoola case."

Gunther smiled and let out one painful chuckle. "You! You followed me? You followed me."

"Yes, I am sorry. I followed you."

"Can I lie down again? I think I need to lie down again."

"I don't know if you should. You are choking. It's a good

thing I followed you. They beat you in that hallway by third base, then they carried you out here and dropped you on the pitcher's mound. I knew I couldn't stop them, so I just hid and waited for them to leave. They left you here on the mound. I think they left you for dead."

"Dead. Killed. Strikes."

"Yes. I ran out here as fast as I could when they left."

"Yeah. So. So, am I struck? Am I going to die, you say? And the score is…what now?" And with that, Gunther fell over, out cold.

Carmella shrieked. She looked around as if there was someone who might help. It was so dark, she could not see the two men leave the last row in the outfield bleachers.

Who knows how much time later, Gunther's eyes opened again.

"Hola," Jefe said.

"Hola," Gunther repeated and looked around the bright, white room. It smelled of medicine. It was a hospital room.

"Hello," Carmella said, walking into his view.

"The young lady? She saved your life," Jefe said.

"Yeah, good thing she was following me like a creepy spy." His speech sounded slurred even to him. He looked through a window. A red dawn appeared to be breaking outside.

"Red dawn, sailor take warning," Gunther muttered to himself.

A doctor and nurse walked in.

"And how are you this morning?" the doctor asked, "after your very rough night?"

"I guess, you best tell me, Doc," Gunther muttered.

"Well," the doctor said, looking into Gunther's eyes with a large, thick magnifying glass, "your face has broken bones. We've moved them back into place the best we could. We have stitched up cuts on your face, neck, arms and scalp. You have some broken ribs."

"I can feel that. Just breathing, I can feel that."

"Your arms are roughed up very badly. Bruised. But we haven't found any broken bones there as yet. There are several hematomas."

"Hema…toma, what?" Gunther ran his hands gingerly over his arms and shoulder. Hand, arms, shoulders, they all hurt.

"Your legs are bruised. Knees look ok. The lady says they took baseball bats to you. She says the baseball team did this. Are you a betting man, or something?" the doctor asked. "Do you owe them money?"

"Not really. Not on baseball. Just some of them were players. Some were ballplayers, yeah, the others weren't… ballplayers. No," Gunther suddenly recalled what happened to him.

Mesha burst into the room, her overweight body forcing everyone aside as she rammed her way to the bedside.

"Oh, Sahib! Sahib!" she declared taking his hand in hers and pressing it to her cheek.

"Hi. Hi, Mesha. Just me. Almost dead again."

"WHO did this to you?" She started to cry when she saw his condition.

Carmella squinted curiously at Jefe, at Mesha's emotional response.

"Mesha, this is Carmella, Carmella, Mesha," Jefe made the introductions, and the two women acknowledged each other with nods.

As Mesha continued to make a fuss over Gunther, Jefe stepped back and explained the relationship to Carmella,

"In India a few years ago, Gunth saved Mesha's life. She became something like his sworn servant. He did not want dis. But, she followed him. When in Afghanistan a month later in a military battle, in a British fort in the Khyber Pass, Mesha found him near dead inside the fort and carried him out of the battlefield."

"She…carried him?"

"She tied him into a chair and dragged the chair miles away. He was about half dead then. She saved his life. Then she nursed him back to health in a British military, Indian hospital. She returned here with him. And, you know, we hired her to work in our office."

Carmella eyes widened, trying to grasp that amazing

story. She shook her head in a sense of wonderment, looking at the two, now holding hands.

"How did he save her life?" she asked.

"Hindus were going to burn her alive at a stake of some sort. Her masters were cult killers. The tradition was to burn the slaves with the masters. He stopped them from killing her."

"Did he save the killers too?" Carmella asked.

"No. He killed the killers."

"Oh."

"And now you have saved him," Mesha said, turning to Carmella, overhearing their hushed tones. There were thick tears falling from her eyes. "Thank you."

"Can I get out of here?" Gunther interrupted the biography lesson.

"I worry about your head injuries, sir," the doctor said, "I would like to keep you here for at least a day and a night. For observation. Maybe two days."

"My wife and Mesha will take good care of him when we get him home. He lives in the back of our office. We live upstairs," Jefe said.

"I will stay with him here tonight," Mesha assured. "He will be safe."

"Well, then, good, but he must stay here 24 hours," the doctor said, backing up and heading for the door. "He needs to drink a lot of water. Take the pain medicines, I've prescribed. And, the police will be around shortly, asking questions, no doubt. Anytime we have someone nearly beaten to death like this, we have to call them in. You know, it's routine."

Gunther wanted to say he understood, but he lost the words. All he could manage was a nod and a raised finger to show he understood.

"I will sleep here tonight," Mesha said, pointing to a couch in the room. "I will go now and pack a bag."

"Good, I think I need you here, Mesha," Gunther suddenly gained control of his voice again. "Good."

"I'll go with you," Jefe said. He turned to Carmella, "can you stay here with him for about an hour?"

"I will. I will be happy to," Carmella said.

"Jefe, bring back a gun, will ya? And we need to order a new Luger. They took mine."

"They did? Those sons to the bitches!"

"Sons of bitches," Gunther corrected.

"Well, maybe we will find that gun again around town?" Jefe said, with a sneer and raised brow.

"I am counting on it. Ahhh, my wallet?" Gunther asked no one in particular.

Everyone in the room looked at each other and either shrugged or shook their head.

"Sons-TO-the-bitches," Gunther quoted Jefe on purpose. "They got my wallet too!"

"Our British spy bought that for me," he said to Mesha, "remember?"

"Yes," she said. "He would be angry it was taken."

They all left except for Carmella. She pulled a chair up beside the bed and instinctively grabbed Gunther's hand. He squeezed her hand. His hand felt cold.

"You have quite a background."

"That ain't all of it. And a lot of time in hospitals."

"What were you smiling at back at the ballpark? When you first opened your eyes and looked at me? How could you smile at that moment?"

"Oh, you don't want to know."

"Oh, I do want to know."

"Well, I was kind of delirious at that moment, you know? Head caved in, and all. I didn't know where I was when I woke up. And, I hadn't felt a lick of pain yet. Kinda numb. I opened my eyes and saw your face there, hovering close over me." He put his hands up over his face, "you were looking down at me. Your…your pretty face, your eyes, all that beautiful black hair hanging down surrounding your face, and all down around mine! I thought I was dreaming, or I thought I got very lucky. I thought you were lying on top of me in bed. And that? That made me smile."

"I see!" Her head jolted back an inch, and she appeared half-astonished, one-quarter shocked and one-quarter smiling. Gunther like the fractions. He'd work out the math later.

"Well, you asked me! Hey, real quick? Can you hand me that trash can over there?"

She did, and as soon as he had it, he threw up.

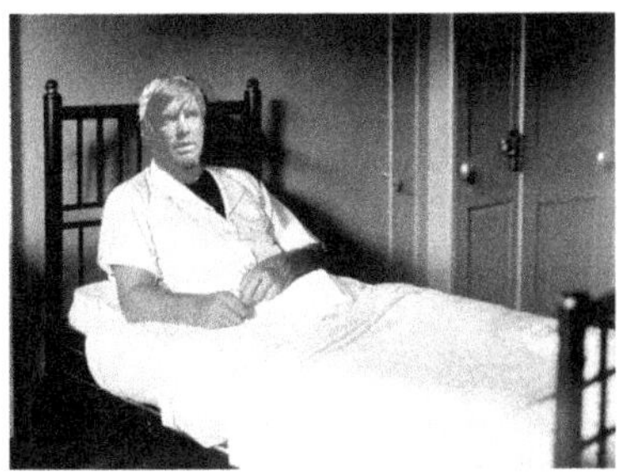

Chapter 12: Monkey Hell

With Jefe on one side of him and Mesha on the other, they guided a weak-kneed Gunther across the office lobby, down the hall and back to his quarters in the Remedies building. He was quite woozy, and he hadn't handled the bumpy carriage ride all that well from the hospital. Carmella followed with a bag of medicine and Mesha's suitcase. They eased him onto his bed, and Mesha slowly removed Gunther's hospital slippers. He was surprised he felt so glad to get prone again, so quickly, and let out a deep sigh.

"That…was my big, short ride for today, and I am bushed," he declared.

Maria, Jefe's wife, appeared in the doorway, leaning against the frame. Some of the kids came to stand beside her, watching wide-eyed and serious.

"I am ok, kids," Gunther said. "Just fine. Look at me. I can move all my fingers and toes."

They watched every appendage articulate. The monkey jumped up on the bed. The small odd creature startled Carmella, but Gunther could tell her tolerance for surprises had increased since meeting him. She seemed less surprised about his lifestyle and his little cadre of friends and co-workers than he'd imagined. A cadre of Filipinos. Indians, spies and now… a small, carnival, organ grinder monkey were not the norm, he knew. The monkey seemed to know Gunther felt weak and hurting. It made its way to his pillow and then reached out and touched his face whimpering.

"Hey there, critter," Gunther said, scratching its shoulder.

"Thirsty?" Maria asked.

"Yeah. Yeah, I don't know what for, though? Water or whiskey?"

"Tea!" Mesha declared. "English tea. No alcohol and none of these unusual tea flavors! Black tea."

Maria nodded and disappeared through the doorway, headed toward the kitchen.

"Tea for me too!" Carmella shouted. "If you don't mind?"

"The bodies? What about the bodies?" Gunther asked Jefe.

"Norman Spinks went to court with Wiley yesterday afternoon. They explained why they needed to exhume the bodies. The judge agreed."

"Good. When?"

"Tomorrow."

Gunther reached into his jacket pocket and pulled out a folded piece of paper. He handed it to Jefe. Then he sat up and gingerly slipped the jacket off and tossed it across a chair near the bed.

"A lawyer and a scientist," Gunther said. "Both up in New England. I had a friend from Texas A & M look them up."

Jefe examined the note.

"Can you find them, call them or wire them, and hire them to get down here, as soon as they can?"

Jefe nodded. He left the room.

"Who are they?" Carmella asked.

"Two legal experts for Torontoola. If I can get them down here for a hearing on the science of the guns and bullets, I think we can spring the sergeant from his penthouse jail."

The monkey sat on the bed, his head turning back and forth toward each as they spoke, as if he were following the conversation.

"And who is this little guy?" she asked.

"Oh, he is Mesha's pet monkey."

"Well, he looks like your pet monkey."

"We get along. Not at first, though. He belongs to Mesha."

"Did you save his life too?"

"Come to think of it, they were going to burn him alive too."

"So you saved his life."

“Saved his life from India, monkey hell.”

“Any other exotic, wild animals lurking around here that I should know about? Any tigers? Maybe a lion? Or perhaps camels?”

“Not a one.”

The monkey heard the kids laughing in the lobby, and he scattered off in a flash to find them.

“He’s a fast one!” Carmella said.

“He’s a blur most of the time.”

Maria brought in a tray with a teapot, cups and saucers and milk. She sat the tray on a table by the bed. Carmella handed Gunther a cup of tea.

“Can you serve yourself, Carmella?” Maria asked. “I have some things to do in the kitchen.”

Carmella nodded and prepared her own cup, with milk and sugar. Mari winked at Gunther and left the two alone.

“You have quite a clan of people here. Doesn’t look like you’re married? But were you ever married?”

Gunther shook his head. ”I am currently unattached.”

“Who could stand being married to you?” she said.

“Any given day you could be beaten to a pulp at home, or in India.”

“I can barely stand myself. I’d smile at my own joke there, but my face hurts too much.”

“Knock, knock,” called a voice at the door.

“Hey, come on in, Wiley.”

The county detective selected a wicker chair from the corner, pulled it over and sat on the other side of the bed from Carmella.

“You…what…jumpin Jehoshaphat. This is what happened to you?” he asked, eyeing Gunther’s face.

“I was jumped by half the baseball team. Their baseballs and their bats.”

“Why?”

“I was asking around about Torontoola and the highway murders. Had a meeting. A bad meeting.”

“With the ball team?”

“Yup.”

“And you rescued him?” He turned to Carmella.

“I did,” Carmella said.

“We can press charges,” Wiley said.

“We cannot,” Gunther said. “No. Not the time.”

“Not…what…time? Oh, what then? When’s the time? You want to just go shoot em all, don’t you?”

Gunther tried to smile, then stopped. His gums hurt and the insides of his cheeks felt like chopped meat.

“Well?” Wiley continued.

“Nooo.”

“No? No, my sorry ass, that is exactly what you are thinking. Catch ‘em and shoot ‘em all one by one, or some such cowboy shit. That ain’t gonna work, Johann. You can’t do that anymore. The gunslinger times are over. This ain’t Dodge City, or, or Manila. This is Fort Worth, Texas. Year of Our Lord 1908.”

“I’m not going to press any charges yet. We need to play around with this some more.”

“You look like you don’t have a play left in ya.”

“The last thing we do is arrest them. When we have run out of ideas? We’ll arrest them. The statute of limitations gives us a few years,” Gunther said as he ran his tongue around the insides of his mouth. “…we’ll arrest them later, Wiley. For a lot of things.”

Wiley shook his head. “Now what? What’s next?”

“Next, we get Torontoola out of jail. We put him on the streets too.”

“How ya gonna do that?”

“With your 1908 Fort Worth, Year of Our Lord, law. We are going to follow the letter of the law, and get him out.”

“Torontoola gets out? You looking for revenge. Mother of God, we’ll have a gang war on the streets.”

“We’ll try and arrange the showdown out of the county.”

“Sheeet.”

Chapter 13: Bull-istics and Loose Cannons

Two weeks later, 213th District Court...

"Bull! Ball-istics? It's BULL-istics!" Assistant District Attorney Bennett Brockman shouted out in disgust.

The crowd in the Fort Worth courtroom fell into an uneasy and hushed silence following Brockman's interruption. They had all just heard a dissertation from the witness, a metallurgy scientist named Dr. Daniel Pinsky from Boston University. It was a speech on the study of firearm barrel riflings and impact marks, the likes of which most had never heard of, and many had difficulty following. This was not a typical bail hearing. To many, it seemed more like a small trial. But, Judge Joshua Dean appeared patient.

Raoul Torontoola, dressed in the striped black and white jumpsuit worn by county inmates and seated at the defense table, had already been denied bond a month earlier by Judge Dean. The people who'd been following the rumors felt he belonged in jail. And according to some rumors circulating the lobby that morning, the trouble-making Johann Gunther had pushed for yet another hearing.

This time Gunther used his own "damn-Yankee-lawyer" Nickoli Hatziz and some "damn-Yankee-firearms expert, by the name of Dr. Daniel Pinsky." And all with the promise of new evidence and all in the name of justice to attempt to change Torontoola's bail status. Most people thought this was just another stalling tactic to try and get Torontoola off on a technicality of some sort. But anyone who looked at him could tell the man was guilty. With his well-groomed hair and finely waxed mustache, he'd been leading entirely too fancy a life for a city police sergeant, and now his life had caught up with him.

Across the crowded room, Texas Ranger Chester Winch sat wearing his usual impatient, surly sneer. Slinky legs crossed at the knee. Gunther eyed his ragged, long, wispy, mustached, profile. Winch probably thought Gunther either hadn't seen him or didn't remember seeing him the other night at the stadium. However, Gunther had no trouble recalling the man literally giggling in the shadows of the ballpark hallway the night of his severe beating. Or, maybe Winch felt himself to be such a cool character, protected by that Ranger badge, that he just didn't care if Gunther knew he was there that night? Either way, Gunther detected no guilt or remorse in Winch's face when their eyes met briefly.

"Your honor," the newly imported defense attorney Nickoli Hatziz said. "I have supplied you and the prosecution with the science and the growing history of courtroom decisions on firearm ballistics." Some from recent cases and rulings here in Texas, such as the well known, Affray vs. Brownsville case.'"

As if to answer Brockman's outburst, "Yup, yup, yup, yup," Judge Dean muttered. "Pray continue, Mr. Hatziz." Carmella Davis quietly entered the crowded courtroom, locked eyes with Gunther in the back row of pews and came to sit beside him.

"Have I missed much?" she whispered. She took a pencil and a notebook out of a tooled leather bag she carried.

"The good part is just getting started," Gunther said. Attorney Hatziz turned to the heavyset, middle-aged man on the witness stand and asked, "And your final opinion, Dr. Pinsky?"

"Upon my examination of the bullet found inside Mr. Justin Trace, I can prove that it is from the same handgun that fired the bullets that killed Mrs. Torontoola, and her maid on the Dallas turnpike in Arlington. Two crime scenes. Three murders. One handgun."

"Bull-istics," muttered D.A. Brockman again. The judge ignored the snide, side remark yet again.

"Further," Dr. Pinsky continued, "I am relatively sure I can prove the bullets are made by the same manufacturer, if appropriate manufacturer samples can be located with which to make the comparison."

"So, there is evidence that one man, or one gun did two crime scene's worth of killing, on two dates, and this man used the same batch of ammunition?"

"Objection. Leading the witness," Brockman said.

"Oh, is this an official comment now, Mr. Brockman?" the judge asked.

The judge and Brockman stared at each other for a moment, until Brockman nodded. "Yeees, Your Honor."

"Overruled to save time, because the defense will only rephrase the same question with a fancier tongue. Proceed, Mr. Hatziz."

Gunther noted that the judge, atop his high perch was often busy reading something during much of the testimony, the subject of which no one at ground level could see. Perhaps it was the Hatziz briefs? But then Gunther saw him quietly try to fold down a large-sized page as low as possible, of whatever it was, and spotted what looked like the tip of a newspaper.

"I think the judge is reading your Whispering Wind newspaper up there," Gunther leaned over and whispered to Carmella. She smiled and put her hand on his knee.

Mr. Hatziz asked, "Dr. Pinsky, have you examined the registered service revolver of my client, Sgt. Raoul Torontoola?"

"Yes, I have."

"Did my client's pistol fire any of the bullets involved in these murders?"

"No, it did not."

"Did you find the ammunition in the Torontoola gun and gun belt to be the ammunition recovered from the body of either of these murder victims, miles and days apart?"

"No."

"That is all I have for this witness," Hatziz said.

"Your witness, Mr. Brockman?" the judge offered.

"No questions of this witness."

"No questions?" Judge Dean asked, looking perturbed.

"You have been moaning and groaning over there like a sissy with a splinter, and now you have no questions?"

"Well, your honor, this is all science fiction, like in a Jules Verne book. How can I possibly take any of this seriously? How can I ask a non-fiction question to a fiction expert? Ok, ok, I do have one question."

Bennett Brockman stood up at his table.

"Mr. Pinsky," he refused to call him doctor. "In your scientific opinion, can a man in Texas, or a man anywhere for that matter, own more than one handgun?"

"Yes."

"Hmmm, no further questions."

"You may step down, Dr. Pinsky."

Hatziz returned to the defendant's table, took a seat next to Raoul and looked over some papers.

"The defense calls Detective Wiley Lewis of the Tarrant County Sheriff's Office to the stand."

The bailiff, an old wounded veteran, limped out into the hallway and shouted out for Wiley.

"How are you doing?" Carmella asked Gunther.

"Well, my brains have quit spinning around like a top. I ate some barbecue last night, and I quit peeing blood."

"All good signs."

"Yes, all of them good signs."

They watched Wiley walk across the courtroom and climb into the tall witness chair, followed by the bailiff walking in his stinted gait. Once seated, the bailiff swore him in.

"Detective Lewis," Hatziz began, "you have worked on the murder of Justin Trace."

"I have, sir. I helped out. It is not my case."

"And what was the date of the murder?"

"June 20th, sir."

"And what is the date that my client Sgt. Raoul Torontoola was arrested for the murder of Justin Trace?"

"June 22nd."

"And he has remained in jail without bond since that date?"

"Yes, sir."

"And you have worked on the murders of his wife Mrs. Torontoola and the Torontoola's housekeeper in Arlington, Texas?"

"Yes I have, sir. Directly."

"And when were those unfortunate murders?"

"June 24th."

"And on or about June the 14th, my client Sgt. Raoul Torontoola was still in custody in the Tarrant County Sheriff's Office?"

"Yes he was, and still is."

"Have you or anyone you know collected any handguns, officially and directly connected to the shootings? Such as guns from the crime scenes?"

"No we have not."

"And have you had the occasion to examine the service revolver of my client?"

"Yes, I have."

"And did any of the bullets recovered, as in just simple caliber alone, from the murders of Justin Trace, Mrs. Torontoola and her housekeeper and maid, match with caliber of the handgun of my client?"

"No they did not."

"So, detective, I ask your opinion on this. If the same pistol and the same bullets were used to kill Justin Trace on the 20th of June and also used to kill Mrs. Torontoola and her maid on the 24th of June, what might you conclude?"

"That the same gun was used in both crimes."

"And, if Sgt. Torontoola was in fact in custody since…, remember he was jailed on the 22nd, what else could you conclude?"

"Well, that he could not have shot his wife. Somebody else did. And that same somebody else and that gun also killed Justin Trace," Wiley said.

"No further questions?"

"Mr. Brockman?" the judge asked.

Brockman stood and asked, "Detective Lewis, in your law enforcement opinion, can you conclude, can a man in Texas, or a man anywhere for that matter, own more than one handgun?"

"Yes, he can."

"That's all, your Honor.

"Anything else? Anybody?" the judge asked.

Gunther waited for the State to produce their secret, star witness rumored to hook Torontoola to the death of the gambler. No such witness, or eye witness was presented. Was the State keeping a witness hidden away for the trial, he wondered?

Hatziz was thinking the same. "Your honor," Hatziz spoke up, "on the matter of discovery, I would like to make sure I have been apprised of all the information against my client. All papers and, certainly all witnesses."

The judge looked over at Brockman.

"That's all there is, Your Honor," Brockman said.

"Is there or is there not, I say NOT, an eye-witness that confirms the defendant shot Justin Trace?" The judge asked, apparently having heard the same rumor.

Silence. Ranger Winch shifted in his seat.

"No, Your Honor," Brockman said, looking down at his table, "we only have several men that heard him threaten the life of Justin Trace a week before the crime."

"Did someone identify the shooter at the scene of the crime?" Hatziz asked.

"Someone did. Someone yelled Torontoola's name out loud at the scene."

"Who?"

"We don't know. The witness ran off. We have the statement of another witness who saw and heard this man identify the defendant," Brockman said.

"Witness to another witness. That second-hand testimony is no…" the judge started to say.

"I know Your Honor, and that is why I have not presented such hearsay here today."

The judge nodded.

"Who is this second-hand witness?" Hatziz asked.

"An insurance salesman…" Brockman slipped some papers about on his desk. "A Charles Sumner."

"If it pleases the court, I would like to have information on the witness. And in closing, Your Honor," Hatziz continued, "and I think you see where I am going."

"I see where you are going."

"The same gun was used in two murder scenes, one of them well after my client was incarcerated, which he could not have done. This is a mystery gun operated by a mystery man. This clearly creates a reasonable doubt in his case. The State has no eyewitness, or really any evidence at all that my client shot Justin Trace. We request a granting of bail."

"Yup, yup, yup, yup. Bail granted at 250 dollars. Sergeant, I cannot reinstate you back into your job, as that is out of my hands and up to your sheriff. Most likely Sheriff Brazzard will keep you off-duty and on leave until this matter is fully adjudicated. But, you, sir,…are out! Next case, bailiff."

"Thank you Your Honor," Hatziz said.

Brockman quietly packed up and left. Ranger Winch tailed after him.

Gunther and Carmella approached the defense table.

"You are a very smart man, Señor Gunther," Torontoola said, smiling in amazement.

"No, Raoul. These fellers here are the smart men. I just found them. I know smart people."

Deputy Hanniken appeared smiling, and placed a hand on Torontoola's shoulder, to lead him away.

"Your bail will be arranged within the hour," Hatziz told him.

Led off to a side door, Raoul whispered over his shoulder to Gunther, with an exaggerated mouth movement for understanding, "gracias, amigo."

Gunther winked at him. He watched Deputy Hanniken walk Torontoola out with an easy hand on the shoulder, more like friends on a stroll, than a guard and his charge.

"That is a very elegant man," Hatziz said, watching him leave.

Gunther laughed out loud. "Elegant! Elegant, sir, does not come to my mind. And now, the steaks and beers are on me."

"Am I invited?" Carmella asked.

"YOU are not just invited, you obviously are the center attraction," Gunther said.

Gunther knew he had just released another loose cannon out onto the battlefield to blast over rocks and maybe flush out some rattlesnakes. Four killings to-date, counting the Louisiana politician. His own near death beating. Six or more suspects. And a real starring cast of circling wagons. Lots of rocks. Lots of snakes.

Gunther kept his smile even when he spotted two men in the last row on the far right looking at him. Looking too hard. They were smartly dressed. Suits and ties. Very fit. Muscular, mid-30s ties, clean-shaven faces. So much so, that they almost resembled each other. One had a serious scar that ran the length of his face. They turned away when they realized he was looking at them. They stood, and Gunther noted they both carried guns underneath their suit jackets. They filed out of the courtroom, and Gunther could see they wore dress shoes, not boots. Two men. Partners, but what was their business? The business that brought them to watch this bond hearing? Were there even more loose cannons floating around than he realized?

Brockman made his way through the people in the courthouse toward the exit, not in good spirits.

Chester Winch, spurs a spinning, skipped up beside him.

"Ranger Winch," Brockman said, with a tone of disgust. He stopped. "I wonder where that eye-witness is you promised me?"

"Bennett, I didn't think you needed him today."

"I need an eye-witness!" he growled, then remembered where he was and lowered his voice. "I need an eye witness immediately. Right away. Not the morning of court!"

"Well, I figured this was a little-ol bail hearing and..."

"Where is this witness?"

"I got him."

"Who is he?"

"I'll get him to you."

"Look, this Torontoola is a cheatin, low-down, corrupt skunk," Brockman moved in inches from Winch's face. "We finally have a case on him, and they just…they just bonded him OUT! Now they won't revoke his bond even with a witness if we have one, but we sure need one for the Grand Jury and that's in two weeks."

"Whatcha need from him?"

"I need for him to testify before the Grand Jury. I need for him to walk into the district attorney's office and give us a signed statement that he absolutely saw Raoul Torontoola shoot Justin Trace."

"Ok."

"Then he needs to walk into the Grand Jury and say the same thing." Brockman stared at him, turned and walked off, shaking his head in disgust.

"Mr. Sumners?" Detective Wiley asked the cultured man answering the door.

"Yes?"

Sumners was a well dressed man, well dressed even lounging around his house in the early evening. About 50 years old with carefully styled hair swept back from his face and molded into place.

"I am Detective Wiley Lewis with the Tarrant County Sheriff's Office and this is Johann Gunther, working for the governor. He's a…special investigator. Can we step in and ask you a few questions?"

"About?"

"About the night Justin Trace was murdered."

"Oh, yes, come on in gentlemen. Maybelline! We have company!"

"Very temporary company, ma'am. No bother." Gunther and Wiley slipped off their hats. The three men sat on the living room furniture, Gunther with a painfully, slow descent. The couch was way soft, too soft, and he floated down deeper than he wanted, wondering if he'd ever get back up again? Maybelline Sumners appeared from the back rooms. She too was well dressed in a white blouse and full dark skirt. She was shoeless, and padded across the floor in her bare feet.

"Something to drink?" she asked.

"Oh no, no," Gunther said. "We are here but only for a

minute. Don't go to the trouble." Maybelline was clearly taken aback at Gunther's bruised face, but tried to compose herself. She eyed him up and down. Then she leaned against the doorframe with her arms folded.

"Mr. Sumner, I have your statement here in my file. You saw the shooting?"

"Yes."

"And you cannot identify Sgt. Torontoola as the shooter?"

"I cannot. I did not see his face."

"You also said a man near you commenced to screaming that the shooter was Torontoola."

"Oh, yes. Adamantly." Sumners lit a cigarette.

"Know this man?"

"No. Never saw him before either, nor have I seen him since."

"You said in your statement that the shooter left, and this man left - the shouting man?" Gunther asked. "And then you heard some kind of machines start up in the directions that these men ran to?'

"Yes. I did."

"Could those machine sounds have been cars? Motorcycles?"

"Oh yes. Motorcycles. That was it."

"You've heard motorcycles before? You know what they sound like?"

"Yes, I have. Around town. Hither and yon."

Wiley stood. Gunther tried to rise from the pillowy sofa, and failed. Finally Wiley offered a hand, pulling him up out of the deep, plush furniture.

"Oh my," Maybelline said, "Mr. Gunther, have you been in some sort of a scrape?"

"That is a very comfortable couch, ordinarily," Gunther said with a half smile. "But, yes I have. I have been scraped pretty good recently - you might say. However, I have been scraped worse than this, so I'm sure it will all heal."

She looked at his open jacket as he stood, and he could tell she glimpsed his shoulder holster.

"Thank you, sir. That is all we needed to know," Wiley said.

Gunther and Wiley put their hats on and both gave a tip of the brim to Maybelline. They walked out to Wiley's open top, police car at the curb.

"Motorcycles," Wiley said, as he climbed aboard. "You have some friends with some motorcycles."

"I do," Gunther said, somehow managing to step up into the automobile. "And they play baseball."

"Ready to file charges yet?"

"Not yet."

"Gunther!"

"Not yet, amigo."

They rolled through a few streets. Gunther took some of the bumps well. Some not so well.

"So," Wiley said, "you do the hokey-pokey with that newswoman yet?"

Gunther shook his head and half-smiled.

"The hokey-pokey? No. I can't even breathe deep yet without hurting."

"Oh, ok. Ok. Just asking. I know about her, you know."

"You do? What do you know?"

"I know this much Johann. She is one hell of a news reporter. She gets her story. She'll do anything to get her story."

"Anything, huh?"

"Anything."

Chapter 14: Misters Gray and White and Mrs. Sumners

Gunther's elbow strikes were blocked and passed off to the side, never hitting the face.

"Dis is what you do. You can stop dis here." Jefe put a cupped palm up catching Gunther's elbow and upper forearm. "Or you can pass it aside like dis." Jefe scooped Gunther's incoming elbow with the back of his other open hand and shoved it aside.

"You try dis," Jefe told the group of 12 men and two women in the backyard. It was Jefe's weekly "Jungle Fighting" Filipino class, taught in the open, backyard of the Remedy's office, a walled in courtyard and stable area.

Gunther and Jefe proceeded to walk amongst the students to help them work the moves. It was Gunther's first day back in training, and he was taking things very slowly and, at times, mostly just watching.

"Johann," Mesha called out, and Gunther turned from the practitioners to see her standing beside two men at the double, back doors of their office building.

"Johann, these men are here to see you."

Gunther turned to see the two well-dressed, mystery men from the courtroom, in much the same twin-like garb as they wore at the courthouse the previous day. Jefe and Gunther exchanged short glances. Gunther, dressed in a dusty white undershirt, tan pants and light brown, deerskin boots, slapped the dirt off his hands and approached the men.

"Gentlemen," he shook hands with each, and they smiled

broadly at him while doing so. "Come on inside." He led them back to a large conference room off the front lobby. He retained a slight limp as he walked.

"Getting around pretty good after that beating you took?" one asked.

"Oh, well, yeah. Still hurts. Still taking it very easy. So, you heard about that?"

"What were you doing out back?" one asked, ignoring the question.

"It's Filipino Arnis. A fighting system from the islands that my friend, actually my partner out there, Jefe is an expert in. Sinawali boxing. Mano Mano. Kicking. Knife and stick fighting. It's his class. I help out."

"That might hurt some to do," one said.

"I'm taking it very easy."

"You have been to those islands," the other man stated more than asked.

"Yes," Gunther said as he sat at the large table in the room.

"We know you have. We have too."

They sat around the table.

"You have?"

"Yes. Army. Like you, Johann. My name is John Gray and this is Frank White."

"Gray and White. Very…colorful names," Gunther noted.

"We are all alum here. We also graduated West Point. Two years before you started."

"You did!" Gunther declared. "Mesha! Let's get some whiskey in here for these men!"

"Sounds just grand," White said.

"So, you've been in the islands in the war. Are you still in?" Gunther asked.

"Oh no," Gray said. "We got out after eight years."

"Eight long years," White added. "More to do on the outside. More money."

"I hear ya," Gunther said.

Cigars were pulled from an ornate box atop the table, all three quickly snipped and lit up like vets. Mesha poured the whiskey, and the men swapped stories about West Point, who was still there teaching and commanding when Gunther passed through, how severe the hazing was for them all, and where they all were in Cuba and the Filipino islands. They laughed. They moaned. They shook their heads. They spoke of the living and the dead. They even asked about Roosevelt and Gunther's official trip to Afghanistan.

"So now that you're out. What are you doing now? What kind of business?" Gunther asked them, eyeing the gun shapes in shoulder holsters under their suit jackets.

"That's the reason we came to see you, Johann. This is a personal visit," White said.

"Off the record," Gray added. "Not business."

"Ok," Gunther said.

"Yes, off the record. Alumni-talk. The reason we came to see you, Johann, is not to talk about West Point and the wars," White said.

Both men shifted in their chairs. Different positions, official poses now. Straight up. Uncomfortable. Gunther just sat there and waited.

"Justin Trace, Johann," White said.

"Justin Trace," Gray repeated.

"Justin…Trace," Gunther said softly, and sipped the whiskey.

"We wholeheartedly suggest that you not look too closely into the matter of his death. Strongly," Gray said.

"We strongly suggest."

"Very strongly," White added.

Gunther stared at them, feeling slightly quizzical.

"The murder of Justin Trace should not be your concern," Gray said.

"Why?"

"We now work for very big people. With very big concerns. The Trace murder concerns them," White said.

"How?"

"Not for the reasons you might think, Johann," Gray said. "You might think it is all about…about some Texas gambling and maybe organized crime? Maybe some mobsters throwing their weight around? Scaring people. Mobsters paying us as henchmen? You might be thinking about crime and criminals."

"It's not, Johann. We are not any of these things. It's bigger. Way bigger," White said.

"We are not in the army anymore but we work for some of the same people connected in different ways with the government instead. We have the success of the United States in mind."

"The…government is involved with shooting Justin Trace?" Gunther asked.

"No. No, it isn't that," White said. "It didn't shoot…we didn't shoot Justin Trace. And make no mistake about that. Trace was supposed to live a long and happy life. Some locals killed him, and we think we know why, and we think we know who."

"Who and why?"

"Now we can't say. We shouldn't say. And we shouldn't have you finding out anymore. We don't want you digging around in the past of Justin Trace."

"Do you think Torontoola shot Trace?"

"No. And now, thanks to you and your witnesses in court yesterday, we know Torontoola did not shoot Trace. Not at all."

"I did see you two in the courtroom."

"We know you saw us. And that is why we decided to come to see you and explain what little we can tell you. Professional courtesy. West Point grads."

"We wanted to keep you clear of this. Keep you on the outside, safe," White said.

"We saw you at the baseball field the night you were beaten," Gray added.

"You did?"

"But we also saw that the young lady was following you too, and that she would see to you. We would not have left you there to die."

Gunther just stared at them, them said, "I am working for the governor on this. And also, indirectly, the governor of Louisiana."

This was obviously news to Gray and White. They exchanged a quick glance. White shook his head.

Gunther continued, "I am working the highway robbery,

the murder of the former judge from Louisiana and therefore the murder of Torontoola's wife, not the Trace case," Gunther added. "But, they are all somehow connected. I don't care a whit about Justin Trace unless it becomes part of that other robbery and murder, fellers." Gunther did not want to reveal all of his cards either.

Gray slid the glass across the desk. It was the cue to leave. White slid his too. They stood simultaneously.

"Ok, ok. Thanks for telling us that," White said.

"That…maybe… can be carved out, Johann," Gray said. "Maybe we can carve all this out. We can do some carving."

"We might even help you a bit if we can carve it just right." White twisted his wrist in the air in a half circle like he held an imaginary knife. "But we work for very big people with a very big plan, and I hate to tell you this, Gunth, I hate to. But don't get in the way of the plan. We have our orders. We have to follow orders."

"Roosevelt big?"

"Not that big. But almost."

"Almost?"

"Same old story, you know, Gunther? We have to follow orders. If we don't, someone else will. Someone will replace us. People you won't know. People you won't like," White said.

"And they won't know or like you," Gray said.

The three left the conference room. The pair left the lobby and building. They smiled at him on the way out. Gunther moved quickly to look out the front windows and watch them, ignoring the pains in his back and leg. He wanted to see where they went. Car? Horse? Carriage? But the two men walked down the street and out of view, their gait in sync, a habit from too much military marching.

There were plenty of nice hotels in the downtown neighborhood in that direction. He sat down and turned the chair to gaze out the windows again, the sun seeped in on him through the plantation blinds.

"What dey want?" Jefe asked, walking in.

"To scare us off. Get us off anything to do with Justin Trace."

"Who are dey?"

"Misters White and Gray! Ha! I can't remember which was Gray or which was White. They are definitely West Point grads, but they sure as hell ain't using their real names. They know I know that. Using colors for names like an old American military spy trick or alias. Said they are working for rich men now. On some government plan they won't explain. Said Justin Trace was working for these same men. Same plan. All in something way bigger than little ol you and little ol me, amigo. And too big for the Fort Worth police."

Jefe sat on the corner of the table.

"We need to order West Point yearbooks. Maybe 10 years worth of them. Like 1887 to 1897. That oughtta cover it," Gunther said.

"Ok. I will do dis."

"I'll look over the pictures, and we'll see who these sons-a-bitches really are. They are not hostile to me. Us. Not yet, anyway. But it sounds like they will kill me if they have to, if I get in the way."

"They said this?"

"More or less."

"And…and, before we go and buy you a new Luger…" Jefe said.

"I know what you are going to say."

"Dis ballistics used in court the other day? Not good."

"I know."

"Not good for us, too. For bidness."

"Yeah."

"If, if dey can start to use this science everywhere? We have to do something different with our guns."

"Buy different guns," Gunther said and sipped the last of the whiskey from the tumbler. "We are going to have to get and stash some firearms that no one knows of. Ammo too. And destroy the guns after we use them."

"I think you can still get the new Luger. Let everyone know you have a Luger and Colt auto pistols," Jefe said.

"And, it's ok to use them for a good shooting, in self defense. But if we think we…"

"I know. Let's get the new Luger, I guess. Let's go

through Daniel Brothers and order another one. Yeah, I am up for a trip to Daniel's. But we do need to be careful. Times, they are a changing," Gunther said. "I guess we need some very common six-guns from somewhere else."

"Yeah. Dere are some good ones."

"And we can't buy them where they can be traced back to us."

"Yeah," Jefe said and stood up. "I've got a few upstairs. Maybe we need at trip to San Antonio, or El Paso to buy some pistols and rifles."

"From Santino."

"Yes, Mexican guns," Jefe said as he left the room. Gunther swiveled the chair back to face the windows. Ballistics was a double-edged sword of justice, making it hard on the last of all gunmen, good and bad.

The front door opened and Jefe went to the lobby. Gunther heard a woman's voice ask for him.

Jefe walked back into Gunther's office and said, "A woman is here to see you."

Gunther waved his hand inward for Jefe to show her in. It was Maybelline Sumners. She was dressed perfectly, with a large hat pinned to her piles of dark hair.

"Mr. Gunther?"

"Yes, yes, have a seat. Excuse our appearance, Mrs. Sumners, but we have been working outside. Come on in here. Come on. What can we do for you? Have a seat."

She did. Jefe did too.

"It's my husband. He's been threatened. He has been beaten up," she said.

"Charles?"

"Yes, Charles."

"Charles Sumner," Gunther said to Jefe, "the man on street that saw Justin Trace killed."

He turned back to Maybelline, "By whom?"

She shook her head in disgust. "A Texas Ranger, Chester Winch. You know him?"

"Oh, I know him, all too well."

"He has been to my house and first, the first time, he just threatened Charles. He wanted Charles to swear that he saw that police sergeant, identify him positively as the shooter of that gambler man."

Gunther was somewhat surprised, but not completely. He and Jefe exchanged glances.

"He has said that he would make Charles' life, our life miserable, even frame him for a crime if he doesn't swear on paper, and swear in court, he saw that sergeant do it."

"He didn't see him, did he?"

"Noooo! My husband was not lying to you."

"I see. But why not tell the police this? Tell that detective I was with the day we came to your house?"

"The police! That Ranger is the police! I can't trust the police! I know about the police."

"Why trust me?"

"I've heard of you. You are not the police. You have this… this Remedies place. You carry a gun, and you have killed men. It said so once in the newspapers. A soldier. And you are still fighting. Look at you. All fresh from the fight. When you walked into my house the other day, I took you for somebody who does what needs doing - no matter what. And you don't follow the rules."

There was a distinct, new toughness in her voice, in her tone and in her expression.

"This crooked Ranger came to my house the first night. He and Charles talked. Then they argued. He came back last night. I was gone. When I came home, Charles was beaten up. Almost looks as bad as you. He told me the damn Ranger beat him up."

She stood and paced the conference room.

"Charles is from Austin. He's cultured. Refined. City. A good man. He can't handle…he can't even begin to handle something like this. Me? Mr. Gunther, I came here 30 years ago in a covered wagon from Bangor, Maine." She leaned on the table, on her gloved fists. "I have killed Indians, and bushwhackers. I…I killed a man in Little Rock who crawled into my sister's house with us, wanting sex. I shot him in the guts so many times his intestines fell out on the floor. My poor Charles knows none of this. He thinks I'm a…a New England queen. I am afraid of what I might do if something happens to

Charles. What I might do will ruin our lives."

Gunther nodded.

She reached into her purse and pulled out a two-shot derringer. "I mean business."

Gunther's eyes widened at the sight. "I know you mean business. What does the Ranger want him to do exactly? And when?"

"In a week and a half, he wants Charles to go to the district attorney's office and testify before the Grand Jury." She laid the derringer on the table.

"Week and a half. We have some time. Does Charles know you've come here?"

"No."

"Well, tell him to agree to go along with Ranger Winch. We have some time. Give me about three or four days or so. I have some plans to make over the next couple of days, then I will see what I can do."

"Keep me from using this gun, Mr. Gunther." She put the weapon back into her purse. "What will you do? He is a Texas Ranger?"

Gunther smiled. "I will think of something. I may just punch him in the nose."

"I'd like that," she said. "I'd like more!"

"Maybe seeing his guts on the floor?"

She nodded. No smile.

"Mrs. Sumner, you look like a beautiful dove, but you have the heart of an eagle. You remind me of a woman I knew once named Lydia. I will do something, so you don't have to do something."

"How much will this cost?"

"The good news is," Gunther said as he slowly stood, "the governor of Texas is paying to resolve this issue. I think this is part of that very resolution, and let's just say he is carrying the tab."

She finally smiled. He escorted her by the elbow to the front door.

"You come back and tell us right away if anything changes."

She stopped at the door and turned to him, "what did this

Lydia you mentioned do?"

Gunther smiled and felt his eyes well up just a bit too fast.

"She…she was a helleva woman. She blew up the front half of a fort at the very top of the world."

Chapter 15: Dead Reckon Road

Hours later, Jefe strode into Gunther's office and reported,

"I am going for a ride by the Farks' house. Maybe even knock on the door."

"Wish I could go with you."

"You best stay here. I want to reconnoiter dat house. I want to go back tonight and watch it."

Then, Jefe left as swiftly as he appeared.

Gunther was indeed still sore. He figured he really shouldn't be helping Jefe on this afternoon recon of the Farks house, nor with Jefe's Filipino fighting classes for that matter. He still couldn't set a horse. He thought if he could keep his involvement in the backyard workouts light, it would do him some good to move around just a bit, but he was still occasionally dizzy and half his bruises still hurt.

He looked over the books atop his desk. He was reading two. England's Winston Churchill's book called the *River War*, about Churchill's observations and involvement in the recent Egyptian wars. It gave him a better understanding of the quixotic world of Southwest Asia, and even his recent, violent past in Afghanistan. And, he was reading Sigmund Freud's *The Meaning of Dreams*. He couldn't wait until the West Point yearbooks appeared on his desk, so he could hunt for the photos of the mysterious Mr. Gray and Mr. White.

He opted instead just to rest, to simply stare out the windows, but Gunther's office windows overlooked the brick law office building next door, just eight feet away, a dry and empty view. He left his desk and limped out to the front lobby and turned into the conference room. He rolled a chair from the table over to the windows and pulled open the sheer, lace curtains. With a grunt he sat in the chair. He leaned his elbows on the window sill and watched the afternoon traffic of Dunston Street and the intersection of Fry a short distance away.

It had numerous business office buildings both wooden and brick, but was not a main street in Fort Worth, just one of the many side streets off the main one. Two lanes of east-west traffic, partially paved at his end, eroded to hard, packed dirt on the far eastern end. Civilized in parts, "country" in other sections.

People moved about on the busy pathways beside the road that warm afternoon. The street itself was coated in horse manure and it stunk. The politicians claimed that the horse would soon be replaced by automobiles and the never-ending problem of smelly, squished horse crap would soon go away. In the summer heat, the smell drifted pungent and frequent on the wind. As he was thinking about this problem, a new car drove by beeping at a horse.

He rubbed his sore and bruised face. Several couples passed by. With this talk of Lydia, his mind spun off as it often did, to the Khyber Pass, to the Star of Africa, as they all called her. He thought of her for a moment. The Star. There could be no one again quite like her. He recalled the first time he saw her, atop a powerful horse on a steep hillside in Afghanistan, leading her band of mercenaries down the slope. As the horse dramatically shifted his front and hind quarters to descend, he rocked her lean yet generous body back and forth with him. Long thick black hair hung over her leather clad shoulders, hair worn long and full almost down to her gun belt. Her face. Her smile and powerful, unforgettable lips. The Star of Africa. In the desk drawer of his office was the diamond and her gold tooth, chopped out by radical tribesman. Handed to him by a man he later stabbed in the throat.

That thrust of his Bowie knife finished off many things.

Many revenges. But, it could not finish off this deep ache. The Star. Their night in her cave where they lingered in the hot springs. He thought of their morning on the mountain top where they stood together overlooking low clouds. He thought of the artistic curve of her legs and delicate arch of her feet. He obsessed about them because those tribal maniacs must have chopped her feet off too, as those murderers did to all at the mountain camp, as so ordered by the madman sheik he killed.

War. It could create a certain distaste for humanity. His head suddenly, involuntarily shifted to the right, like the tiniest inkling of a panic attack. He reigned himself in. He took a deep breath that hurt his ribs.

Somewhere people are making sheer lace curtains, like the ones slightly waving before him, he thought. And somewhere else they were chopping off feet. Survival is so often just a question of simple geography. Inches, feet, yards, miles. Continents.

Out of frustration he sat back in the chair, a pointed finger supporting his chin. He'd been with many women around the world, and they all moved on again, or he did.

He considered his failure to find commitment or even contentment of any sort. Carmella of the Whispering Wind showed possibilities, but he knew she would soon pass from his life too. A sad fact, but he just knew it. It was this way. He was this way. Like a curse in a way. A curse made worse now by his dream of the irreplaceable Star. He somehow seemed to quickly forget all the other women as they disappeared, but not the Star. This precious, unique one still lived on in his mind.

Settling. Settling in. Settling down. Is settling the best word? It sounded to him like 'settling for,' and not settling down to him. Could he settle for someone else? At night, he dreamed of her coming near to him. Not often, but often enough. Her body was complete, as alive as he knew her to be, he felt her beside him in strange abstract dreams, passing in and out of his story lines. He could smell her unique scent and feel the texture of her hair in these moments. She never spoke in these dreams. She looked at him. Just looked at him in each one.

A thousand words were passed in those looks. Yet all unanswered. Of waiting. Of wanting. Of aching. What would Sigmund Freud make of all this dreaming? Was there an answer in his book of dreams?

Was there some kind of heaven, he couldn't help but wonder? Was she there? In some heavenly cave in a breathtaking valley, of some God-like making? Made for her? For them? Would it be somewhere else? Something else? A place like from an H.G. Wells or Jules Verne story?

The monkey ran into the room and jumped onto the window sill and looked at him, with an expression as much as if to ask, "what are you doing?"

"Hey, messy," he whispered. "You remember the Star, don't you? You were there too, huh?"

The monkey dropped from the window, and crawled onto his lap, sitting and curling its tail around its legs for warmth. It sat there and looked out the window, too—cozy. He rubbed its head.

"You remember too," he whispered.

So Gunther sat, and resumed a gaze through the windoww. His mind wandered. His vision flattened out into a slight blur. And that is when he first saw him. The man. The man in the tan bowler hat. Standing there on the far side of the intersection corner. Gunther looked at him like you hunt for a man or an animal, how you draw your focus back to take in the big picture, how you sense the wind, the natural movement of the scene, all as the mind seeks to define the normal so it can spot the abnormal. The man was watching the Remedies office. Gunther watching all around him, saw the normal flow of people, cars and horses and then spotted this man in the bowler who stood out separate from the others.

He walked at a different pace, his focus directed toward the Remedies office. He stopped and stared. He ate food from a brown bag. Then he walked off. He came back. He came back again. Same pace. Same head-twisting study of Remedies.

The office was being watched. Was it so ordered by Mr. Gray and Mr. White? Was it by the Whispering Wind newspaper? He set the monkey down, walked to his private office and got his binoculars. He took a good look at the man from his office windows. A white man. A city suit, shoes. No cowboy. If Gunther hadn't felt so tired and bad, he would have confronted him in some way. If Jefe didn't have such important plans for the Farks' house...

"Amigo. Amigo!" he shouted to Jefe when he heard him run down the stairs.

Jefe appeared. Gunther handed Jefe the binoculars. They were several feet back from the window.

"The guy in the bowler on the corner? He's watching us."

Jefe stood deep in the room and looked out the window.

"Yes. Yes, he is."

"Seen him before?" Gunther asked.

"No."

"Neither have I. He's either with Gray and White. Or, with the newspaper?"

"Or with the gang."

"Or with the gang. You've got a big night. Let's leave this be until tomorrow. He or somebody will be around. I wanted you to see his face before you left."

Jefe set the spy glasses on the table and moved back down the hallway to continue his packing.

On Reckon Road...

Jefe tugged on the right rein and turned his horse, Kipling, off of Zella Avenue onto Reckon Road and on down to the listed home address of missing, wounded or dead Billy Joe Farks. The Filipino Jefe was dressed like a Mexican, as he was so often called, yet as a señor of some stature in a black suit and black, flat brimmed hat, with expensive tack on Kipling. Under his jacket was a .38 revolver. He kept his gaze about the neighborhood casual and the pace very slow. Aimless. Out for a walk. The street had many houses on both sides, usually single-story, wood, but some of brick and even some adobe. Old. New. Some made by construction teams and others by one or two men as if they were still an ongoing project. This was not an upper-class section of Fort Worth, though some houses were quite nice. Some had stone sidewalks out front, others did not. Some had gardens behind the house, and some not a stitch of green, just dirt and rocks. A few even had small barns. On larger lots sometimes goats or horses grazed behind white picket fences, maybe even the occasional cow or two. Just a few cars were parked here and there along the street.

The Farks' house was coming up on the left. It too was wooden, but in real need of a good sanding and fresh paint. No fence. No manicured lawn. An uneven, worn, front porch ran the length of the house, also in need of repair. The front double doors stood wide open. Men were inside talking loudly, with the wang of drunken blather.

They talked with slurs and easy laughs. But, what made this house different on this weekday afternoon were the motorcycles. Out front on the street, were seven parked motorcycles resting in a row on their kickstands.

Through the open door, Jefe could see a group of men and one woman standing inside the house. He saw some seated at a large table. On the far wall, he saw a giant, round sign, a banner of some sort. It read, "The Home Run Kings." It was the artistic logo Gunther had described to him. And other designs too were present that Jefe couldn't identify before he lolly-gagged out of sight again.

The last bike parked in the line on the street had two leather saddlebags over the rear fender. The same logo of a skull and baseball bats were embossed into the saddle bags. This time he could distinguish two rifles along with the two ball bats in the design.

Earlier that morning, he'd entertained the idea of walking up to the front door of this house, knocking on it and just asking for Farks, but this was no ordinary house to do such a thing. No wife or child would answer here. No mother, or grandmother. No, this was like a clubhouse. A hang out. An unlicensed bar. Jefe took quick note of a small field between two houses almost directly across the street. Brush. Trees. Tall grass. He could return here at night and spy on this very odd house. Once at the end of street, he turned Kipling for downtown and their Remedies office.

The sun set at about 7:00 p.m. and 30 minutes later Jefe nestled into his dark place in that grassy field, almost far enough away to need his small set of binoculars. As the darkness fell completely he would get closer and closer to the house, perhaps even get close enough to listen inside. He wore dark brown boots, pants, shirt and thin jacket. He carried a leather rig and bag in dark brown. He had carefully chosen a flat black pistol so it would not reflect light.

There were five motorbikes out front and one horse, but by 7:50 p.m. the horseman left. The doors stood wide open again. Three women in loose fitting dresses carrying bags and boxes of what looked like food, walked slowly up the street, laughing and talking, then went into the house.

At 9 p.m., Jefe crawled to the first clump of bushes across the street from the house, leaving his bag of gear back by the second line. He watched more people come and go. Some rode bikes, some walked. The revelry on the inside remained at a low din. A man fitting the description Gunther had given Jefe of Spanky and another man, dressed in their baseball uniforms, probably coming from their late afternoon game, drove up on motorcycles. They entered the house, spent about 20 minutes inside, then left.

Two men walked out onto the porch and lit cigarettes and talked. Jefe could eventually smell the marijuana. Jefe cupped his ear toward them, desperate to hear any news. They spoke about hard times which led to specifics.

Man on right, "so, what's cooking?"

Man on left, "sheeet. Not much. I warned you not to go hog wild with that batch of money."

Man on right, "my shop is gonna fold any day. Any day now. I bolstered it as best I could. That's all I did. I didn't waste any on nothing."

Man on left mumbled something that Jefe couldn't hear. Man on right continued,"…these two _ like federales _ figured _ they's agents of something. Spank says…says we need to ___ be taken care of such bidness."
Jefe just couldn't catch the whole message.

Man on left, "Yeah. Yeah."

They wandered back inside. Jefe could only assume they were discussing the two mysterious "military" or 'federal" men, Gray and White.

At 10:30 p.m., Jefe checked north and south then bolted across the street to the side of neighbor's house. Then he dashed east to the side of the Farks' house moving in a half crouch and finally laid out prone right beside the front porch. There was an inset, under an overhanging wooden planks, and he felt pretty good under there. He still could not hear inside well enough though. Men and women laughed and talked in mumbles and someone started playing the piano.

An elderly couple walked up the street for an evening stroll, but with grimaces and glares, cut a wide swath around the front of this house. Jefe laid there on his back, staring at the dirty wood planks just above his head, planning his return tomorrow night, thinking about his approach and any possible ways to hear more clearly the goings-on inside the house. The house itself set about two feet off the ground and he thought about getting right under it, under the floor of the big party room itself.

Then, he heard a quiet foot shuffle and spotted something down the street. It was not the elderly couple returning, as they were long gone. He slowly moved his head. He turned slightly to his side.

Two men! Crouched. Running. Two men dressed in dark greenish/brown outfits with black bandanas wrapping the tops of their heads, like the ones of his Filipino homeland. Each wore a mask over their nose and mouth. They both had long guns! Jefe could see as they drew close they were shotguns. And the men wore military-style, pistol belts with two handguns, one on each hip. And while they each held a short shotgun, another shotgun hung over each of their backs in a sling.

Each man also had a dark canvas sack of some kind wrapped by a strap around their shoulders. He instinctively knew by the very nature of their surreptitious approach that if he so much as moved or was spotted? If they saw him? They would blow him to kingdom come. So, he laid still.

One of the men almost walked right by him as he climbed

the side of the porch. He wore very soft, dark shoes. The other circled the back of the house. Jefe soon saw the second man's feet from under the far side of the porch. He'd circled the house. Jefe peeked over his edge.

The two men were now on either side of the open doors. They nodded at each other and burst into the front room barrels first.

Jefe sat up. Then stood up. There was a window to this room and he wanted a look. But, the explosions came quick. Shotguns roared in a nightmare of slaughter. That window Jefe approached exploded outward just before he got there. He threw an arm up against the spray and collected glass in his sleeve and arm. There were screams of shock, then pain inside. There were yells of agony. A back door burst open and, gasping, desperate people bailed out of the house and tore off into the darkness beyond the yard. Someone opened a window and dove out. Jefe ran back to the side of the neighbor's house, far enough away to see into all the windows on the south side.

The two marauders methodically, quickly searched the house, ripping into cabinets, drawers and closets. They had one man and one woman contained in the back kitchen area. One yelled at them. The couple pleaded and begged.

"I don't know. I don't know," he heard each of them yell.

One of the gunman shot the woman in the knee. She collapsed out of Jefe's sight under the window sill.

Dogs barked up and down the street. The resident of the house he hid by, a young man craning his neck, came out on his porch, holding a rifle in the crook of his arm while fastening a pants suspender.

"Get inside!" Jefe commanded. "Get inside, now."

The man's gaze was glued on the house next door and he didn't seem surprised to find Jefe standing in his yard. Jefe ran up on his porch. A woman in a loose nightgown appeared at the screen door. Jefe grabbed the man's arm and pushed him back inside through the door, and pushed the wife back too.

"Get low," Jefe whispered. "You want no part of this. No part."

Other neighbors in various stages of dress, ventured out into the street. Jefe ran out to them.

"Get back inside. Inside! If they see you, they'll shoot you!" he shouted. Some listened.

Jefe was no match for these killers with just his six-shot revolver. He looked toward the darkness of the field where his gear bag lay. Ammo. A small rifle.

Almost any military vet such as Jefe would recognize the low rumbling sound that precedes a big, rolling fireball of an explosion. Jefe dropped to one knee just as the back of the Farks house exploded red, yellow and white like a huge fire bomb. Jefe felt the heat on his face as he kneeled on the porch next door.

Jefe saw the two killers leap from the front porch of the house next door. Hitting the front yard at a dead run they made their escape headed south down the street. The very sight of these two men frightened away any neighborhood spectators as they yelped and clamored toward their own porches.

A man jumped on a bicycle and yelled, "I'll get to a call box!"

Jefe popped up and ran across the street to the front lawn of another house and fretting onlookers. He saw the two men pass in front of him. One glared at him. At the end of the street they turned right and west running. Jefe darted across the empty field of his first perch and snatched up his gear bag. On his run westerly, he pulled his lever action rifle from the sack and dropped the bag. He caught glimpses of the men between the houses to his left on the next street. He paced them in the field, hoping to emerge on the next street the same time they did. He would only have to run out the other side of the field to see them.

Out on that next street, he worked the lever action and turned south. No men!

"Hold it there, Jefe!" a voice came.

It took more than a few feet for the swift-of-foot Jefe to reduce his pace to a halt.

"Drop that rifle," the man ordered.

The two masked men had ambushed him at the intersection. They were kneeling, 10 feet apart.

"Who are you?" Jefe asked, but he thought he already knew.

"Drop that rifle. Drop any pistol you have. This is over. Don't make us shoot you."

He knew these men would shoot him. He did drop the rifle. Metal clanked onto the paved avenue. The pistol fell next.

"Get over here."

Jefe put his hands up and walked toward them. One of the men transitioned over to his pistol, letting the shotgun drop to sling's length at his side. He was now security for any close fire, as his partner guided Jefe over to the porch of the corner house.

"Put your hand between these bars," he said and producing a pair of handcuffs from his canvas sack.

Jefe did. The masked man handcuffed him to an iron railing of the porch.

"We saw you ride by this afternoon. We saw you in the field. But we couldn't wait. This had to be done tonight."

Jefe stared alternately at the man's eyes inside their masks.

"This is not your fault. This is their fault. We are all only doing our jobs," one said.

Then they dashed away. They disappeared into the darkness of the next intersection. Bells clanged from distant fire trucks approaching.

Had one called him "Jefe" just a minute ago? Yes! Yes, he had. They knew him. They saw him ride by that afternoon. They'd been watching the house. Watching him.

They had to be the two West Point grads. Gray and White. Today's morning "visitors." Special soldiers. Perfect executioners. Execution! And why kill those people? Why blow up the house?

A motorized fire truck raced by, followed by two, horse-drawn fire trucks. Dalmatian dogs barked and ran beside the wagons. Jefe vaulted over the porch rail in one lunge and sat in disgust on the porch steps.

The front door of the house opened behind him. An elderly woman in a robe, holding a lamp emerged.

"Young man? Young man! Can I help you?"

Jefe turned toward the light of her lantern and tried to smile, "yes my lady, could you please have someone call dey police and get dem here? I chased de men who set fire to dat house around the corner. The one dat da fire engines are going to. I tried to catch them, but, as you can see? Dey have caught me instead." He raised his handcuffed hand and the other cuff rose up to the top of the iron porch rail. "I don't want to break your nice porch rails. I am afraid I have done enough damage for one day."

The following afternoon, the authorities converged upon the crisp, smoldering ruins of the Farks house on Reckon Road. The fire had been contained to only that house, as if from a controlled explosion. The Tarrant County Medical Examiner and some of his crew sifted around the rubble looking for bones, bodies and whatever other evidence they could find. Detective Wiley scoured around the scorched back yard.

Gunther walked the perimeter of the mess. Jefe, his right forearm bandaged to cover the wounds he sustained when the window blew out, leaned against the Remedies coach across the street. The news reporters were there, to include the quick response, bicycle crew of Whispering Wind, all held at bay by some uniformed police officers assigned that very task. The reporters were busy trying to outdo their competing news teams and photographers by climbing trees and the balconies of neighboring houses for superior, front page photographs of the carnage.

Then Ranger Chester Winch rode up on a horse, ignoring the officers without so much as a wink, a nod or a smile. He passed through them, dismounted, took time to sneer at Gunther before walking over to the wreckage and to a local fire marshal. Gunther watched him, filled with contempt.

Rattling engines approached. A unique sound and everyone turned north to see three men on motorcycles roll up to the line of police on the corner. They turned their machines off. The lead biker stepped off his bike, removed his goggles and skull cap. It was Spanky Runyan. Jefe slowly stepped to the rear of the coach, not wanting the men to see him, should he decide to follow them. Gunther followed Jefe's lead, not wanting them to see him either.

Spanky wanted through the police line, but the officers held him at bay. He pushed a shock of black hair off his forehead, put his hands on his hips and grimaced, his big head bobbing up and down in frustration. Another biker dismounted, de-goggled and struck a pose beside him. The third man remained on his bike, goggled and helmeted. They conversed with the officers, and an officer pointed to several locations, answering their questions.

Then Sgt. Raoul Torontoola, looking every bit like a go od working detective in a black suit and bolo tie, black hat, and black gun belt, walked up the center of the street, opposite the bikers. He struck a solemn figure, his eyes glued to the splintered wreckage as he approached. With the recently freed lawman appeared, the bikers spotted him and the duo backed up, climbed back aboard their bikes, kick-started the engines and all three rode away. Apparently, they didn't want Torontoola to see them.

Torontoola stopped to stand beside Gunther at the rear of the Remedies' carriage. The two men barely exchanged glances, their eyes on the wreckage.

"Horrible," Torontoola whispered.

"Yep," Gunther said.

"How many?"

"Jefe can only guess. Eight? Ten? Some women."

"Just terrible." He turned and nodded hello to Jefe, his sometime matchstick poker player between the bars.

"All this is over Justin Trace. The mystery…that is Justin Trace," Raoul said.

"It would seem so. Still suspended?" Gunther asked.

"Yes."

"Still have a badge in your pocket?"

"I do."

"I have several badges. The chief only took one. What is that son of a mother's dog doing here?" Raoul asked, jutting his chin out toward the Ranger, who was kicking around in the rubble.

"I don't know. I guess he is either real nosy about crime; or, he knows this is connected to your wife's murder. I suspicion the second."

The men stood still for a moment. Then Gunther shifted his hips and pulled his hat brim down to eyebrow level.

"We really need to get into Trace's office, or wherever he lived."

"Yes, we do."

"We won't tell Wiley. We might have to do something he wouldn't want to do, or do something he shouldn't know about. Can you find out where that is?"

"I already know where he was living. He lived at the Grand Guthrie Hotel."

"You on a horse or in a car?" Gunther asked.

"Horse."

"I got this coach," Gunther said. "Let's split up here and meet at the lobby of the Grand."

Gunther and Jefe climbed into the coach.

"You are going to make Misters Gray and White very mad at you," Jefe said, as the coach left Reckon Road.

Ranger Winch watched from the corner of his eye as the men went their separate ways. He spit his tobacco chaw into the dirt.

Gunther, Torontoola and Jefe approached the hotel desk of the Grand Guthrie. It was indeed a grand place, like the name, and expensive rates even for one night.

Torontoola waved his hand to draw a clerk over.

"Hello my friend. I am Sgt. Torontoola of the county sheriff's office. Is your manager here? Or nearby?"

"One moment, sir." The clerk reached for a phone, cranked the box handle and spoke into the mouthpiece. He explained his need to a switchboard operator.

Within seconds a door opened behind the desk and an older, thin, well-groomed man emerged. He motioned for the three of them to come around the desk and enter his office. Once inside, he eased down into his chair. Torontoola found a chair, but Gunther and Jefe remained standing.

"Augustus Milligan. Whatever can I do to help the police?"

"Thank you for seeing us!" Torontoola said, displaying his city badge. "A long-term resident - Justin Trace…"

"Yes."

"Had a room here…"

"Yes, a suite."

"He was murdered…"

"Yes. Yes, by a policeman."

"I can assure you, sir, he was not murdered by a policeman."

"Oh? Well. I do not follow such business. Didn't even read the newspaper article, but I did hear about it."

This would explain why he didn't recognize the name Torontoola, thought Gunther, who decided not to enlighten the manager.

"Uh-huh. Has anyone come to look at his suite since his passing?"

"The police. Sad. The night of his murder. To investigate the burglary."

"The…burglary?" Torontoola repeated.

"Yes, sir. Only hours after Mr. Trace was shot. Someone broke into his suite. Broke the lock on the door."

"They did?"

"Yes."

"You have me at a disadvantage because I work for the City and perhaps the County police came to investigate?"

"No detective, even more powerful. The State."

"Ohhh…the State?"

"Yes, sir. The Texas Rangers."

"Oh I see. One Ranger or several?"

"Just one, Ranger. He came right after the shooting to check out Mr. Trace's residence and, as I understand it, he found the door broken. He came down and told us about the break-in."

"I see; and I assume he said he would take care of it all."

"Yes. Make the burglary report and investigate the burglary."

"Do you know the name of the Ranger?"

"Oh, yes. It was Ranger Chester Winch. He comes in frequently. He has a beer at the bar every now and again."

"Did he find any evidence that you know of?"

"By the time the clerks came to my room to wake me and I made it to the lobby, he'd left. The clerk said he had a duffel bag of evidence. I don't think he had much in that bag though. He said he found the suite door locks broken when he got there."

"A duffel bag?"

"Yes."

"Of evidence?"

"How about two men? Two men in fashionable suits.

Clean-cut men. In their late 30s or early 40s?" Gunther stepped forward and asked. "Have you seen them visiting Mr. Trace? Or his rooms?"

"Mr. Trace had many visitors, and maybe such men came to see him while he was alive. He held many meetings in the lobby. Our restaurant. Our bar."

"But not to look over the room after his death?" Gunther asked.

"I wouldn't allow it, except for the police," Milligan said, nodding to Torontoola.

The suite? Is it still as it was?" Torontoola asked.

"Oh, no, no Sergeant. We cleaned it all out. We fixed the door. A couple with children, moving here from Omaha, currently occupy the rooms until they can purchase a local house."

"I see. I see. Did Trace leave anything behind? And, if so, where do you have the rest of his things?" Torontoola asked.

"There were clothes, yes, and some other items. We have them in boxes in the basement. We'll hold them until someone contacts us, or his next of kin show up to claim them. I just wish we could do something about all that cereal."

"Cereal?" Gunther asked.

"Yes. Yes. Mr. Trace was a cereal salesman by profession." He looked confused that the enquiring trio didn't know this. "You…you didn't know this?"

"No," Torontoola said.

"And he has his wares shipped to him, right here, from

West Texas."

"What sort of wares?" Gunther asked.

"Well, cereal, sir. Breakfast cereal. We have a whole skid of cereal boxes down there now. And we have no idea what to do with it. Shipping and receiving collected the order, and it's all sitting in the basement."

"Do you mind if we see it? Perhaps we can help rid you of this problem?" Torontoola said.

"Oh, most surely," Manager Milligan said with a certain glee. He stood up and tugged down on the bottom of his vest to better cover his protruding belly. He peeled a key chain off a hook behind him and made for the door.

"This Texas Ranger?" Gunther asked as they walked out the door. "Did he see these cereal boxes too?"

"Oh, no, sir. It seems he didn't know or care about them. He just looked over the Trace suite."

"Not the basement."

"No."

In the basement, the manager directed the men to Trace's remaining possessions and the pile of boxes.

Shoes. Dress boots and a stack of rather elegant looking clothes in a box set on a canvas tarp, in an open area surrounded by piles and rows of hotel and restaurant equipment and canned food stored on wooden shelves. Milligan pointed out the cereal pallet.

"If you could possible take the entire mess off my hands I would be grateful," the manager said."

And he departed.

"I have never heard anything about Justin Trace and cereal. A cereal salesman?" Torontoola said.

The three men circled the cereal boxes. There was a cloud of small, slow moving, black gnats circling above it. There looked to be five rows of boxes with about 10 in each row. Jefe picked the clothes off the tarp and Gunther grabbed several boxes of cereal. He pulled a knife from his belt line, cut off the box tops and poured the contents onto the tarp. This made the gnats very happy.

"Cereal," Torontoola muttered.

Then the three began cutting open every box. Cereal, and

more cereal. Several greasy rats appeared from under the shelves by the wall.

"Get away!" Jefe shouted at them and tossed an empty box at them. They scattered, all but one. A brave rat larger than the rest remained in place nearby sniffing the air.
Jefe returned to his chore. Cereal and more, then…

"Allah be praised," Jefe said in a gasp.

Gunther and Torontoola, both ankle high in cereal, crunched over to him. Jefe extracted a handful of money held together with rubber bands from one of the boxes. He passed the stack over to Gunther, then turned the box upside down. Stacks of money tumbled out! They exchanged glances, and continued their work, this time with the fervor of gold-miners.

When they finished, they all three sat on the tarp, in a large pile of breakfast cereal and about 20 thousand dollars. Twenties and hundreds in banded stacks of a thousand each. The center boxes of the lower two rows where full of money, not cereal. Gunther leaned over on one elbow and thumbed through the nearby stacks.

"All new. They all look like new bills."

"This much new money?" Torontoola said. "New? Here? How?"

"I don't know."

"We could ask Harold Wiskowski about brand new money," Jefe said.

"Yes," Gunther said and turned to Torontoola. "He is the president of the Trail Dust Bank. Our bank. He handles all of our money. And, I have worked some cases for him. He was a regulator in Washington DC and worked on Wall Street in New York for awhile, as well as the London stock market. He will have an opinion on this new money."

"Meanwhile, what will we do with all this," Torontoola asked. Maybe we can store it at my house?" The brave rat crawled onto the edge of the tarp and began eating around the outskirts of the cereal pile.

"No. You are in enough trouble," Gunther said. "And they may search your house again for evidence and find all this there. I don't want it at our place either. We'll put it in a locked safe somewhere."

Jefe spotted something and stretched out to his left side to fetch a piece of a paper that must have fallen earlier from the stack. He read from it aloud.

"It is a mailing receipt. Fifty boxes of Morning Glory Cereal. To Justin Trace. From Morning Glory Cereal, Bendigo, Texas."

"Bendigo City. That is south of Amarillo," Torontoola said. "And so this is where this skunk was getting all of his money. Hidden in cereal boxes. But why? Why?"

Large doors burst open across the room from the same direction they'd entered earlier, and two men talked casually about getting some food ready as they came toward the trio.

The three tossed all the money stacks into one pile threw a tarp over it and quickly sat back on the floor as they had been only seconds before, surrounded by piles of cereal.

The two approaching men, chefs by the look of their hats, stopped cold in their tracks when they saw the pile of cereal and three grown men stretched out on the floor in the middle of it. Even the rat looked up with a combination of surprise and guilt at them.

"Surprise cereal inspection, gentlemen," Gunther said. "We are here from the Breakfast Board."

"All is well! Not to worry my friends, all is well." Torontoola declared. "You have passed! Carry on."

The chefs stood with their mouths open too shocked to speak and watched as the men stood up and brushed the loose cereal off their clothing.

Gunther, as casually as possible, picked up the four corners of the tarp containing the cereal boxes of money and heaved it over his shoulder—something like a Santa Clause bag; and he, Jefe and Torontoola left the basement the same way they came in.

Chapter 16: A Cluster of Thieves, Den of Traitors

"It's a fake," Harold Wiskowski said. "Hand me another."

Jefe passed another bill to the bank president. Harold stood at his office window, shades up, the sun glaring in, the money pressed against the glass with his hands.

"And?" Gunther asked.

"Hmmm. I think it's fake too. They are damn good, though." He reached across his desk and grabbed a handful of the cereal box money Gunther gave him, looking the bills over closely. Then he laughed. He walked to his chair and sat down. He pulled a magnifying glass from his desk, turned his desk lamp on and looked over the bills again. Then he sat back.

"I think they're fakes, Johann. They are almost perfect, Holy Saints be praised, but I think they are fakes."

"Fakes," Gunther mumbled.

"Fakes made on very good printing presses. Presses and paper the likes of which the government uses. If you hadn't walked in with a suspicious story, I probably never would have noticed. They are that good."

"All of this?" Gunther waved his hand over the bundles laying on the tarp on the floor.

"I'll have to take a good look."

"It looks so real," Jefe said.

"Counterfeit money problems go back a long way. Hundreds of years. People made fake coins back in Europe.

Here, they began printing fake money right after we signed the U.S. Constitution. It was all a hardy mess. States made money. Banks even made their own money. And criminals started making their own money too. In 1861, the government started to print one standard money. Made the artwork very complex. But the paper is really the key. There's a secret to it, and no one outside the government can really get the right paper. That's the trick. Criminals can get the engraving plates, but not the paper. But this is damn good.

The Secret Service was created in 1865 to fight counterfeiting. Investigate and destroy counterfeit operations!"
The three men sat silently as if a bit dazed by the many different potential scenarios. Want to know what to do?" Harold asked. He started to roll a cigarette on his desk.

"I guess so," Gunther said.

"Call the Secret Service, that's what."

"Why? Why would someone come to Fort Worth and give all this money away? Not buy something? Well, he did buy a big gambling house…" Gunther said.

"There ya go. Gamble and lose nothing."

"It costs something to make these fakes," Gunther said.

"I mean, losing is still losing."

"Well, that's true. You know, the U.S. Attorney General Charles Joe Bonaparte issued an order a short time back to staff at the Office of the Chief Examiner," Harold said.

"They might work on this too."

"But…but, he also gave away tons of money. Why do that?"

"Well, I don't know. I do know that back during the Revolutionary War, the Brits ran a counterfeit U.S. money operation to de-value the new American dollar. It worked, for while."

"So, Justin Trace wants to destroy the American economy? Destroy the American dollar?" Gunther said. "Right here in Hell's Acre, Fort Worth?"

"I don't rightly know. Where does this money come from anyway?"

"Amarillo," Jefe said.

"Amarillo! Well, the plot thickens," the banker said.

Gunther pulled a bundle from the tarp on the floor, and handed him more bills. Harold took them and gave them a once over.

"A plot is hatched in Amarillo to destroy America. Something ain't right with these bills. They are damn, damn good, but they ain't right. I tell ya right now, Johann. Better call the U.S. Secret Service."

"Not just yet."

"Not yet?"

"This money is connected to a series of murders here in town, Harold. We don't need the Federales sniffing around just yet."

"Murders!"

"Murders. And I am working for the governor on this. It's official business from the top. Can we keep this money here for awhile?"

"Here? Is anybody looking for it?"

"It sat in a hotel basement for almost a month. Right out in the open. Right in the cereal boxes. Just like it was delivered to Justin Trace," Gunther said.

"The murdered man?"

"The murdered man."

"I have a personal safe here in my office. I guess I could lock it up here. And if the governor's involved…I guess I could help out. The bills are so good, I could say I thought they were real, if anybody asks. Or, I could say agents of the governor asked me to secure it."

"If anybody asks, tell them I brought it here. Tell them the truth."

"Morning Glory Cereal?" Jefe said.

"Yes!" Harold said. With a huff, he got up and walked over to the open tarp on the floor and picked up another of the boxes. "Morning Glory Cereal." With a box in hand he walked over to a table near a massive set of thick books on shelves. He took two books down and returned to his desk.

"Ooookay," he said. He opened one book and flipped through the pages.

"Ooookay. The business is on the stock market. Several markets. It is a farming business, and a cattle business, and this cereal business. Yup. Amarillo, but officially near Red Gun City, south of Amarillo."

"It says Bendigo, Texas on the box," Jefe said.

"Bendigo on the box. Ok. Let's see…and the owner, well, the chairman of the board of the Bendigo Corporation is a Clyde Bendigo."

"Have you ever heard of him?" Gunther asked.

"Ohhh my, yes. He built a small city and incorporated it. Named it after himself, being the rich coot that he is. He's in the train business, but he created and runs a health clinic there. A spa. People go there to lose weight. From all over the world they come to take the cure. Get in shape. Cure sexual problems. Cancers. Here, look. I got this awhile back from my sister." The banker shuffled through his desk drawers and pulled out a pamphlet and handed it to Gunther.

Gunther looked at the one-page advertisement.

At our sanitarium, the Morning Glory Spa, you'll learn about the latest, most successful diet and exercise regimens, cleanse your body with frequent herbal enema treatments to remove toxins, and more. We'll introduce you to a low-fat, high-protein diet of whole grains, fiber-rich foods and nuts that will increase energy, enhance sleep and improve sexual desire and function. Daily fresh air, exercise, and healthful hygiene are practiced religiously at Morning Glory Spa!

And it went on,

…methods comprising hydrotherapy, phototherapy, thermotherapy electrotherapy, mechanotherapy, dietetics and physical culture. To assist with diagnostics and evaluation of therapeutic efficacy, various measures of physiological integrity are utilized to obtain numerous vital coefficients especially in relation to the integrity and efficiency of the blood, the heart, lungs, liver, the kidneys, stomach, intestines, brain, nerves and muscles. People come from all over the USA and Canada. A few from Europe. One of my friends told me he even saw some Chinese people there.

Gunther handed the flier to Jefe.

"Bendigo is, needless to say, – rich. He takes baths in pasteurized milk. A pretty woman cuts his fingernails for him.

He wears socks from France. The boy is rich. He hobnobs with the richest, rich. He works with and is on the board of the Texas Bank Commission. Agriculture Commission. He travels to Washington a lot. He has his own train and train car. He knows yer buddy, Teddy."

"Roosevelt?" Gunther asked.

"Yup. A 14-karat, hob-nobber. Sit a spell at the library and read up on him, in the newspapers on file. You'll see him in the middle of many wheels and deals. He built his own city! Houses. Stores. A court house. He has contacted church leaders in an effort to build various denominations of churches out there. I read last year that he ordered 350 trees to be delivered just to line the streets."

"So, Clyde Bendigo, or people in Clyde's business, sneak boxes of fake money to Justin Trace here in Fort Worth to just… well, what? Give it away?" Gunther muttered.

"Looks like it. But, he is rich enough to give away real money, a lot of it, to charities. Which, I think he does, if my memory stands. Are you still going to wait to call the Secret Service?"

"Yes I am."

"Whatever will you do?"

"I am going to Bendigo, Texas. Gonna see a man about a breakfast," Gunther said.

"You're a dern fool, then. You are going to ride into a cluster of thieves or a den of traitors, one way or the other."

Chapter 17: The Wind Will Whistle Right through It

Two a.m. and Beau Kershaw appeared tired. All that drinking and cavorting after his blues gig at the Bociferous Night Club had likely taken a toll on him. A hired coach dropped him off, and he slowly climbed the stairs of the dark, quiet Ebbie Holland boarding house.

He didn't spot across the street, just inside a patch of trees, Gunther and Jefe, who could hear him humming and singing a drunken, jazz-like melody.

"Heeee got nobody, nooobody but him. He got no…"

He entered the unlocked front door as Gunther crossed the street and circled the two-story wooden apartment building. Gunther had eaten dinner at the Holland House before and was familiar with the layout. Jefe remained back a ways working a larger circle around the house from a distance. Gunther moved around the porch that surrounded the entire building until he saw an electric light come on inside a window, the room of the newly arrived Mr. Kershaw. Gunther slipped up the back porch steps and made his way to the window. He could hear the vocal baffled only slightly by the glass.

"…when youuu got nobody, nobody's got you."

Jefe found some trees to sit among with a view of that window and the building. Gunther pushed up on the window. He carefully opened it an inch or two, took out his revolver and stuck the barrel under the glass. With one hand and a barrel he lifted the window up and stepped into the room. He heard Kershaw in the adjoining bathroom.

"...so it seems in your dreams, you say..."

Gunther stood beside the window. Kershaw walked in, half dressed.

"the dreams...huh, this cannot be..." Kershaw gasped and froze at the sight of Gunther, with gun out, standing in his room. "What? You? What?"

"If you have a gun in the room somewhere, Kershaw? I suggest you pull it now and save yourself a lot of grief," Gunther said softly. "Shoot yourself with it."

"Wha?"

Gunther approached him and cracked the side of his gun barrel across Kershaw's face and head, knocking him off his feet. His bare feet flipped about as high as his head had been. He hit the wooden floor, stunned. He crawled like a drunken scorpion away as best he could, from the intruder.

"Now, now wait a minute dear, dear, can we...we can discuss this," the man mumbled.

Gunther kneeled down and whispered in his ear, "Kershaw, here's what we'll discuss, you sorry sack of shit. About you setting me up. How's that for a discussion we can have tonight?"

He drew back, put his pistol away and pulled out a knife from his belt. He stuck the tip about an eighth of an inch, through Kershaw's white ruffled shirt and into his rib cage. Just about an eighth of an inch. There was an instant gasp, followed by a small bloodstain on the cotton shirt.

"I ain't here for jazzy bullshit. I want answers, or I'll gut you wide open. You won't see morning. Thanks to you, I was just about beaten to death by your buddies with baseballs and baseball bats, robbed and left for dead, and I'm thinking about popping open your lungs right here, all while you're watching me do it."

Kershaw shook his head, gasped again and stammered some grunts. Gunther kept the pressure on the rib cage.

"What in hell is going on?" Gunther asked.

"Goings on?"

"Yeah, you French prick. Goings on. What the fuck is going on with you and those sons of bitches?"

"Spanky and dem boys, all dem boys, they are just a pack

of highwaymen. Dey work the streets looking for jobs to do. Monies to steal. Beatings for hire. Killings for hire."

"Jobs? You mean crimes."

"Crimes, yeah. Jobs. Dey, dey hears of something, some kind of an angle, dey work it. Dey're a gang Gunther, like… like bank robbers or something, or, or train robbers of yester-year days. Like Butch Cassidy's Hole in the Wall boys. Dey take anything dey can get. Outlaws."

"You give them angles?"

"Ugh, yeah, yeah, I give dem some angles, sometimes. Yeah. Stuff I hear from the clubs. Dey pay me something. I hear something juicy, you know, a possible job? An angle? I tell them and, if it pans out? Dey pay me. Yeah."

"And I was an angle."

"ahhh…ahhh"

"The Torontoola murder and robbery. The Justin Trace murder. What do you know?"

Kershaw rubbed his bleeding forehead. "I did not work that. But yeah, yeah, well. Dem boys you see, well, you see they are afraid of this Torontoola lawsman, because he would arrest dem if dey crossed his path. Maybe even rob dem because he's bad, and he dirty law! He dirty law! Dey know he's dirty, and dey know he collects payoffs. Big payoffs. Dey know he's got a gold mine of money stashed somewhere. Dey want it. Dey's been wishing, watching and talking about hitting him for about a year now. Then…then dey heard about the bank run to Dallas every Tuesday by him and sometimes the missus. Dey wanted to rob dis run, but didn't want to face Torontoola in no gun fight on the turnpike."

"You tell them about the Tuesday money run to the dallas bank?"

"Nooo, no, no I did not. I don't know nothing about that. Somebody did. Somebody else."

"Go on."

"One of dem boys heard that Torontoola…he threatened the gambler Justin Trace out in the open, in public one night. In front of some folks. Said he would kill Trace, out loud in front of witnesses. Dey figured if Spanky dressed up like dat Torontoola, all in black and all, Spanky could gun down

Trace some night and get Torontoola thrown in the jailhouse for it. Once he was in jail? Long enough? Long enough so dey could rob Torontoola's money on the bank run. Wear masks and rob the monies."

"So it was all a big set up. Kill Trace. Set up the cop. Rob his wife while he was in jail."

"Yeah, yeah a big setup. A job."

"Name the men."

"The men. Name the men. The men. I don't know for sure. I ain't no witness to it. I wasn't there or nothing. Well, you know Spanky. You know Spanky already. He always dere. He da boss. Deres, deres…Chiseler Kovaks. Dey call him "The Chiseler" because he steal bases."

"He's on the ball team."

"Yeah, not all of dem are ballplayers in the gang, but Chiseler is. He plays shortstop. He get on base? He steals second. He steal third. Sometimes even home. They call him The Chiseler. Dey got Henry Bloodpainter. Dats his real name. They call him on baseball roster 'Henry Painter,' but he a half-breed, and his real name is Bloodpainter. Dere are Indians playing ball all over the league but dey hide dere real names with da white folks names. Dey got other bums, too."

"Billy Joe Farks?"

"Yeah, him too. He don't play no baseball. He works at the meat house."

"Farks alive?"

"I don't know, like you asked me before, I don't know, but I ain't seen him. Not since that robbery."

"Abbott Sureline?"

"He, he one of them. He makes saddles by day. But he in deep."

"Who do you think threw the balls at me?"

"Johnny Cleveland. He be the pitcher. He a robber, yeah. He be a killer. From Minnesota."

He looked down at his gut. Gunther still had the knife tip in him. The blood continued to seep out onto the white shirt.

"Dey got a whole gang you know. Dey ride motorcycles. Dey got a name like other gangs, like the famous old 'Hole in the Wall Gang.' They call themselves the 'The Home Run

Kings Gang.' Dats dere name ya know. 'The Home Run Kings.' Dey got peoples a coming and a going out of the gang, but them ballplayers are the main ones. Dat house dat got all burned up the other night was the Farks' house."

"Justin Trace."

"Huh?"

"Tell me about Justin Trace."

"There was something going on with that Justin Trace feller, Gunther. He ain't right. He was too rich, and the people who sent him here from West Texas? Spanky and da boys figured as soon as they killed him, dey would rob his hotel room. Maybe get a stash of some of dat cash from the room."

"Did they?"

"Don't know. I don't know. He had money somewhere. To open up dem gambling houses? Spread all that money around? That Trace had money from somewhere, somehow. Whoever it comes from, they sent two men in, white boys about two weeks ago. Fellers are in from West Texas, only dey ain't from West Texas themselves. Dey from up North ways. Yankee boys. Like Army boys. Dey are sniffing around. Asking about Justin Trace. Spanky and the boys? They are getting afraid of these West Texas people. Maybe Spanky will kill them two, too."

"Who are they?"

"Two gentlemen types, but they rough looking under dem suits. Look, walk and talk like soldiers in suits. Like you. Straight up tall. Yeah. Two guys snooping around, I tell ya. Look like they are the military or something. Act like, look like they are police or Federales or something."

"You wouldn't tell me all this the other night?"

"Well, why Gunther?" he pleaded, almost crying. "How could I? Why should I? You understand? You a stranger. I mean why would I? I don't know you. You ain't no police. I knows dese boys. I have a thing with dese boys for a couple of years now. And they take care of me."

"That Texas Ranger. Winch. He was there, wasn't he?"

"Uhm who?"

"The…Ranger," Gunther asked with a growl and that knife tip touched in a little deeper.

"Oh. I…oh. Yeah, yeah, the Ranger. Yeah, he was there. He was there, too. He knows dem boys good too. He got your wallet."

"He did?"

"Yeah, he did. Right outta ya pants."

"Winch. Trace. Did Winch get money, a whole duffel bag of money from Trace's room?"

"I don't know dat."

"How much they give you to turn me over?"

He was silent, and Gunther gave his knife a slight twist.

"Aghhh! They, they paid me."

"How much?"

"Three. Three dollars."

"Three dollars."

Gunther leered at him. He grabbed Kershaw's right hand and held it up, his palm away from Kershaw.

"I oughta kill you right here."

"Nooo, but…"

Gunther looked at Kershaw's hand.

"Nooo. No! I…I plays the piano! No! That's my living!"

Gunther laid the blade on his palm.

"Get another living."

"AGHHHHH!" Kershaw moaned sinking into a deep shock.

Gunther stood.

"I don't like to shoot a man in the arm," he said slow, in almost a growl. "Or the leg. Leave him behind alive. Some men get revenge crazy. And I don't like stabbing them in the hand, either. Leaving them behind. Alive. Because if you do? They come back for you. So, let me tell you something, you little wimpy, skunk, fuck bastard. I am leaving your hands alone and you alive, and I don't like it. As you can tell, I'm not to be crossed. You have really fucked up, crossing me. So, you leave Fort Worth. Leave Texas. If I see you anywhere, ever again I will drop you cold like a dead man's shit. I will shoot your skull so full of holes the wind will whistle through it. If you tell your friends about our talk? My visit here? You know they'll just kill ya, too. They'll kill ya, or I will. You leave Texas."

"What'll I tell people about…"
"Your hand?" Gunther walked over to the window. Tell them you fell on some voodoo, bad luck. And you're going back to New Orleans and study Cajun cooking, or some such shit."

Kershaw just stared at Gunther, probably just hoping he'd climb back out that window and leave him alone. Not change his mind and finish him!

"Who's got my Luger?"

"Spanky. Spanky does. He carries it in a shoulder holster."

Gunther sneered with that answer.

"I know you're running girls. Send them home," Gunther said, and he stepped out the window, and out of Beau Kershaw's life.

At this point, Jefe perched on the porch, by the window, his back to it. He'd no doubt heard the whole conversation. They trotted across the field, through the crisp night air across Jacksboro Rd. and through the treeline to their horses.

"You stab him?" Jefe asked.

"Just a little bit," Gunther said. "He's leaving or I;I'll stab him deeper.

"He won't be playing jazz tomorrow night at the club," Jefe said as they saddled up.

"No. No, but he'll be singing the blues."

Chapter 18: Stinking Foot to Mouth

Next afternoon, Ranger Winch's house, Fort Worth...

Naked, Betha slid off the top of the boney, half-dressed Ranger Winch. He let loose a big sigh. No matter how many bathes he took, every bit of him stank to her from his feet to his mouth. For the life of her she could not figure the cause. Truly, she couldn't tell which inch of him she disliked the most. But she would never tell him how much he stunk or how terrible she hated him. She actually felt scared to death of him, but he favored her and paid well and regular. Winch leaned over to the nightstand beside the bed and took a sip of beer from a dirty glass.Betha sat on the edge of the bed.

"You know that Kershaw's gone."

"You don't say?"

"I say."

"Where?"

"Don't know. He left. Said he was leaving Texas. Goin home."

"You don't say."

"Said he was going home. Sudden like. Scared acting. Told me and our girls to go back to Midlothian. I said what would we do there? He said the same as here. But the church folk would burn us at the stake back there. Our old church. They're thumpers and they'd tar and feather us and set us alight."

"Well, then you can't go."

"Well, then, we are alone here."

"You ain't alone, Betha," he sat up and stroked her long brown hair down her back. Then he leaned back on the bed and scratched his balls.

"How about you scratch my balls, will ya?"

Betha turned and leaned her thigh upon the bed and lightly scratched his balls with the tips of her long nails.

"You ain't no help. No real help. I need real money. Regular money. Like a job. You know where I could get one?"

"A job?"

"A job."

"Can you get me a job?"

"I can get cha a blow job," Winch said with a shit-eating grin.

"That ain't funny, Chester. My cousins and me, we'll be starvin soon enough! We're gonna be kicked out of our rooms now that Kershaw is gone."

"Kershaw. He was all shook up."

"Hmmm. He mention anybody's name? He mention a Johann Gunther? He mention Raoul Torontoola?"

"No. He just up and left us, with his hand in a sling."

"Hmmm. Look…you can always be my thang, little lady. I can help you a bit. I can't help your two cousins though. But you have a job with me. Doing me."

She stopped scratching his balls.

"We are like sisters. Deeper than sisters. I have to stick with them."

"You do?"

"It's my fault they're up here in Fort Worth, doing what they doing."

"Can't hep 'em."

"Can't or won't?"

"Both. Looky, I am sweet on every turn of your body, missy. But I can't be housing no three whores to my house! I am a got-damn Texas Ranger, and everyone will know that I have three whores stationed at my address. I can't fade that heat."

"Look at what else you do! Everything else you do and nobody knows you're up to no good."

He stared at her. She saw many emotions pass through the muscles of his unshaven face. She didn't like any of them. Any one of them could mean instant trouble to her, like a slap or even a beating.

"Now you watch yer mouth, little lady. With me, or with anybody. I can protect you only so far. You could get a baseball bat up beside your head for talking about what we talk about. Fer what you might have overheard at the clubhouse."

He got out of bed. He still had his wrinkled shirt on. He walked through the open door of the bedroom closet. He came out with a handful of change.

"Take this."

"Coinage?" she asked.

"Take this. There are dollars of coins in there. Take it. It's the only specie I got here."

She formed a cup with her hands, and he poured the coins into them. She did see dollars in there!

"Now go on. Go on. Geet. I gotta get out of here and go to work," he said.

She piled the money on the bed, got up and picked her cotton dress up off the floor. She put it on. Winch watched.

"I like woman with no underwear," he said, grinning, a little shiver running through his shoulders.

"You got a bag or a rag or something for this money?" she asked.

"We need to get you a purse, you know? No underwear, but a nice, purse bag." He stood up again and pulled a red-checkered neckerchief from a drawer. He gave it to her. She curled her lips as she put the coins into the neckerchief.

"Oh, remember I got that Catholic preacher man thing in the workings. I'm meeting the alter boy tonight and I will let you now."

"Messing with a priest," she said. "I don't Chester."

"You'll. Now geet!"

"Goodbye, Chester."

"Goodbye, Betha."

Betha left the house, and sure enough several neighbors spied her and made foul faces. Maybe Chester Winch was right? Maybe she and her cousins couldn't stay at Chester's house without rumors and gossip and trouble from the Texas Rangers?

She walked the 10 blocks to her favorite teahouse, "Chin's." It was run by Chinese, and they didn't care much about who came in and loitered as long as they paid for tea, or coffee or food. Her two cousins waited inside for her.

"What he say?" cousin Sadie asked.

"He ain't helping us."

"He ain't?" cousin Hillary said.

"Food here!" Betha shouted to the Chinese lady at the counter. "He just ain't helping us. He will help me for screwing him until the cows come home, but he ain't supporting all of us."

They sat in silence.

"He seemed worried about two fellers I have heard him and the boys talk about. Joe…Joe something Gunther and that rich, 'Mesican,' lawsmens Torontoola," Betha said. They have been fussing on about them for weeks now at the clubhouse. When I told him about Kershaw's hand being busted up? He axed me about them two fellers. Like they'd done it to Kershaw?"

"Did they burn down the clubhouse?" cousin Sadie asked.

"I don't know. I don't think so."

"Can we go to Joe or the Mesican cop and geet us some money for something?" cousin Hillary asked.

"Rattin?" Betha said.

"Yeah, rattin. I heard the police will give people money for rattin. I hear there is a lot of money for some rattin."

Betha's head bobbed up and down. "I guess so. Some money. If Torontoola is as rich as they say, I think we need to see him. But Chester said thay's beat us in the head with baseball bats if we talked too much about anything."

"We have to geet the money and go!" Sadie said.

"Geet up and go?" Hillary said.

"Dallas maybe? Houston? Right away? I heard from

Ebbys' cook that Ebby's kicking us out of the house by Friday. She needs the room for the horse races this weekend," Sadie said.

"She don't care nothing about us," Hillary said.

"She don't. I will find that Mesican, lawsmens and tell him he can buy some rattin' news," Betha said.

"How?"

"I will call the police station and tell them I need to talk to Torontoola," Betha said. "Matter of life or death. Lawsmens always worry about that kinda talk."

Chapter 19: Peter Packed a Pence

Later that evening, Downtown Fort Worth, TX...

Texas Ranger Winch sat at a picnic table outside of Clandy's steak house with a big mug of Pearl beer. He anxiously awaited the arrival of Theodore Smickle, alter boy. His fingers drumming on the table were interrupted.

"Ranger."

"Kid."

The teen sat eyeing the beer.

"Don't be looking at my Pearl. How old are you?"

"Fifteen."

"Yeah, you can have ya a milkshake. What about the preacher?"

"The Father has girls in..."

"Hookers?"

"Yes, prostitutes, about once a week."

"And you said you get these women for him?"

"I do. At Hell's Half Acre."

"Helen! HELEN! Get this young man a Pearl."

"Well, with the big fire down there, a lot of the girls left.

"Yeah."

"So that's how I can...we can...sneak our girls in and do this deal. New girls left over from the fire."

Ranger Winch smiled and said, "You ahhh...you a little ass con man, ain't cha?"

The waitress Helen delivered the beer. The kid's eyes lit up. He took a big gulp and it was apparent it was not his first.

"And he likes em two at a time?" Winch asked.

"Oh he do. He lets me watch sometimes."

"Whooowe! Well, I will get you enough money to get your own girls and maybe let him watch. When?"

The alter boy took another refreshing cold swallow and said, "Two nights from now. 7 at night."

"Lucky 7."

6:45 pm two nights later, near the Benbrook Catholic Church...

"You bust in fast! I don't want to be sexen up no preacher man," Betha demanded, as they walked down the street behind the Catholic Church.

"I'll bust in there when I get in there," Winch said. "Looky, he's got to get the two of ya naked and doing something, infla-greatio, to get him on the hook."

"I was once a Bible girl!"

"And I was once a Lutheran. It don't make no never mind, today. We all is once-was-ers,' and that is no excuse to do nothing until you die. Ain't you ever seen Hamlet?"

"Hamlet!" She looked puzzled.

"Hamlet. It's a Limey story about a yesteryear prince who spends the whole play thinking and reciting poetry about what to do, what not to do. When he finally does something, the idiot gets killed. You don't know no Hamlet? To be and all not to be questioning?"

"Nope."

"I think that God made the British just so's we could have quotes. Look, we is gonna catch a big money fish. You get yer money up front from him. Get the clothes off of em. You and yer friend get naked and I interrupt the carnal she-bang-bang. You and her leave, and I give you even more money afterward."

"How much money?"

"Well, I don't rightly know yet, darlin. I'll see what he's got. But, you get before and after money. That's tonight in the palm of yer hand, my dewy-eyed princess."

"That a promise?"

"From a former Lutheran to a former Bible girl. To be-est or not to be-est."

They approached the back of the church.

The second girl wandered up when she saw the two.

"There. There. Knock on that door, there." Winch pointed to it across a parking lot.

She frowned and shook her head. She and "Girl 2" strutted off. He watched them on the cobblestones in their high heels and tight dresses. He'd unwrapped Betha from cheap dresses several times before and might try it again tonight if and when this scheme played out.

Monsignor Hoolahan answered the door. He was a tall thin man with fuzzy grey hair, dispatched somewhat forward to cover its recession. He grinned at them with some good teeth. He was already drunk. Betha could smell it all on him. He let them in.

"Monsignor," Betha said.

"Oh my darlings, don't cha be looking lovely tonight, lassies."

She smiled.

"Shush now darlings. Sussshhh. We have to pass by the nuns' rooms."

They went down several narrow hallways. Up some stairs, and Hoolahan turned and winked at them when they approached a big brown door. He opened it and let them in. He shut it behind them with both hands leaning with his back against the door like he just caught the prize pheasant. He rested there for a second.

"Lassies, what in God's name do you have packed under that dress?"

He felt of Betha first with his two big hands, up and down and all around. Being good at what she did, she smiled and rolled with his rhythm.

"Should I call you Monsignor?" she asked.

"Yes. Yes, call me that all night, no matter what I do to

you. No matter what we do. I am your Monsignor. You lassies, are my novitiates."

"Novitiate? I have been called many things, but never that." She stepped away and lit a cigarette from her purse. She sat in a velvet chair, crossed her legs. With a subtle pull she showed a lot of leg. She kicked a high-heeled shoe off. His gaze followed its bounce. Girl 2 did the same.

"Yes, a novitiate. It means you are a novice in religion. A novice nun." He poured them both a drink of whiskey. The glasses were intricately cut, thick and magnificent. He handed one to her.

"My job is to spoil you for the nunnery, my dear novitiate. Introduce you to so many, many wonderful, screaming things that you give up on God, and you become…you become full-bodied, full blooded, women."

"Not the…normal work of a priest, I might say," Betha said.

"I save women. I save women from the nunnery."

"I save money, Monsignor." She flicked ashes into an exquisite and clean ashtray, while blowing smoke. "And we need five dollars from you, before anything else gets saved around here."

He opened an ornate marble box on a hand-carved table. He pulled out five dollars. Grinning all the while, he handed her the bills.

They stripped naked. There wasn't much under those dresses. Betha spread her legs. Girl 2 stepped over and began undressing the priest.

"Go ahead Mr. Monsignor. Save me," she whispered.

He dropped his black pants. He went after her. He tried to save her. But after only a few minutes the door knob twisted right and left. Distracted, Hoolahan glanced at the locked door.

Then, the lock area splintered open.

"Texas Rangers," Chester Winch declared, but not too loudly. His engraved Colt revolver was out and aimed at the man of the now, half-cloth. Hoolahan, now clad in only his black shirt, fell fully back on the floor.

"Oooh, oh laddy."

"Common, prostitutes, Monsignor?" Winch declared with disgust. "We have been a follering this lady of the night on a hooker case. And she has lead us here to you," Winch said, again with a low voice. He closed the room door behind him.

"It is my weakness. I have sinned, My Lord!" the Monsignor howled. "Oh forgive me, Lord!

"Put something on for Christ's sake. Yer disgusting to see."

Hoolahan reached for his pants.

"I have sinned, My Lord!" he said, whimpering as he dressed. "My Lord."

"Ah shut the hell up. Yer just got caught, red-dicked. Caught in the act, and now yer a crying and praying about it. Just cause yer caught. If you were never caught? You wouldn't whimper a peep."

"You," Winch pointed at the ladies. "You two get outta here, you tarts." Turning away from the preacher, he half-smiled and winked at them. "Beat it!"

The girls played the game, acted scared and snatched up her clothes and shoes from the floor and ran out the door. She too closed the door behind her.

Winch turned back to Hoolahan. He grabbed a chair, and straddled the seat. He pushed his hat back on his head.

"You know, Your Soiled Holiness, as a Texas Ranger, I am duly bound to report this."

"Ohhh my Gawd!"

"And I am also duly bound to arrest you."

"Nooo, oh no, Sweet Jesus."

"And when you geet arrested, yer name, and this…this rectory here, this church will be listed in the newspapers as the unholy scene of an unholy sex crime. Ain't you supposed to be married to Virgin Mary er something? What is this?"

Winch snatched up a bottle near the bed and read the label.

"Whiskey! The devil's brew. And the smell of you! There is the odor of this whiskey all about you!"

"I have sinned!"

Winch took a swig from the bottle.

"Can…can you help me, sir. Can you forgive me?" Monsignor dropped to his knees and crawled over to Winch. "What can I do?"

"QUIT yer sniveling!"

"Yes. Yes, sir."

"I know all about you and yer kind. Destroying the names of good priests and Catholics everywhere. Your tomfoolery will be heard of all the way to yer Vatican. Yer Pope himself will read about this."

"What can I do? Please? Anything to save the grace of the church."

"Sheet. You mean save your stinking ass. Maybe I can make a deal?"

"A deal? Yes? Yes. What do you want?"

"Money," Winch said calmly. He laid the shiny pistol down on a thin table nearby.

"Money? Money. I have some money saved."

"How much?"

"About 75 dollars."

"SHEEET!"

"What then?"

"Real money, preacher! Like. Like how much money does this church take in per week?"

"Ahh…ahhh… about 50 dollars."

"Sheet, you say. That's nothing!"

"Oh God, Oh God."

"I mean real money, big money."

"You ever hear of Peter's Pence?"

"Peter's who? Pecker what?"

"Pence. Peter's Pence. Tis the money we all send to Rome. Tis the purpose of the Peter's Pence Collection to provide the Holy Father with the financial means to respond to all those a suffering as a result of wars, oppressions, natural disasters and disease. "

"You memorized that didn't ya? And spit it out like a… like a mindless fool."

"We raise the money from…"

"Yeah. I see the likes of the people in your church. Poor Mesican families that the got damn Spanish came here and tortured and tamed into church slaves. Sheep! They give you their hard earned money every Sunday and you mumble some jumble."

"We have some well-to-do benefactors…"

"God made the Heavens and God made the Earth. He just seems to have a problem with money. He can't get enough. And Rome! Rome money. How much Rome money then? Now we are talking turkey. Gobble on."

Every year, each church sends an offering to the Vatican. It…is voluntary…it…"

"Sit up in the damn chair, will ya? Get off yer knees." Hoolahan did. Winch took another swig and then handed the bottle to the Monsignor. The Monsignor reflexively took a big mouthful and swallowed it like water.

"Go on," Winch said.

"We send a yearly offering to his Holy Grace."

"How much?"

"About five thousand dollars."

"Tsk-tsk-tsk. What church sends in the biggest amount of money?"

"Our Lady of the Pure Sacred in San Antonio. It is the biggest in Texas. It sends in over 10 thousand a year."

"To the Pope! What does he really do with it?"

"He…he…"

"He spends it! That's what he does. He spends it on gold-plated shit and high living. All those eye-talian, red-robed, big hat, mother-fuckers eat steaks with sharpy-little silver knives, and sleep in…in big, big feather beds in golden palaces while the whole got damn world goes to hell. Starves. You seen those creepy pictures of skinny people in Africa and…and where the Chinks live? One got damn gold plate would feed a whole village fer an entire month."

They stared at each other. Hoolahan took another drink from the bottle and handed it back to Winch.

"Are you a religious man? Do you…"

"Don't you even start in on that with me," Winch said, pointing a finger at Hoolahan's red, bulbous nose. Then he zeroed in on the proboscis.

"These church people don't look at that big, red, balloon nose of yers, and don't assume you are a drunkard?"

"Well, no."

"They are blind as bats in a cave. Now, that San Antoine church sends in about 10 thousand? When?"

"It ships out September 15. We all do this."

"How?"

"First by train to Galveston. Then by boat to Miami, Fl rida. Then ship to Italy."

"Train. Boat. Ship. Guards?"

"Guards?"

"Yeah guards! Guarding the money!"

"Yes. Every church hires armed guards for the Peter's Pence. I know many of my brothers in San Antonio. They hire U.S. Marshals to pick up and transport the gold by train to Galveston. Of course they are all Catholic Marshals."

"And before the delivery, where is the money kept?"

"In a church safe. In Monsignor Hensen's office. "

"A monsignor…like you," Winch said, bobbing his head up and down.

"Like me. Monsignor Hensen. He's a fine gentleman."

"His office attached to the church? Where is his office?"

"It's in a building behind the church. Tell me, where is this all going, sir?"

"Going? I will tell you where this is all a going." He leaned forward. "I am gonna rob that fine ol gentleman, and deprive the Pope of his San Antonio, Peter's Pecker Pence. And when I get that money, when I prove you ain't a lying to me? I will release you of your sex and alcohol crime here tonight."

"Oh, oh saints be praised, but you won't hurt anyone will you?"

"If they don't get in my way, they will be alright."
One more sip each.

"You savvy?" Winch asked.

"I…savvy. I savvy."

Winch slowly picked up his pistol, aimed it at Hoolahan's head and cocked back the hammer. The Monsignor's jaw dropped.

"Now, *you're* safe. Where is it?"

"It's over there." He pointed to a large desk.

"Uh-huh. Open it."

He stayed still and in shock.

"Go on!"

Hoolahan got up and walked over to the safe. Winch followed. Mumbling, praying, trembling with fear the Monsignor opened the safe.

"You pull a gun out of that mother-fucker, and I'll cut you down."

"I have no such gun. I am a man of peace."

"You're a man of pussy and booze, I know. Now give it here."

Hoolahan laid a pile of money on the desk.

"How much?'

"About…about 250 dollars."

Winch smiled. He grabbed it all.

"What will I ever tell the church?" he mumbled.

"Tell em you spent it all on hookers and booze, and — while right in the middle of the act— you done got hijacked. You see, those robes will get you a lot of pussy, but it'll take just one pussy to get your robes."

Winch turned, put the gun in its engraved holster and walked to the door, but stopped there and faced Hoolahan once more.

"Mr. Monsignor. You can tell I am a man with no rules. But I am a man with all the rules behind me." He flicked the Texas Ranger badge. "I suggest you conjure up a good tale about where this money went. And, if this San Antonio story turns out to be a fairytale? I will ruin you, ruin this church, and bust you up later with a baseball bat. Ta-ta."

And he left. Hoolahan leaned back on the desk. He looked at the grandfather clock, its pendulum ticking away. The ladies came in at 7:30. The ranger came in at 7:40. It wasn't even 8 p.m. yet. That whole tornado swept through in about 18 minutes.

It was all enough to cause a man to get religion.

Chapter 20: Mister Nope-Taint-Neither

It was a warm late summer morning. Reckon Road. Gunther and Jefe dismounted from their steeds. Dressed for dirty work but still packing weapons under their light jackets. Their mission was to sift through the ruins of the clubhouse. Jefe pulled two rakes from the long canvas saddlebag on his horse. He handed a rake to Gunther and the two stepped into the gray rubble. The police were long gone now. Even the Fire Department was gone. It was their turn to kick around the ashes, to look for some items the others would not know to search for.

They studied and raked around the terrain, moved and plowed for about 45 minutes before Gunther said, "Look at this."

"What?"

Jefe walked over to the kneeling Gunther. Gunther picked up a shredded, wet piece of cardboard about six inches by six inches. It was part of the front of a Morning Glory Cereal box. They dug around in the immediate area and found some more pieces of boxes, and all this not in the former kitchen area of the house where common cereal would be found.

"We can guess that these are the boxes the illustrious Ranger Winch carried out of Trace's hotel room in that duffel bag," Gunther said. "Too many boxes and not in the kitchen area. No sign of burned money though."

"He's such of the snake," Jefe said. "You would think he

would keep the duffel bag money all for himself?"

"Maybe he's too afraid of the gang? Maybe he's a dedicated part of the gang?"

"Maybe…he is the leader of the gang?" Jefe said.

"Maybe."

"Question is, do they know the money is counterfeit? Do they think it's real? No matter what, hitting Trace was a gold mine for them. Then they hit Torontoola's money run."

"HEY! Hey, what you doing here?" demanded a voice.

Gunther and Jefe turned toward the street. A gaunt man, just eight feet or so away, round-shouldered, head slouched forward, stared at them. His arms down motionless at his sides, he wore a blue and red plaid flannel shirt under a brown jacket, brown pants and brown boots. A tan felt hat dwarfed his head. In the opening of his jacket, they saw a buckle of a wide gun belt. His lip curled, displaying a row of buck teeth. He was near-death looking, his face had an ashen gray quality to it. He looked like an odd, sick, crazy man. He looked damn near like a ghost.

Gunther smiled at the man. Jefe, rake in hand, immediately stepped off to the right several steps, opening a gap between himself and Gunther. They saw no horse, no car, no motorcycle on the street. The man just seemingly materialized.

"I said, what are you doing here?" The man asked again, with a growl.

"Well now, you must be Mr. Farks, the owner?" Gunther asked.

"Nope."

"No? Oh," Gunther said and he started to rake around the ground again. He knew Jefe had him covered on the flank.

"Then you must be from the insurance company? Checking on the property?" Gunther continued.

"Taint neither."

"I mean who else would even care about this piece of property? Well then, Mister Nope-Taint-Neither. Who are you, to be so worried about this piece of property?"

"Who are you to be scratching it all up with them tools?" the man asked.

"Oh, let's say we're just treasure hunters. Treasure hunting for leftovers. Maybe we'll find some diamonds, or a chunk of gold here?"

"You won't find such here."

"How do you know? You know who lived here before?

Maybe we'll find a stack of money from Mrs. Torontoola's purse here?"

The man's eyes widened at the name, and his head moved an inch down and to the right at the mention of her name. His right hand twitched. That hand flipped back to the right side of his jacket. That hand reached for…

"NO!" Jefe shouted. Jefe's revolver was out and aimed at the man. The man froze, barely touching the handle of his gun.

Gunther released the rake. The rake slowly fell over. He walked up to the man and stopped. Jefe closed in more from the side. Gunther stared at his face. Then he moved the man's right hand aside and tugged the pistol from the holster. Now with the man's handgun, he stepped back several steps.

"There's some confusion here," Gunther said. "If you aren't the owner, why do you care if we are here raking up this place, and why do you want to pull a gun when I mention the name Torontoola?"

"I live up the street," he said. "It ain't right, and it ain't Christian that you is here stirring up the ashes of the folks what died here."

"Oh," Gunther said as he unloaded the six gun. He took the gun by the long barrel, reared back and flung it as far as he could. It spun off quite a ways and landed on the front lawn of the house next door. He tossed the six, loose rounds back over his shoulder.

The man leered at Gunther.

"Go on then," Gunther said."Just get on outta here."

The man shrugged those poorly-postured shoulders, turned and walked off with a very stilted gait to the neighbor's yard.

Gunther retrieved the rake and continued raking. Jefe started raking again too, but his gaze followed the man. "He's heading for the gun," Jefe said quietly. "Not a good idea to toss it."

Gunther shook his head.

The man got to the pistol, kneeled more than crouched over to get it, like he was protecting some injury or a bad back he had. He stood up, and started pushing bullets out of the loops on his gun belt. He loaded the cylinder of the pistol.

"He's loading up," Jefe warned.

"Shit," Gunther quietly groaned.

Once loaded, the man spun the cylinder, looked up at them and with a sudden gangly, looping dash, charged them, pistol in one hand. He lifted the pistol barrel. He let out a war whoop.

"Damn," Gunther cussed as he and Jefe drew their pistols and broke off in a run in opposite directions. The strange man opened fire, but poorly, not really knowing who to shoot first. After a few steps Gunther and Jefe dove to the ground, chest down and started firing prone at the crazy man.

Mister Nope-Taint-Neither's run was interrupted as each round pelted into his chest, arms and legs. His arms flinched with each hit. His torso bucked. Finally his legs gave out, and he hit the ground headfirst.

"Damn!" Gunther said.

"Oh! Oh, you really screwed that up," Jefe complained.

"I know."

"I know, you know."

"Dammit."

The two remained flat on the ground, still a bit shocked at what had happened.

"You don't take a pistol from a man with a crazy face like dat and den throw it away! He will just go get the pistol back and start to shoot you."

"Well, what was I supposed to do, Jefe? Steal the gun from a grown man? Keep it and send him home? Mail it to his momma?"

"Yes. Yes, dat is one thing to do. Yes. It would be better than dis!"

"Yeah. Well, remember in Omaha, Nebraska when I took the rifle from that plumber? I threw his rifle away down by that creek. He got it, and he left."

"You have dis…dis mistake in your brains about throwing guns away like dis. You really screwed up dis time."

"Jesus, I hope we didn't shoot some old lady in her house cross the street knitting! Good God!" Gunther muttered as he sat up on the ground. "DAMN!"

Some neighbors started to come out of their houses. Jefe saw a woman on a porch, "Hello! Hello, ma'am. If you have a phone, can you call the police? Or go get the police?" he shouted.

She waved in acknowledgment. Within a minute, a young boy on a bicycle burst from the yard en route to convey that message.

"Dis is the second time I have asked a neighbor here to call the police," Jefe said aloud to no one in particular. Gunther, now seated on the ground, took a look behind them and tried to imagine where Mister Taint-Neither's bullets ended up. About four, maybe five or six rounds! There were houses and open lots behind them.

In about half an hour a police car pulled up. Some foot patrolmen jogged up and joined them. Then Detective Wiley showed up on a trotting horse.

"What in hell's bells happened here?" Wiley asked as he slipped off the horse.

They told him the odd story. Obvious self-defense. But, they did not tell Wiley they were looking for boxes of counterfeit money on the grounds, but rather just looking the scene over for clues. Wiley left them on the street and joined the four officers investigating the body on the burned lot. The officers had to almost strip the man to find some identification.

"Gunth!" Wiley cried out.

Gunther and Jefe walked over to them.

"Looks like you shot somebody interesting. Looks like you shot…the missing Mr. Farks."

Gunther's jaw dropped.

"Looky here. These are some papers from his wallet. He's got some receipts made out to Farks. And lookie here. Look." He bent over and rolled the now shirtless dead man over.

"This boy's been shot a short while back. Shot bad. Treated badly. Look at all that discoloration. Front and back. The wound from the robbery. It's healed poorly over the weeks. Poorly!" Wiley gasped. "If I was guessing on it, I'd say some gangrene was about to set in or has already started."

"The judge's rifle shot went clean through. So he did survive it," Gunther said.

"It is no wonder he was walking dey way of a cripple," Jefe said.

"You fellers have caught and killed one of the six gunman. By got-damn accident you have."

Gunther shook his head. "I killed a suspect we could have questioned is what I did. Damn! Now let's see if we accidentally shot anybody else. He shot at us this way. We shot at him that way."

"You take the north side, we'll take the south," Wiley said.

In a half-hour canvass, they found no other casualties.

"We have a lot to tell Ranger Winch, don't we?" Wiley said to Gunther.

"Yes, we do indeed," Gunther said. "Let's set that up. Besides, he's got something of mine I want back."

Chapter 21: Spurs that Jingle-Jangle-Jingle

"He's up on the roof with the birdies," a county deputy told Gunther at the police station.

Gunther was directed to a stairwell. He climbed the stairs alone. Each floor felt quieter than the last. Finally he reached the top. Just a narrow, rooftop, room with a door. He opened the door and felt the cooler air and sun on his face on the rooftop.

Wiley sat inside a giant cage of…sure enough…birdies, on the flat roof.

"Hello Johann," Wiley said, roaming about inside the giant cage amongst what looked to be about 50 or so pigeons.

"Hello!" Gunther walked up to the cage. "Whatcha got going on here?"

"These are my birdies, Gunth."

He tidied up the floor of the cage with a little hand broom.

"You ever let them out?"

"All the time."

"And they don't…escape?"

"No, sir. This is their home. And they love me too much."

"Ok."

Wiley stepped outside and closed the cage door.

"About 20 years ago, the then sheriff here, the sheriff in Little Rock, Arkansas and the one in Hattiesburg, Mississippi, were conspiring to create federal laws against the Ku Klux Klan in Washington." Wiley wiped his hands on some towels. "They figured out that some of the telegraph operators were in cahoots with the Klan and were sabotaging them. They needed to communicate and plan without them. So they started sending messages with these birds."

Gunther stepped closer to the cage and eyed the birds.

"We have kept them every since. The laws didn't pass, but we kept the birds."

"What do you use them for now?"

"Pets! Pets really. They are my pets, and the sheriff here now likes 'em too. Oh, you know, we enter races."

"Pigeon races," Gunther repeated.

"Yeah! Competitions. There are clubs. I take care of them, and one of the deputies likes them too. And my daughter comes up here after school and looks after 'em."

Gunther nodded with a smile. Somehow he liked Wiley even more than before, watching him clean up and worry over his birds. And now he knew the investigator had a daughter. He wandered to the wall near the edge of the roof. He gazed out over the city. He saw where the big fire had burned a swath across town. It looked like a twister had touched down and ripped a splintered trail. All the splinters were cocked at odd angles, charred black.

"Homing or carrier pigeons have been used as far back as Genghis Khan. They teach ya that back in West Point?" Wiley asked.

"Must a missed that day," Gunther said as he wandered back near the coop.

"Well now!"

There was a large table and about 12 chairs on the roof.

Wiley sat on one chair and Gunther sat across from him.

"We all come here once in awhile and sit. Smoke. Have a beer," Wiley said. "Some play dominos up here. Depends on the weather."

"It's a …it's a good view." Gunther said. In this still moment he could feel the cooler air, the slight breeze blew away the horse dung smells that the street level generally offered. He could see all of the city unfolding around him.

The courthouse nearby. The Trinity River. The smokestacks down south.

They talked and waited for the third in the trio to show up. Gunther did not plan to mention the counterfeit money to either of them. It was too hot an issue just yet. The roof door was left open for their special guest.

"All the bigwigs here are happy we found…you found… Billy Joe Farks," Wiley said. "Doc Bunyon is doing the autopsy on Farks. It's crystal clear, self defense. One down. Five to go, hot shot."

"It sure was a surprise."

"I suppose you are planning on gunning down the whole lot of them? Like a gunslinger?"

"I'm not planning on anything."

"The hell you say."

Then they heard the spurs ringing on the stairs through the small rooftop hallway room's open door. Then some wet coughs.

"Here he comes, ol Christmas Party Spurs," Wiley said.

"Jingle, jangle, jingle," Gunther said.

And onto the rooftop he strutted. Texas Ranger Chester Winch, a bit winded. He appeared in his full and usual regalia. Hat, ornate vest, white shirt, two tooled, overlapping western belts, not one but two engraved pistols. That special star of a badge pinned to his shirt. When he stepped outside, Gunther got up and closed the rooftop door behind Winch, all the while eyeing Winch's back pocket closely. He made a quick nod to Wiley as Winch sat down. Gunther sat too.

"It's about time," Winch said with a sneer. He put his fists on the table. "I very much want this meeting. You damn sure better have something for me. And it better be good. And what in hell are we doing up here on the got-damn roof?"

"This is bird feeding time," Wiley said calmly.

"Bird-feeding time? First it was monkeys! Now birds!" He turned to Gunther, "you have been pulling rabbits out yer ass and haven't told me a damn thing. I've got a governor to report to."

"What is it about the Judge Rufus Hofferman murder that I haven't told you about?" Gunther asked.

"How about finding that killer's horse, and finding out who owns the horse?"

"I thought Detective Wiley here would tell you that," Gunther said, pointing to Wiley.

"Hell, I thought Gunther would tell you," Wiley quipped back.

Winch studied the two and frowned, "Well ain't you two bird-brains something. What about catching and shootin down one of the robbers!"

"That just happened yesterday, Ranger," Gunther said.

"That was tantamount to an accident. He charged me with a gun. And now, here you are the next day. Then too, I've been busy working on the Justin Trace murder," Gunther said. "No surprises for you there though, right? You saw me in court. You have nothing to do with that though, right Ranger? Though, you were in the courtroom the other day for Torontoola's bond hearing."

"I am interesting in what's going on in my bailiwick. That's part of my job," Winch said staring at the birds and picking at the pressed creases on the thighs of his jeans. Then he snorted.

"You are interested in a lot of things. Course you investigated the burglary of Justin Trace's hotel room the very night of his murder," Gunther said. "That was timely."

Wiley squinted with this news.

Winch sneered at Gunther and remained silent.

"I wonder though," Gunther asked, "I wonder where I might find a police report on that burglary you found there? Wonder what became of that duffel bag of evidence you collected?"

"I don't report to a total nobody like you."

"How about a somebody then, like a report to County Detective Wiley Lewis? Wiley, would like to know about that hotel room burglary of a homicide victim the night he was killed?"

"I would, very much so," Wiley said.

"I report to my Ranger Captain." Winch stared ahead, not looking at either man.

"I'll bet you five dollars your boss Ranger Captain knows

nothing about the Trace hotel room burglary," Gunther said, leaning toward him. "Bet if I marched over there to your captain's office he'd know jack-shit about it. A whole bag full of money is missing."

Nothing. Silence.

Gunther smiled.

"Yeah. About finding that horse," Gunther asked, "do you know anything about the owner of that horse, Billy Joe Farks?"

"No."

"Never met him?"

"No!"

"Never. Hmmm, oh, I thought you might, because you know all his other friends real well?"

"What?"

"You know his compadres. You've been seen with them."

"Horse manure."

"Yeah? Manure? You were out at their burned-down, clubhouse the other day. The Farks' house."

"Like I said, I keep track of crimes in my area. Make your point, nobody!"

"My point? Well, hey, you know…you know what? Stand up," Gunther told him with a half smile, like tease.

"What?"

"No, come on, just stand up for a second," Gunther said with a big grin.

Winch grimaced and stood. Gunther stood up too, still smiling. Gunther took one step forward and then suddenly, like a coiled spring, shoved Winch about two feet across the roof and up against the stairwell enclosure.

"You Dutch bastard! What the…" Winch gasped, as he caught himself with his hands, just before his face hit the wall. He sneered, turned and reached for an engraved revolver, but before his fingers could touch the handle, Gunther flipped back his jacket and pulled his own .45 semi-auto out, and held it hip high on Winch. Winch froze aghast, knowing he could not beat that.

"You're a heartbeat behind, ain't cha?" Gunther said calmly. "A lifetime behind."

"Are you going to shoot a Texas Ranger on the roof of a police station? What, are you crazy? Are you seeing this?" Winch asked Wiley. "Are you seeing this, detective? Pushing and then pulling on a Ranger!"

Gunther reached over to Winch's right back pocket and pulled out the big, leather, tooled wallet.

"On, what? What you hijacking me, now?"

"Just taken back what's mine."

"What?"

Gunther examined the wallet.

"Yeah. Yeah, you see this tab here? This wallet was handmade for me in India, Ranger. India! A gift from an Englishman named George Hall."

Gunther put his gun back in his holster and growled, "Now, how do you suppose my stolen, Indian wallet wound up in your back pocket?"

"I…I bought that from a vendor at the Oktoberfest."

"Shit, I say," Gunther said. They were facing each other now.

"Shit! You think you can get away this? I know the DA. I know the governor."

"You know a lot of people," Gunther said with a smile.

"Yeah. And I know a lot of people. And I know a little bit about you, Chester Winch." Gunther looked him over with a sneer. "I know they rounded you up outta some alleyway for a posse about 10 years ago in Laredo. Killed some Mexicans down on the border. Slaughter's more the term. And then… and then some Ranger Captain made the sign of the cross over the whole scummy lot of you and, like magic, you're all Texas Rangers. Poof!"

"So?"

"You've never been a lawman. Never had any training. Probably can't even read nor write. The Texas Constitution, to you, is taking a daily shit. And here you are 10 years later, all shiny and all starched up, running the streets like a little fucking, lawless dictator. But the real you?"

Gunther stepped even close, "I know the real you. You're an illiterate, back alley bastard. A back shooter. And look at cha. Veins all poppin out on your thick empty skull. You're not used to people so much as disagreeing with you. Everybody's oh so scared of you. But we know. We know here. You're just a petty, little, punk thief. I ain't scared of you. The very likes of you breathing just pisses me off."

And Winch started breathing heavy. He shot glances at Wiley.

"Where did you…" Winch started, but Gunther interrupted.

"I know the governor too. In fact I know the president. Listen up here, you little prick, son of bitch. I also know witnesses. How do you suppose I was found alive on the pitcher's mound three weeks ago? How do you suppose I didn't die out there?"

"How the hell should I know?"

"People saw me beaten up, that's why. Witnesses. Witnesses saw you there. Witnesses saw you take my wallet."

"What…what people?"

"People that will testify. You think I'm gonna tell you the names of my witnesses so you can rough em up and scare em? I will tell ya one witness name, though." Gunther stepped in yet even closer, now almost nose-to-nose with Winch. "ME! Yeah, me. I saw you there."

"You…you can't do this to me. I…."

He pushed Winch's head up against the wall, with a hand on his throat. Winch's big hat fell off.

"Speaking of a witness names, let me tell you a witness name."

"Wha"

"Sumner."

"Sumner?"

"Charles Sumner."

"Wha…huh?"

"You leave Charles Sumner alone. You leave him alone, or I'll make you swallow those fancy spurs you're wearing."

"Yeah?"

"Yep." Gunther pulled his fixed blade knife from the sheath on his belt and stuck the very tip up in Winch's left nostril. "You leave Charles Sumner alone. He won't lie for you. And you don't want to die slow over him. Bother him again, and I will kill you."

Winch was speechless at first, gasping. His eyes darting across Gunther's eyes. Then he muttered to Wiley, "you seeing this detective. You hearing these threats?"

"I ain't seen ner heard shit, Ranger. All I've seen so far is a Texas Ranger who has somehow, in a very strange and obtuse manner, returned a man's stolen wallet back to him."

Gunther backed up, put his knife on the table and opened his wallet for another look inside.

"I've got papers in…" Winch said.

"You can have your damn papers. I don't want em." Gunther emptied the wallet's contents on a nearby table. There was no money inside it.

"I had about six dollars in here when you took it. Get yer shit and get out of here," Gunther said.

Winch did. He scooped up the pile of papers and shoved them into his pockets.

"You and me? You and me," he said in exasperation. "We'll meet again you Dutch, smart-ass. We'll go round and round."

Gunther smiled, "oh yeah, you bet we will. You still owe me six dollars."

"Fuck you," Winch said. He opened the door on the roof that led to the stairs and disappeared down the stairway spurs jangling.

Gunther and Wiley grinned at each other.

"That was fun, wasn't it?" Gunther said.

"Yup."

"Good to see you're feeling better."

"Oh, I am. But I ain't all better yet." He sat down. "I'd say you've lost a precious contact in the Texas Rangers office around here," Gunther said.

"Many words come to mind, but precious ain't one of them. Precious he ain't. It's like Torontoola said. Winch is greedy, corrupt and trouble," Wiley said. "What's this about a bag of money?"

"The night Trace was shot, Winch went straight to Trace's room and left with a big duffel bag. I'd say it contained money. He is probably skimming off what Spanky and the boys are working. Probably also setting up some plays for them. Getting a cut, like my piano-playing amigo, Kershaw," Gunther said.

"Like a gang of outlaws," Wiley said. "And on motorcycles! Like a motorcycle gang. That's a first. What's the story with Sumner now?"

Gunther sheathed his knife. "That son of a bitch went to see Sumner. Beat him up! Tried to make him lie that he saw Torontoola kill Trace."

"No!"

"Yes."

"No!"

Sumner's wife came to see me and told me."

"Why wouldn't she come to me?"

"Don't trust ya. Can't trust the police."

"Sheeet. Well, can't say as I blame her. Well, Gunther, watch out for Winch. All of them. Watch yer back, man. You have made a conniving enemy today."

"He's already tried to kill me once. With a group. He won't take a stand alone."

"You're not thinking of killing him are ya? Because that ain't right. This ain't the Wild West around here anymore."

"So, you've told me and told me."

"He's a Texas Ranger!"

"So he is."

"Sweet mother of Jesus," Wiley said. "You know what? Thinking about it. I ain't so sure Winch ain't the leader of all of them."

"Hi, daddy!" Wiley's daughter arrived on the roof.

"Hello darling. Your timing is impeccable. This is my friend Johann Gunther. Gunther, Remick."

She looked about 13 years old, wearing a floral, printed dress with schoolbooks held together by a belt strap slung over her shoulder.

"Remick. Hello." Gunther shook her hand. "I guess everyone tells you what a unique name that is."

"They do. How are the birdies today?"

She dropped her books on the table, dashed toward the cage and went inside. The two men looked at her. Gunther could tell she was thrilled to be in there.

"Did I tell you my very first police investigation," Gunther said," back in Paris, Texas years and years ago, was a case of three stolen school books. With that Stinky Moses name you heard me mention."

"Adventurous," Wiley said.

"Yeah. The little thief was just desperate to read," Gunther said.

"Uh-huh. Look at you now. Sticking a Bowie knife up a Ranger's nose."

"Yeah, just look at me now," Gunther said.

"Daddy! Charlotte's leg is healing up fast!"

"I know honey!"

Vaudeville Club, Fort Worth, Texas...

Spanky Runyan bit down on the very edge of the champagne glass. He remained smiling with that giant, face-splitting grin of his, like he enjoyed the taste.

"Disgusting!" a man cried out.

"Oh my God," a woman gasped.

There were but a few patrons of the Vaudeville Club who were busy talking in booths and ignoring the unique demonstration of glass eating going on at one of the tables.

Spanky made wild faces, like an ape, as he munched the glass rolling it around in his mouth before swallowing it. Then he took another bite and began to chew! He bit off still another section of the glass and crunched away.

"Oh, stop it, Spanky!" a woman begged.

He didn't. At one point he took a big swig of beer and said, "aaaaghhh." Then he picked up the half-eaten glass and nibbled some more.

Chester Winch walked into the club, spotted the commotion and came toward the table of onlookers.

"Go! Go! Go!" a man cried out.

And Spanky did just that. Chester could see that Spanky was drunk. Spanky chewed and grimaced and at one point suddenly cried out in agony.

"Ahhh!"

Everyone stepped back, some clasping their own faces in empathetic shock. Then Spanky let out a giant laugh to the relief of all. Everyone laughed with him, except Winch, who shook his head.

Spanky chewed the glass down to the stem. He held the stem up, in his fingers, spinning it around like it held a reflective treasure or message. Then he cried out, "Bar tender! Another glass!" to everyone's, clapping delight, except Winch.

Spanky stood and made for the bar, in amongst all the backslapping. Winch followed him over.

"Arthur, oh ye named after a grand king," he said to the barkeep while leaning a big arm on the bar, "let's have another beer."

"Someday you'll shit out all that glass and bleed to death," Winch said.

"Naaah. It's all in how you bite it. Gnash it. And let me tell ya, I know what glass I can and cannot do it with." He got his beer in a big mug. "This mug? Now that would kill me or break my teeth."

"Listen, two things. Member that preacher I almost had on a hook?"

"Yeah."

"I hooked him good last night with Betha as bait. Y'all play San Antonio weekend after next? Right?"

"Yeah. Two weeks."

"A Catholic church down there has about 10 thousand in a rectory safe. In the Monsignor's office. All stacked up to be sent to the Pope. You could hit it before or after the games."

"Sounds mighty fine. I'll send Sureline down there to check it all out. Sounds like another good deal."

"But look, we gotta do something about this alien, Ditch bastard, Gunther. You won't believe what he just did to me."

"What? What'd he just do?"

"He braced me up against the wall and stole my wallet."

"You mean his wallet? Did he get his wallet back?"

Spanky almost smiled.

"Right at the got-damn police department. He did."

Spanky fished a small shard of glass out with a careful

tongue and spit a little chunk of glass gristle from his mouth onto the floor.

"I still have his gun!" Spanky said, opening his jacket and displaying Gunther's Luger in a shoulder holster. "He ain't braced me for his gun back!"

"Well, bully for you. He pulled a replacement pistol out on me and said he'd kill me if I tried to stop him."

"He did! Pulled a gun on you! Yeah, yeah, you are right. We gotta do something."

"He killed Billy Farks! He gunned Farks down on his own property," Winch said.

"Yeah."

"And who's to say he and his little Mex didn't burn down the clubhouse!"

"Yeah. We need to kill him," Spanky said. "You do it?"

"Me! I'm a got-damn Texas Ranger, I… "

"Chester, come on! After all you've done before and you are gonna…"

"This is different, Spank. This has two governors involved. And a dead judge who was a congressman. If it percolates up, the governor's liable to assign the whole company on the case. No, sir. No sir, I can't."

"Yeah, yeah you're right."

"And you can't do it neither. Too much heat."

Spanky nodded. "Yeah, we all need a sterling silver alibi the night they put a bullet in Gunther's head. We need a hit and run guy. Somebody who'll pull the trigger and disappear. I got some honchos I'll call in Kansas City. See if they'll send somebody down."

"Will it be dear?"

"It depends. We'll just give him a whole special box of Morning Glory Cereal. Ya know, I'm hungry, let's eat. Let's get a steak at the Stockyards. We can discuss the details of this San Antonio church job."

Winch shook his head. "You'll be pissin glass someday and screaming like a stuck pig."

"Yeah! But not today!"

"Masterson's View On
Timely Topics"
A column by Bat Masterson

Chapter 22: The River Styx Leads to Hell

"Joooohann, Carmella is on the phone," Maria shouted from the lobby.

Gunther walked over to the conference table, interrupted by some shooting pains in both his legs, lingering souvenirs of his ballpark adventure. Gasp. He finished the trip with a limp. He picked up the telephone ear and mouth piece.

"Hello?"

"Hello, cowboy. You called for me earlier?" she asked him.

"Yes, I did indeed. Carmella, I was thinking about you again. Thinking I need to take you out on the town," Gunther said.

"Well Mr. Gunther, that is a good idea."

"How's about a romantic and exciting…baseball game tomorrow night."

"I see your devil's mind spinning. I've become very interested in the league, recently," she said.

"So have I. This time you don't have to follow in the

shadows behind me."

"I am moving up in the world."

"Yes, you are. And we might get lonely at the park. Does the Whisper have at least one sports writer you know and trust? Someone to bring along and tell us the sports scoop on each player?"

"Yes I do. Ramp Hempstead."

"Yes… Ramp. Mister 'Eyes and Ears on Sports' column. Would he join us and tell me all the insider rumors on baseball, and all the insider talk about the home team players?"

"Yes, he would. He's at every game. We merely have to join him in his box seats."

"Good."

"And, he already has a very special guest at every home game this week with him too."

"Oh?"

"A rather famous sports writer and fellow ex-lawman. Perhaps you know him?"

"Oh?"

"Oh yes, I'm sure you've heard of him. Bat Masterson."

"Bat…"

"Yes, Bat Masterson. He's in Fort Worth lecturing on some of the books he's written."

"I had read that in the papers. Well, that will make for a very interesting evening."

"You two will have much to talk about."

"Oh, maybe so? I don't know. He is a New York sportswriter now. And he's popular, almost a living legend. Me? I'm an unknown, desert son."

"He's never been to war in Afghanistan. He doesn't have a pet monkey whose life he saved. That is all very legendary sounding to me."

"I told you, that is not my pet monkey. He just lives with me."

"Bat and Ramp will want a beer before the game. Your treat."

"Ok. Ok, let's go back to that Sir Lancelot's. Where my physical troubles began… the British pub place across the street from the stadium. See if anyone winces when they see me walk in, alive and kicking."

"I'll call tomorrow and tell you what time," she said.

"We'll meet there. Ok. Adios, then."

"Bye."

Gunther hooked the earpiece on the metal stem of the phone and set the whole rig down on the table.

"Bat Masterson," he mumbled.

"Huh?" Jefe said from nearby. His arms were full of boxes.

"Bat Masterson. Friend of Wyatt Earp. Heard of him?"

"What? You crazy in the head? Of course I know dese men. Did you forget that your friend here was an Illustrado? A Los Indios Bravos! In College in Spain?"

"Ohhh, yeah. So you know who Earp and Masterson are?"

"Ohhh, yeah I do. What about dem?"

"I am going to the ball game tomorrow night with Carmella and Masterson."

"Masterson!" he said in a gasp. "I am going too. To meet Bat Masterson. He is now in Fort Worth on a book tour."

"Well then, so be it."

"American baseball. Bat Masterson. Anyway, I want to see who beat you up." Jefe hustled off with his heavy load.

"Me too," Gunther said aloud to himself. "Just from a different angle."

Gunther recalled that Jefe was sent off from Manila to college in Europe in the 1890s. A certain group of these wealthy, smart dispatched students were called the Illustrados – or the "rich Intelligentsia." And, a group within that group became fascinated with the American Wild West, as depicted by books and the traveling Wild West shows they'd seen overseas, and then, to some extent, history even further back to the American Revolution. Most Illustrados identified with the American Indians more than the cowboys, as did the Los Indios Bravos, yet another name they called themselves. But Jefe was equally interested in cowboys and lawmen of the West too, and he and others became enamored by "cowboy" horsemanship as well. Many of this Intelligentsia would later become involved in Filipino revolutions, favoring America against the Spanish.

This love of the American West was actually a touchstone for Gunther's and Jefe's deep friendship. When Gunther was stationed in the Archipelago, Jefe was a Filipino Army officer attached to Gunther's unit, and when Jefe first learned that Gunther was a former lawman from Texas, he saw all the adventure and mystery of the Old West in the American officer. And as the years proved out, Jefe was not disappointed. Gunther chuckled out loud thinking that, no doubt the one and only Bat Masterson would receive some of this same shine he first got, tomorrow night.

Sir Lancelot, Fort Worth, Texas...

Jefe and Gunther opened Sir Lancelot's front doors. No one took notice of them, and the pub was not as crowded as the last fateful night about four weeks earlier when Gunther had wandered in with his new Cajun acquaintance, Mr. Kershaw.

Carmella waved to them and the two joined her and two men at a large, square, wooden table, but not without Gunther noticing the same auburn haired, piano player, tickling the keys over in the corner.

"Ramp Hempstead…this is Johann Gunther and Jefe. This is Ramp and Bat Masterson."

The four men shook hands.

"Carmella has been telling some tales about you two," Masterson said. "You have a private detective company here in Fort Worth?"

"Yes, we do," Gunther said. "Remedies. Sometimes, some folks need a remedy that they can't get anywhere else."

"I understand completely, sir. And you travel some I hear? India. Africa. England. Afghanistan."

"My gun is my passport, as I have had to say a time or two."

"Ha! You should stamp that phrase on a business card. But I won't forget you, in case I need some help down around here. Of course, I am but a simple sports writer now. But, on again, off again, some of my friends need help. Hell, I need help sometimes!"

"Thanks. This time around, I am rather preoccupied with

a problem here in Fort Worth," Gunther said.

"As Carmella has explained to me. And you have the bruises to show for it. And, this very pub plays a part in the problem?"

"It is unfriendly territory. That it is. The worst ass-whoppin' of my life started here in a back-room plan. This place is kind of that horse that threw you down and you gotta get back up on it to move on down the road. So… I'm here."

"Mind f I call you "Dutch?" I call all men from Germany and thereabouts - Dutch."

"Well, sir, Dutch isn't exactly a German connection. It's close. But, go right ahead. Wouldn't be the first time. They called me Dutch a lot in the Army."

Masterson nodded. "Just call me Bat."

Gunther noticed that Jefe was hypnotized by Masterson, which caught Bat's attention as well.

"You must excuse my partner, Bat. He has been a long-time, historian of our Old West and has read quite a bit about you and your friends."

"Yes, sir," Jefe said. "From as far away as Manila, the Philippines. I went to college in Spain, and my friends and I were very interested in the American West. You are a famous man for many people in many countries."

"Isn't that odd?" Masterson said with genuine exasperation, scratching the inside of his right ear with a finger.

"How could a bags of bones like me, skeleton-thin, skeleton-dry, and living on the edge of civilization, be so damn interesting to people on the furthest sides of the world?"

"Books," Jefe said.

"Yes, those Blood and Thunder books. Write them myself. I have worked with some good men, indeed. They deserve some fame. Earp's got most of it. I suspect Wyatt will never be forgotten. If they ever get around to writing a book on Earp, that'll be a show stopper. Like Custer or that Kit Carson. Now Wyatt's over in what they call 'Hollywood,' making motion pictures about some of our doings. Or versions of our doings, at least. Wyatt told me there are more outlaws in Los Angeles than in the Arizona Territory. Well, God bless 'em all. The living and the dead. The poor dead," Bat said looking down into the foamy top of his beer, as though he suddenly lost even the energy to raise it for a toast.

Jefe refused to even bat an eyelash at Bat, missing a second. Gunther could only smile at that.

"You were a lawman for many more years than Mr. Earp. Have you seen Mr. Earp lately?" Jefe asked.

"Yes, I have…"

And while they talked, Gunther turned to the other sports writer in the group. "Ramp, see any of the ballplayers here now?" Gunther asked.

"No. No it would be too close to game time. They are all over at the stadium getting ready."

Gunther nodded, and said, "Will you all excuse me for a moment."

He got up and walked over to the piano player. He pulled a nearby chair up beside the piano. The woman looked at him calmly, never missing a note in her classical piece.

"You know, "Gunther said, "the last night I was here, I saw you play. Beautifully. And you had a beer setting there, and you reached for it and drank that beer with one hand, and continued to play your piece flawlessly. You downed that beer and your hand returned to the keys and the song like a…like a melted…I don't know…what. Snowflake ….or something. Right back into the song."

She chuckled. "A good musician knows her piece well enough to know when she can or cannot pick her nose or 'drank' a whiskey."

Gunther chuckled. Her mastery of the opus classics apparently did not match her upbringing or language skills.

She laughed, louder this time and smiled.

"You're joshing with me, ain't cha?" he asked.

She looked back at the piano. She changed tunes to something Gunther could not recognize. Or maybe she thought so, anyway.

"Listen, the last time I was in here, I was here with a feller, well, he is a piano player like you, named Kershaw."

"Oh?"

"Yeah. You see him lately?"

"No."

"Well anyway, he came over to you that night and you two spoke. Then you looked around the pub here and pointed and nodded at some folks. And then it seemed like you made some kind of a plan. You sent Kershaw off to speak to a tall, lanky feller."

"Oh?"

"Oh, yeah. Yeah. His name is Johnny Cleveland. And that lanky som-a-bitch tried to kill me later that night."

"Oh?" her eyes remained on the ivory keys. She remained disinterested.

"Oh, yeah."

"I don't know nothing about no nothing…about that," she said.

"Hmmm. You say you ain't seen Kershaw around?"

"No."

"There's reason for that, Lady Beethoven. He's gone, thanks to me. But, you might just find yourselves together again someday. Both gone, picking each other's nose somewhere else far, far away. Far up the River Styx maybe? You know where the River Styx is?"

"No."

"I think you do. But you like to play it dumb. It's the fucking river to hell, lady."

With that, Gunther stood and when he did, he slammed his hand down hard on all the keys his spread fingers could reach on his side of the piano to support his rise to his feet. The crash of ivory proved quite disruptive for everyone, but Gunther smiled at all the bartenders and customers, like he had stumbled. He walked back to his table, painfully riding his limp.

Just as Gunther sat, Ramp spoke up, "I think we need to get over to the stadium."

With that, Masterson guzzled down his beer, but Carmella and Jefe looked sternly over Gunther's shoulder. Gunther's eyebrows raised, but as Masterson and Ramp stood so did he, somehow knowing that for whatever reason they were looking over his shoulder, he'd best be standing up for it.

When he did, he turned to see two large brutes in black suits coming up to stand beside him.

"You've been bothering our piano player," one brute said. Both were as large as Gunther and country-boy strong, judging from the strain their muscles put on the neck collars of their shirts. Bouncers.

"We were just about to leave," Gunther said.

The man put his palm on Gunther's chest. Gunther did not look down at it. He smiled at him and sighed. "You know what, bubba? The last time I came in here, a few of your patrons almost beat me to death across the street. And I'll tell ya, I almost can't raise my left arm above my shoulder from it. Still! And I still can't really see too straight. Really. So if you want some kind of rough house show…" Gunther pulled his jacket open and displayed a black semi-auto pistol on his belt line. His smile slowly eroded. "I will gut-shoot you here and now. And then you be dead."

"You can't threaten me, Sharpy….I..."

Then Masterson, to Gunther's right, opened the side of his jacket and flashed his holstered handgun too. The two brute's eyes shifted and they saw a second hog leg. And Jefe, ever the militarist had already wandered off to the men's right flank, no doubt ready to slay them both, six-different-Filipino-ways, with three of the knives he had concealed in his clothing.

"So, we are going to leave here and go watch the ball game," Gunther said. "Unless you want a huge mess in here of which your guts will be a big red-ass, part of all."

"You...you don't scare me."

"Oh-no, don't want to scare ya. Just want to shoot ya."

The two finally did step aside. Gunther winked and smiled at them, and the five left, headed for the front doors, Gunther continuing to hide his limp.

"You! Ahhh…you are barred. Don't come back here," the bouncer shouted after them.

Gunther did not turn around. He said, "Bubba? Oh, you can rest assured, I will never return to this piss house again."

He nodded at the workers as he passed them. The threatened Miss Beethoven kept right on playing, her back to him. A well-dressed man stood, grimacing from behind the bar, too groomed to be a bartender, obviously the owner?

"Cheerio," Gunther said to him, on the way out.

They all walked out to street and turned toward the stadium.

Masterson sidled up to Gunther as they walked. He continued to look straight ahead as he spoke to Gunther.

"I like you, Dutch," Bat said quietly.

"I like you, too, Bat," Gunther said, not turning either.

Carmella slid in and hooked her arm through Gunther's.

"Bat Masterson and Dutch Gunther. Showdown in a cowboy bar," Jefe said.

"It was a British bar," Gunther corrected.

"A limey bar," Bat said. "Get your derogatory slang correct, or you'll never truly understand good, sports writing."

"Ohhh boy," Gunther said.

Ahead, hundreds of people, maybe even a thousand, were gathering. Men, women and children milled about, most dressed as if they were going to church. Folks were walking in from the train yards, others from their parked cars, buggies and horses, left scattered on the surrounding fields wherever they could find the space.

"Big night," Ramp told them. "We're playing the Cleburne Railroaders."

"What's your interest in these Texas League games?" Jefe asked Bat.

"I'm doing a story on how railroads have built baseball and how they will continue to do so."

"De railroads have built everything," Jefe said.

"Yes, but I am just a sportswriter, so I view the world through a sports writer's glasses. They say that this Year of Our Lord, there will be eight million fans at ballparks around the country. Many brought there by train."

"Eight million," Jefe repeated.

The group entered the grounds and had to veer toward the very hallway to the center of the stands where Gunther had been beaten. They walked in, and Gunther took a good look around the hall. He felt a chill. And a stink, whether real or imagined.

"You ok?" Carmella asked him.

"Reckon so. Reckon so," Gunther muttered.

But he clearly was not. He was reliving what he could remember. And even remembered some of what he'd forgotten. The look of the cement walls, up really, nose close. The lamps spinning overhead. Were he stood. Where he fell. He could see it all now in the flashes of each bat swing. Ones that missed. Ones that deflected. Ones that landed. He fell there. He dodged here. He collapsed there. And the laughing. The coaxing –

"Get him Spank!"

Swing.

"Get him Spanky! Ha, ha ha…"

Swing.

A flash of that punk Chester Winch.

Then…then he suddenly saw in an ugly flash in his mind's eye, back to the Afghan mastiff. The mouth of the big giant, evil killer dog that got him and got him good back in the fort at the Khyber Pass. Its monstrous head roared and snarled in a picture of his death, just inches from his face. His neck. Death in the mountains connected to death in the ballpark. Gaspingly close.

They approached the end of the long hall. Not a second too soon. His throat felt crushed and dry. He took a deep, breath. He stopped, because he had to. People filtered in all around him.

"Ok, where are we going?" he said, to cover the reason for his sudden pause.

"This way, ladies and gents," Ramp said from way ahead. He led them to a section of seats close to the field labeled with a placard that read, Whispering Wind, Box 12.

"Peanuts! Beer!" a young lad called out from nearby as they took their seats.

"Yeah, yeah, here!" Gunther called.

The boy delivered five beers and some cans of unshelled peanuts. Masterson insisted on paying. But Bat was eyeing Gunther. He appeared to smell the angst in the air. He handed Gunther a beer.

"Here ya go Dutch, this will freshen you up."

"Thanks."

Someone in the outfield bleachers stood up and started singing "Take Me Out to The Ball Game." Immediately, everyone chimed in, even Carmella and a smiling Bat Masterson and Ramp. Gunther and Jefe didn't know the words.

When finished, Bat turned to Ramp and said, "Baseball is making that song a national hit!"

And the game began. Ramp and Masterson chatted on about sports. Gunther studied the players on the field. The baggy uniforms, the small, brown leather gloves. The big caps. He took it all in.

The Chiseler walked up to home plate, encouraged by cheering fans. He was one of the ones there at his beating, Gunther knew. How much of a criminal was he? A real outlaw? Did he partake in the killing of Mrs. Torontoola?

"What's his background?" Gunther asked Ramp.

"He's from Uvalde, Texas. He's played all over the Texas leagues. Been here now four years. Short stop. He is jackrabbit fast. He's getting a little long in the tooth, but still quick. He'll end up here. No chance for the big leagues in the big cities that Bat covers."

"How's the pay here?" Bat asked.

"Oh," Ramp said, "You can live, but you can't live good on it. Not good."

Crack! The ball left the bat and lined into the outfield. The Chiseler dashed to first base like lightening and rounded the base with athletic jumps and jolts as if he'd try for second base.

The next batter, a stranger to Gunther, walked up to the plate and took a hunched-over stance.

The pitcher reared back to throw, and the Chiseler disappeared off first base. The ball hit the catcher's mitt, and the runner was well on his way to second. The catcher threw to second. The Chiseler dove head first and sliding into the base, well before the ball arrived. The fans hooted and hollered.

"See?" said Ramp. "Fast little fucker."

Gunther nodded.

The batter struck out.

A large, broad, man emerged from the dugout with a face

as flat as a pan. Spanky Runyan. He strolled up to the plate, swinging a bat as he walked. The crowd cheered.

"Go Spank!"

"Kill em, Spank."

And Gunther could hear in his head, "Get him Spanky!" but not from this crowd.

"The big hitter. The big man," Ramp said. "Spanky is bound for Chicago or New York," Ramp leaned over to Masterson - "we're gonna lose him and we're gonna miss him. He's a good hitter and pretty decent fielder. He's a home run hitter, he is."

Gunther and Jefe exchanged glances. They didn't know how. They didn't know when. They didn't know where. But they were going to kill that son of a bitch.

After three pitches, Spanky Runyan smacked the ball into the outfield. The Chiseler rounded third base and scored. Runyan jogged up to second base. He took off his hat and slapped it on his thigh a couple of times, exposing that full thick head of black hair, with a hairline so far down on his forehead, he looked like it was poorly painted on by a caveman. He grinned at the stands, cracking that pan-face open like the smile on a cheap wooden puppet.

The crowd roared.

"Perfect ladies are screaming like a batch of Coney Island barkers," Masterson said, looking around. "This guy's got something special."

"Yup," Gunther said. He...they were gonna kill him. And Gunther sat there dreaming again. Another kind though, that involved Spanky and the River Styx.

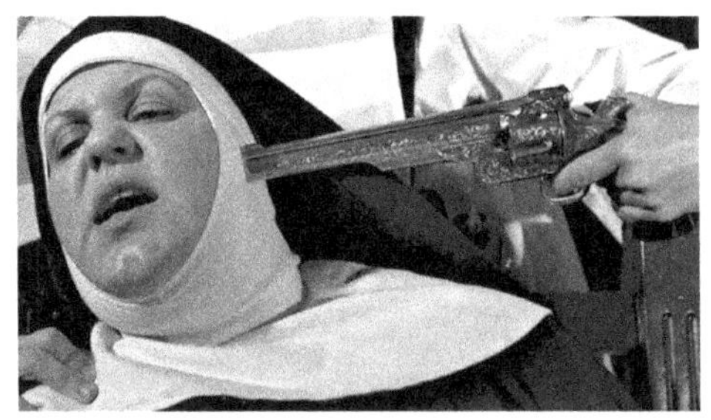

Chapter 23: The Night Mother Superior Gurgled

Sunday night. San Antonio. The boys had just played Saturday and Sunday series. A double-header on Sunday. They were cranky, and they were tired. They lost two, won one over the weekend. But some of the team still needed to finish some work.

The day before, Saturday morning, Abbott Sureline rented a canvas-covered, business wagon with a team of two horses. He brought with him, or also purchased, some gear, the collection of which would convict any person with the charge of criminal conspiracy. He pulled the wagon up to the Jose Moreno Park. The park was just behind the Apples Hotel where the team stayed when in town. Inside the wagon, on the floorboards lay five shotguns, five pistols, and five hats. And five ski masks he got from a Sears Catalog. Five coverall uniforms Sureline bought in a downtown Austin store, that resembled those of a common city sanitation worker, were rolled up on the side benches. He also had five gray canvas bags with drawstrings for the shotguns. Sureline had procured this type of criminal inventory many times before for the team's traveling robberies.

He climbed down from the buckboard seat and stood by a metal and wooden wheel. His fingers drummed the wheel. They first thought about hitting the church on Friday night before the games, but then they realized the take would be better after the Saturday Midnight Mass and Sunday services, especially, the Sunday services. The boys and the team would be in town on Sunday night too, anyway, …tired, scheduled to leave for Fort Worth on Monday morning.

The wind brought the cool with it. Then Sureline spotted them, briskly walking up the side street under the swaying tree limbs. They crossed the avenue and strolled up to Sureline and the wagon.

"Ready?" Cleveland asked.

"Ready. It's all in the back."

They climbed in the back and sorted out the uniforms and weapons, then looked at Sureline.

"We'll park this heap a block back from the rear of the church. I walked around there yesterday during the afternoon when the church still had some people mumbling prayers as they sat in the pews. I even saw the back of the place."

"You know where the Monsignor's office is?" The Chiseler asked.

"In the back."

"Phone?" Spanky asked.

"Yeah. They got two phone lines. One to the church. One to the office. We'll cut them, pronto. I know where the hookups are," Sureline said.

The fourth man, the half-breed, Henry Bloodpainter remained quiet, as was often his way. No questions. No comments. He just pulled on the coveralls.

Once dressed, Sureline and Chiseler walked to the front of the wagon and climbed aboard the front seat.

"Beautiful horses," Chiseler said.

"Yup. Not the normal rental type. I gotta get them and this rig back to the stable by Monday noon. Told them I was a furniture mover."

He pulled the wagon out on the avenue and made toward the church about 20 city blocks away. Sureline parked the wagon on a street heavily lined with trees behind the church. The roads were paved, the front lawns of the houses spacious. They piled out and began their march to the avenue ahead. The back lot of the church appeared empty, and they all stopped there to pow-wow. Sureline pulled a big knife from his belt line and trotted up the sidewalk of the brick office building separate from the church. He chopped the phone line in two, a thick black wire running from a street pole to a wooden box. As he did this, the others scanned the building. It was dark and appeared unoccupied.

Then Sureline ran across the lot to the rear wall of the church and cut that phone line there as well. Tension gone, it snapped and slid across the lot.

They would have to enter the church to find the Monsignor. They traveled down the side of the church and around to the front doors. The street seemed quiet. They entered. Inside, a few people kneeled in the pews most in prayer with their heads bowed. Rows of candles burned with wavering flames to the side of the alter. Hallways ran down the right and left sides of the sanctuary, and Sureline led the way down the right side. The hallways were dark, small, candle lit and, as they moved, the men pulled on their masks, and drew the shotguns from their sacks. No one in the pews seemed to notice them. By a closed door in the hallway near the alter, they stopped.

"This is as far as I got," Sureline said quietly. "I think the quarters are all down this way."

Spanky had made a study of the windows and church configuration as they walked by outside. He took over with a hand wave. He opened the door and walked in. The others followed. They entered a long hallway, lit by dim light bulbs. They immediately heard women talking. The muffled sound of voices drifted down the hallway toward them from a bit of a distance.

They approached an open door, a kitchen door, and saw two nuns working over a large metal sink that was suspended from a wall.

"Ladies," Spanky said.

The nuns turned from their dishwashing, one in mid-sentence, and froze at the sight of his gun barrel aimed directly at them.

"Ladies," he repeated.

All the men stepped into the kitchen.

"Ladies, where is your Monsignor?"

"He's not here," the heavyset one said.

"What do you want with him?" the other asked.

"Where is he?"

"He's performing a wedding."

This was a stumper for a moment.

"Who is left in charge here?" Spanky asked.

"In charge?"

"Your Mother Supervisor," Chiseler said.

"You mean Mother Superior?"

"Yes, Superior," Chiseler said.

"Sister Helen."

"Where is she?" Spanky asked.

"She is…she is…"

"Speak up ladies," Spanky said, "your time on Earth grows short."

The two looked at each other, and gulped. Five men pointed shotguns at them!

"She's in the rectory."

"What's your name?"

"Sister Mary."

"Sister Mary. A perfect name for a sister," Spanky said.

"My friends here will stay, while you and me go to the rectory and find Sister Helen." He lowered his shotgun and handed it to Johnny Cleveland. "If you call out, Sister Mary? We will crucify you, Helen, and all the nuns here. Now come on, let's go find your Mother Superior."

The men cleared the doorway and Sister Mary and Spanky Runyan stepped into the hall. Spanky flicked Bloodpainter's arm as a motion to follow. The three walked down the hall, turned through a large waiting room and into what looked like the living quarters.

"Sister Helen?" Sister Mary called out. "Sister Helen!"

Sister Helen walked into view, an elderly, plump lady in her dress black uniform, pale faced and serious, holding a stack of white, thread-bare towels. She stopped when she saw the two masked men approaching.

"Wha…"

"Hello, Mother Superior Helen," Spanky said and raised a pistol and pointed it at the head of Sister Mary. "Here's what I'm guessing. By the looks of ya, I'd say you don't care about yourself. You're the drive boss of these women, and since you are married to Jesus, you will die willingly rather than fuck things up. Am I right?"

Mary gasped.

"So, let's cut to the chase. Can you open the safe in the Monsignor's office? Can you get us the Peter's Pence? Or am I going to shoot off Sister Mary's head right here, and then kill you and everyone in this church?"

Sister Helen slowly set the towels down on a nearby chair. The fluffy, white stack teetered but did not fall over. Without a word she walked off to a large set of back doors. Inside her cowl, she jerked her head for them to follow as she passed. Inside his mask, Spanky smiled. The four walked out the door, across the back lot they had previously traversed only short minutes before and to the front door of the back lot building.

She glared at Spanky, almost daring him to do something, and then reached a hand deep into her habit pocket. Spanky raised his pistol at her, expecting a weapon draw? She grimaced and pulled out a set of keys attached to a long cord of twine. She sorted through them until she found the one she wanted and unlocked the door.

"After you, Mother Superior," Spanky said, and all four walked inside.

They followed her into an office filled with large, old, ornately carved cherry furniture. She pulled a cord and several electric lights flickered on. There beside the desk, sat a large black, Leo Duran floor safe. The safe rested on thick wheels.

Sister Helen walked up to it and pivoted toward Spanky.

"This money was donated to feed the poor," she said through gritted teeth.

"I am the poor, you tough ol bird. It will feed me and my poor friends," he said.

"You are not the poor."

"Neither are you, Sister. Spin, spin, spin," Spanky said, twisting his open left hand in the air.

Sister Helen knelt and began to turn the dial, entering the combination. It did not go unnoticed by Spanky that Sister Mary, now in the grips of Henry Bloodpainter, edged back and up against him. Spanky extended his gun hand. The Sister let go of the dial and reached over for the gold colored handle. She twisted it downward. It clunked into place. She opened the big safe door with a pull. The nun's large habit covered most of this action. She stuck her left hand into the safe. She turned and stood holding a large revolver in that left hand.

Spanky Runyan shot the nun high in the chest one time. She shot too, but she shot after he did, and the impact of his bullet caused her arm to rise too high. Spanky rushed forward and clubbed her in the face with the barrel of his pistol. She fell. Spanky grabbed her pistol. She hit the floor and lay, still conscious, but unable to move on the throw rug in front of the safe.

"Oh, Sister. Did I fail to tell you that this is not my first rodeo? Not my first safe job? And that I know everyone keeps a gun in their safe, thinking they will shoot a robber with it? Even Sister Mary here saw that coming," Spanky said.

The Mother Superior gurgled.

"But thinking is different than doing it."

Mary fainted.

So there were two gunshots. The men exchanged glances, worried about the noise. Bloodpainter watched the door as Spanky looked inside the safe. There were stacks of cash in there. A lot of cash.

"You…will…be….damned," the Mother Superior gurgled.

"A shooting nun," Spanky said, filling his canvas sack with the money. "You know, only out here in the Wild West would you actually find a shooting nun. Kill a man to save the Pope's Pence." He shook his head. "If you had shot me and my friend? You might have starred in a dime-store novel back East. Helen, the Shootin' Nun. The Blazing Guns of Sister Helen."

He emptied the safe. With his bag full of money and some gold jewelry, he stood and looked over at the unconscious Sister Mary. He backed up a bit taking a couple of quick steps he kicked Mary in the head. Her head snapped back, and her body rolled across the floor.

"A half-assed faint ain't as good as a full knockout," he

said to the gurgling, Sister Helen.

Then he leaned over her.

"Let's see you," he said. "Yeah, you'll be dead soon, Mama Sister. Safe in the loving arms of your heavenly husband at last. I hope it was all worth the wait."

"You…will…be…" and she died.

"I know. I know. Damned," he said. He leaned in even more for a closer study of her face. Blood came from her lips. "Ha. The Shootin Nun of San Antonio."

He and Bloodpainter left the building.

Spanky stood outside the back door of the church with the money bag and told Bloodpainter, "We got it. Knock out that nun in the kitchen. Use the butt of a shotgun. Knock her out good. We need the getaway time. Shit, knock out anybody else that you see. We can't shoot again. I'll be over there waiting." He pointed to the dark corner of the lot where they first arrived. "Get the boys all out of there. This shit's done."

Bloodpainter nodded and ran inside. Spanky walked slowly to the far corner and stepped back from the streetlights underneath some trees. He thought a moment about the last game. He struck out with a man on second base that afternoon. He grimaced. It was a curve, not the fastball he anticipated. He got a burn in his gut thinking about it. His hands shook and the bag shook in his hand. Oh well, oh yeah - there were thousands of dollars in the bag. Thousands. He was overcome with joy at the thought.

"I got the joy, joy, joy joy, down in my heart. Down in my heart. Down in my heart," he sang quietly.

Chapter 24: All for One and So On…

Tipping over the cardboard box, Jefe emptied the West Point yearbooks onto the conference room table.

"I will look too, but you saw them better. Longer," he said to Gunther as he sat down, picked up a hardcover book and began to leaf through it.

Gunther looked at the years on the books and picked the last year in the batch. He took a sip of Hawaiian coffee and found the section he sought. There, he scanned the faces.

"What about him?" Jefe asked spinning a book across the table toward him.

"Close, but no, amigo."

Time passed. Mesha brought in more coffee.

And then, it happened.

"Kranepool," Gunther whispered. "Marion Kranepool. Look."

Jefe got up and came around the table.

"Yes. I see it."

"Kranepool, from Battle Creek, Michigan, is Mr. Gray."

Gunther stuck a strip of curled, shipping paper from a nearby box between the pages to mark the picture. He continued. But only for a few more pages.

"Same years, and Mr. White right there. Jacob Seavers. From the Seavers clan in Boise, Idaho."

"Yes. Yes," Jefe said. "Now what? What do we do now?

What more do we need to know?"

"I don't know," Gunther said, leaning back in his chair. "It remains to be seen how this will all develop. I don't know what else we need to know about them, yet. At least now we know their real names. They actually are grads, were officers, are war vets. They told me all that. And now they are men paid for hire. Gunmen. Mercenaries or something like that."

"So are we," Jefe said.

"Yeah, I guess we are. We're damn sure not going to Michigan or Idaho to do a background on them. I guess, now we know who they really are and that's that. If I see em again I'll say 'howdy Jacob, howdy Marion' and for one brief second seem to be one clever son of a bitch. Then I'll drop back down to stupid."

"We'll see them again," Jefe said.

"It won't be pleasant the next time."

Jefe shook his head, made a sour expression and said, "Well, bout time to head out to Torontoola's. Are you ready for the long ride?"

"Yeah, yeah. It's the first long one since I got the crap beat out of me, but I think I can make it. How about in an hour?"

"Yes. An hour. He called again this morning. He said he has a very big surprise for us when we get there."

Gunther's eyes widened. Then the two got up and headed for the stables out back.

The Torontoola house set on the outskirts of the west side of Fort Worth, and it was a sight to see. It rose up, a grand terra-cotta colored hacienda towering over the surrounding landscape, surrounded by stately, tan adobe walls. Even the cracks and chipped paint looked like the careful plans of a Santa Fe architect or painter. The scrolled metal gates at the front were drawn open in welcome, awaiting their arrival. Once inside the walls, Gunther and Jefe admired the Spanish style architecture and an artfully landscaped courtyard with a fountain splashing water musically at the center of it all. They glanced at each other and both raised their eyebrows.

"Opulent," Jefe mouthed.

"Indeed."

Gunther recognized the cat that as it wandered out onto the front porch as the one keeping Torontoola company at the jail when he visited. It ignored them, as cats do, and picked that time to clean its shoulder with a vigorous tongue.

They dismounted and tied off their reins to a metal hitching rail at the front of the main house.

Gunther pressed his face against the side of his horse's head, wrapping it with his left arm and said quietly, "Will you wait for me here? Huh? Big Freud? Will you wait for me?" Then he gave the horse a fond pat.

Freud, Gunther's horse bobbed his head up and down and slightly snorted as if they shared some profound understanding between them.

The cat, now atop a front porch bench, did not stop to watch them, but instead moved away as they approached the open front double doors, clearly more interested in the horses than in the men. As they waited at the front door the cat scampered down the steps and rubbed up against Freud's legs in greeting arching its back with pleasure. The horse lowered his head and nuzzled the cat, eyes drooping with gentle curiosity and affection.

An elderly, well-dressed, Hispanic man stepped into the doorway and shouted inside, "Raoul!"

"Please come in gentlemen," he welcomed them inside.

"My heroes!" Torontoola shouted as he walked down a flight of spiral, interior stairs. He was dressed casually but regally in black well-pressed trousers and white shirt, not unlike the wardrobe he sported while roosting in the jail.

"Come in. Come in. This is my father-in-law, Reynaldo. Papa, could you bring us some Sangria?"

Reynaldo nodded, but before departing for the kitchen, he shook their hands and added, "I want to thank you two for what you have done for Raoul, and…my daughter, God rest her soul." He made the sign of the cross over his chest. He left the living room for his alcoholic mission.

"I have a surprise for you. Come with me. Johann, do you remember back when I was in jail, I told you that Kershaw was running some women, some ladies of the night from Midlothian? One woman was named Betha, and the other two she says are her cousins?"

"Yes,"

"Allow me to introduce you to...Betha."

They walked into a lavish den to see three young, well-dressed women sitting side by side on a red velvet sofa.

"I have fed them. I have clothed them, as they were about the size of starving goats. And due to their circumstances, they stayed here last evening. Betha called me, and we couldn't dare have some switchboard operators listening in on such a conversation. I sent a coach to fetch them. They are here to share some information."

"Ladies," Gunther said, and they all nodded.

"Speaking of feeding, our mounts outside sure could use some water," Gunther said.

"It is being done while we speak, my friend. They will also be relieved of their saddles. Yes, Betha called me yesterday morning. She has information about our mutual interests.

"You have money? Rattin money?" Betha asked Gunther.

"Rattin...money?"

"Money we get for rattin on outlaws and such."

"Oh, that. I do. I have rattin money."

She brightened up considerably, flashed a smile and exchanged knowing glances with the other two women.

"I've been sexing with some of the Bobcats' ballplayers and with that dirty smelly ol bastard, Chester Winch."

"Winch, the Ranger?" Torontoola asked with a certain delight.

"My condolences," Gunther offered.

Betha gave him a confused glance and paused a moment, then continued, "And I have heard them talk about a lot of things. Crimes and such. Sins."

She proceeded to describe the group as a gang of outlaws, plotting crimes and sins in other cities often in coordination with the team's away games. She explained how Chester Winch helped the gang. She also said how she overheard them whispering and bragging about killing Torontoola's wife and killing Justin Trace.

"We already know all this, Betha," Gunther said.

"Well, I know...I know something else. These boys are

plotting the next big job. I heard it."

"What job is that?" Torontoola asked.

"They are going to rib a chuch in San Antoine of come money a going to Pope in the Vatican. If they ain;t done it already?"

The men exchanged glances.

Looky, they got cereal boxes of money after killing Justin Trace. Lots of money from his hotel room. It sounds crazy I know, but that man Trace was a cereal salesman. His company sent him money in them boxes, not cereal. There was money stacks inside all those boxes. They figured the plan was for Trace to buy up the town. Chester got the boxes from the room the night they killed Trace."

"Did they know about dis money then?" Jefe asked.

"No. Chester just wanted to rob the room. He came one night to the clubhouse with a big bag of money boxes. They cooked up a plan. The cereal company must be filthy rich and must be dirty. They's all going out West to play a series with a team in Amarillo next week, and they are planning to go rob the cereal company out there."

Gunther looked at Torontoola, then back at Betha.

"Are you sure?" he asked.

"Oh yeah, I'm sure. That's what they do, ya know? Before the first game or just after the last game of a series, they rob em someplace."

"Chester....Winch. He the boss? Or is Spanky Runyan?" Gunther asked.

Betha thought about it for a few seconds.

"I don't rightly know. Sometimes it seems like one is bossin the other. Then that changes."

"Betha, all this money. You've seen some of it?" Gunther asked.

"Yeah, I seen it. I geet me some of it, from sexing and all."

"Is it real money?"

"Real money? Yeah, it's real money."

"Ok. Just asking, cause it's a lot of money."

"Those boys ain't no fools," she said. "and I got some of it, and I've spent it downtown. I spent some money at

Leonard's Department Store. It's all real."

"Ok. Ok," Gunther said.

The room fell silent.

"Where's Kershaw?" Gunther asked her.

"He done left. Sudden. Chester Winch thought it might be you or Sgt. Torontoola that done that to him. He axed me if I knew."

"Whatcha say?"

"I don't know. How would I know what you done? Did you fellers…did you fellers burn down the Farks' clubhouse?"

"No we didn't," Gunther said.

"On account a, on account a we've seen two men snoopin' around us. The boys seen them too. Snoopin around. They got the look like lawsmen, or maybe Federales?"

"Thank you ladies," Torontoola said and stood with a clap of his hand.

"Do that deserve some rattin money?" she asked.

"That certainly does," Gunther said. We'll figure out how much, Betha, but I can tell you it will be a decent amount. And…you girls know you cannot stay around here. You have to leave."

"We know," she said. She looked pleased, as did the cousins.

"Now, we men will adjourn to the smoking room, ladies. So I must leave you for a time," Torontoola said.
"Feel free to make yourselves comfortable for a while longer until payment can be arranged."

The men moved to leave the room in favor of another at the front of the house, but just before he passed through the doorway, Gunther spun back around.

"Betha, let me leave you with an idea."

"Ok."

"If you will stay, if you will stay in …touch….with Chester Winch, as you…do. I think we can pay you even more money for information. I have to ask a county policeman about it first."

"What about my cousins?"

"We'll take care of em."

"Ok. Ok then, I'll think on it."

"Only if it's safe," Gunther added.

"Ain't a moment safe with Chester Winch. But I know how to work him so far."

The men continued out of the room toward the room at the front of the house where they settled into rich, dark leather upholstered chairs behind closed doors.

"I think Wiley thinks Chester Winch is a gangland boss. Maybe of several gangs. I think Wiley will pay Betha to…rat on Winch. If he needs the money, I will use the governor's money to pay her. I think it is curious that when he found the boxes of money, he went to the clubhouse."

"He could have kept all the money for himself," Jefe said.

"He has a …special connection with these men," Torontoola said.

They quickly discussed the banker's news and advice. Torontoola was stunned with the news of the counterfeit money and its possible implications.

"Madre de Mia! That is why you asked her if the money was real?"

"Yes. We needed to know if they think the money is real. Would they steal counterfeit money? But they must think it's real."

"Yes, of course!"

"And what of this shooting of Farks?" Torontoola asked.

Jefe explained the odd incident, highlighting with a sneer how Gunther disarmed Farks then threw away the pistol for Farks to recover a moment later.

"He was almost dead anyway," Torontoola said, "recovering so poorly from the robbery shooting. And now, we found him. Uno dead cucaracha of seis."

Jefe nodded. He continued with the discovery of several burned pieces of Morning Glory Cereal boxes at the Farks' house, confirming Betha's words.

"Carmella knows nothing of this counterfeiting," Gunther said. "If she did, it would be all over the newspapers. We have to keep her out of this as long as possible. Neither does our Detective Wiley know. I am keeping all this from the police and the governor too until we can figure out what in hell is going on here. I want to have more information to report to the governor than more unanswered questions left for the Secret Service to hide from us. The government may take forever and then they will never tell us anything anyway. And you need more information and evidence for your defense."

"So…we do not tell the Federales," Torontoola said, nodding his head.

"No. We should, I know. I know. But I think I have no choice but to go to Bendigo, Texas and kick over some stones at the breakfast cereal company," Gunther said. "I need to go. And now we need to warn them of this robbery attempt."

"I agree. What will you…" Torontoola started to ask, and then he blurted out, "I will go with you!"

"You shouldn't go," Gunther said. "It's all too close to your case. It may taint your legal efforts. And we need Jefe here in Fort Worth to work these other tips and take care of some business we have pending. We have other cases we are working. I will go alone."

"I understand, but I cannot let you go alone. I already owe you my life, and I would not dream of you journeying alone on such a mission. The idea that something may happen to you is too much for me to bear when I could have been there to help you. Look at me! Look!" He waved his hand over his body. "Most of the day I am here in my pajamas!"

"Amigos," Reynaldo said, approaching carrying a red tray topped with a pitcher of Sangria and several clay cups. When he set the drinks down, Gunther noticed a copy of the Whispering Wind newspaper also on the tray.

"Since we have learned about the duplicity of this baseball team, I have been following them." Reynaldo said. He opened the paper and folded it over once to the sports page. "Mira!" His fingers pounded the page. "The Fort Worth baseball team is playing the Amarillo Angels this weekend. In Amarillo."

"They will take the train," Jefe said.

"And so will I," Gunther said. "The same train, but a day early to set things up. I really need to take a train out there anyway. Too far to ride. I'll put my horse, Freud, in the horse-box car. Get off at Amarillo and ride south to Bendigo."

"Yes," Torontoola said. "We will get on this train out West. You cannot go alone. They will see you eventually. You need my help."

It looked like Torontoola would not take no for an answer. Gunther and Jefe exchanged glances at his word

"we." Jefe nodded.

"Yes, you're right," Gunther said. "I do need help." Reynaldo poured the Sangria for the others, followed by a cup for himself. He said quietly, but with a dark low growl uttered through clenched teeth, "you men must avenge the death of my daughter."

"Papa, they have killed one of them already."

"Muy bueno," he said solemnly.

The men reached for and took up their cups. Gunther smiled at this. "Are you familiar with The Three Musketeers?"

Jefe, the graduate of a European college was quite familiar, but not the others.

"But there are four of us," Torontoola said.

"As it was with the musketeers," Gunther said, raising his glass to the others and then they sipped Sangria.

Remedies office, Fort Worth...

"Hey cowboy," Carmella called out from the Remedies lobby.

"Yeah, hey! In here!" Gunther called. He had just arrived back at his office intending to collect some papers. Jefe's family, as well as Mesha and the monkey had gone to the open-air market and the Remedies Office felt unusually quiet to Gunther without them.

Carmella walked into the office.

"Hey, Carmella," Gunther greeted her. He picked up his hat, placed it on his head and slipped back into his jacket. "I was just about to leave!"

"Glad I caught you. I came by this morning and you were out. Ramp Hempstead found out some news about the ball team. He thought I should tell you right away."

"What's that?" Gunther came over to stand beside her, a thinly disguised effort to catch a whiff of the unique fragrance she always wore. The fragrance remained the single good memory of their time together on the pitcher's mound.

"Well, he said that all the team's troublemakers are leaving early for Amarillo this weekend. Days early. Ramp heard talk at the clubhouse that they were going early to stay at the Morning Glory Spa south of there."

"They are?"

"In Bendigo. Ramp said they were up to no good going there. Lots of rich people from all over stay there. He thought it sounded like some kind of robbery plan."

"Hmm."

"Have you heard of this spa?"

"Oh, I've heard of it. Yes."

"Ramp has to go cover the game. And Bat wants to go too. And I'm going. There is no way I will miss that. We'll all stay at the spa."

"You have convinced me. I'll go too."

She moved a little closer to Gunther with an extra little sashay. A lazy smile spread across her face, and she canted her head back and looked up at him. Eyes wide. She inched a little closer still.

"Are you still peeing blood?" she asked.

"Well, I believe that's just about the most romantic thing a woman has ever asked me."

She grabbed the collar of his jacket and pulled him down until their lips almost met, but not quite.

"But everything is working just fine now, down there?" she asked.

"Yes…?"

She peeled the hat off his head and tossed it back onto his desk.

"Prove it," she said.

So...he locked the office door…and did.

The next morning Gunther asked Mesha to call the Toron-toola house. She told him when the call was ready by way of the telephone operators, and he walked to the wall phone, taking the ear piece from her. Careful not to tip anything off to any nosey, eavesdropping switchboard operators, he began a conversation…

"Hello, Raoul?"

"I am here. Yes. Hello my friend."

"Raoul, I have some news that changes our plan. Our old friends are checking into the place on Thursday. I think we need to get there on Wednesday. You see, we need to check in early too."

"I see."

"We can reserve the rooms by telegraph. And I have found out that there is a train to take us south, right where we need to go. We need not bother with our horses."

"Sounds good. We will take this train."

"We will need to pack heavy."

"Very heavy."

"I'll make the reservations and see you at the downtown platform at noon Wednesday?"

"Yes, I will be there."

They hung up.

The Morning Glory Spa. The Morning Glory Cereal factory. From the pictures in the marketing material, Gunther knew the two giant complexes stood side-by-side. Scores of rich people staying in one, and tons of counterfeit cash squirreled away in the other? Gunther had no idea what he and Torontoola would do when they got there. He just knew there would be armed robberies and bloodshed at one or both places. Would Misters White and Gray be there? To help? Or hurt?

He packed heavy.

Chapter 25: The Pleasant Gawdy Shirtz

Four men rode through to the southern California vegetable farms. They rode slow. The man in the lead was dressed in a tan suit and bowler hat. He was the local connections man. Second in line was a man named Gawdy Shirtz. He sat tall and heavy in the saddle but rocked with it like an old hand. He too dressed in a citified suit and wore a short brim Stetson. His cheeks were clean shaven, despite the many rolls and lumps in his face that made shaving without bloodshed difficult.

The other two men, cronies of the Los Angeles gang, rode behind them. One looked damn uncomfortable astride his horse.

"I am sorry Mr. Shirtz, it is not easy finding these Chinks and Japs in the field on any given day."

"Not a problem, Barnaby," Shirtz said. "It's not too often this old Oklahoma boy gets to set a horse anymore. I am enjoying the view. And, fact is, the land here looks a bit like parts of Oklahoma."

"You see that stand of buildings over there?" Barnaby said. "I think that's where they set up shop to talk turkey. That's where they will have their meeting."

"A pleasant place to pow-wow," Shirtz said.

The men turned toward the work buildings. As they approached they could see in among the buildings and barns stood a tall, clean, new gazebo. As they drew closer they could see the oriental design and craftsmanship in the way the corners of the roof flared at the ends and in the intricate wood carving of the posts and supports.

Shirtz looked at his pocket watch. About 2 p.m. The meeting was scheduled for 3 p.m. Then he started to spot some Chinese workers in the nearby fields, picking fruit.

"So all these Chinks work for Japs?"

"Yes, they do. Japs and Americans own this land. The Coolies and the Mexicans pick the fruit for the Japs and the Americans."

"Pleasant. Hello! HELLO!" Shirtz yelled and waved a hand. The workers stopped their work to look. Some waved.

The four men stopped at the oriental gazebo and tied off their horses to the rail out front. The gazebo looked large enough to accommodate maybe 20 dancers and contained tables and chairs, most now folded and stacked to one side, all atop a carved platform with half a dozen steps leading up to the wooden floor. An older Japanese man came running out from a nearby house, followed by a younger one, and invited them to sit at a table inside the gazebo.

"Plez. Plez you come," the older one said waving his hands.

"Mr. Tokyo," Barnaby nodded and climbed the stairs. The man's name was not Tokyo, but the boys in L.A. gave him that nickname. They called the younger one "Little Tokyo." They had no idea if he was a son or not.

All three settled into chairs in the gazebo. Gawdy Shirtz remained at ground level, walking around looking first at a distant view, then close by, at the horticulture.

"What they want? I don't know," Mr. Tokyo said.

"They want money is what they want," Barnaby said. "What else does a Tong want. A piece of this action out here. But don't you worry, you pay us for protection, and we'll protect you."

"I know dis, but how much percentage? They are like the Yakuzi of China."

A Japanese woman appeared with a tray of beer and saki. The men sipped, but Shirtz remained on the outside, alternating between sitting on the steps and even a walk over to the rows of cucumber plants alongside the gazebo. He got down on all fours and looked a few over up close.

"Dis Chink bastard, he show up here with his Tong friends before," Mr. Tokyo said. "He have a big paddle board with a handle. You know, like one you make bread. Dat size. He carries it out here."

"A paddle board?" Barnaby asked.

"It have all kinds of Chinese carvings on it. Who knows what it says. He come here and walk around and he beat my Chinese out in the field with this board. My Chinks they scream and cry. Bend over and squat down and they beat them. They don't hit back. Afraid of the Tongs."

Then about 2:45 p.m. a car drove down the dirt road. A convertible. It pulled up to the gazebo. Four thin Chinese men were inside, their hair wild, dressed in the high fashion of L.A. They got out of the car. Some laughed. They shoved each other a bit. When their jackets parted, gunmetal flashed in the sunlight. The leader wore a concealed gun as well and also carried the aforementioned paddle board by the handle. Three of them walked up the gazebo and stood by the table. The tallest one lingered back and away.

"Jap," the Chinese man said to Mr. Tokyo.

"Chink," the Japanese man said back to him.

The Chinese man giggled and set the edge of the paddle board on the table, then said, "so these are your bosses from Los Angeles," he pointed to Barnaby and his men.

"Did you tell them what we want?"

"Money. I told them," Mr. Tokyo said.

"Dats right. We are the Wang Ze Tong," he shouted loud enough for the pickers to hear. "We own very much of Chinatown. We own very much of everything Chinese people do when they come here. It is tax. A Chinese, American tax."

"And you want money from these farms? How much?" Barnaby asked.

"We want....ahhh....30 percent."

"Thirty perCENT!" came the voice from ground level. Gawdy Shirtz took a few steps up the gazebo steps.

"That's almost one-third. Not a lot left for my Japanese friends or my Los Angeles friends."

"We don't care about your Los Angeles friends."

"Ahhh, you don't know me. My name is Gawdy Shirtz. You kinda…kinda stuttered when you said 30 percent,' though. Kinda like, kinda like you were going to say something more like 20 percent? But then got real braggadocios and said 30 percent."

The man stared at Shirtz.

"You thinking that you and your three zoot suit buddies are such hot dogs that you will shoot us all down, if we try to run you off this place?"

Now, all the men in the gazebo stared at Shirtz.

"Let me guess, you are stuck on some — Merican words. 'Braggadocios.' 'Hot dogs.' But, they don't really mean much given these proceedings."

They all stared.

"Braggadocios. Well, it means, it means bragging. Just bragging. It means thinking, sounding like you're bigger than yourself. Trying to impress EVERYONE around you and convince them you are a hot dog. Hot dog, that's the second one. Being a hot shot, a big deal. But you know there is nothing but meat-shit inside a real hot dog. It's a shit of meat."

"You cannot run us off this place," the paddle man said.

"Oh we won't try to run you off," Shirtz said. "We'll just kill ya off."

Shirtz pulled a revolver from under his jacket. With one hand, without taking much serious aim, he shot the man standing to the rear. Twice. Once in the head. The man collapsed to the floor in a noisy bundle.

Then Shirtz turned slightly, raising his revolver higher and shot the two men behind the leader two times each. This sudden action and these massive explosions caused such a distraction that no one saw him pull the second big pistol from his belt. All the field workers now stopped their work to watch.

The other three men with Shirtz hadn't a chance to even move. Neither did the paddle man, whose face went pale with concern as he stared at Shirtz.

Shirtz climbed the last step up into the gazebo; his gun pointed at the heart of the Tong and approached him slow.

"Say, funny boy, what's all…what's all that gibberish on that paddle?"

"It says 'beware the Wang Ze Tong.'"

"Oh. Beware the Wang Ze Tong. How pleasant," Shirtz said eyeing the carving. "It sure seems like it says a lot more than just that, what with all that sliced, gibberish on there. Holy cow. That how Chinese looks written out?"

"That is what it says. I can go back to Los Angeles and tell…"

"So…you been out here hitting coolies with that paddle? Like they was your stepchildren or something?"

Silence.

"Huh? Step children. Huh? Been hitting coolies?"

"They…they will learn obedience."

"Ohhh. Obedience. What a good, big, —'merican word for you to know."

Shirtz slowly took the paddle away with his right hand, looking it over. He turned it sideways and smashed the edge across the Tong's face with a mighty arm swing. Hard. This took him down off the chair, and onto his back. But it didn't knock him out. The blow contorted the Tong's jaw causing it to project in a misaligned and shocking angle away from his face. It twisted over to the right side. The Tong whined, but couldn't speak.

"Well Mr. Chinese bully? Meet Mr. American bully," Shirtz said, walking up to him. "I like to beat people up too! Something about it makes me feel good. Especially that magic moment when you have won. And there is nothing left but a scared little man to look at. Or woman. Or child, even. That's my prize. That moment. So, I share with you this moment, paddle boy. And imagine us meeting and us getting together here like this today. This beautiful southern California day. Two bullies. An, American bully, and a Chinese bully. I guess it's inevitable there will be some bullying going on here," Shirtz turned to his friends at the table, "huh fellas?"

Shirtz dropped the big paddle on the Tong's chest.

"Annnnnd look here! Herrrre's that exact moment!"

He shot the paddle three times. The bullets cracked the wood apart and tore into the man's chest. The man screamed as it happened, at least as best he could with a broken jaw.

He leaned over the Chinaman to take a good look, grinned and said, "Pleasant."

Then he turned to the men at the table. Even though they were on his side, they were scared to death of him at that moment, each dodging his penetrating gaze.

"Oh now," Shirtz said, addressing Mr. Tokyo, "dammit to all hell, we have made a complete mess of your pretty new gazebo. Soap and a good brush. Like the nuns say. Soap and a good brush. Not one of those metal kind of brushes that'll…that'll just scar up the wood. A coarse boar bristle brush—that's what ya need. Maybe even some sandpaper? It will be a pleasant enough gazebo again after you apply a little elbow grease." He put both his guns away and walked off the gazebo. Workers in the fields gaped.

He went straight to his horse and got aboard.

"Looks like you got a new car," he said to Mr. Tokyo. "But if I were you? I'd drive that car to the front gate? And I'd set it afire? And leave it there for the next stupid batch of Chinkos to see when they drive up. See their paddle boy's car all fired up."

The other three took this cue and vacated the gazebo in favor of their horses.

"They will come back!" Mr. Tokyo said.

"Then our Los Angeles friends will have to post armed guards out here. There's a world full of bullets and only so many Tong, Mr. Tokyo. If I have to come back? I'll come back."

"Thank…thank you, Mr. Shirtz!" Tokyo said.

Shirtz turned his horse toward the gates.

"Have the rest of a pleasant day, Mr. Tokyo."

The men slowly rode off. This time Shirtz rode in the lead.

"Some of these areas out here do remind me of parts of Oklahoma. Imagine that. California looking like Oklahoma. And, covered with Japanese Chinkos fightin over land."

Chapter 26: A Gawdy Threat

Remedies Investigations...

"A Sgt. Barry Astler," Jefe said, holding the whole phone, stand and all, in his hands. The extra long wire allowed him to walk into Gunther's officer with it and place it on his desk.

"Barry…?"

"Barry de Cane. From Los Angeles Police Department," Jefe reminded him. "You remember, Lake Tahoe. De detective we gave money to?"

"Hello, Barry the Cane!" Gunther said into the mouthpiece. "How goes it out West?"

It's all the same out here Johann. Drugs, Booze. Sex. Guns. I swear it's like the Civil War here every day. And I'm stuck in the middle of it."

"What can I do for you here in Fort Worth, Texas?"

"Listen, see…I called to tell you something. Can we talk on this line?"

"I don't know, Barry," Gunther said with some frustration. "It's chancy, so many operators between us, but go ahead."

"I'll try to keep it simple, then. You know I work doing a small job or two with Mooney Rick. Remember me telling you about him?"

"Yeah, I do."

"Yeah, well, he's having some troubles with the Chinese Tongs nosing in on his fruit and vegetable picking, farm deals and some drug deals here. So, Rick and these boys, you see, they are connected with the Kansas City mobsters..."

"Mobsters…"

"Mobsters. It's a word, a word they just started calling gangs of criminals. Outlaws. The Mob. The Mob is what some inside people call the organized crime gangs from Italy."

"Ok. Yeah. Like the Black Hand in New York City."

"Yeah, that's the ticket. Yeah. See, you are going to hear that word a lot in a few years. Mobsters. Like gangsters? But mobsters. And their gunmen. These gunmen are not like the cowboy gunslingers you are use too, Johann."

"Ok."

"…and Rick just hired a guy, a killer named Gawdy Shirtz, on loan from the Kansas City gangs to shoot some of these Tong out here. They are starting to call them gunmen now. What you wild westers would call gunslingers. These gunman will kill in public or private, and walk away."

"We've got some gunslingers like that too."

"I know, but these hitmen - a hit is what they call a paid for murder - area a different breed. The mob also uses the word 'painter,' from the east Coast and Chicago. They shoot you and the blast paints your blood on the wall."

"Okay."

"Shirtz has done some work in our area. Well, in my dealings with the Mooney Rick boys, I overhead that Kansas City wants Shirtz back, see. They want him back to send him to Fort Worth and kill some private detective. I heard them say that the detective was from another country, Germany, and nobody cared round there if he got iced."

"Hmmm. Gawdy Shirtz."

"Shirtz with a 'z.' S-h-i-r-t-z," Barry spelled it out.

"With a 'z' on the end?"

"I figured out, it had to be you."

"It probably is, Barry. I'm in the middle of a big ugly mess. What else do you know about him?"

"I know he is a stone-cold killer. He's dropping Tong like stink flies out here. Originally from Oklahoma. An orphan.

The story goes that when Shirtz was two years old, he was

dropped off on the porch at some Catholic orphanage. On the porch. Standing around. The nuns found him, see, when they opened the door. The kid had no name. Nothing, see. He did have a small paper bag of clothes dropped off with him, just setting on the steps. They took the kid in. They had to give him a name real quick for the records. He tells the story that a nun said that the paper bag of clothes was mostly shirts, and they were all awful looking. Terrible colored. Loud. This nun quick-named the kid Gawdy Shirtz. She put a 'z' on the end so that maybe the last name might sound like a normal name for somebody."

"That's quite a story. Do you know when he's coming to Fort Worth?"

"No. He might go to Kansas first. Or take the train to Fort Worth, through Phoenix. That's the route he'll likely take. I saw him here in Burbank two days ago. That's the last time I saw him around here."

"What's he look like?"

"He's about six foot tall. He is stocky. Ugly. Brown hair. Lumpy face. Out here he might dress like a Los Angeles pimp. But sometimes like a cowpoke if he needs to be. Down there by you, I don't know? You know?"

"Un-huh."

"He's a talker. He talks to people before he kills them, I understand. A smart ass. But, when he decides to pull the gun and pull the trigger, it surprises everybody. They say he's fast on the pistol draw. They say…they say that if he tells you his name? If he introduces himself to you? You're dead. he likes to do that."

"Ok, well, Barry, you might have saved my life by telling me this. I thank you. Your debt to me is paid, I…"

"No. No. My debt to you is never paid off, my friend. You know the word - kindred?"

"I do."

"You and me, buddy, see, we are kindred."

"That we are."

"When you decided to help me out in Lake Tahoe, you… you saw a kindred-ness in me, see. You made your play to settle things up because you read we are kindred spirits."

"I understand," Gunther said.

"Don't get yourself killed, Johann."

"I won't Barry. You neither. And, thanks."

Gunther put the earpiece on the hook, cutting off the call. He realized that Jefe was still standing in the room.

"He says that…"Gunther said.

"I know. He told me first. They have hired a killer to kill you. He called him a mobster gunman."

Gunther nodded and sat back in chair, "Guess I'd better be careful."

"Guess so."

"Careful around here too. All of us."

Jefe folded his arms.

"Sometimes, Jefe, I think we have to worry about all of us living here together. You know?"

"We do have to think about dis," Jefe said. His kids were right behind him, out in the lobby, playing.

"At least we could make some plans for emergencies. Other houses. Safe houses when we work the complicated cases. Maybe it's time I got that cabin built up on the lake." Jefe nodded.

"Gawdy Shirtz," Gunther repeated in a whispering sigh.

"Shirtz with a z."

Gunther walked out on the roof of the county sheriff's office to find Wiley, once again, enjoying his favorite pastime with pidgeons. Wiley had his back turned toward Gunther. His jacket lay across a chair, but he still wore his gun in a belt, a big Colt and a run of bullets in loops across the back. His shirt fluttered half untucked from reaching to all the levels of pigeonry.

"They said you'd be up here." Gunther walked across the rooftop.

"That I am," Wiley said, not turning.

"I am here to file an official crime report. A report of a threat to my life."

Wiley turned and looked at Gunther with one squinted eye.

"That supposed to be something new?" He wiped his hands on a white rag, then stepped out of the big cage. "A threat?"

"Yeah. I got word from a police sergeant in Los Angeles…"

"Los Angeles? California?"

"Yeah. This sergeant told me that a hired gunman is coming in from California to do me in."

Wiley put a foot up on a chair rung and said, "A gun...man. Okay. They don;t call them gunslingers?"

"I guess not anymore. The killer's name is Gawdy Shirtz."

"Gawdy Shirtz. What kinda name is that?"

"With a "z". It's a made up name given to him at orphanage in Oklahoma."

"Let me guess now, he wore gaudy shirts."

"That's about right. Something like that."

"Who sent for him?"

"Who do you think? Somebody here with connections to the Kansas City mob."

"Mob. That new too?'

"Short for mobsters. Reckon so."

"What do you want me to do about it?"

"Right now, nothing."

"Nothing again."

"But I want this threat on report, " Gunther said.

"Nothing. Nothing, so's you can gun-man him down yourself."

Gunther didn't answer. They looked at each other. Wiley shook his head.

"I just want this on report," Gunther said. "On file here. From a police sergeant named Barry Astler, a reliable source, a Los Angeles detective, learned of this threat and called me to warn me."

"And you don't want us to do nothing about it."

"Maybe something. Later. He's not even here yet, far as I can tell."

Wiley just stood there.

"Ok, well, I will consider it reported," Gunther said, and

turned for the stairs.

“No, no, no, hold on,” Wiley said. “Let’s go downstairs and make an official written report.” He grabbed his jacket and followed Gunther down the stairs.

Chapter 27: The Guns of Johnny Cleveland

Fort Worth train Station...

High noon. That big downtown fire had even ravaged a part of the Texas Railway Station, gutting a part of its eastern section. The area was roped off and teeming with construction workers.

Gunther waited at the Fort Worth train station with a big travel trunk. He, dressed in a white Stetson, tan suit and brown boots, looked like any other well-heeled traveler. Different from the others perhaps only because of the Colt revolver and Bowie knife under his jacket.

The 12:30 p.m. train, the one that ran the Albuquerque, New Mexico line sat puffing in the station as if impatient, as trains were want to do. This train would carry him as far as Amarillo where he'd change to another train, for the final leg of his trip to Bendigo with many stops along the way. Passengers who arrived to the station early casually boarded the common cars and stepped up into their elite, luxury compartment cabins. These special cabins even had doors that opened out to station platforms for easy on-and-off access. Gunther had reserved one such compartment for himself and Torontoola.

About 10 minutes later a small, diverse crowd appeared, dressed to the nines or down to the ones. Within this timely group, Raoul Torontoola emerged rolling his own travel chest on a low wooden dolly. Gunther waved at him, pointed to a cabin and started for it.

The doors for the compartments were all open and Gunther lifted and slid his trunk across the floor of their numbered cabin. Torontoola approached with a smile, but he saw Gunther suddenly pre-occupied with a sighting off to his right.

"What?"

"Look over there. See that tall guy? Three-piece suit? Brown derby?"

"Yes."

"That is Johnny Cleveland. The pitcher. He must be heading out a day early too."

A porter loaded a large chest into a luxury suite for Cleveland. Cleveland paid the porter, apparently handsomely due to the man's joyous expression. He stepped aboard into his cabin.

"Johnny Cleveland," Torontoola repeated. "heading out early like us."

"A scout."

Torontoola and Gunther stepped aboard themselves. They quickly took window seats and studied the rest of the crowd, looking for other teammates.

"Will he recognize us? You?" Torontoola asked.

"I don't know. It was dark that night. I was quickly knocked off my feet. Beaten. I don't know. I'll bet not."

"What will we do?"

"I say we have to pay him a visit," Gunther said. "He might recognize the both of us on this train anyway and call the raid off. Or they might hit the health spa guns blazing for the robbery? I'd rather something bad happen on this train than at the spa."

"Madre de mia. What will become of this surprise visit?"

Gunther shook his head. The men sat in their cabin and waited. Whistles blew. Porters hollered. Platform staff shut all doors. The train rocked and moved forward. Within 30 minutes, the ticket taker, a portly woman wearing a man's uniform, knocked on the door, opened the door and Gunther handed her the two tickets. With a metal punch hooked by a silver chain to her belt, she punched a large hole in both tickets and handed them back. She left, slamming the door.

Then Gunther followed her out in the hall and stood by a window looking out. He waited there, pretending interest in the terrain outside until the woman had not only left Cleveland's cabin, but had also left several others in the car, then he motioned through their cabin window for Torontoola to follow him down the hall. Bouncing slightly left and right with the rocking train, the men marched down the hall.

He found Cleveland's cabin door unlocked. Gunther turned the door latch and he and Torontoola quickly entered. Cleveland looked up at them from the sports page of the Whispering Wind newspaper, his head jolting back an inch in a surprise.

"You fellows have…"

"Hello," Gunther said, sitting on the bench seat across from him.

Torontoola sat down next to Gunther, with a smile on his face.

"Can I…what…?"

"Can you do what?" Gunther said.

The three sat quietly for a few seconds. Cleveland laid the paper down across his lap, his hands underneath it.

"If you knew who we were," Torontoola said, "you would find this to be quite an inescapable nightmare."

A wave of concern did pass over the pitcher's face.

"Then who are you?" he asked.

"This man, this man is Johann Gunther. About a month ago, you threw fast ball pitches at his head, and your teammates almost beat him to death with bats at your stadium."

Cleveland's gaze cut toward Gunther's face.

"You cannot recognize him in all this daylight," Torontoola said with a chuckle and a wave of his hand. "As you are a low-life coward of a weasel who does his best work in the shadows of the night."

"I…"

"And me?" The smile disappeared. "My name is Raoul Torontoola. I am the police sergeant you and your friends framed for murder. And then…and then you robbed and killed my wife."

Silence. Each of the three men in the cabin waited for one of them to make a move. They all sat stone still. For they all knew, the next physical movement on any of their parts was toward a gun. That meant a quick or slow death, but death regardless.

"So, you see, Señor, you see what kind of nightmare I am talking about?"

"I don't know what you are blabbering about."

The newspaper spread across Cleveland's lap started to slowly move.

Gunther wasted no time. He drew the revolver tucked in his belt line under his jacket, holding it low, aiming it at Cleveland's chest.

Torontoola reached over and yanked the newspaper from the pitcher's lap. Cleveland's hands were atop each leg, empty and palms down.

"Oh, none of your baseballs?" Torontoola said.

"You think you are gonna shoot me dead right here on the train? I am a sports star heading to a game."

"You are heading to the Morning Glory Spa, one day ahead of your gang. What are you going to do at the spa?" Gunther asked.

Cleveland remained silent.

"I would not sit like such a fool," Torontoola said. "This man has very limited patience. I know. The other night he ran a man out of Texas. Kershaw? So, when he asks you a question, you should answer him. And you? You may never play baseball again either."

"We are going to the spa to rest up before the doubleheader in Amarillo."

Torontoola stood up and pulled down the three shades of the two windows and the door.

"You all are up to no damn good at the spa," Gunther said. "You all are going there to rob and kill."

Cleveland could say nothing.

Gunther reached up and pulled down the chest from the upper rack behind him. He found it locked.Torontoola pulled his long silver Colt and pointed it at the pitcher.

"I am not going to take your pistol off of you yet. In hopes that you might try to pull it," Raoul said.

Gunther slid the Bowie from his belt line sheath, which caused Cleveland to tense with concern. Gunther cracked open the hasp on the suitcase. He opened the lid. He pulled the everyday clothes out.

"No uniform?" he asked.

"That comes with the team crew."

Then Gunther saw a sawed-off shotgun and a simple black leather, pistol belt with two handguns. He saw a black hat and finally a black mask with eye holes. He saw boxes of ammo.

He pulled the shotgun out.

"You need this for baseball?" Gunther asked, checking the weapon. He found it loaded.

"A man has a right to protect himself," Cleveland said, "from fools like you who barge in on him."

"Mask too?" Gunther pulled the mask out with his two fingers through the holes. "To protect yourself?"

"I use that for sex. I like to play more games than baseball."

"You used that mask to rob and kill my wife," Torontoola said. Seeing the mask affected him. Death was in the air and in the tension of Torontoola's gun hand. His pistol even inched forward, his face twisted with the emotions of both hate and sorrow.

Seconds ticked by. Seconds. Gunther stood up and unlatched the door to the outside world, filling the cabin with drafts and wind.

"What? What? You gonna push me out? What?"

"Who are you going to rob? What are you going to steal?" Gunther asked.

Cleveland remained silent.

"Do you know the money kept there is all counterfeit? Fake?" Torontoola said.

Cleveland's head tilted. One eyebrow went way up, the other way down.

"Counterfeit?" Cleveland said. "What's counterfeit?"

"The money that Ranger Winch brought you all in that duffel bag. All the money from Justin Trace and all the money at Morning Glory is fake," Gunther said.

"Counterfeit," Cleveland said again and his gaze fell to the floor.

"You don't know, do you?" Torontoola asked.

"Nah, that money is real!" he said.

And with that subtle confession, Gunther stood and with a free left hand, grabbed a handful of Cleveland's jacket at his upper arm. He pulled him up and over by the wind and howl of open door. The shotgun remained in Gunther's right hand.

"You two fools don't scare me. You can't shoot me. You won't shoot me."

Torontoola lifted his pistol and sneered. A few more seconds past.

"Johann," Torontoola said softly without turning his head, "do you remember our conversation back in the jail? Do you remember when I told I…I could not just shoot a man down in the coldest of blood?"

Cleveland's eyes flashed back and forth at their faces. Was he to live through this? With the shotgun on the pitcher, Gunther slowly bumped Torontoola aside.

Cleveland's eye left the double barrels, looked at Gunther's face, saw the death therein, then back to the barrels.

Cleveland whispered, "swing low, sweet chariot."

Gunther pulled the trigger. The scattergun's double blast blew a hole in Cleveland's gut, shredding his clothes and flesh. It doubled him over; and within a second, like a puff of smoke, Cleveland disappeared right out the open door and flashed away. Gone.

Gunther stepped up and shut the door. The quiet resumed. He took a look around the door frame and window frames, running a finger along the borders. Cleveland took the full blast.

Torontoola's gun hand dropped to his side. Wanting to ask if he was ok, and then not asking, Gunther sat. Torontoola sat. Gunther shoved the shotgun back in the chest and closed the lid, but there was still the smell of it in the small cabin.

"Best put that up in case someone heard the blast and comes a checkin," Gunther suggested about the pistol. "Pull some shades up."

Torontoola holstered his weapon and pulled all three shades up.

"I have shot men before, but not…"

"Yeah, I know. Let's not revisit that whole conversation. I still trust ya," Gunther said, leaning to the left and opening the outside windows as wide as they went.

"I could not, but you can." Torontoola said.

"I can. He wouldn't be the first son of a bitch I shoot off a train. Or pushed?"

"You have?"

"Yeah, some KKK members. Somewhere...oh... in Missouri or Nebraska. Thereabouts."

"Two of the six," Torontoola said. "You have killed both of them."

"I have." Gunther said.

"And we will we kill all six?"

"I don't know. I hope so." Gunther clasped his hands together between his legs and rotated his thumbs one atop the other.

"You hope so?"

"Yeah," Gunther said. "We have no case against them. No evidence. What else is there to do?"

Torontoola grunted. "I did not hire you to kill them."

"No. No you didn't. And I don't get hired to kill people. But, sometimes I just do things on my own."

Torontoola nodded. He understood. And, all these men did try to kill Gunther in a horrific way.

"We need to pitch all this stuff out," Gunther said, collecting the clothes he'd scattered. "This is pretty desolate land out here. May take a long time to find that body. Maybe some railroad linemen may find him. Eventually. A dressed up set a bones and maggots I hope."

"Yes."

"We are keeping the guns and ammunition," Gunther said. "You can't go to a gunfight with too many guns or too much ammo."

Gunther stood, and opened the door to the hall. He casually stepped out and looked out the row of hallway windows again to the bleak, dry landscape to the north. He looked up and down the hall. No one in the hallway. He returned inside.

"If he had reached for his pistol, I would have shot him," Torontoola said.

"Yeah, yeah. I know."

"But he didn't."

"I know."

"I thought he would. Out of desperation. If I just waited long enough."

Gunther nodded. He started collecting the clothes and stuffing them in the trunk. He placed the chest on the floor, near the door. Every 10 minutes, he opened the door a bit and threw another article of clothing out, low so each piece might not fly up in view of the other cabin windows behind them.

"I think he was surprised that the money was counterfeit," Torontoola said.

"I think so too. I could read it all over his face."

"The gang thinks they are robbing a robber baron." Gunther continued to toss items out of the door at intervals.

"I guess a ballplayer truly loves his glove," Gunther said massaging the soft leather of the glove. The glove was the only baseball item he found in the trunk. He considered it for a moment. It was the last thing he sent sailing out the door.

Gunther cut a name tag off the handle of the suitcase and shoved it in his pocket. The ballplayer's trunk appeared non-descript enough to keep for awhile. The only items inside the chest now were the shotgun and the pistol belt.

"The guns of Johnny Cleveland," Torontoola said looking at them. "One or both of these pistols may have been the one used to shoot my wife." Then he closed the lid.

They each grabbed an end handle and left the empty compartment, bound for their own cabin. Once inside their room, Gunther emptied Cleveland's guns and ammo from his chest and put them into his own. He took his jacket off and put his feet up on Cleveland's chest. Both the men were quiet for the next few hours.

Gunther pulled out a book from his trunk and started reading.

"What are you reading?"

"Die Traumdeutung. It's a book by Sigmund Freud. On

dreams. Symbols. Memory. What they all mean."

"Is that in German? You read German?"

"Yes. I was born in Germany. My parents are German, and I spoke and read German until we moved to New York City."

"What do our dreams mean?" Torontoola asked wistfully.

Gunther laid the book on his lap.

"Something. I am not sure we can ever know. But they are your mind's way of working out the problems of your day. Your life."

"And this Mr. Freud is a dream reader?"

"He tries."

"I dream of my wife often."

Gunther nodded.

"And whatever do you dream about, Johann?"

"Nothing. Nothing, really. I don't seem to dream much at all."

"You sleep well?"

"Yes. I think I do."

"I should think you have much to work out. With your work. With what you…do. Perhaps you work out all your problems while you are awake? Problems like…with Señor Cleveland."

"Perhaps." He picked the book back up.

"I should think I will never sleep well again," Torontoola said.

Gunther looked up at him.

"You…do you still…cry out at night? Like you did back in the jail?"

"Yes, I do. Not every night. But I still do."

Gunther didn't know what to say. Then he said, "Thanks for the warning." He smiled.

"Not as…not as loud, you know? Perhaps I will meet Dr. Freud someday and he can help me sleep," Torontoola said.

"Perhaps. There must be some of, what these doctors call, closing the case."

"Closing. Ha!" Torontoola repeated. "Closing in. We are closing in."

Gunther nodded again. He returned to his book.

About 10 minutes later he heard a snort and looked up. He saw Torontoola deep asleep in his seat, his head laid uncomfortably to the left side, mouth wide open. Getting some sleep. Getting some closure if even by Gunther's hand. Gunther did dream about a woman too, sometimes. The Star of Africa, but what sense would it make to explain all that to Torontoola?

Two down and four to go. Closer to closure. What would Sigmund say about his methods for closure?

Chapter 28: Death Moves Fast

"Can I help you sir?" The man behind the Morning Glory Spa front desk asked.

"Yes you can, sir," Gunther said. "Two things. First, I need to see Jacob Seavers and Marion Kranepool."

"Are they guests here, sir?"

"No they are not. They are employees."

"Were do they work, sir?"

"They work directly for Mr. Clyde Bendigo, your owner." Gunther asked.

"I am afraid I have no knowledge of them to tell them anything."

"But you do have knowledge of Clyde Bendigo?"

"Oh, yes I do, sir."

"Clyde Bendigo will fry your ass on a pole if he misses this important message for Jacob Seavers and Marion Kranepool…Mr…Mr…" as he looked close at the name plate on the desk. "Mr… Sean Bruner."

Mr. Sean Bruner contorted his mouth and stared at Gunther.

"Get a message to Clyde Bendigo's office that a Johann Gunther needs to see Jacob Seavers and Marion Kranepool. It is a matter of life and death."

Bruner began to write on a note pad before him, repeating "Johann Gunther. Jacob Seavers. Marion Kranepool. A matter of..."

"Life and death," Gunther finished for him.

"…and death. I will pass this on."

"Not through normal channels. Not through that message tube thing you've got behind you. Pick up that phone and call. Call now."

The man lifted the phone. He read the message aloud. Gunther watched him closely. Bruner spoke and listened. He looked up at Gunther.

"Mr. Bendigo's assistant asked if you are checking in?"

"That…is the second thing. Yes. A Mr. Raoul Torontoola and myself, Johann Gunther, have reservations." Gunther pulled his wallet out.

"Raoul Torontoola and yes, this is Mr. Gunther himself right here in front of me, ma'am. Yes. Yes."

He hung up and said, "Mr Bendigo's assistant says that you need not worry about paying for your rooms. A Misters White and Gray will be meeting you at your room…" he handed Gunther a key for Room 117, "…in 30 minutes."

He handed Torontoola a room key for 118. He snapped his fingers for a bellman.

Gunther nodded, "I thank you, sir. You handled this odd request professionally."

Off the men went headed for the elevator, passing the grand room off the lobby. At least 50 people stood by various tables all laughing in a random melody of sorts. Over to the side in the room, a man in white medical clothes, with a megaphone to his mouth, orchestrated the laughing song.

"Ha, ha, ha, ha, haaaaaa, ha-ha…"

"I feel oddly compelled to laugh," Gunther said, as they followed the bellman with their luggage.

Amongst the chorus, stood Carmella! She spotted Gunther and ran to him, kissing him on the cheek.

"Are we having fun?" Gunther asked her.

"This is a very strange place..."

"Let me guess, it might make for a good story."

She smiled coyly, "Yeeessss."

She shook hands with Torontoola.

"Señorita," he said.

"Are Ramp and Bat here too?" Gunther asked.

"Yes, they are not singing though. They are in the health

bar, trying to find something that will inebriate them. They are doing their best to dodge all the clinic people trying to get them to sign up for electronic massages and enemas."

Gunther laughed out loud at that one, as they all proceeded to elevators.

"Listen, you keep on singing. We have a meeting scheduled with Bendigo."

"Already?"

"Yes."

"Can I come?"

"No. I should think he wants as little publicity as possible. I will meet you all later at the health bar."

Thirty minutes later, a knock sounded at Gunther's door. Gunther answered.

Mister Gray and Mister White, AKA Seavers and Kranepool stood in the hallway, dressed in their usual, near matching suits and demeanor. The three stared at each other for a moment.

"Johann," Jacob said.

"Jacob and Marion, come in," Gunther motioned them in. By calling them by their real names, he'd had that special moment, thanks to the West Point yearbooks where they knew that he knew. Gunther regretted Jefe had missed it.

The two men were nearly smiling at Gunther's accurate ID. Nearly. They eyed him and Raoul Torontoola studying them from head to toe. Torontoola stood and shook their hands.

"My name is Raoul Torontoola. I was the one framed for murder."

"Not by us, sir," Jacob said.

"I know."

"You found us, Johann," Marion said.

"And to what end?" Jacob added. "You are here. To what possible end?"

"We are here because we think you are about to be robbed by a gang of professionals," Gunther said.

"And in a very big and bloody way," Raoul added.

"We have been investigating the events back in Fort

Worth. The baseball team of outlaws…" Gunther started. "and Justin Trace," Raoul said.

"…and we know about the counterfeit money. The team thinks the money is real, and they are going to mask up and shoot up, probably the cereal company office for sure, maybe even the spa. They'll likely shoot you and anyone at either place that gets in their way."

Misters White and Gray exchanged glances.

"And you are telling us this because?" Jacob asked.

"Because these men are killers, and they will kill again. Maybe many customers here in this hotel will be killed? Or workers at the factory," Gunther said.

"What about the counterfeit money you mentioned?" Marion asked. It was a dodgy question, with no ownership to the subject matter.

"Right now, I don't care about the money. I'm trying to close out the murder case of this man's wife and the murder of a retired Louisiana judge. I am not a lawman. I don't care about the money. I am doing a job. Your business needs to be warned."

The men looked at Torontoola.

"I…I want to kill the men who shot my wife. If you have looked into me. My past. You have found, señors, that I am not, as you might say, pristine. I am not pristine, but I do a good job for justice when people have been hurt or wronged. There is no question about this. In my spare time, I protect some gambling operations. What is gambling? Who is hurt from gambling?"

"Why not shoot them down in a Fort Worth, beer joint?" Jacob asked.

"Because! Because I am not the kind of man that does that," Torontoola said calmly. "And I would not shoot Justin Trace down in the street, and I would not shoot these men down cold either, or shoot them in the back. I want to catch them in a crime and do…do what is right. I may take money for influence, but I am not a cold-blooded killer!" He gulped a few time as if he felt his throat burn with this declaration, perhaps realizing by his denial that he'd inadvertently just called Gunther one.

Marion walked over to the room phone, took the earpiece off the hook, put it up to his ear and hit the lever several times. Then he spoke into the mouthpiece.

"Extension 28," he said. "Elizabeth, this is Marion. Is Mr. Bendigo… Yes? Yes? I need to…yes. Mr. Bendigo? I am in Room 117 on our property, with Johann Gunther and Raoul Torontoola from Fort Worth. Yes. Yes. No. They need to tell you something. No. No. No, sir. Yes."

Marion hung the earpiece onto the lever.

"Follow us," Marion said, and the four men left the room and took the stairs down. Leaving the lobby by the front door, they got into an enclosed, black private coach hitched to a team of two horses. He told the driver to head for the Morning Glory office.

The men remained quiet for the half-mile journey. On the ride to the office, Gunther saw what appeared to be a small, very modern city. New. Clean. But without a soul anywhere. No people on the streets, in the restaurants. No one.

"Is this the city Bendigo is building?" Gunther asked.

"Yes. There are schools, churches, stores, houses. A government building. Restaurants. It's a real city," Jacob said. "Parks. A community swimming pool. A small hospital. There's a horse racetrack underway on the south side."

"No people," Raoul said.

"No people yet," Marion said. "Employees will soon move in. Mr. Bendigo is busy contacting people to move out here. They are building a power plant on the south side. Once you build everything, then people move in to work everything, and they need…everything."

"It is…" Torontoola said, gaping out the window, "…like a ghost town in reverse. The people leave first and buildings decay. Here, the buildings come first. What is the name of the city?"

"Bendigo. Bendigo, Texas," Jacob said.

"Of course," Torontoola said.

The coach stopped. The men hustled out into the large Morning Glory lobby, up those stairs, to two ornate double doors. Inside they found an office larger than Gunther had ever seen before. A trim man, near bald, in a three-piece suit, in his 50s stood from an ornate, hand carved chair in position behind an elaborate wooden desk. His right arm was in a white sling.

"Have a seat, gentlemen," he said, motioning a welcome with his good arm.

Gunther and Torontoola advanced as Kranepool and Seavers took up positions behind them in chairs along the wall, which was a bit unnerving to the visitors.

"Sit. I am Clyde Bendigo. You…" he pointed to Gunther," must be Johann Gunther. And you must be Raul Torontoola, the police detective. He walked around to stand, leaning against the front of his desk. We are going to have a conversation here, gentlemen. And make no mistake, what we say, what you say, will decide whether or not you leave this room alive." Bendigo looked dead serious.

Serious, but Gunther smiled at the threat. Torontoola lowered his head, widened his eyes and half-smiled.

"And this warning is somehow funny to you two?" Bendigo asked.

A voice from the rear, Marion's voice chimed in to break the mood, "Sir, ahhh, Johann here is a veteran of three wars and various other scrapes. He doesn't scare easily."

"And you Mr. Torontoola?" Bendigo asked.

"I have been threatened so many times, señor. Faced my own death so many times, what you say matters little to me. My beloved wife is dead." He shrugged his shoulders. "What do I care if you kill me now?"

Bendigo stared at him a bit taken aback, then nodded ever so slightly in understanding.

"Sir," Marion interrupted. "The motorcycle gang of outlaws, the ballplayers from Fort Worth we were dealing with. The killers of Justin Trace, they are on their way for a stay at the spa. Johann is convinced they are coming here to rob the spa and maybe even the office. Gunther and Torontoola are here to warn us, sir."

"They want to help," Jacob added.

"Help?" Bendigo said.

"One of the gang members stole a duffel bag of money from Justin Trace's room the night he was killed," Gunther said. "When your men, here," Gunther threw a pointed thumb over his shoulder, "...pillaged...killed and burned their clubhouse, some of the money was there. We found some burned Morning Glory boxes in the rubble. The gang doesn't know it's counterfeit. Thanks to Justin Trace, your identity fell into their realm of awareness. Now, they're coming to get all your money," Gunther summarized.

Bendigo, Marion and Jacob didn't utter a sound. Bendigo, standing in front of his desk, turned, walked back around his desk and sat down in his chair. Gunther could tell from the other man's face that what he said revealed that he knew entirely too much about their business, in Bendigo's opinion.

"Their realm of awareness," Bendigo repeated slowly.

"Yes sir, that is how they operate. Very personally. They get a whiff of a weakness. A hint of money, and they are on top of it."

"You follow the markets, Mr. Gunther?" Bendigo asked.

"Yes. Somewhat," Gunther offered.

"You? Mr. Torontoola?"

"The fruit and vegetable markets, señor. I deal only with the cash in my hands." He rubbed the fingertips of his right hand together.

"Have you men...well, of course you have, have you heard of the San Francisco earthquake? About a year and a half ago?" Bendigo offered the men a cigar, when they declined he selected one for himself and lit it. Inhaled deeply.

The two nodded.

"Thoughtful men, men in money, like myself, began to fear all things financial in 1905. There was a serious strain on the world's capital supply and credit. When the earthquake hit San Francisco in April of 1906, hitting also its key financial institutions - San Fran was the financial center of the whole West. Horrible. 350-500 million dollars of damage. It hit the stock markets here in the U.S., and then the world. Anyway this was the straw that broke all of our backs. A million dollar straw, that, if coupled with the world's capital supply and credit problems. And..and gold problems. And that bastard Heinze and the copper mining...well, it screwed us all into what we call The Panic of 1907. You are familiar with this Johann?"

"Quite."

"The Panic?"

"Yes."

"What it means? People ran to their banks, demanding their money. Here in Texas, we lost 11 national banks and over 40 state banks. People shot themselves. People jumped off tall buildings. Rich people became hobos. People were arrested for stealing food. Put in mental institutions because they went crazy. This panicking, it got worse and worse, affecting everyone. And, it all affected me, here, too. The poorer a person is, the less they want or can eat breakfast, least of all my cereal. But poverty affects every business. It shaves, it skins your business. Any gain you've sweat to make, any profit that finally sweats out of the skin, a crash like this, is like a razor. It just…just shaves that sweat off, and your skin comes off with it."

"Are you suggesting, sir, that you gave people in Fort Worth piles of counterfeit money to buy your cereal?" Gunther asked.

"Ha! Ha ha! In a way. In a way." Bendigo leaned back in his giant chair. "You are friends with President Roosevelt?"

"Yes. From Cuba. But I work for him once in a while. If he doesn't need me? I rarely hear from him."

"My wife would say the same thing about me."

The fear and threat in the air dissipated a tad as Bendigo seemed to visibly relax back into his chair, and he spoke, "The President has been on the warpath against big business. Robber barons he calls us. We wanted to work with him, but he made it impossible. So…myself and many of the richest men in the county decided to save this country without the president's help. Take my friend JP Morgan. He, like my other friends, did what we could. We bankrolled cities in bond issues. We created corporations to create businesses. But everything we did, openly, was still within the rules. Within the money system we muck around in. Robbery?

There were times the, so-called, evil Morgan was shipping wagon trains of gold bullion and greenback cash to banks. Now there was the time for a robbery, Mr. Gunther. But no one knew about the shipments. But, none of us alone, not even all of us together, had enough money to save our country. And we have a lot of money. And we are patriots, you know. We love this country and want it to grow, despite what Mr. Roosevelt thinks of us. So…we decided to do something else. Something outside the system to save our country.

And President Roosevelt doesn't know this. Not a bank in the country knows this. Not a single government official knows this. And there you have it—that ugly word you used 'counterfeit.' A cheap word. A criminal word. Your counterfeit mystery solved, Misters Gunther and Torontoola. My friends and me, evil corporate monsters that we are, have gotten together and mustered our forces to save the country.

From my humble factory outside," he pointed his cigar to the windows, "I have been making our money. We, and by 'we' I mean the aforementioned wealthy men, have amassed the greatest mint, the greatest paper moneymaking machines we could build outside of Washington DC. We have made the greatest looking money ever made. other than the original."

Gunther and Torontoola exchanged glances.

Bendigo continued, "When a country, our country, any country, prints more money, it is money of record. International record. Every financial system in our world, every government knows how much the government prints, and the world sets the value of our dollar. Essentially, usually, the more money you print, the less your money is worth.

A government is incapable of printing empty paper, enough to stop a panic like the one in 1907, or any panic. If people find out about the printing then the dollar becomes worthless. So, we, not the government, we made the money. Money that no one knows about. No one. Certainly not the banks of this country. The banks of the world. There would be a lot more money in the system, money for food, cars, houses, yet no devaluation of the dollar on any market. Genius, don't you think?"

And with that, Gunther instantly understood.

"So, Justin Trace was not alone," Gunther said.

"No, he was not alone. Far from it. There were…hundreds of Justin Traces. A thousand? We, my business partners and me, dispatched them to every major and minor city we could, coast to coast. In San Francisco we sent several, giving away business grants to rebuild old companies and build new ones too. In New York the same. Omaha. Chicago. Denver. Everywhere we could.

We also fed money into gambling. Because gambling money is unrecorded money. We have bolstered the economy with millions. Millions I say, of unrecorded dollars that no one in the world knows about. An internal wealth and prosperity, off the books, away from taxes, away from the damn banks in London and Europe that would de-evaluate our dollar. And Mr. Gunther, money was spent in your Fort Worth, and since you asked, I can presume that here and there, some of that money was actually used to buy my cereal. Now, can we trust you? Can we trust you with this our secret?"

Gunther rubbed his chin and sat up a bit straighter in his chair. "Well…I am only interested in solving two murders. I do not work for the Federal Government, or any law enforcement agency. So…I don't care about all this extraneous money stuff. Frankly, at first blush, Mr. Bendigo? I must confess to you, I think it's a damn fine idea."

Bendigo smiled. He looked to Torontoola.

"I am a simple man," Raoul said. "I am afraid that I do not understand the workings of international finance. Frankly, I do not understand a single word you just said. I am here only to round up the men who killed my wife. Then I wish to return to my simple life in Fort Worth. I do, however, wish to live in a very prosperous Fort Worth, with many, many happy people, gambling, and building and working, and eating cereal every morning."

Bendigo's eyes flashed to his Misters Gray and White. Then he nodded.

"I am building a small city out there. You must have passed it," Gunther said.

"We saw it, sir," Torontoola said.

"The money and printing presses are still in the bank. In the back."

"Still?" Gunther asked.

"Yes. Yes, there is no more counterfeit money. It's gone.

But the rare paper. The ink. The printing plates and the presses. All still there. A professional print shop manager could look it all over and be able to print some money again if necessary. We decided the operation was over about three weeks ago. We dismantled the presses, but haven't disposed of them yet."

"Maybe all that could be distributed and hidden around the city," Gunther said.

"We shut down when the public learned that a massive shipment of more that 12.4 million dollars in gold had arrived from Liverpool, England aboard the Lusitania. Our U.S. Treasury issued about 40 million in gold bonds to national banks. And we all, we horrible rich people and robber barons, donated millions above the table, and sneaked many millions more in below the table with our secret deed. The Panic of 1907 has turned the corner. It took more than a year, but it turned."

"With this counterfeit money gone," Gunther asked, "if these robbers were successful, how much could they get from you here?"

"Just a few thousand of real money. We don't keep mush cash here. The real cash we keep in an Amarillo bank," Bendigo said. "We can't tell the Amarillo County Sheriff about this raid. If they come out here? Well, word may somehow leak about the counterfeiting. We'll have to handle this…ourselves."

"They will then turn to the spa after the bank and rob whatever they can," Kranepool said. "We'll have to keep five men at the spa, and three... four…that's seven of us here."

Gunther nodded. "Weapons?" he asked.

"Shotguns. Revolvers," Seavers said.

"Seven of us?" Bendigo asked.

"Gunther said, "Count us in."

Torontoola nodded.

Bendigo's brow wrinkled, then he smiled.

"You know Bat Masterson?" Gunther asked.

"Bat...Wyatt Earp's friend?"

"He's now a newspaper reporter in New York. Mostly sports. He is my friend, he is here at the spa and I'll bet he will help us too."

"That is very interesting. He was at the OK corral?"

"No sir. He missed that one, but he's done a lot elsewhere."

"How many men you expect?" Kranepool asked.

"Well, I don't know. There are six outlaws on the ball team. Were, I should say, I killed one of them on the train, coming out here earlier," Gunther said, which caused a ripple of energy, however silent, around the room. "He was one of the team's pitchers, a Johnny Cleveland. A scout. A front-man, look-out for this raid. he tried to kill me a few weeks ago and I returned the attempt. But they have more members in the gang, not all on the ball team. Could be, as many as eight, I would say."

Gunther looked at Torontoola and Raoul nodded in agreement.

"This is Wednesday," Torontoola said, "they will get here Thursday. They will play ball in Amarillo on Saturday and Sunday. We expect the robbery to be on Friday."

"We get the idea that they think the money is real. They found the money in cereal boxes so I reckon they will come to the cereal factory first," Gunther said.

"Sir, you will have to leave," Seavers said to Bendigo. "We'll pack you up and escort you to Amarillo tonight. Within the hour. We'll get some county detectives to look after you at the Ritz, and I'll come back here."

Bendigo didn't argue with the logic. He stood up and came around the desk. Everyone else stood.

"Then we'll be off." Bendigo slipped on a light suede jacket, letting it hang over the shoulder of his injured arm. All the while he looked at Gunther with a curious eye.

"Polo accident," Bendigo said, alluding to his injured arm as he maneuvered the jacket on his shoulders. "You look like you might play polo, Mr. Gunther."

"Seen it. But never played it," Gunther said.

"Fell off my horse," indicating his arm. "You are a strange man, I think, Mr. Gunther. You have placed yourself right in the middle of all this. Why?"

"Doing a job, sir."

"Doing a job. But you work for yourself. You are your own boss. To hire. To fire. To stand down. My friends here advise me you were in the Army. Were you a lawman once?"

"Yes, sir, I was. Once. For a few years up in Paris, Texas."

"Hmmm, that explains some of it, I think. And you left?"

"I left because…justice moved a little too slowly for my liking, you know? Life moves real fast. Death moves even faster. Justice? She moves real slow."

"Hmmm, like the economy."

Gunther nodded at that.

"Like the economy. What's in this for Mr. Torontoola?"

"These men killed my wife and framed me to murdering Justin Trace," he said matter-of-factly.

"Hmmm. I see. I do. I understand. You know, I mentioned people jumping off buildings a minute ago? Suicide?" Bendigo said quietly to Gunther. "My son jumped off a New York City rooftop a year ago. Almost took his whole family with him. Tried. Tried to take them all because he felt ashamed at the financial decisions he'd made. Shame. What a terrible thing, to shame a life away. My…my little grand kids will never know their father. They...they watched him jump."

Gunther nodded again, staring at Bendigo.

"You…you might think me a criminal or a robber baron," the millionaire said, "but…every dollar that passes hands, every single dollar has a human story attached to it. It strengthens our country, and makes for businesses and customers."

"We've got to go, sir," Seavers urged.

"I won't forget this help, gentlemen," Bendigo said, looking at both Gunther and Torontoola, then he walked over to the door and beyond with Seavers. Kranepool remained.

"We have work to do," Kranepool said, after his boss and a team member left. "So, we have eight men."

"I think maybe we have one more coming," Gunther said.

"Who?"

"My partner Jefe Cocoy. You fellows already know him."

Bat Masterson sipped his herbal tea and ate his prune Danish.

"This is just hideous," Bat said to Carmella and Ramp, each dissecting and shoving their own bitter little pie around a plate with their fork.

They looked at their evening desserts with shocking distaste, and across the dining room there were not many pie-takers among those sitting at the other tables either, obviously veterans of the prior night's menu.

"You can shove that around all you want, but I wouldn't put it in my mouth if I were you," Bat warned.

"But it's supposed to bolster your constitution," Ramp said.

"I spoke to a feller from Portland, Oregon this morning," Bat said, "who flat out told me that they sank him in a tub of water and sent Edison's electricity all through the water and him. God all mighty only knows what's in that Danish. I've heard of the electric chair, but not the electric bath."

Bat looked up and saw Gunther, Torontoola and a third man in an expensive suit approach from across the dining room at a brisk walk.

The men pulled up ornate chairs and sat down with them at the table.

"Dutch, you look like you saw a ghost and have a scheme to catch it," Bat said.

"Bat, I think we need your help," Gunther said.

"Help? Why not have some of this prune pie with me and we'll talk about it. It'll help your constitution."

Gunther gazed at the plate, then back at Bat.

"Come on Gunther, you'll hurt my feelings if you don't!" Bat smiled an evil smile.

Gunther shook his head and continued, "Looks like the robbery will be late tomorrow or anytime Friday. We think it will be at the factory first, or the bank; and if not stopped there, they will return here and rob the spa, maybe these people here in it."

"How do you want me to help?" Bat asked. "I thought you'd never ask. How many are there?"

"Eight? Maybe?"

"Ok. Ok. I have my pistol with me, but I would like more guns."

“We have the guns from the train,” Torontoola said.

“Two pistols and a shotgun,” Gunther offered, knowing he spoke of Johnny Cleveland’s guns.

“Shit, sounds to me like I have guns then. Do I have bullets?”

“A box of shotgun shells. Two boxes of pistols rounds.”

“Sounds like I have bullets too,” Bat said, dropping his pie filled fork on his plate with a clatter. “Now if I don’t have to take a shit in the middle of the gunfight from these old prunes, I’m good.” He looked at Carmella and said, “Oh, I am so sorry for that feisty language in the presence of a lady, ma’am, but when you get me out West a ways a whole layer of civilization seems to peel off.

“Bat…Bat Masterson?” Kranepool asked.

“Bat Masterson,” Gunther said.

“Call me Bat, son,” he said. Standing, he leaned over to offer a hand.

“Marion Kranepool,” Marion said, shaking Bat’s hand with a kind of reverence.

“Carmella,” Gunther said, “we need you at the train station in the morning. When you see these men come in and head our way, call us. There is a working phone there.”

“There’s also a café. You can sit and wait in there,” Kranepool said. “The phone is inside the Western Union Office.”

“They have half of Thursday and all day Friday to rob the place. The game is Saturday,” Ramp said. “Is there anything I can do?”

“Ramp,” Gunther said, “I reckon no matter how this turns out, you’ll be writing something.” He looked at Carmella too, “you both probably will be writing about the baseball game in Amarillo that never happened because half the team consisted of an outlaw gang, and they got themselves shot dead.”

Carmella grabbed Gunther’s forearm and squeezed it. He could see he had her full anticipation.

Chapter 29: The Most Modern of Ghost Towns

"Johann?"

The telephone connections, operator to operator finally came through.

"Jefe..." and Gunther explained the latest developments to his partner.

"I will come. I am now free. Free until Monday. If the robbery is on Friday, I can get there in time. You will need help," Jefe said.

"How will you get here?"

"The train."

"Tomorrow? You'll be on the train with the ball team."

"They have not seen me. They do not know me. I will go in deep disguise as a peon."

"Disguise?"

"Yes. I will put my horse on the train, and when we stop I will ride out to Bendigo."

"Ok. Ok. I'd feel much better if you were here. Ride to Bendigo, and..."

"I already have a map."

"...ride here and follow the signs to the business office, not to the spa. I will be staying in the offices out of sight tomorrow."

"Mañana, mi amigo."

"Mañana, my friend."

Thursday noon. Amarillo Train Station...

The Dallas, Fort Worth train chugged in, and Carmella put down her tea cup and stood from the rustic table at the cafe. She strolled out onto the platform in time to hear the singer and cello player tune up for his welcoming instrumental. A beehive of people disembarked from the train. People wandered to the exits and out onto the Amarillo streets. Others lingered waiting for connecting trains. Still more followed the signs and red arrows to the Bendigo line for transport to the spa. She saw no sign of the ball team. Nor did she spot Jefe.

She walked up to the train and turned to look first one way then the other. The length ran far back down the line, much farther than the length of the passenger platform. She maneuvered through the people and made her way to the far eastern corner of the platform. In the distance, workers were disconnecting freight cars and other routine duties. In her dress and dress boots, she dropped off the platform and walked south. Then she decided she needed to see the far, right side of the train. She walked to the handrails in a space between two cars and hoisted herself up, lifted one leg and then the other over the hand rails. She did the same to exit the right side and dropped to the ground with a spring in her step. She stepped out and walked casually across the open yard among the scattered workers, an oddity for sure on these grounds, but she wandered around as though she were taking in the sights at a county fair.

Eventually, she spotted them, the ball team. They were sorting out their luggage from among other men of various ages and clothing — from ranch hands to suited up, tie wearing businessmen. They were about eight cars down. Men lowered a ramp with ropes and some workers untied horses inside the cars and walked them down the ramps, turning over the nervous, prancing animals to their owners.

Then, other workers began to roll a collection of motorcycles down the same ramp. First one, then another. Eight motorcycles in all were removed from the car. Some of the passengers gawked at the machines; a few even kicked the tires. Eight men approached their rides, joked with the horsemen and pushed the bikes about 20 feet away near a pile of luggage they'd already sorted. Carmella could recognize several of them as ballplayers, and she certainly recognized Spanky Runyan among them.

A wagon, rented, she deduced by the sign on the side, hitched to a team of black, bony horses drove up to the ballplayers, with two male drivers on top. The men jumped down and began loading the luggage into the wagon. Carmella felt for the horses that no doubt had a full load and long haul ahead. The men prepared for their ride too. Some put on leather caps and goggles. They laughed as they slid their hands into leather gloves. They talked.

When the workers finished loading the wagon, the bikers bid the workmen goodbye and, one by one, kick-started their motorcycles into life. The engines roared. They shouted to each other, and Spanky led the group through the work yard riding his bike. The wagon followed. Horses shied as the bikers passed them, often bucking and dragging their owners out of the way. The bikers showed no concern for the stir they created and even gunned their motors more as they rode out of sight.

The men that remained worked to settle down their horses, then pulled their saddles from the train cars and made ready for their departure as well. A man dressed in rough homespun pants and shirt of a native Mexican and wearing a large straw hat, from a distance, resembled Jefe to Carmella. He jumped on a horse loaded down with gear and trotted off in the same direction as the motorcycles.

Carmella watched as they all left, first the bikers, then the wagon, then followed by Jefe at an even slower rate. She watched as they crossed the tracks and headed off southwest, more south than west. Then she could no longer see them, but the noise of the engines reached her for some time. She jumped through the same space between cars once more, made her way to the platform and found some rickety stairs to climb. Just beyond the restaurant where she'd had tea, she located the Western Union Office and the phone, paid the clerk a few pennies and started the process of calling the

Bendigo spa lobby.

"Call for Mr. Johann Gunther!" The bellboy shouted.

Gunther stuck a finger in the air and made for the lobby's row of wall phones.

"Here, sir," the boy held out the phone receiver.

Gunther took the dangling earpiece and spoke into the mouth piece.

"Hello?"

"The gang is on their way Johann," Carmella reported. "They are riding their motorcycles in. A wagon is carrying their gear behind them. There are eight of them in all. I think I saw Jefe too. He is ok. He's on a horse and following behind them all, looking like a Native Mexican."

"Okay. If you can, tell him not to go to the Spa, but to head to the cereal company office, further into town. See you later," Gunther said, and he hung the phone.

He walked to the table where the othe men sat - Bat, Reed, Jacob and Marion.

"They're in. They are riding their motorcycles in from Amarillo," Gunther told them. "They got a supply wagon following them with luggage."

Marion stood and called for some bellmen. He pointed them to the trunks on the floor. "Charles, get this luggage and run these two men down to the office lobby, won't you?" Marion handed him a dime.

"Yes, sir," the bellman said.

"We'll see you men later," Gunther said.

4 p.m. Thursday...

In a surprise announcement, the front office and lobby personnel of Morning Glory Cereal, were all given the rest of Thursday and all of Friday off. A sudden, four day weekend! Instead of the usual well-dressed and articulate ladies that worked the front lobby, it was now manned by one tall man in a black suit standing behind the long lobby desk, and one man seated by the front windows in a brown jacket, tan shirt and brown pants. A tan Stetson rested on his head. Three pistols rested under that jacket and nearby, a lever-action 44-40 rifle.

The desk man threw his booted leg up on the counter, and pulled up his pants leg. He scratched his calf furiously.

"My pappy said there is no greater pleasure on Earth then scratching a chigger bite."

Gunther by the windows smiled and said, "I reckon so."

"By the way, my name is Holloway Loomgloom."

"Loom-gloom," Gunther repeated slowly, working his tongue around the unusual syllables. "My name is Johann."

"I know." Loomgloom pulled down his pants leg, stuttered with the thought of some scratching again, then put his foot down onto the carpet. "I've worked security for Mr. Bendigo here at the plant for eight years. Security. I am perfect for this job here at the desk - to lure those men from here over to the bank, you know, and act dumb, cause as a joke? I can play a pretty, stupid hillbilly. I do it all the time to the delight of my friends."

"Well," Gunther said, looking over the man and his long flat face and bottom lip that protruded to the left, "don't work to hard at it. They may rough you up, toss you around, then ask you where all the money is. They'll be masked. They all have guns. Probably some will stay outside. But I think a few will come in here and brace you up."

Loomgloom nodded.

"If it looks like they are going to kill you? I'll stop them. I will be right up there, watching everything." Gunther pointed to the second floor that surrounded and overlooked the lobby. "Peeking out that door there." He pointed again. "And, while we are all trying to get ready this afternoon, but we really expect them to come tomorrow."

"Anywho…I know who you are because Mr. Gray and Mr. White said you were a good man. That you all went to West Point. Said, you have been to the wars in the Pacific Ocean, and the Atlantic Ocean and damn all the way to China."

"Yup."

"They said you knew all about what was going on here. I was kinda hoping you might have a war map for me here. If I can just point to the bank, or if I lead them to the bank myself, walking, and then if they let me go? I would sure like to get me a pistol or something over there, to help you all out."

"Where's your pistol?"

"It's a company pistol. It's in the back room in a satchel."

"Ok. Why don't I run that satchel to the sidewalk across the bank and just leave it setting there by the front door. What a business there?"

"Bakery. It ain't open. Ain't nothing open really. This place is the dangdest dream."

"Bakery front door. That way if they do march you over there, and you do get the chance, if they set you free, ignore you, maybe you can get over there to it. I am waiting for my partner to show up. When he gets here we'll walk that gun over."

"Fine."

"Then I have a third pistol in my belt. I will leave that pistol in the room behind you. So if you need to run, if you can back there, it will be there for you."

"That sounds fine Mr. Johann. You can…you can count on me. I will help if I can. I want no harm to come to Mr. Bendigo or any part of his business. You can count on me because I have shot men."

"You have?"

"Yes. I was police officer in Lampasas. One afternoon I had to kill two men trying to make off with a wagon of drapes in front of a curtain store..."

"Drapes you say?"

"Yessir. The owner caught them trying and pitched a fit with them. They gunned the old man down with old-timey, ball and cap pistols. Magine that? I showed up just as they shot him, and I had to shoot both of them cusses, out on Lancaster Avenue. Detectives found out that they were planning on hijacking that wagon and selling all the drapes up in Wichita Falls."

Gunther and Loomgloom stared at each other for about 10 seconds.

"Magine. Magine dying over winda draperies," Loomgloom said.

"People will steal anything."

"People will. People will steal anything and buy anything. My grandfather was a constable way back when, and he said an Apache raiding party stole a wagon load of drapes bound for Laredo once in south Texas. When the Rangers caught up with them, they was all wearing the floweredy drapes like dresses. He said they all looked like they were wearing Greek togas. Looked like…looked like a Dallas Lady's Ball. Can you —'magine that?"

"I can imagine it."

"Yeah. Yeah."

They sat quiet.

"Reckon it would be nice to live far, far enough away from all this, huh?" Loomgloom said, with a pinch of regret in his voice.

"Reckon so. But I don't know how far away that would be. I've been far away, and it's all the same, Mr. Loomgloom," Gunther said; then he looked back out the window.

"Oh, you don't have to call me mister."

"Oh," Gunther said softly, still staring out the window, "I believe I do."

The potential city of Bendigo had the very latest, evolved concoction of asphalt on its vacant streets. Gunther heard a horse's hooves clicking along as the horse approached walking on the pristine pavement. Gunther stood, walked to the north windows and took a look.

"My friend's here," he told Loomgloom.

Gunther walked out the double doors and looked up at Jefe as he approached on his horse, Kipling. He'd ditched the peon clothes and straw hat and wore his usual outfit. He veered Kipling over to the front of the office. Jefe wore a black gun belt with a pistol on each side.

"I thought you said you were coming in disguise?" Gunther said, "Coming in as a peon."

"I did. I changed at the station."

"You did. You look like a singer in a Mariachi Band."

"This is Bendigo?" he asked, ignoring the snide comment. "This looks like an empty city of the dead like in one of your science fiction books."

"Go around back, amigo. There is a big garage with a corral next to it there. Good place for Kipling. Water. Hay. Meet me back here, and we'll go for a walk through this modern ghost town.

Gunther went back inside.

"Let's plant that gun by the bank. Can you get the satchel for me, and I'll plant it."

"Sure, I see your Mexican friend got here."

"Filipino. He's Fil-i-peen-o."

"Oh. Ok. Fillia-peenio. Gotcha. Yeah," And Loomgloom turned toward a hall that led to a back room.

He came back with a canvas satchel and handed it to Gunther. Gunther reached inside his jacket and handed him a Colt revolver.

"Stick that in the next room, or wherever you want it."

"I will."

Gunther stepped outside and within a minute, Jefe showed up.

"Where we go?" Jefe asked.

"We're going to plant this pistol in this sack, across the street from the bank. This way if they force our man down there to show them where the bank is, if they let him loose once there, he might get his hands on a gun and help us."

They walked down the center of the street. The bank was a long block away. They took note of buildings. New designs in wood and brick. The fresh signs above the empty stores. "West Texas Clothiers." "Peking Duck." "Oil Digger's Eatery." "The Electric Company." "Waterfall Steak House."

"There are street lights here. I wonder if dey work?" Jefe asked.

"Probably. This is Bendigo's dream. I guess he will hire people to run all these places. There's a bunch of new, empty houses west of here. Live here. Work here."

As they got closer to the bank, Gunther recognized its European architecture. Raoul Torontoola stepped out into the street from the bank doors.

"Como Esta, Jefe!" Torontoola shouted.

"Muy bien, e tu?"

"I am hiding here with some very nice gentlemen guarding the bank. I cannot be seen at the spa because I could be recognized."

Gunther laid the sack with the gun by the door of Zanzibar Outfitters, the business across from the bank, but still not too close to potential lines of fire.

Bat Masterson stepped out of the bank, shotgun in hand.

"Hola there, Jefe!" Bat said.

"Hello, sir!" Jefe said, obviously impressed with Bat's presence. He just stood there, grinning.

"Glad to see you join our little hunting party."

"We thank you for your experienced help!" Jefe said.

"I put a gun there over for Loomgloom," Gunther said, "in case they haul him down here to point out the bank. If he breaks free? He'll make a move for it."

"Sounds like a plan." Bat nodded.

Jacob stepped out, dressed like an armed Westerner, not the usual city slicker outfit. "Chow is at 4:30 p.m. They'll run a chuck wagon round back with grub and coffee. We plan on sleeping in shifts tonight in case they try to burgle the place."

"And, I have seen these shifts," Bat said, "and while not all together un-masculine pajamas, they look damn uncomfortable to sleep in."

Nobody but Gunther got the "shifts" joke. He chuckled with a head shake.

"We'll be eating in shifts too!" Bat took the pun to the next level. Still unnoticed - the writer's curse. "Oh, the lonely, lonely life of a wordsmith," Bat said with sigh and he walked inside.

"It's gonna be a long night," Jacob said, when he got the pun.

Gunther and Jefe walked back to the office.

"Why are dey talking about pajamas?"

"It's an English thing, amigo. Word play. Like a language joke."

"I will not sleep in pajamas. I will remain dressed. What if they come in the night?"

"We are not changing into pajamas. We are sleeping in shifts."

"Nor will I change into some kind of shift to sleep in"

“You are not…”

And off they went to the office lobby, bantering back and forth about the English word “shifts,” in shifts.

Chapter 30: A Showdown in Bendigo

In the Friday afternoon stillness, they first heard the motorcycles' rumble. Jefe, Loomgloom and Gunther looked at each other. The sounds got louder, then louder still. Multiple engines roared in an irritating harmony. They buzzed around the outskirt streets first, out of sight, like a swarm of angry wasps. This surely alerted all in waiting at the bank that the crime was brewing. Then, suddenly, in the not too far off distance, the machines stopped.

They waited a very long 10 minutes, then eight men in long coats and big hats, with long guns slung across their shoulders walked into view of the Bendigo office lobby windows.

"They come," Jefe said, "all eight of them."

Jefe and Gunther made for the stairwell. Halfway up, Gunther pointed a finger at Loomgloom. No words were needed. Loomgloom nodded.

Jefe peeled off to the right and Gunther to the left. They stepped back and away from the balcony railings and knelt down in the open, office doors, ready to retreat even farther back if needed. They could still see the street through the windows, but once the men entered, all they could do was listen in at first.

The men stopped just outside the office. They looked every bit like the raiding party. They didn't climb the porch stairs onto the elevated sidewalk. They milled about there for a few seconds. Talked. Looked. Then all lifted bandanas from their necks and covered their faces. Three men trotted up the front steps and into the lobby.

"Can I help…" Loomgloom said, acting surprised."Now, what the…? Fellers? What?"

"Money," a masked man said.

"Money?"

"Money."

"Fellers there ain't no kind of money here. None kept here."

Gunther felt like the lobby had been scoped out by now, so, hatless, he peered over the edge. To Gunther this man ordering Longbloom around was the size and shape of Spanky.

Two masked men stood at the door. Spanky near the lobby desk. Gunther held up two fingers and pointed to the door for Jefe. Then one finger and pointed below them to the desk. Jefe nodded.

"All the money is at the bank, just down the street. We don't…."

"Come around from there," the man by the desk ordered Longbloom in a crisp bark.

"Ok, Ok."

"Where's this bank?"

Loomgloom walked toward the front windows.

"Look. Look, you make a left right there and walk about a block. A long block. The Bank of Bendigo is on the right. The south side of the street. Other side of the street."

"You alone in here?"

"It's Friday afternoon, mister. Everybody's off. Half a day on Friday. Cept me. Yes, cept for me. I gotta answer the phone and deal with…and deal with…walk-ins. I guess like...like you?"

"Yeah. We're walk-ins and outs alright. Mr. Bendigo upstairs?"

"No. Mr. Bendigo is in Galveston, Texas."

"Bank open?"

"Till 4."

"You know what you get for lying to us?"

"Gut shot! Or something. It don't take very dang much to imagine what I'd get."

“Get down on the floor there,” Spanky pointed to the floor below the front windows.

This sounded like an execution? Both Gunther and Jefe peeked over the edge. Loomgloom laid spread eagle. The three men talked in whispers. Spanky and one man left, leaving one man in the lobby, no doubt as a look out and to watch Longbloom. No doubt keeping him alive in case they needed more information.

Gunther and Jefe crawled back a few safe inches. They could still see the street. The two men told the other five about the bank, gesturing down the next street. They all marched off, fanning out as they went.

“You lay there like a good momma’s boy,” the remaining robber told Loomgloom, “and you may see supper.”

“I will do just that,” Loomgloom mumbled, his face and mouth pressed into the oriental carpet.

Gunther and Jefe exchanged glances. The same thoughts went through their minds. They could not shoot this man for fear of noise. To shoot this robber down cold in the lobby would alert the other gangsters and ruin the bank ambush and turn this whole mess into a scattered bloodbath. If they startled him in a charge he could also freely shoot with that shotgun he held, alerting his gang. To not take action against him would mean three armed men could not quickly join the bank fight from a flank and even the odds. Could they wait? Should they?

Jefe put down his shotgun, and pulled out his Bowie knife. Gunther’s head shook with the exaggerated message of “no.” Throwing a knife was always risky, and there was no guarantee the robber wouldn’t still fire his gun if he was hit and stuck somewhere in his body even one that big. But in a second it became clear that Jefe was not going to pitch the knife the 20 feet below. He tiptoed along the railing to get above the robber and with a leg up, hopped a foot on the top rail.

Gunther was aghast. He stood and leveled his pistol at the robber for cover. Jefe leapt airborne, diving and dropping through the air from the second floor! His knife held in an ice pick grip.

Jefe, knife first, hit the man like a boulder with the Bowie piercing deep into the back of his neck. The robber collapsed to the floor with an animal grunt, in a spasm, and lost his grip on the long gun entirely. Jefe hit hard too, atop the back of the robber, he tried to roll off but couldn't completely. Gunther darted down the stairs.

Loomgloom got up and repeatedly kicked the robber in the head, "no...supper...for...you, you...tick!" He said a word with each kick,

"You alright?" Gunther said.

"No," Jefe said. "No. My ankle."

"Broke?"

"Nada. But not good." Jefe looked pale. He sounded breathless. He felt of his left ankle. "Not broke. Moving my toes. But not so good."

Loomgloom took all of the robber's weapons. He shoved two pistols in his belt line and took the shotgun, checking it for ammo.

"That was loco. Loco!" Gunther said.

"Loco is better than nothing. It was a fast idea. A good idea, up until I hurt my ankle. Give me uno momento. You Go. Go on. I will catch up," Jefe urged. "I just need a minute."

"Are ya bleeding?"

"No! Go. Help our guys."

Gunther nodded and stood. They couldn't wait, or Jefe's daredevil dive would have been for naught.

Gunther and Loomgloom stepped outside and took a look around. Their end of town looked empty. They dashed across the street still out of the view of the bank, and up to the corner where Gunther peered around the building. The robbers were near the bank, stepping cautiously, signaling to each other as they looked into every empty business along the way. With each closed store and vacant office, they became more and more suspicious of…this town.

"This ain't a town. There's nobody anywhere either!" one said in a half shout, "It's like a ghost town here."

But the bank was still their target and, as they approached it, they crouched, barrels up. A robber peered into the bank corner window. He nodded vigorously to signal it was occupied. Open.

Spanky, yelled, “Go!”

Three men hit the double doors of the bank pushing through, yelling like crazed fiends. Spanky and three others stayed behind, just outside, scanning the street.

In the lobby, Marion, Bat Masterson, Torontoola and a Bendigo guard immediately opened fire in a blasting blaze from four angles.

The two robbers who entered first collected most of the malicious ammo, and they were shredded red. The third, behind them, cut loose with his shotgun in a horizontal spray, causing the security team to duck. He too was hit numerous times, but continued pumping and pulling until his head split open.

Instantly, Spanky and the three men outside, spread out evenly across the street in front of the bank and opened fire on the windows and interior, laying multiple fields of fire into the bank lobby, making the protectors duck even farther down after their successful first second or two.

One outsider reached in the double doors and grabbed the coat collar of the third wounded man in the lobby, and yanked him outside under this cover fire. They took off for the far side of the street, shooting over their shoulders every few steps, hauling their wounded man behind them.

Gunther and Loomgloom ran down the sidewalk shooting their pistols at the fleeing group. They could tell some of the shots were landing on flesh and bone. One man tripped, yelled out and fell, but got up and continued. One dropped right in the street, face first on the new pavement.

The escaping robbers disappeared around the corner of a street.

Silence.

Marion, Torontoola and Masterson carefully stepped outside the bank, trying to reload as well as stay alert. They walked onto the sidewalk at a slow pace, eyes looking ahead, they spaced themselves several feet apart. Gunther and Loomgloom jogged up beside them on the street.

“Any of you hurt?” Gunther asked.

“One dead,” Masterson said, ”That poor fella, Bendigo’s

guard. Took one in the forehead."

"Josh?" Loomgloom said.

"Yes," Marion answered.

"Oh, Lordy *Jesus*," Loomgloom whimpered.

Ahead, there was an opening between the buildings and long sign hanging from an overhead platform that read,

"Bendigo Garage and Corral."

Gunther could hear moaning, cusses, shouts and other sounds coming from inside.

The men angled out in a line and Marion became the point man out in the street. Then Masterson. Then Torontoola. Gunther. Loomgloom.

They passed a downed man, who lay rather still. Gunther shot him in the head anyway as they passed not wanting to turn his back on him in case he revived. Every few feet Gunther spun to check their rear in case some of the robbers might have circled around through the buildings to ambush them.

And then they swung into the open area of the garage corral. Gunther could get the full view. A vision of hell unfolded before him. Bloody men, scatter-brained from a botched counter-ambush and bullet wounds, lay on the ground, some kneeled, some walked about or tried to mount their motorcycles. Some unhurt moved quickly. They were a sorry looking, confused and shattered lot. Some had ripped off their masks exposing their identities. Gunther saw Spanky.

"Drop your guns! Put your hands up!" Torontoola shouted, as several riders managed to mount their motorcycles and start them.

"Fuck you to death!" one declared. And that started it. He raised his pistols. Others followed suit.

Now within shotgun range, Gunther and all the men opened fire. Gunther and Marion dropped to one knee, then spread prone on the ground, but the others remained standing against the aimless, chaotic and desperate fire of the escaping gang. Masterson shot as he stepped to his left, seeking the protection of the corner of a nearby building.

His five shotgun rounds soon done, Gunther pulled his pistol and fired away. The robbers in the front took the heat in waves of lead as two bikers in the back raced down the side alley of the garage and nearby coral. One of the potential escapees looked like the big and athletic Spanky Runyan. The two went full throttle.

Gunther ran to a bike and shoved his pistol in his belt line, kicked the engine into a roar and, spinning the back tire, took off after them.

Past the buildings, flat and rocky country quickly spread out before them. The spa to the northwest and grounds soon faded away into only a silhouette and the bikers headed for the desert not looking back. Spanky took the lead. The second biker, followed quite a ways back. He wobbled every 10 seconds or so causing Gunther to think he might be wounded.

Gunther poured on the gas. He hit a few cracks and dips in the ground that almost flipped him! But he steadily gained ground on the second man. When he got within some 15 feet, with his left hand, he pulled his pistol from his belt and shot the man twice, in the head and the back.

The robber went down dead, and the bike flipped up and spun crazy in a cloud of dust, narrowly missing Gunther, as he veered off to the side to avoid it so fast he just couldn't get control of his bike again. With a sudden surprise thud and crank of the front wheel in a dry crack in the ground, Gunther found himself airborne.

He lost his pistol. Lost his bike. Lost his balance. Lost his mind.

He didn't know how long he lay knocked out cold in the dirt. He awoke to the feel of dusty, gritty sand on his lips, a slight wind blew through his sweaty hair and heard only silence other than his ringing ears. After a few moments he heard someone approaching, the rhythm of a horse trotting up.

He moved his hands and feet. Shook his knees. Rolled his head from side to side. Nothing seemed broken...yet. Who was coming? He reached for his pistols, one at a time but all were gone. He went for his knife.

"Johann!" a voice called out.

It was Jefe. Jefe, atop Kipling closing in on him at a trot. Jefe pulled Kipling to a halt nearby.

"Are you alright?" Jefe asked.

"I...So far. How about you?"

"Ok. But you have to get up here by yourself. I cannot get down off this horse. I mean I could, but I don't think I could get back up."

Gunther slowly stood, then realized what had just happened. Gunfight. Chase. Escape. Bike crash. He craned his neck and looked off toward the tan and blue horizon.

"He's gone," Jefe said. "That was Spanky. Well. Spanky is as far gone as his petrol will carry him."

Gunther limped over to the horse and took a big deep breath. He stood beside Kipling for a second to muster the balance necessary to climb aboard. Jefe leaned over and grabbed Gunther's jaw with his right hand and tilted his face up. He looked at Gunther's mouth, nose and eyes.

Then he twisted Gunther's head to the left and right looking at his ears, checking the head for bleeding. Gunther, trusting his old lifelong compadre, just let him look.

Then, after Jefe seemed satisfied, with a groan, Gunther stepped on Jefe's foot in the stirrup, the unhurt ankle side and slung his leg over Kipling, seating himself behind Jefe.

Jefe turned the horse. They around rode in silence for a bit looking for Gunther's gun. Failing to find it, they continued on.

"You did good, my friend," Gunther said.

"So did you, my friend," Jefe answered. "Where shall we go? The city or the spa?"

"I know we should go back to Bendigo City and help pick up the pieces; but right now, the spa is where I want to go. Let's go to the spa. Marion is the man in charge downtown. Let him sort it all out."

Jefe pulled Kipling's reins directing the horse away from the shallow city of Bendigo, now occupied by more dead people than live ones, and headed toward the spa of healthy, happy people laughing and torturing themselves with tasteless foods.

A short time later, Gunther and Jefe limped into the lobby. Gunther did not recognize the desk workers. No Sean Bruner in attendance.

"Name's Gunther. You should have a letter on file from Mr. Bendigo. An 'anything goes' letter?" Gunther rested his dusty, dirty arms on the tall counter in a fit of exhaustion. He knew he looked awful, and the guests walking by seemed shocked to see the pair.

"Yes, Mr. Gunther. We do."

"The best suite in the spa, please. I was in Room 117, but I need to move to the best suite you have. And one for my friend here, Jefe. Steak dinners to each room. Massages at 7 p.m. Great red wine…immediately."

"Mexican beer for me," Jefe chimed in.

"Wine for me. Beer for him."

"Yes, sir. Of course, but, sir? The clerk leaned forward with a short smile, "Ahh, sir, we…we don't allow for Mexicans in here. I am sorry."

Gunther ran a swollen, sore hand over his face and hair. He touched a sore spot, sighed and said "It has been a bad day," he said. "First, he is not Mexican, he is rich Filipino."

"I am Filipino," Jefe added with a smile.

"So, on a technicality, he ain't no Mexican. In fact he's here partly because he fought for your prissy ass in the United States Army in several countries. Second…second…" Gunther actually reached for his holster. His fingers came up empty. He reached for his shoulder holster. Found that empty too. He turned to Jefe, pulled a revolver from Jefe's holster, and put his elbows back on the counter, and causally aimed the gun at the clerk, inches from his face, between his eyes. This was something the clerk and cliental had never experienced.

"I will shoot your fucking nose off if I don't get two suites," Gunther said.

"Ahhh sir, sir. I have to call security."

"Your security here? Your security here now is me and my best friend, the Filipino."

"Well the sheriff would…"

"Son, if the sheriff comes all the way out here? Trust me,

he'll have more to worry about than your missing nose."

They stared at each other. The clerk re-read the letter from his boss Bendigo.

"Yes, I see. Everything is in order. Please put the pistol away."

Jefe took the gun back.

"Two suites. Two steaks. Wine. Beer. Two massages," Gunther said and rapped his knuckles on the counter. "I trust we can wander down to the hot springs anytime we want?"

"Ahhh, yes, sir. No appointment necessary."

"Goooood."

"You seem to have a dozen doctors running around here like a pack of happy squirrels. We need a doctor to have a look at my friend's ankle."

"Yes sir. Right away."

"Johann!" He heard Carmella. She ran toward him across the lobby. "What? How? What happened?" she asked as she eyed the disheveled pair. "Are you okay?"

"Darling. It's over. They are dead, but Spanky appears to have gotten away on a bike."

"Is everyone ok? Bat? Raoul?"

"We lost one guard that's all. Listen, I hate to ask this but, can you go down there and tell them where we up are, and that we are ok?"

"Oh yes," she said enthusiastically.

"It'll be ugly down there."

"I'll bring my cameraman Tobey. It's part of the story."

Gunther should have remembered she and Tobey were in the ugly business of news reporting.

"So it is. Then, I'll be in…" he turned to clerk.

"Room 412."

"Room 412. Come see me right away when you get back."

"I will." And off she went.

Gunther watched her cross the lobby and yell for Tobey, "get your camera equipment!" Jefe watched Gunther watch her.

"You know she is not in love with you. She really just wants the story," Jefe said.

"Yeah. Yeah, I know. But, she's kinda in love with that

part of me," he said as he got the keys.

He reached out an arm with a key to Jefe, "here, my rich, Filipino friend." he with an acted Filipino accent.

"Muchas gracias, amigo" Jefe said, while glaring at the clerk.

Chapter 31: Some Heroic, Local Volunteers

Carmella never made it to Gunther's room that night. He waited as long as he could, then, exhausted, fell fast asleep on the couch.

The next day, limping, and on some pain meds supplied by the spa doctor, Gunther and Jefe went by coach to the ball game in Amarillo. The Saturday match up. They couldn't resist the idea. Onlookers grumbled that a portion of the team of stars had gone missing and scorned the nobodies who played in their places. They watched the burly Spanky Runyan play in the field and bat. He looked downtrodden and, in their estimation, he constantly looked around like he wondered if the police might arrive and arrest him every time he advanced into the dugout. he couldn't see Gunther and Jefe in the stands and given the confusion of the Bendigo Corral shoot-out, it was possible Spanky didn't see them there.

"What we do with him?" Jefe asked.

"Getting arrested was too good for him," Gunther said.

He had something else in mind for Spanky, something far more permanent, and Jefe knew exactly what that was.

For that night and the next day, Carmella, Bat Masterson and Ramp Hempstead worked almost in unison inside a meeting room at the spa, pounded away on their typewriters. They created a shared byline for the New York Times and the Whispering Wind newspapers. No doubt the headlines would run starting that Sunday and several days in a series serial. These stories would be picked up as far away as Seattle, Washington and then London, England.

"Fort Worth Baseball Team Masquerades also as an Armed Robbery Gang!"

"Four Baseball Team Members Dead in Bank Robbery Shootout!"

It read, "for Spanky Runyan, it was just another day, just another ball game in Amarillo, but members of his team didn't show for that Saturday afternoon game. The second-stringers played beside him, losing both Saturday and Sunday's game."

With no workable evidence connecting Spanky, the writers had to keep him legally clear of the crimes. The trio wrote the torrid tale of an outlaw gang of baseball players, pillaging their way through minor league cities on the innocent pastime's schedule. How they mixed with some evil fans. How they drove motorcycles in a motorized biker gang. A sports nation empathized with poor Spanky.

It was a Pulitzer Prize story for sure. But Bat, Carmella and Ramp were also in the dark to a degree. They hammered their keys in the proverbial dark about any counterfeiting operation. The fake money was still a secret. The writers also did not mention the name Johann Gunther, Jefe and the mysterious Misters White and Gray.

Armed Bendigo security agents were the only heroes said to have saved the day. Even Bat, a surviving gunman in the fray, decided not to allow them to include his name or his part in the battle, fearing his reports would be tainted by involvement. Only one Times staff editor knew he was actually there, but they both agreed to keep it a secret. As far as the police record was concerned, all the robbers were shot dead by employees of the business and some unnamed, "heroic local volunteers."

Misters White and Gray indeed did clean up the bloody mess at the corral. They did call in the county sheriff and reported the attempted armed robbery. Wagons and cars of county deputies, along with the county coroner and two funeral homes arrived the next morning to dispatch the mess.

The sheriff even had afternoon tea with Mr. Bendigo himself while all their men did the dirty work. There was no mention to the authorities about an escaped fugitive.

Bendigo paid for the funeral of his slain guard Joshua Mullhouse. He gave the family a tidy sum, an amount unknown to the public. He promoted Loomgloom to a supervisory position over cereal product convoys to the Texas and Oklahoma cities.

Gunther quickly summoned his science and ballistics team back down from New England. Over the next three weeks of toiling with the gun ballistics of all the robbers' pistols, in the welcoming Amarillo police laboratory, (a political path cushioned by Mr. Bendigo) there was clear evidence that three of the pistols collected from the dead gangsters were used in many other crimes. Those crimes? The murders of Mrs. Torontoola and her housekeeper, the murder of the distinguished Judge Rufus Hofferman and the philanthropist Justin Trace. Just who and which of the deceased owned those pistols? No one could tell for sure from the mess of moved bodies as the weapons were dropped or released when the shooters fell. The guns were all collected by police, dropped in a big bag by a deputy ignorant of modern, forensic breakthroughs. All the police cases in Texas were cleared and closed…by death of the suspects. Which dead suspect actually shot who was not a matter for the District Attorney.

With these results broadcast in the papers, the charges against Raoul Torontoola were dropped, and he was immediately re-instated by the city police department, with back pay as well as his prior rank and position.

Within a week of the big Bendigo shoot-out. They had all taken the train back to Fort Worth but, once there, Bat Masterson remained behind at the station to transfer to a train bound for New York City. On the station platform, he shook everyone's hand and said goodbye. He saved shaking Gunther's hand for last.

"Dutch, I want to thank you," Bat Masterson said, "you

know, I missed the Gunfight at the OK Corral; but by God, I didn't miss the Gunfight at the Bendigo Corral. And I'm glad I didn't."

Chapter 32: A Crackerjack Killing

Betha looked again at the note from Chester Winch. The scribbled address.

Come to 106 Rose Avenue at 5:45 p.m.

She walked up the street looking at the house numbers. It was getting dark early now and the addresses on the houses were difficult to read. Most of the old houses stood empty. This wouldn't be the first time Winch summoned her to an odd or different location for one of their trysts.

At times as he worked as a Ranger, watching criminal people and businesses he was stuck in certain places for days and he sent for her to pass the time, so such a request was not unusual.

One zero six! She found it. What a terrible old house, she thought. Broken furniture on the porch. One front window broken. She wondered what sort of bed they would be in this time. He was disgusting enough, now this.

She didn't knock. She opened the door and stepped in.

"Chester. Chester?"

"Come on in, honey blossom," came a voice in another room. But this voice did not belong to Chester Winch.

She walked into what was once a large den and saw a strange man sitting in an old, ripped chair.

"Who are you?"

"Hi!" the man said.

"Look mister, I don't do switches..."

"Switches? Do you do snitches?"

"Huh?"

"Are you a snitch for the police?"

"What are you saying? Who are you?"

The man stood up. He was stocky, wearing winter clothes and his hair hung in long brown strings around his face. His face looked lumpy with acne scars.

"I don't switch sex with no stranger like this," she said. "You may know Chester…"

"You don't know me, but my name is Gawdy Shirtz."

"So?"

"And I am here to settle up on some business, that's all."

"Well, my slit don't pay off Chester's debts. If he owes you money then you get real money from him."

"Chester has paid me already. Paid me well."

"Well, then what in bejesus do you want?"

"He has paid me to kill you." He smiled big. "He is sure that you told the police about a robbery out West. He is sure you been telling secrets to the police."

"I ain't spoke to no lawsmens about no nothing."

"All manner of secrets. Yup." He still smiled and looked her over. "I am still gonna kill you, Betha."

He walked closer, and she backed up.

"No sense walking," he said. He pulled a pistol from under his jacket. It was a small gun.

"You gonna shoot me with that little crackerjack?"

"Why yes, ma'am. It makes a small, pleasant sound. And I do not want to disturb any neighbors left out here on this empty street."

"I knew I shouldna come out here to this place," she said, backing up to a wall.

"No matter. I'd a gotcha somewhere else."

Her dress was long, but Gawdy Shirtz shot her once where he guessed her right leg was. And it did indeed hit her leg. She shrieked, spun and slid down the wall.

"Who you been snitching to, ma'am?"

Silence, mostly from shock.

"Your loyalty, however pleasant is misplaced, Madame."

She gasped.

"Since I am the last man, the last person you will ever see in this lifetime....look at me...look at me! The last! Any ounce of loyalty should now be directed only toward me. Your very last seconds. Your very last look at life. Me, the man with all the God-awful power of life and death over you. And you know...pain. The pain. You want to die in pain too?"

He smiled again. He shot her in the other leg. She yelped. Gasped. Her breath was wet and growling in fear and came like an animal in ragged gasps as she neared death.

"WHO you been a talkin too, lady?"

"A police detective named Wiley. And another man with money. Gunther!"

"Gunther. Johann Gunther?"

"YES!"

"Pleasant," he said, and shot her in the face.

She went still. He looked her over. He lifted up her long dress and took a good peak.

"Nice flower-edy underwear."

He walked to the front windows. He put the small pistol in his coat pocket and extracted his big revolver, to see if there might be any other witnesses he might have to kill for snooping around outside. None.

He went back in the den and looked Betha over again for any whisper of life. He picked up the chair in the room, and with a sudden rage and a roar like a maniac, he charged her and threw it down on her, looking again for any signs of hidden life. Nothing. He felt disappointed. The chair stayed half on top of her, and he liked that. Pleasant.

He walked out the back door, dropped off the back porch and untied and mounted his horse. He said to no one except maybe his horse? "Winter is sure a coming."

He pulled up his collar, and tugged the reins toward a trail that leads to and from the back of the houses through some black walnut trees. Darkness had fallen, and in seconds he vanished into the night thinking about Johann Gunther.

Chapter 33: An Omen in Tweed

The annual Track and Field sports event, sponsored by Texas Christian University, was quite the important competition, placing athletes in positions as high up as the Olympics. Gunther attended the three-day event every year, sometimes even sponsoring some promising candidates.

The convention center at the college was a gathering place for such spectators and investors, a giant hall full of tall wooden tables and matching chairs, where people might congregate over beer and pretzels before the events began in the neighboring stadium and fields.

Gunther, wearing his white Stetson and tan suit, stood out from the crowd who were mostly dressed in black with tall black top hats or bowlers. Gunther was, of course, armed with a short-barrel .38 in a holster on his belt, and sheathed knife on the other hip.

"Gunth!" he heard a voice. He turned to see Ramp Hempstead from the Whispering Wind.

"Ramp," Gunther said, making his way through the crowd to shake his hand. Ramp balanced a pretzel atop his beer mug and returned the grasp with his empty hand with equal warmth.

They found two seats at an empty table.

"Too bad Bat didn't hang around for this," Gunther said.

"Yes. He left New York for Chicago two weeks ago. The Cubs and the Worlds Series."

"Ohhh, yes."

"How is Carmella?" Gunther asked.

"Are you asking me?" Ramp said, surprised.

"Yes."

"Oh, oh."

"I haven't seen her in weeks," Gunther said, "not since Bendigo."

"Oh. Hmmm, well, she is very busy Gunth...with a new story," Ramp said with his mouth half full of soft pretzel. He coughed. It was a bad one, like he had food stuck in his throat.

"You ok?"

"Ahhh. Yeah. Yeah." He caught his breath and took a swig of beer.

"Yeah, I understand. Seems my big story is…over."

"She is story-driven, my friend. And I guess then you don't know?"

"Know?"

"She's moving to Kansas City. After the big news story? An important newspaper up there offered her a job as managing editor."

"They did?"

"They did. Lots of money, too. Do you want a beer?"

Out of the corner of Gunther's right eye he caught a glimpse of a walking omen wearing a three-piece, brown tweed suit. The omen rested its right hand on the corner of their table near Gunther and leaned in on it. Gunther raised his head to the omen in tweed. The man was six foot, broad with long reddish-brown hair under a short-brimmed felt hat. Lumpy face. The man's jacket fell open and Gunther saw the heft of a thick gun belt inside it, not a thin dress belt.

"Hello, Johann Gunther," the man said musically, "you don't know me. My name is Gawdy Shirtz, and I…"

"Shirtz with a…z," Gunther muttered instantly, as they stared eye-to-eye. Detective Aster's tip!

And then, instantly, they knew they had to kill each other.

Gunther felt he had nowhere to go but forward. He dove into the gap between Shirtz's arm leaning on the table and his body. His left shoulder hit Shirtz's right arm. His right shoulder hit Shirtz's torso, as he leapt through him. And as he turned, he pulled his short-barreled pistol. And as he fell to the floor, mid-air, he twisted and shot Shirtz in the torso. Right side.

Shirtz let out a grunting grasp as the round pelted into him. He too fell to the floor not so much from the bullet but from the impact of the blast and his need to get out of sight. He dropped, scratching at his jacket, searching for his pistol, he hit Gunther's empty chair as it fell backward.

The entire hall went from the solemn calm of a gentlemen's club into a thrashing madhouse of people fleeing. The interior, rocked as men scrambled away from the epicenter of the gun shot. Dozens and dozens of tables and chairs were tipped over and flew in a ruckus and roar among escaping, startled men hiding or running. Once grounded, Gunther and Shirtz lost sight of each other, with tables, chairs overturning and human legs scrambling together between them.

Gunther remained down, low and on his back, crawling backward, shoulder walking and shoving off with the heels of his boots. More tables and chairs fell in between him and Shirtz. He tried to see the faces of the men nearby to predict exactly where Shirtz was, but their wild eyes were only searching for their own escape routes.

There! Ten feet away! Gunther saw the top of Shirtz's head and hat! Gunther aimed as best he could at the brim. BANG! The edge of a chair splintered as Shirtz ducked in time, but his bowler hat was hit and flew off his head. The now invisible Shirtz opened up, firing from a few inches off the ground, hoping to cut through the furniture and hit Gunther, or set him to run. He blasted away and the wooden pieces splintered apart, exploded and spinning—each one with lethal potential. Six shots! Six! Was Shirtz reloading? Did he have a second pistol on his other hip? Gunther did not pop up to find out. A professional killer would not empty his one gun in such a manner without having a second.

Most of the men in the hall were gone now. Except for a few distant shouts, the room grew quiet. Gunther still proceeded to shoulder-walk back and to the left, looking, scanning, searching the tan horizon of downed furniture. He had four rounds in his gun and six more in the belt loops at the small of his back.

Suddenly Shirtz rose up like a sea monster in an ocean of wood, his hair wild. He growled. He thrust himself forward first at a low crouch, then rising up he hit a full run, his guns blazing.

"Death to YOOOOUUUUU!" he growled.

He charged a few degrees to Gunther's right not knowing where he was. The shots were blazing but methodical. Paused. Timed. Right gun. Left gun. Controlled to the last. The bullets filleted the furniture to Gunther's side, all this in scant seconds.

With an extended arm, sights at eye level, Gunther, still off to the left of the killer's bullets, fired twice — right into Shirtz's center mass. They hit hard. Shirtz jerked as though he'd been struck by lightning. His arms came back tight to his chest as he clutched his brace of guns. His head turned to Gunther, baring yellow teeth, then he collapsed out of sight in the rubble again.

"Death to you too, you son of a bitch," Gunther whispered, rolling and shuffling to change his position.
Gunther replaced the four rounds. Then he rose to one knee.

A tall, overweight man charged in through the main double doors. He was dressed in dark blue with a badge, a blue hat and a shotgun. Security.

"Hey!" the man shouted, pointing his gun at Gunther.

"Get down!" Gunther ordered.

"Drop the gun!" The man demanded.

"Get down! He will shoot you!" With his free hand Gunther pointed to the spot he last saw Shirtz. He curved his finger downward, as much as to say the real target was hiding just ahead.

The guard got the message and crouched, turning his barrels away from Gunther and to the center of room. Gunther saw it was a double-barrel shotgun and short barrels at that. He shook his head, but then he too was in the middle of a gunfight with just a two-inch revolver.

Shirtz stood up like a ghost and fired at the guard. The guard let loose his two rounds, but over such a distance it did not do much. Freshly pelted, his face shred red, Shirtz stood his ground and blasted away. The guard was hit, hit and hit again, once in the face and he melted away down to the floor.

Now Gunther charged from the left, shooting with one hand. It was just the right moment to charge, as any good infantry or cavalry man instinctively recognized such a moment. His knees knocked away the tables and chairs like a tidal wave. Bang! Hit! Bang! Hit! Bang! Hit!

"Dammit!' Fall! Bang! Hit again! FALL "Dammit!" Shirtz contorted. Shirtz yelled. Shirtz could not bring his guns up, perhaps from wounds in his arms. The guns pivoted down, and blasted into the floor, throwing splinters.

Gunther hit him like a freight train. Body into body and the two went sprawling, tumbling over the furniture. Gunther lost his pistol and drew the knife with his left hand. He was half atop Shirtz. Shirtz now became a babbling raging, wounded buffalo. Blood spurted from his mouth. Eyes spread wide. Hands scratched at the air.

With an ice-pick grip, Gunther plunged his knife into the man. Again and again, in the neck. In the face. Finally…the beast stopped moving. The beast died. Gunther looked for any sign of life. Nothing. He slid off the body and laid on his back, gasping for some air.

"Hold it!" another man in blue with a shotgun yelled at him.

"Held," Gunther said with a smirk. "Best check on your friend over there."

"We did. He's dead," the guard said. Then another guard showed up in view.

"Well, this man here tried to kill me. He did kill your friend."

"Give up your gun," the new man said.

"Gave. It's…it's laying around here…somewhere."

"Then…then drop that knife."

Gunther flipped the knife in his hand. He held the tip. He threw it about seven feet and stuck it in an overturned table.

That brought silence. Gunther sat up and looked at the door, as more and more people filled in. Ramp Hempstead came back in, spotted Gunther and shook his head. And who did Gunther spot next by the door peeking in? Texas Ranger Chester Winch.

Gunther stood up.

"WINCH!" Gunther howled in an angry roar. He pointed a finger at Winch, his arm as though he held a gun, his torso twisting forward.

Winch grimaced and backed out of sight through the door.

Gunther shook his head and leaned against a standing table. He looked over the area.

"There," he said, pointing to his pistol.

One of the guards retrieved it, not knowing yet what to do with it.

And then Detective Wiley showed up in the doorway, talking fast with Ramp and the guards, then he jogged over to Gunther.

"You alright?" he asked.

"I think so," Gunther said. "There lies one Gawdy Shirtz."

"Hummm-dig," Wiley said. Looking over the bloody rubble.

"One tough country boy. Took a lot to put him down. Shotgun. Pistol. Knife," Gunther said.

"Boys, I got this," Wiley told the guards. "This was in self defense. This man had threatened Gunther's life and was coming here to kill him."

The guard gave Wiley Gunther's pistol. The men backed off and hovered near their fallen compatriot.

Wiley looked over the gun in his hand then at Shirtz.

"He, I presume started this?"

"Well, Wiley, what do you think? The jerk is here to kill me. Paid to kill me. He came all this way to…"

"Yup, yup. Yup. Ok."

"Did you see Winch outside?"

"Saw him," Wiley said.

"He knew this was going to happen."

"No doubt."

Ramp walked up, with a beer from an unmanned stand, and handed it to Gunther.

Gunther took it and gulped a few mouthfuls, then sighed.

"Ramp, you are the smartest guy in here," Gunther said, probably about the beer delivery.

"I don't know, Gunth. I didn't help you! I ran out."

"That is why… (another gulp)…why you are the smartest guy in here."

Chapter 34: The Bigs

Under a long drooping canvas, storefront awning, his Stetson pulled low, his jacket collar up, with a boot heel braced against the wooden wall ledge of the shop, Gunther stood in the dark. He stared at the Dalliance Night Club across the wide, dirt street, a place in Hell's Acre, Fort Worth where the ladies stripped and the men gambled, fondled, drank, snorted and smoked. Men and women came and went. Some laughing. Some talking. Some silent. This night motorcars parked on the street, horses were tied off on hitching posts, and wagons were hitched, and there beside all these modes of transportation, sat several Indian motorcycles.

So he waited. This was his 14th night of waiting. Not just at the Dalliance, this off-road night club, but at the other hot spots in and around the city. Riding his horse here and there, walking here and there, watching here and there and waiting here and there. Prowling the Fort Worth streets for Indian cycles and his one target.

Then a big man in a big tan hat and a long gray jacket stepped outside and sucked in a big gulp of crisp night air like he'd die without it. He yelled "YEAH!" out loud, to no one. He coughed a wet lung cough. Then he stumbled across the cement sidewalk to one of the motorcycles. It was Gunther's man. Gunther's target. The man he was waiting for. The man threw a leg over the bike, got it off its kickstand, then he and the bike promptly fell over.

"Gaaaat damn!" he slobbered. He lay there fairly still for about a minute.

Gunther slowly stepped off the store's porch and walked up the wooden sidewalk to where his horse was tied off on a balcony column. He stood on the far side of Freud and over the saddle, under his hat brim, he watched the man slowly struggle to get up, to stand the bike up and dust himself off, all with the great, sloppy effort of a solid, total drunkard.

He kicked the kick-starter and the engine cranked. Gunther climbed into his saddle. The bike took off slowly and wobbled severely at first. Gunther heeled his horse off to follow. The man turned the corner. He heard the engine rev, so Gunther galloped to the corner and lost sight the bike. But he could still hear it. He galloped down the empty street and to next corner, following the sound. Then the running engine sounded muffled. Different. Then it raced like the rear wheel was free. Gunther turned the bend of the road and saw the man and bike down on their side again. He stopped his horse and watched.

Gunther spotted the broad, stumbling figure turn off the bike. Then the man took off walking onto the dark city street ahead of Gunther. The man's right shoulder rubbed against the store windows and front walls of the establishments as he walked. It seemed like he was talking to himself. In a space between two stores, a narrow alley, the man slipped off the street.

Dismounting from his horse and tethering him, Gunther crossed the street with his eyes on the alley. From the opposite sidewalk he could see the man huffing and spitting up. Gunther walked across the street and stood before the alley.

"Hey…hey…," the man said to him as he leaned against the brick wall. His clothes were disheveled as though he'd fallen several times, more than the two falls Gunther witnessed. One collar up. Tie askew. His bowler hat tilted far sideways. Jacket open. His white shirttail out of his pants. His big, fat face was pouring sweat despite the night chill.

He peed on the wall. He looked at Gunther, almost cross-eyed.

"Spanky Runyan," Gunther said matter-of-factly as he stepped into the alleyway.

"Hey. Hey. Yeah. I ….know you? You know me?"

"Of course I know you. You are famous. Been drinking, Spanky?"

"YEAH! Hey. That. That, and HA! A little more. A little more than that too. Haa." He put himself away, failing to button his pants, then tried to pull a cigarette out of a pocket. "Yeah. I'd shake your hand, but I just peed on my hand."

He put a cigarette into his mouth. He rested against the brick wall and tried to light a match from a small matchbox.

"I'm celebrating. Celebrating. Yeah!"

"What are you celebrating, Spanky?" Gunther asked.

"The majors. The Bigs!" The cigarette fell from his mouth. The match fell. "They are sending me up. Up! I'm gonna play in the big leagues next year."

"No, you ain't," Gunther growled. He pulled the revolver from his belt and shot Spanky right in the chest. Spanky's shirt flapped. The blast of the gun bounced off Spanky and sent a puff of wind blowing back on Gunther. Spanky fell back against the wall. Jaw dropped. He was as shocked as he was drunk.

"Wha? Who…who?" He slowly slid down the wall. He gurgled. "This can't be. I'm finally…finally…."

"Dead. Is what you are? Finally—dead."

Gunther stepped back and peered up and down the street from where he stood at the entrance of the alleyway. Nobody. Nothing moved. Now Gunther leaned against the wall, gun down at his side.

Spanky was so drunk and drugged, with a demonstrated high tolerance for pain, he didn't understand what had happened to him. He looked down at himself, swiping a hand across his shirt. Gunther leaned over and reached into Spanky's jacket. From under his left arm, Gunther yanked out his German Luger. He looked it over and then pushed it back in Spanky's holster.

Spanky ignored him. With his fingers he dug through the

hole in his shirt deep into the hole in his chest. With a grunt, he stuck his finger into the bullet hole and pulled out the bullet, holding it high in the air.

"What?" He gasped. His finger was red. He brought it close to his eyes to see it better. Then he looked at Gunther. "I know you? You know me?"

"You won't know nothing in a minute."

"Why'd you shoot me?"

"Because there are just some sons of bitches that need killing," Gunther said.

"Oh."

"Yeah."

"Oh. I'll be…damned."

Spanky gurgled, wheezed, shook and died. Gunther spat on the sidewalk and left the alleyway. He passed the downed motorcycle and walked the long, lonely street back to his horse. Remaining afoot, he walked his horse down to Throckmorton and then turned toward downtown. He climbed onto Freud and took the quiet side streets back to Remedies.

He felt a great sense of accomplishment, peace and relief. Spanky wouldn't be robbing and killing anyone else. He unlocked the back gate, and put Freud in a stall, rubbed him down, watered and fed him, then threw his saddle across a short wall in the barn. He touched his face to Freud's and closed his eyes taking in a deep breath and smelling the familiar scents of the horse and barn. The comfort of the familiar seeped into him. Then he walked to the back of the house. Another key unlocked the back door of the Remedies building, and his home. He stepped inside, passed the empty rooms in the hall, through the lobby into the dark, conference room. He took off his jacket, his hat and his gun belt and dropped them on the table. He rolled a chair up to the window, sat and looked outside.

This place. This office. This home for him and Jefe. It was time to break up the family. A man was hired to kill him. What if the killer walked into the office, a building where children played? Where workers and relatives toiled. Half of Jefe's whole family from the Philippines lived here.

What if members of Spanky's gang had come here to settle the score? What if Ranger Winch came here to shoot him? What if a gunfight….

He shuffled his feet, feeling claustrophobic again. This was not the first episode. The British doctor in India told him to take slow deep breaths when he felt things closing in. He did this now. It was too risky to have this big family home and office all together. The office must be only for work. Nothing more. Nothing more.

"Gunth?" Jefe limped down the dark stairs.

"Yeah."

Jefe picked up the gun belt by the holster and smelled the pistol. Gunther noticed that Jefe was wearing only a long, sleep shirt.

"Are you sleeping in shifts?" Gunther asked.

"Very funny. Lucky tonight?" Jefe asked.

"Best of luck."

Jefe sat too. The room remained dark. Only the streetlights shined in through the sheer curtains.

"Jefe, we are going to have to break this household up," Gunther said, staring out the windows.

"I know."

"Someday, it may become too dangerous to have your wife and kids here."

"I…know."

"Too dangerous for Mesha to be here."

"I know. Where will you move?" Jefe asked

"Cabin by Eagle Mountain Lake. Bout time I built it."

"I have to consider dey schools," Jefe said. "The school for my kids. I have to stay near here."

"Maybe…maybe you keep this as your house. We'll make a new office somewhere else. Your kids love it here."

"They love you here my friend. You are more than an uncle to them. Like a father to them to "

"I know."

"And, they will miss Mesha. She is like a second mother to them. Everyone will miss everyone."

"Yeah."

"I will pay you for your half of the building."

"The hell you will. If I move it's is all yours. You've earned it 10 times over. Anyway, in the future. Something to think about."

"It will be very boring…the two of us just sitting in an office all day by ourselves," Jefe said. "Think about it." Gunther said with a smile.

"Oh, I have thought about it. Boring as hell."

"I am going to bed."

"Yeah. Yeah, me too."

"And anyway," Jefe said while standing, "dis case is done. Done for us tonight, huh?"

"It is, as they say, closed. Tonight. I will go to Austin and report to the governor later this week."

Jefe stopped at the bottom of the stairs, "I hope…I hope he knows the toll of all of dis. The cost to all of us."

"Jesus. Jesus, It was costly. It was, huh."

"Mañana."

"Mañana, amigo."

Chapter 35: Last of the Gunslingers

The next morning, Jefe, Rosa, Mesha and the kids made ecstatic noises in the lobby. Gunther left his desk and his office to discover what all the commotion was about? With hammers, Rosa and Mesha were taking apart a tall, slim, wooden crate. Jefe stood nearby with his arms folded and with a giant smile on his face.

Whatcha got there?" Gunther asked him.

"It's here, Gunth. A vacuum cleaner."

"A vacuum…" He'd read about them but had never seen one - a machine, an electric broom actually, with a motor inside that somehow sucked up dirt, right off the floor.

Gunther heard an automobile chug up, outside. Through the windows he could see it was a police car, driven by Raoul Torontoola. The car tires squished a pile of horse manure on the street. Torontoola got out, in his full black suit and hat, carrying a small, brown, canvas sack and jumped and skipped over the manure to alight on the sidewalk.

Gunther made for the front door and opened it before Torontoola could knock.

"Mi amigo," the re-instated, Sgt. Torontoola said and nodded. He checked the soles of his boots, first right, then left, then walked in.

"What's going on here?" he asked.

"Jefe bought his wife, and the office, a vacuum cleaner."

"A vacuum cle…what is this?"

"Cleans up dirt with electricity. Spinning. Somehow. Like a top. Like a…a man-made tornado in a fat pipe. What's in the sack?"

The kids yelled out with glee as the last board of the shipping container was pried loose, exposing the new wonder machine. Rosa clapped her hands in delight.

"Come on in here," Torontoola said, leading Gunther into the conference room.

He laid the sack on the table. He reached in and pulled out a German Luger.

"Mine?" Gunther asked, playing dumb.

"Of course. Who else do you know has such a thing around here? And has one…missing. This was recovered form the body of Spanky Runyan who was mysteriously shot in an alley."

Gunther picked it up and looked it over, "no worse for wear."

"No worse for wear."

"I will not ask you…" Torontoola said.

"Good. Don't," Gunther said.

The two men went to stand in the doorway of the office looking back into the lobby just as another man appeared at the front door. At first he was taken aback by the party-like activity going on in the lobby. County Detective Wiley Lewis.

Maria plugged the cleaner into a wall socket and pressed the big red, start button. It roared. She jumped back. She started to move the machine over the throw rug and wooden floor. The children dropped flat on the floor, inches from the machine, eyes straining trying to see, at ground level, the amazing magic that occurred. The monkey scrambled onto the top of the bookshelf and sat looking down, holding the end of its tail and petting it for comfort and screeching, eyes wide. Mesha tore off an end from the newspaper and dropped it on the floor. Rosa rolled the machine on its four wheels over it, and the paper disappeared to the excited and happy delight of the screaming children.

Wiley walked up to the Gunther and Torontoola, tilting his head toward the lobby, "What's that?"

"A vacuum cleaner," Gunther said.

Wiley pointed back into the conference room. The three walked back into the room to escape some of the noise in the lobby.

"Listen," he said. "Bad news. Betha, you know the girl you sent me as an informant?"

"Yeah," Gunther said.

"Well, shit. She's dead, Gunth."

"Dead?" Torontoola said.

"A real estate salesman was showing an empty house out on the south side. It stunk. They moved a chair and found the girl's body. I mean all stunk up. Maggots and everything."

"Oh no, Betha?" Torontoola said.

"Yeah. The cousins identified her. Identified the clothes she wore. Shoes. What's left of the face. We are sure it's her."

"Oh," Gunther said. "Oh," with a deep breath. "That's… that's on me. Damn."

"It's on me too," Torontoola said. "How was she killed?"

"Shot. Shot in the legs. The face."

"If you can, connect the bullets with the guns of Gawdy Shirtz," Torontoola said.

"Yeah," Wiley said. "She was a strange kid. But she helped us. Now we have no one to testify on Chester Winch's doings."

Wiley looked at the table and saw the Luger.

"Read about Spanky Runyan this morning. Mysteriously shot dead in an alleyway. That your Hun gun?" Wiley asked.

"My Hun gun."

"And let me guess. From Spanky Runyan's corpse."

"Yes," Torontoola said. "My captain heard the whole story. Thinks the two comancheros who blew up the Farks' house probably killed Spanky."

"Hmm, two comancheros," Wiley said, looking at Gunther's profile.

"Gang fights," Torontoola said, "such a pity. Gang revenge."

"I see," Wiley said. "The docs downtown are checking out the bullet that apparently killed him. I don't suppose a slug from him will match any brace of pistols you own, using your fancy bullet science?"

"Not a chance," Gunther said.

"Of course. You know, I know what you did, Gunth," Wiley said, still staring at Gunther's profile.

"You do?"

"You killed off the whole gang."

Gunther turned to him, expressionless, stared at him for a few seconds and then back to watch the miraculous vacuum sucking up every granule of dirt in the lobby. Wiley shook his head turning away from Gunther and watching the machine, doing what it was designed to do and doing it well.

"I didn't kill the whole gang," Gunther finally said.

"Jesus, Joseph and Mary Lou! You know you have to stop this, Gunther. You can't work like this anymore. We're civilized now. We are growing more civilized, day after day after day. You can't go around like some gunslinger…like the old days! Those days…those days are over."

"Oh," Gunther said quietly. "We may have seen the last of the old gunslingers, but I think we have seen the beginning of the gunmen. A new breed of criminal. Men like Gawdy Shitz."

Mesas finished vacuuming the lobby and steered the machine down the hall to the living quarters. The kids followed in a giggling gaggle, dancing a hustle. Even Torontoola and Wiley walked behind them to further witness the newfangled contraption work.

After everyone left, Gunther strolled aimlessly into the conference room. He grabbed the back of a chair and rolled it over to the window. The curtains were already drawn. He sat in the chair. He lifted his legs and caught the window sill with the heels of his boots.

The monkey jumped down from the bookcase in the lobby. It scampered into the room, looking over his shoulder in fear, in case the noisy machine returned. Satisfied it was safe, for the moment, it climbed up into his lap and sat holding the end of its tail. It looked up at him, then looked out the window too. Gunther mindlessly scratched the monkey's head and looked over at his luger on the table.

And they both just sat there. Sat there looking out the

window. Cars and trucks beeped at each other trying to get through the once easy passable intersection outside, while coaches and men on horses stopped or sidestepped to get out of the way.

The End

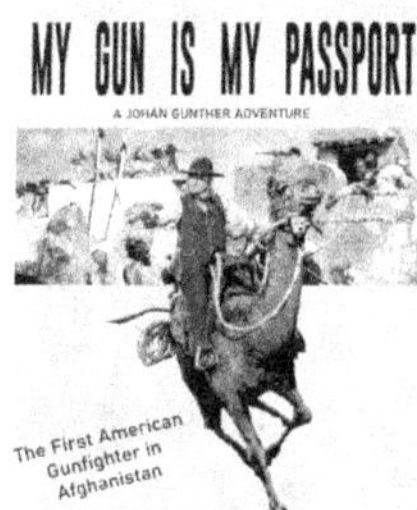

The Johann Gunther Western Hero Adventure Series. Ebooks, Paperback, Audio.

Coming in 2024

"The Horse Killers"

Get the rest of the Johann Gunther western adventure series. Look it up on the Internet by title and author name.

They Killed the Chinese Ambassador's wife. To cover it up, they had to Kill an N.Y.P.D. detective. They shot him in the head, but he didn't die. They just made him...crazy.

Really Crazy.

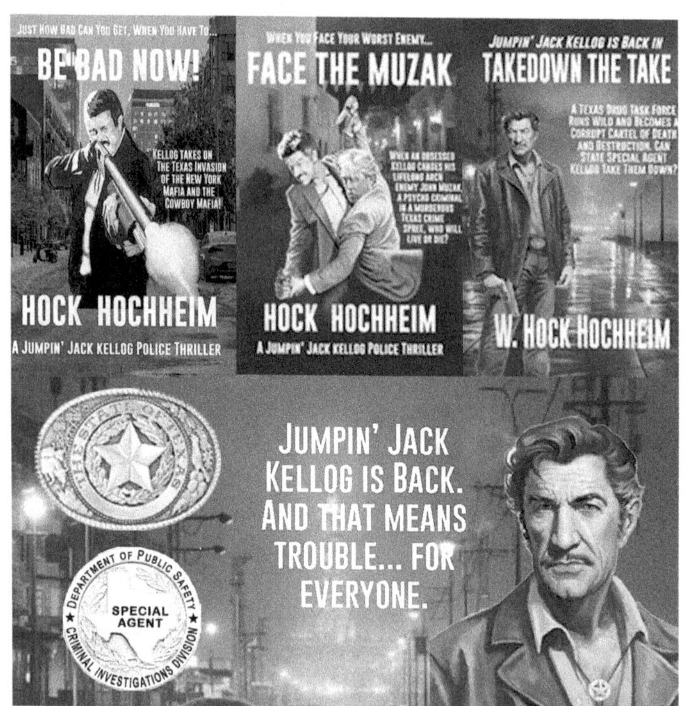

Get the Jack Kellog Texas detective series. Look it up on the Internet by title and author name.

TRUTH IS DEADLIER THAN FICTION
DEAD
RIGHT
THERE
TRUE STORIES OF CRIME AND JUSTICE IN
THE ARMY AND ON THE STREETS OF TEXAS
HOCK HOCHHEIM